JOSEPH'S DILEMMA

Return to Northkill, BOOK 2

ERVIN R. STUTZMAN

HERALD PRESS

P R E S S

Harrisonburg, Virginia

Herald Press
PO Box 866, Harrisonburg, Virginia 22803
www.HeraldPress.com

Library of Congress Cataloging-in-Publication Data
Stutzman, Ervin R., 1953-
  Joseph's dilemma / Ervin R. Stutzman.
    pages ; cm. -- (Return to northkill ; Book 2)
  ISBN 978-0-8361-9909-3 (pbk. : alk. paper) 1. Amish--Fiction. I. Title.
PS3619.T88J67 2015
813'.6--dc23
                                   2015005811

JOSEPH'S DILEMMA
© 2015 by Herald Press, Harrisonburg, Virginia 22801. 800-245-7894.
    All rights reserved.
Library of Congress Control Number: 2015005811
International Standard Book Number: 978-0-8361-9909-3 (paperback)
    978-1-5138-0169-8 (hardcover)
Printed in United States of America
Cover design by Dugan Design Group, layout by Reuben Graham

Unless otherwise noted, Scripture text is quoted with permission from the
King James Version.

21 20 19 18 17   14 13 12 11 10 9 8 7 6 5

To Ruth Py and Rusty Sherrick, descendants and interpreters of the Lenape-Delaware Indians, and Becky Gochnauer, director of the 1719 Hans Herr House & Museum and the Lancaster Longhouse, with admiration for the way the three of them have bridged cultural divides to tell the story of Native peoples with dignity and respect

Contents

Author's Note

Jacob Hochstetler of the Northkill stands tall as a hero of faith among the Amish, largely because he stood the test of nonresistant Christian faith during the French and Indian War. The story of the attack on his family has been recounted through various media over many generations. Far less has been written to interpret the meaning of the Indian captivity experienced by Jacob and his sons Joseph and Christian. I attempted to address that gap by recounting the story of the attack and Jacob's captivity as a novel in *Jacob's Choice*, the first book in the Return to Northkill series.

Joseph's Dilemma—the second in the series—explores the meaning of captivity for Jacob's son Joseph. Although this novel can stand on its own, there are many allusions to Jacob—or *Dat* (Father)—and other characters and events in *Jacob's Choice*. The clash of cultural perspectives between the ways of the Amish and the Lenape—or Delaware—is writ large in these pages.

Archaeologists believe that the Lenape (which means "original people"), as they called themselves, have lived on American soil for thousands of years. They were Algonquin people who comprised three fraternities, which in English are called the Wolf, Turtle, and Turkey clans. The Lenape were both matriarchal and matrilineal, a sharp contrast to the white colonists who settled on native lands.

Beginning in the seventeenth century, the Lenape were called Delawares by white colonists, since they lived near the Delaware River, in what is now the state of Delaware. The name *Delaware* was given in honor of Lord de la Warr, the first governor of Virginia. The descendants of this Indian tribe use both names. The most extensive written history of the people is entitled *The Lenape-Delaware Indian Heritage*.

Both *Lenape* and *Delaware* appear as words on the official seal of the tribe today, along with the images of a wolf paw, a turkey, and a turtle, to signify their three clans. To avoid confusion between the two tribal names, I have chosen to use the name *Delaware* in this novel, although I could rightly have used *Lenape* instead. That's likely how they referred to themselves during this time period. The online dictionary of the tribal language uses the term *Lenape*.

The Delawares during the French and Indian War lived in a variety of dwellings that may be variously described as wigwams, longhouses, lodges, huts, and/or cabins. I have chosen to use the term *wigwam* for two reasons: it derives from an Algonquin word, and it can be broadly used to describe any Native American dwelling.

As much as possible, I used the known names of the people in this story—the protagonist Joseph Hochstetler and the members of his Amish family, as well as Chief Custaloga, Tom Lions, the prophet Neolin, Chief Pontiac, and the various British characters named in the story.

There are few known facts about Joseph's life during the period 1757–64, so I used my imagination to put the flesh of this story on those bones to create a plausible account of what may have happened. The Delaware generally gave their captives new names, so I had them assign the name Swift Foot to Joseph. However, to avoid confusion for the reader, I called him Joseph throughout the entire novel, regardless of the character's point of view, except in the direct thoughts and speech of his Indian captors, when I use the name Swift Foot.

I relied extensively on scholarly research to assure an accurate portrait of the history and culture of that time. Any errors or conflicts with known facts are mine.

—*Ervin R. Stutzman*

-Prologue-

October 1757

Touching Sky swung her feet off the wooden ledge that served as her bed. She felt the familiar ache as she glanced toward the empty spot in the wigwam where her son had once slept. *Will I ever adjust to his being gone?* Her little daughter, Runs Free, murmured something unintelligible in her sleep and shifted under her blanket. Touching Sky moved quietly so as not to wake her.

Grandfather Sun warmed Touching Sky's face as she stepped outside into the morning light. She swept back her long black hair and raised her hands to the sky.

"Great Creator," she prayed, "give the warriors success. Protect them from the enemy. Help them find a captive to fill the empty place in my heart."

Touching Sky tried to imagine where the warriors might be. Had they reached the settlements on the far side of the Susquehanna? Had they encountered the enemy? The raids with the French commander were becoming more risky now that the Pennsylvania province had built a string of forts along the *keekachtanemin* (the endless mountains). Many British soldiers patrolled the woods, and the settlers took refuge in the closest fort when they were warned of an impending attack.

The whites! They were so rude. Before the war party had left Custaloga's Town on the raid more than a moon earlier, Touching Sky had heard Walks Proud tell about a German woman who had refused food to several braves on a peaceful visit several summers earlier. Didn't the whites understand that refusing to give food to a stranger was an insult?

"I'm going to get revenge for that disgrace," he had said. He also had mentioned that the family had several sons.

11

Perhaps Walks Proud could capture one of them to take the place of the son I lost in battle, Touching Sky thought. *Several other widows in the village have benefited from captives. Why not me?*

She sighed, thinking of the winter ahead. Who would hunt game for her and her six-year-old daughter? All of the meat she'd preserved was gone. If she didn't find someone to replace the son she had lost in the white man's attack on Kittanning, how was she to survive the coming winter?

Yes, her brother Tamaqua and her friend Walks Proud had shown her kindness over the past several months. More than once they had provided venison or small game in trade for her sewing and weaving. And yes, they'd given her a doe hide that she could tan. But she needed more.

She wrapped a blanket around her shoulders to stave off the chill and went back inside to stir the embers of her cooking fire into life. For the first time she could remember in her thirty-eight summers, she dreaded the onset of cold weather. The thick pelts of the otter and beaver that the hunters had brought in over the past several months hung in the village as omens of a hard winter ahead.

When it got really cold, the warriors would slow down or cease the steady raids of settlers' properties. There would be no white captives left from whom she could choose to take the place of her lost son.

How would she keep going?

I must have help. I need a son.

PART I

-1-

October 1757

Joseph Hochstetler yanked at the hemp ropes that bound his wrists. *Ouch!* They only dug deeper into his raw skin. He had tugged at them often during the forced trek for hundreds of miles through the Pennsylvania woods. No luck. He glared at Tom Lions, the rear guard in the war party. Tom repaid him with a twisted grin.

Two of Joseph's captors took off their moccasins and splashed through the shallow water to pull the boats onto the bank where the Deer Creek emptied into the French Creek by Custaloga's Town. It was just a day's journey north of Fort Machault, the French fort at Venango. The three bateaux—wooden flat-bottomed vessels twenty feet long and three feet wide with a point at each end—had carried the war party with their four captives and a cache of supplies up the creek for several days.

Lou, the French captain and head of the war party, climbed out of a bateau and strode into Custaloga's Town with a determined gait. The rest of them disembarked and followed.

Joseph's anger welled up as he thought of all that his captors had taken from him. They had killed his mother, Lizzie; one of his older brothers, Jakey; and his younger sister, Franey. Then the warriors had burned down most of the buildings on the farm. Now they held him prisoner, along with his father, Jacob, and younger brother, Christian.

To add to the indignity, the warriors had disgraced the three of them by shaving their heads, leaving only a long, hanging lock from the crown. They'd plucked his father's beard as well. All Amish men wore beards, and this was an equal blow to Amish dignity.

Joseph blamed his father. In the tense moments after a cadre of Delaware and Shawnee Indians had attacked their home under the command of the French captain, Joseph's father, Jacob, had refused to use his gun to defend his family. Worse yet, he'd kept Joseph and Christian from warding off the attackers.

Joseph's anger boiled as he recalled the incident. *Dat* knew *Mam*'s deep fear of the Indians. Joseph's sister Barbara, now married with children, had confided to him that *Mam* hadn't wanted to come to America because of it.

Both he and his brother had loaded their guns and started to aim when their father spoke: "Joseph, put your gun down."

"Why, *Dat*? I can get a good shot off from here."

"You know why." Yes, *Dat* had explained the principle of nonresistance many times.

"But *Dat*, we can't just let them shoot at us!"

"Joseph, that's enough." Turning to Joseph's younger brother, *Dat* said, "Christian, I mean that for you too." With that, they had surrendered their firearms.

Not long afterward—in the predawn darkness—the Indians had set the house on fire. By taking refuge in the cellar, the family had escaped the flames. For a while. Joseph helped pull his mother's stout frame through the small window in the wall. The whole family reached safety outside the burning house not long after the Indians had disappeared into the woods.

But then, a young Indian named Tom Lions spotted them and let out a bloodcurdling war whoop. The warriors rushed back to the house. Joseph outran the warriors and hid behind a log, not knowing they'd seen his hiding place. The war party murdered three of his family, then slipped back to surround and capture him.

Joseph's recollection of the attack was interrupted by the sharp poke of a rifle barrel in his ribs. He sucked in his breath. It was Tom Lions.

Show-off. Joseph wanted nothing more than to whip around and land a hard blow to the guard's jaw. Maybe that would teach him. After nearly three weeks on the trail, Joseph's nerves were raw. He was utterly weary of being forced to do things against his will.

Joseph picked up his pace to avoid another poke in the ribs. *As soon as the Indians trust me enough to take these ropes off my wrists, I'll run away. They'll never catch me again. I'll take one of their rifles and shoot to kill if need be. No matter what* Dat *thinks.*

The war party made its way up the slope toward the village. The warriors fired off several friendly shots as they approached. Several shots sounded in return. Joseph was used to the routine by now, having heard it at every village along the way.

The war party strode toward a group of twenty dwellings built in a random pattern around a central lodge. Most were round or oval wigwams covered with bark. A few looked like cabins with a peaked roof, but they were covered with mats or bark. Some of the homes had a small hut in the back. Everything looked so different to Joseph from the houses back home.

An imposing man—probably the chief, Joseph thought—stepped out to meet them. He led the captives to the center of the small village.

People began to gather. Joseph hung his head, unsure of how to respond to the stares. One thing was sure—he would never cooperate. He would escape at his first chance.

Touching Sky started at the sound of rifle shots. The raiding party must have come home.

"Aw-oh! Aw-oh!" they yelled. They hammered on the "Aw" sound and then leapt an octave to the "oh," holding it out as long as possible. It was a scalp halloo—an announcement that they'd returned with several scalps.

And maybe some captives, Touching Sky thought. She laid down the pestle she was using to grind corn and moved toward the center of the village to watch the action.

Several men threw logs on a fire. Others begun drumming and dancing to celebrate. There were more than a dozen warriors, both Delaware and Shawnee, with a French commander in the lead. Tom Lions guarded the four captives—two men and two boys. All had their heads and beards shaved clean except for a scalp lock. The oldest, a white man with a broad forehead and round cheeks, kept his head bowed, looking at the ground as he marched in line with his hands tied. The other man jerked at his ropes and swore as he stumbled along, his eyes smoldering with anger at his captors.

Touching Sky fixed her eyes on the two young boys. The younger one had blond hair and the older one had brown. The older of the two marched with his head down, flexing his muscles against the ropes that bound his hands. His linen shirt was stained with mud. He must have seen about thirteen summers, she thought. The younger one looked around as he walked, taking in everything around him. When he met Touching Sky's gaze, she saw that he had clear blue eyes.

If only I could adopt one like him!

All of the warriors but Tom sat around the blazing fire. Several people danced to the rhythm of the drums. The captives were shoved into place among the others. Tom stood behind them with his rifle, watching their every move.

Children celebrated the capture by chasing each other around the clearing. One at a time, the warriors told the story of the raid against a white settlement called the Northkill, a former Delaware hunting ground.

I must ask Tamaqua if that's a place our father used to hunt, Touching Sky thought as they described it. *We may have played there as children.*

Walks Proud, a warrior from the village, held up a scalp that was mounted on a hoop. "A British scout tried to stop us," he said, "but we stopped him instead. I mean to turn this in for a good scalp bounty at Fort Presque Isle."

A warrior with a scarred face spoke next. "We took three scalps from a German family. The scalp bounties will help buy a new rifle." Touching Sky noticed that the captives looked away as he waved the scalps on a pole. Two of the scalps had the long hair of women. *Perhaps they belonged to a mother and her daughter.*

A wave of sympathy washed over her. But she pushed aside her pity. The whites deserved the warriors' revenge.

After all of the warriors had taken a puff on the pipe that made its way among the celebratory circle, a few women from the village offered them a simple meal of fish.

It isn't fair, Touching Sky said to herself. *They have husbands who can fish and hunt for deer. If I had a husband, I'd have meat to give to the celebration as well.*

She watched as the warriors ate. *I could contribute some of my popcorn,* she thought. She walked back to her wigwam with long strides and took down several ears of corn that were hanging up to dry.

"What are you doing, Mama?" Runs Free had followed her.

"Come and see," Touching Sky said as she unbraided the husks and wrung the dried kernels off the cobs. She put the kernels into a kettle and headed toward the site of the celebration. What better way to celebrate than to share some of the corn she'd recently picked in her garden?

Touching Sky popped the corn over the fire. The children gathered around, clamoring for their share.

"Here, then," she said, scooping it into their hands. She portioned out some for the warriors, then made sure that each of the captives got a handful as well, lingering over the older boy. He refused to meet her gaze, but greedily gobbled it up. *I wonder when they last ate,* she thought.

They were finishing up the crumbs when Walks Proud pointed to the older of the two boys they had captured. He said to the chief, "This young man they call Joseph is a very fast runner. He almost escaped us when we raided his home— but we were faster! We call him Swift Foot. I'd like to see him race the boys from this village."

Chief Custaloga nodded. "Yes, let the young men show us how they can run."

Walks Proud strode over to the boy he called Swift Foot. He loosened the hemp rope around his wrists and yanked him to his feet.

The boy got up and looked around at the group seated near the fire. Touching Sky saw anger in his eyes. *Perhaps he is a warrior at heart.*

The young Delaware men wore deerskin breechcloths and moccasins. Joseph wore linen pants and a shirt, along with a pair of old moccasins that looked too small for him. Only Chief Custaloga stood taller than he. The hair on his chin and upper lip was fuzzy, like the skin of a peach.

The chief pointed to a painted post some distance away. Then he motioned to show that the racers were to run to the post and back to the starting line, which he drew on the ground with a stick. He pointed to Tom Lions. Tom handed his gun to another warrior and walked over to join the race.

Touching Sky grimaced as she stood up to watch. What a braggart Tom Lions was! He claimed to be the fastest runner in the village. How could a white German captive wearing pants and tight moccasins possibly win a race against the boys from the village? With young Tom Lions in the race, the captive wouldn't have a chance. At least the race would show the captives that Indians were superior runners.

She was surprised to see the one they called Joseph kick off his moccasins as he approached the starting line. *So he's going to run in his bare feet. That will be of no advantage.*

Everyone fell silent. Chief Custaloga raised his hand. The runners tensed. He signaled—they were off!

But wait. Joseph was slow getting started. *Perhaps he didn't understand the instructions.* Yet Joseph looked undaunted. He was making up lost ground, pumping his arms vigorously and running with long, hard strides. He caught up with the last runner in the pack, and then slowly gained on the others. Soon only Tom Lions was ahead of him.

Touching Sky held her breath. Joseph caught Tom Lions at the post. They both wheeled around and headed back. Joseph was in the lead!

Joseph crossed the finish line a stride ahead of Tom. The warriors whooped and cheered for the white captive. *Perhaps this was the son I have been praying for,* Touching Sky thought. With such a gift for running, he could be a great warrior and a winner in the village games. Maybe he could teach Tom a touch of humility as well. She could see by the smiles on the faces of the warriors they were as tired of Tom Lions's bragging as she was.

She watched with admiration as Joseph strode over to the older man and spoke a few words to him. *That must be his father,* she thought. *If it is, he must be proud of his son. I surely would be.*

The competitors milled around, smiling and laughing and recounting the race. Touching Sky walked quietly over to Chief Custaloga, who was talking to Walks Proud. She waited impatiently as they finished their conversation.

Custaloga looked at Touching Sky expectantly. "Yes?"

"I wish for Swift Foot to be my son," Touching Sky said.

It was a bold request—had the chief not been her younger brother, she wouldn't have dared. He looked at her, considering.

"You'll have to speak to Walks Proud, since he captured him. And we must first deliver Swift Foot to the French fort at Presque Isle."

Touching Sky's face fell. "Do you mean the French will decide where the boy goes?"

The chief nodded. "I'm afraid so."

"If you went to Presque Isle with the war party, might they let you bring him back?"

"Perhaps. But I won't be able to go."

"Could you send an emissary to speak for you?" Touching Sky asked. "Someone like Tamaqua?"

"If he is willing." Tamaqua had a good reputation in the village and could well serve as an emissary. The chief turned and motioned to their brother, who was sitting near the fire. Tamaqua rose and came to stand with them.

"What do you think of that young man named Swift Foot?" Custaloga asked.

"He just put Tom Lions to shame."

"Touching Sky would like to take him into her home," Custaloga said. "I want you to accompany him to Presque Isle for her sake. See to it that he is returned to this village, if at all possible."

"He really belongs to Walks Proud and his son, Tom," said Tamaqua. "They may not want him in the village after he beat Tom in a race. But we must ask."

The chief motioned to Walks Proud, who was engrossed in conversation by the fire. Walks Proud, seeing the chief wanted him, left the group and joined them.

"Tamaqua says that you captured the young man—Swift Foot," Custaloga said. "What do you intend to do with him?"

"If the French allow it, I shall release him to Thitpan, who desperately wants a captive to assist her in gardening and hunting."

Touching Sky's face fell. *Thitpan!* Her name meant "bitter," and that was what she was like. *She doesn't deserve a young man like this*, Touching Sky thought. *She wouldn't treat Swift Foot well.*

"If the French allow the boy to be brought back here, the council of women shall decide his fate," Custaloga said.

"I shall accompany you to Presque Isle," Tamaqua said to Walks Proud. "I shall see to it that no one else claims him and that the young man returns here safely."

Touching Sky glanced at Joseph, who was looking at them. Did he suspect what was happening? Would he cooperate?

"Be gentle with the young man," Touching Sky said to Tamaqua. "I see fear behind the fire in his eyes. If you treat him well, perhaps someday he will want to become one of us, with a red heart and mind." Tamaqua nodded.

Just then, the French captain gave a command and Tamaqua joined the war party as they headed for the creek.

She reached down to take Runs Free's hand.

Will I ever see Swift Foot again?

Tom Lions's rifle poked Joseph in the back—hard. *Tom is going to make this trip a misery. I shouldn't have run so fast. Now he's going to treat me worse than ever.*

One of the men from the village said a few sharp words to Tom and got into the bateau with Joseph. He looked to be about the age of *Dat*, with his dark hair tied into a scalp lock and a small leather bundle hanging around his neck. When the man squinted at the sun, small wrinkles formed around the corners of his eyes. Joseph wondered who he was.

When all three bateaux were loaded and ready, the captain of the party barked instructions. One of the warriors took the ropes off Joseph's hands and handed him a paddle. He called out a rhythm as Joseph took up the routine he'd learned the previous day. Rowing was tiring, but anything was better than having his hands tied.

As they rowed along, the man who had joined them spotted a deer standing at the edge of the woods by the creek. He pointed to the deer. "*Achtu,*" he said, and motioned for Joseph to repeat the word.

"*Achtu,*" Joseph said. *It sounds like a sneeze,* he thought.

The man dipped his hand into the water. "*Mbi.*"

"*Mbi.*"

The man pointed to himself. "Tamaqua," he said.

Joseph repeated it back to him, then pointed to himself and said, "Joseph."

The man shook his head. "Swift Foot," he said.

Swift Foot, thought Joseph. *I have lost everything, even my real name.* But he pointed obediently to himself and said, "Swift Foot."

Joseph wouldn't have repeated the words for Tom, but Tamaqua said them so gently that Joseph didn't mind. Perhaps if he got to know the Delaware language, he could overhear their plans and find a way to escape.

It took two days on French Creek to get to Fort Le Boef, where they unloaded the bateaux and struck out on land. The path was so marshy that someone had laid down logs to form a wide path for portage. Joseph shaded his eyes against the sun and looked ahead. The bumpy wooden surface stretched for miles. The captives and most of the warriors walked, but Captain Lou, who had led the war party all the way from the Northkill, rode in a wagon piled high with the supplies they had brought from Fort Machault.

As the sun dropped low in the sky, seagulls circled overhead and the marshy meadow gave way to a shallow bay. Beyond the bay was a body of water as far as Joseph could see. The smell of the water was somewhat like the ponds that Joseph had encountered, only stronger.

The captors quickened their pace as the group neared the water. "Presque Isle," Joseph heard the captain say. A narrow strip of land arched into the immense body of water. Was this the Lake Erie *Dat* had talked about, where the French shipped furs down to New Orleans?

A wooden fort stood close to the water's edge with a ragged French flag flapping in the stiff breeze. A small creek wound its way around the edge of the fort and emptied into the shallow bay.

The warriors marched briskly toward the fort, which was surrounded by an *abatis*, a wall of defense made of branches stacked on their sides with sharpened ends pointing outward. Unlike Fort Le Boef, the walls of this garrison were made of heavy squared timbers laid upon one another in the manner of a log cabin. The wall was perhaps twelve feet high and one

hundred twenty feet long on each side of the square enclo-
sure. Bastions jutted from each corner to enable soldiers to
fire at the flanks of an enemy storming the walls.

The war party marched through the wide gate that opened
toward the path. An officer stood to greet the captain. By the
tone of their voices, Joseph knew that the officer was happy
with what the captain had brought with him.

Joseph stood watching for a few moments as the warriors
handed over the scalps they had taken. The officers wrote
something on a piece of paper about each one, and then
handed the warriors money.

Joseph felt pain stab him like a knife. So that's what scalp
bounties were about—cash for the lives of his loved ones.
Franey. Jakey. Mam. *What had they ever done to deserve to
have their scalps sold like beaver pelts?*

One of the officers barked an order and a soldier stepped
up to untie the captives' wrists. Inside the walls of the fort, the
prisoners had no place to run. A soldier stood guard at the
gate with a gun. As Joseph rubbed his wrists in the chilly air,
the blood rushed back into his hands and warmed his fingers.

The officer led the captives into a large structure made of
rough-hewn logs with a roof of cedar shakes. A young soldier
with a French uniform directed them inside a small room,
where a half dozen other captives were kept.

That night, Joseph and Christian started to lie down next
to *Dat* on the dirt floor to sleep, but the guard poked them
with his rifle. With a wave of his hand, he made them move to
opposite corners of the room. *Just for once*, Joseph thought as
sadness rose in his throat, *I'd like have a chance to say a few
words to* Dat *and Christian.*

It was a long night. Joseph woke up sweating several times,
even though the room had no heat to ward off the October
chill. Was fate about to deal their family another cruel blow?
Was this the place where the French were rumored to sell
captives as slaves? What was going to happen to him? And to
his father and Christian?

The next morning, Joseph swallowed a few bites of dried corn the guard doled out before leading the captives outside. Tamaqua and another warrior shouted at each other while an officer in a French uniform stood nearby. The officer pointed at the captives, then barked an order and walked away.

With that, the warriors motioned for the captives to line up, with *Dat* and Christian in a different group. A sense of terror grew in Joseph's chest. They wouldn't separate him from his father and brother, would they? He edged cautiously toward his *Dat* and Christian.

Tom scowled at Joseph, but Tamaqua said something to him under his breath. Tom turned away.

Dat spoke quietly to Joseph and his brother in the Swiss-German dialect. "Boys, if you are taken so far away and are kept so long that you forget the German language, do not forget your names. And say the Lord's Prayer every day."

Christian's eyes widened as he gave voice to the question stirring in Joseph's mind. "Where are they taking us?"

Jacob put his hand on Christian's shoulder, glancing at Joseph as he spoke. "It's hard to tell. As far as your conscience allows it, always treat the Indians with respect and do what they ask. God will give you wisdom."

Joseph trembled as a warrior stepped between Christian and *Dat*. "Come, Stargazer," he said to Christian in broken German. It was the name they had assigned to him when they cut the captives' hair at the great island, likely because he was so intrigued by the night sky. They yanked him away and bound his hands behind his back.

Tamaqua stepped up to Joseph and motioned for him to follow.

Ever since he had been taken from the farm, Joseph had steeled himself for the chance that he'd be taken from his family. But he was far from ready. Joseph saw *Dat* nod and raise his hand slightly in a parting wave. He struggled for something to say to his father and brother, but no words came. Joseph's eyes blurred with the terror of what was happening, and a silent scream opened his lips. He turned and fell in the line with the captives. Tom Lions smirked and took his place in back of Joseph.

Gone were the days, before the attack, when he wanted to be independent from his family. *Is God punishing me for wanting to disobey my father's orders during the attack?* As much as he begrudged his father's unwillingness to protect the family by shooting at the Indians, he would gladly trade his resentment for *Dat's* gentle presence now. And Christian's too. To see his eleven-year-old brother dragged away by a party of warriors was more than he could bear.

Will I ever see either Dat *or Christian again?* The question plagued Joseph as he stumbled along on the uneven logs of the portage path that had brought them to the fort the previous day. Would they be tortured to death in an Indian village, as some escapees from captivity had reported? Would they be sold as slaves in Canada or some other French territory? Would they be held as ransom?

At least Dat *and Christian won't have to put up with Tom Lions,* Joseph thought as Tom prodded him sharply in the back with the muzzle of his gun. *Dat* had gotten the worst of it for weeks on the trail. He remembered the brief exchange he'd had with *Dat* and Christian on one of the rare moments they were alone on the trail.

"I hate that guard named Tom," Joseph had said through clenched jaw. "I'd like to put him in his place."

"Me too," Christian said. "He's evil."

"*Naw geb auchdt* (Be careful), boys, he has weapons and you don't," *Dat* said.

"I could lay him out with my fists," Joseph said, his face hot with blood.

"That's what he wants," *Dat* said. "If you hit him, he'll kill you with his gun."

"If I show him what I can do, maybe he'll respect me."

"No, you'll be acting just like him. Show him a better way."

He could still feel the anger with which he'd told *Dat*, "If you'd have let me shoot when the Indians attacked, we wouldn't be in this trouble."

"Joseph, I—"

That was when Tom swaggered up, glowering and threatening them with his flintlock. Joseph hadn't talked about it since. Would *Dat* ever get the chance to finish his sentence? To apologize for the way he'd held Joseph back and brought the family such pain?

Joseph's thoughts were so occupied that he didn't realize he'd slowed his gait until he felt another painful jab in his ribs from Tom's weapon.

"Ouch!" the word escaped before he could stop it. Voicing his pain would only give Tom more pleasure.

He picked up the pace, but inside he felt like kicking Tom's teeth out. *Beating Tom in that race has only made things worse. The next time he pokes me with his flintlock, I'm going to pay him back in a way he'll never forget. And* Dat *won't be here to stop me.*

Tom relented over the next few days, stirring Joseph's hope that the worst was over. But when the war party disembarked their canoes on the lower mouth of Deer Creek and started the short walk into Custaloga's Town, Tom rammed his gun into the back of Joseph's shoulder. Hard enough to hurt his body as well as his soul. Hard enough to prompt Joseph's resolve to get back at his tormentor—right away.

Even though his hands were tied behind his back, Joseph wheeled around and kicked Tom in the chest with all the strength he could muster. Tom saw it coming just in time to dodge—enough that Joseph's foot glanced off without doing much harm.

Before Joseph had time to regain his balance, Tom swung the butt of his flintlock hard at the side of Joseph's head, catching him high on his right cheek. The pain in his head exploded into bright colors.

Then everything went dark.

-2-

Touching Sky glanced at the five scalps swaying on a pole in the slight breeze atop the village's central lodge. Warriors from the village had won them several winters earlier in the French victory against General Braddock of the British. The scalps served as reminders of the harm the white man had done to her people. She was bone-weary of the conflicts that had dragged the Delaware into the war that raged between the empires of France and Britain.

Touching Sky was ruminating on her losses when Runs Free slipped through the door of the wigwam and stood next to her at the fire.

"Mama, may I have some *sapan* (corn gruel)?"

Touching Sky's heart melted as she gazed into the little girl's plaintive brown eyes.

She picked up a wooden plate and laid a piece of *sapan* onto it.

"Thank you, Mama." When Runs Free smiled, the broad dimple on her chin accented the small dimples on her cheeks. Runs Free was a lovely child, as free-spirited as the wind that stirred the dried-up leaves hanging on the oak trees at the edge of the clearing.

She's so much like me, Touching Sky thought to herself. *I only wish her life were as carefree as mine was at her age.*

When Touching Sky was a child, her father, Straight Arrow, had often gone hunting west of their home near the Delaware River. Then their fellow natives, the Iroquois, had traded away their land and forced her people to move west of the *keekachtanemin*.

As though that wasn't enough of an insult, the settlers built houses and trading posts along the Susquehanna

River—beyond the boundaries agreed upon in the treaties. Over the past few decades, the Lenape-Delaware—her people—had suffered the loss of the territory they had used for generations. The settlers who moved onto their hunting grounds were mostly British subjects greedy for land. Most troubling was the treaty the Iroquois had recently forged with the province of Pennsylvania. They traded away the hunting grounds along the Susquehanna River valley in blatant disregard for the Delaware and Shawnee who lived there.

Touching Sky glanced down at Runs Free, who had finished her *sapan.* "Do you want more?"

Runs Free nodded and handed her the empty plate. She piled on another generous helping. Although they had little meat, at least they had sufficient corn to feed the two of them. In some places, the white army had burned the Delawares' corn crops or driven them away from the ripe fields.

Touching Sky thought of her tribe as a peaceful people. Yet Custaloga and his fellow chiefs fought to stop the white man's encroachment. Chief Custaloga had thrown in his lot with the French army since they seemed more respectful of the lines that marked off the boundaries of Indian territory. After the Delaware people helped rout the British general Braddock, they joined the French and the Shawnees to form raiding parties on the settlements along the Susquehanna, and as far east as the Tulpehocken Creek. Most times they picked their targets carefully, attacking those who had refused them hospitality or slighted them in transactions.

At first the war went well. Custaloga's warriors returned home every moon or so, celebrating their victory and waving the scalps they had taken. But as the war dragged on, nearly all of the Delawares abandoned their villages in the Susquehanna River valley and moved west into Ohio territory. And then the French ran short on supplies, leaving the Indian villages without adequate firearms, blankets, or food.

Touching Sky wouldn't have cared about firearms except that the men depended on guns and ammunition to shoot game. She could do with less of some things, but she couldn't bear to tell Runs Free that there wasn't enough meat. Last winter, they had run out.

Far worse than the food shortage was the loss of her son, Suckameek, just over a year ago. Suckameek had accompanied a small war party to the village of Kittanning about a week's march from Custaloga's Town. They'd gathered there with other Delawares to raid the frontiers under the orders of Shingas, Captain Jacobs, and King Beaver—the Indian chiefs most feared by the white man.

On the day before the raiding party was to leave Kittanning, Colonel Armstrong launched a surprise attack. It was the first time the British had entered a Delaware village in the Ohio territories. Although the Indians made a valiant defense, nearly all of the thirty homes in the village were destroyed. The ammunition magazine—which boasted enough gunpowder for years of battle—exploded with such force that the sound was rumored to have reached Fort Duquesne, several days' walk to the south and west. Dozens of Delaware lost their lives in the intense engagement. Others lost their homes, their ripe corn fields, their loved ones, and about a dozen white captives. One of the surviving villagers brought the news of the crushing defeat to Touching Sky's village a few days later.

Touching Sky felt tears forming as she recalled the day she received the news.

Runs Free looked up, "What's the matter, Mama?"

"Nothing. You may go and play with your friends."

Runs Free frowned. Touching Sky hugged her daughter and smiled. Relieved, Runs Free ran outside into the sunlight.

Touching Sky often depended on her daughter's carefree spirit to brighten her depression. After Suckameek's death, bitterness had welled up in Touching Sky's soul, followed by a determination to avenge his death against the rapacious white settlers who were scrambling for land. If only she could have Swift Foot to work for her and Runs Free this coming winter, to serve them in place of Suckameek and satisfy her sense of justice. Would Tamaqua succeed in convincing the French to let the young German come back to the village? If so, could she convince the women of the village to give her custody of the young man? *If so,* she thought, *I think I could face the future with hope.*

When Joseph came to, his head was throbbing. He opened his eyes. Tom Lions held the barrel of his gun at his throat. Tom was arguing with Tamaqua. How Joseph wished he could understand what they were saying!

Tamaqua pushed the barrel of Tom's gun aside and motioned for Joseph to get up. Joseph forced himself onto his feet and then reeled and fell over. His head spun with pain. He paused momentarily on his hands and knees, trying to clear his head. Blood ran from his face.

He was struggling to stand when Tom kicked him hard in the side. *Oompf!* Joseph fought for breath.

The warriors half-dragged him toward the guardhouse, lifted the door flap, and pushed him inside. It was dark and cold inside the small wigwam, and the wide pieces of bark that made up the side smelled like stale smoke.

Tom and another warrior forced Joseph to lie facedown next to the wall and bound both of his feet to one of the wall supports that arched from floor to ceiling. They tightened the ropes around his wrists and then stood talking for a few moments before ducking out of the door opening and leaving him alone.

Joseph lay with his face on the dusty floor. His cheek oozed blood and his nose ran as he began to cry. He desperately wanted to wipe his face. Although he strained at the ropes on his wrists, he couldn't relieve the discomfort.

He tried to shift into a different position. His cheek felt swollen and his jaw hurt when he opened and closed his mouth. He thought back to what had just happened.

It was time for Tom to learn his lesson, Joseph told himself. *If only he hadn't dodged, I could have broken one of his ribs. Or at least knocked the wind out of him.*

What would *Dat* do in a situation like this? Of course, *Dat* wouldn't have kicked Tom, so he wouldn't have ended up in the guardhouse with his hands and feet tied.

Maybe I should have taken Dat's *advice not to hit Tom,* Joseph thought. *But I'm not* Dat. *I have to make my own decisions.*

As his eyes got accustomed to the dark room, he saw a mouse scurry across the dirt, then disappear into the bark. Ugh! He hoped it wouldn't come any closer.

He felt light-headed. *I wonder how long they'll keep me tied up here. And when are they going to bring me food? Or will they let me starve for fighting back?*

He shifted on the floor, trying to take the pressure off his aching ribs. Pain shot through his side whenever he tried to take a deep breath. *If I ever get my hands on a gun, I'll kill Tom and run away.*

He was half-asleep when someone raised the flap in the doorway. A beam of afternoon sunshine flashed into his eyes. He squinted. Two people stepped into the small room. Tamaqua! And the woman who had made the popcorn. She held a small wooden bowl in her hand.

They spoke softly to each other for a few moments before the woman squatted down on the floor beside Joseph and washed the blood off his cheek. The raw wound burned a little as she scrubbed off the dried blood, but he was glad for her ministrations. If only he could understand her gentle words as she worked.

Tamaqua and the woman talked quietly for a few moments, then left.

Joseph was alone again. It was almost dark when he heard the rustle of the door flap. Tamaqua came in with a burning brand. He went to the pit at the center of the room and used the brand to start a fire. When the fire was burning well, he sat cross-legged on a mat near the fire not far from Joseph. The smoke wafted upward through the vent hole in the roof.

Joseph watched Tamaqua through narrowed eyes for a time, pretending to be asleep. The fire barely threw out enough heat to reach Joseph, but he was grateful for the little that came. *Maybe I can get warm enough to stop shivering. If only I could get off the ground, I wouldn't be so cold.*

His mind went back to the scene three days earlier when he'd last seen *Dat* and Christian. Were they together? Were they in a guardhouse like he was? If so, *Dat* would probably be saying his prayers, since it was the time of the evening they would have gone to bed back home. Dat *told me to pray the Lord's Prayer every day,* Joseph thought. *I haven't been doing that. Maybe it would help me get out of this trouble.*

He closed his eyes and imagined the scene with the family gathered around the table back home at the Northkill, with *Dat* leading in prayer. *Unser Vater in dem Himmel! Dein Name werde geheiligt,* he started off, saying the words silently in his head in his native German. He paused at the phrase "Give us today our daily bread," when his mind went back to the taste of *Mam's* good bread. Tears rimmed his eyes as he imagined her at the oven, pulling out the fresh-baked loaves in the summertime, sweat dripping down her face from the heat. He felt her push him away, telling him to wait until the bread was cool enough to handle.

His stomach growled at the thought of bread, and he realized how hungry he was. He hadn't eaten any bread since the attack, nearly a month earlier. All he'd had was ground corn. *Don't the Indians bake bread?*

He was so hungry now that he'd settle for most anything, even if it were made of corn rather than wheat. It wouldn't even need to taste good. Something to make his stomach stop begging.

He was on the verge of falling asleep when a woman opened the flap and came in. Her face shone in the glow of the firelight. Tamaqua grunted in recognition and exchanged words with the woman. Joseph recognized her voice; she was the one who had washed the blood off his cheek earlier. What did she intend to do now?

Again Joseph watched through slits in his eyes, pretending to be asleep, as the woman walked over and threw a light blanket over his body. She paused for a moment, said a few words to Tamaqua, and then left the wigwam.

I'll have to pray more often, he thought as he felt the warmth of the blanket on his shoulders. *I'll never get away from this place with my feet tied to the wall. Maybe if I cooperate with that woman, I'll be able to get out of here before long.*

Touching Sky stood close to the fire with others who came to witness the fate of the recent captives. The village would seek consensus.

Never had she felt such a desire to take a captive into her own family. The tall young man with the green eyes could fill part of the gaping hole left by the loss of her son.

The group fell silent as Chief Custaloga spoke about the recent raids and where the captives had been captured. "Our war parties went to the settlements on the far side of the Susquehanna," he said. "We found one of our captives there. Farther along, we raided an Amish farm not far from the path to Philadelphia. We took the rest of our captives there."

Then Custaloga brought each of the captives into the center of the lodge in turn, beginning with the oldest. Touching Sky looked over each one carefully.

Her heart quickened when the chief brought Joseph into the center of the circle. He did not look down as most of the captives did, but he looked around at the faces in the crowd. He was wearing a linen shirt, full-length linen breeches, and Indian moccasins.

"Take off his shirt," someone said. "We cannot see what kind of man he is with a shirt on."

Others nodded in agreement, so the chief motioned to Joseph. The boy looked confused.

Impatiently, the chief mimed removing his shirt. Joseph blushed. He bashfully opened the front of his shirt. His chest was mostly bare, with a few sparse hairs. The assembled villagers tittered. A couple of warriors whooped.

An elderly man stepped up and tugged on Joseph's sleeves, and then pulled off his shirt. Joseph stood there, his white skin showing a sharp contrast to the brown skin of his captors.

He will get darker in the sun, Touching Sky thought. *Bear oil will make a difference.* She gazed at the corded muscles on Joseph's arms and neck. *He will be strong one day.*

"We captured this young man along with his father and brother," the chief said. "He is a very fast runner, as he showed in a race with our young men not long ago. He can jump as well. He will do well in the games."

He's the perfect son for me, Touching Sky thought. *Almost like Suckameek.*

"Is there anyone who would like to take this young man into their family?" The chief waited. Touching Sky quickly stepped forward, as did Thitpan, a woman two summers older than she. Runs Free quickly skipped over to where her mother stood and clasped her hand. Thitpan glared at Touching Sky and her daughter and then folded her arms. Touching Sky tried to look confident.

"I see that we have two women who would like to lay claim to this captive," the chief said slowly. Then he smiled at Runs Free. "Perhaps three!" Runs Free giggled and the crowd laughed. The chief continued, "The women's council may gather now to decide which one will get this prize." An old woman hobbled forward until she stood directly in front of Touching Sky and Thitpan.

"Thitpan, tell us why you think you should adopt this white boy," she said.

Thitpan spoke. "As you all know, ten years ago I lost a small child to smallpox, the spotting sickness brought by the white man. I deserve to have a young white man to replace my child, who would be about the same age by now." Her eyes glistened slightly and she sniffed a few times.

Touching Sky watched the people nod their heads in affirmation. She looked at Joseph, who was watching the exchange intently. *I wonder if the young man can understand anything in our language?* Touching Sky thought to herself. *Does he know what Thitpan said?*

After a few more questions for Thitpan, the older woman turned to Touching Sky. "Tell us why you would deserve this young man as an adopted son."

"All of you know that early this year, I lost my only son, Suckameek, in one of the raids against the settlements. He was young, but he was strong and very brave. Because his life ended so soon, I would like to take Swift Foot to fill my son's place." She looked around at the women as she spoke, taking care not to show undue emotion. "Runs Free needs an older brother to look out for her as well."

Out of the corner of her eye, Touching Sky saw a few approving nods. *Good.*

Touching Sky held her breath as Thitpan muttered loudly: "Although she has lost a warrior son, she still has a young child in her home. I have no one."

Touching Sky heard moccasins scraping the ground. No one spoke. She glanced again at Joseph, who stood with his arms crossed over his chest. Tentatively, she smiled at him. He turned his head away.

Runs Free let go of Touching Sky's hand and walked over to Joseph. She smiled at him and held out a piece of jerky.

He hesitated for a moment.

"Take it, Swift Foot," said Runs Free. "I want you to be my brother! If you were my brother, we could share lots of things."

Touching Sky saw that Joseph didn't understand the words, but he understood Runs Free's kindness. He crouched down until he was at eye level with the little girl and looked her in the eyes. Then gently, he took the jerky from her and said something in a language that they couldn't understand. But everyone understood his smile. It was the first one they had seen from the white captive.

Touching Sky hadn't realized she was holding her breath until she released it. She looked at the women's council. They were nodding with approval. The old woman hobbled over to the other women. Together, they talked in low tones. Finally, they motioned for Chief Custaloga.

"Touching Sky shall have custody of the captive," he said a few moments later, then paused. "And Runs Free."

The group applauded—all but Thitpan. Her countenance fell, and she scowled. Custaloga continued, "Touching Sky and Runs Free, you may take Swift Foot into your home tonight."

Touching Sky could barely contain her excitement. Runs Free jumped up and down, clapping her hands. Touching Sky beckoned to Joseph, who came toward her. She reached out her hand and bade him stand beside her. Excitement coursed through her veins. No one could replace Suckameek, but this would be a new beginning for her little family.

Joseph stood stock still as Touching Sky stepped up to him with a turkey feather in her hand. He didn't flinch as she smeared vermillion-colored paint, mixed with bear's grease, onto his cheeks, chin, and forehead. He remained still as she hung a string of wampum around his neck, speaking in the language of the Delaware.

He motioned that he didn't understand.

She pointed to herself. "Touching Sky," she said.

He repeated it as best he could.

She smiled, and he could tell she was pleased. She pointed at the little girl. "Runs Free," she said.

He repeated her name, and the little girl who had shared the jerky with him grinned. She was missing two of her front teeth, just like his little sister, Franey, who had let him pull a loose tooth just a week before the capture.

Then Touching Sky pointed at his pants.

Joseph looked at her, confused.

She mimed taking off his trousers, more urgently this time.

Panic gripped him. He had no underclothing, and he had never undressed in front of a group of strangers, least of all women. What did this mean? He was about to bolt when a man came from behind and swung his long arms around Joseph, locking them tight against his chest. He yanked Joseph up and back, lifting his feet off the ground.

"No!" Joseph yelled as two other men came forward and pulled off his trousers. He flailed his legs as the villagers roared with laughter. Touching Sky stepped up and held a breechcloth in front of him, motioning for him to let her fasten it on him. He stopped kicking as she passed the soft deerskin leather between his legs and hung it over the belt she tied around his waist.

The villagers cheered as Touching Sky adjusted the leather so that it draped evenly in front and in back. It hung about three-fourths of the way to his knees.

Joseph relaxed ever so little now that he was covered. How was he going to stand the strange feeling of the soft leather pressing against the inside of his legs, the sense of exposure on his thighs?

A drum and a rattle began to beat out the rhythm for a dance. The men in the village lined up and began to move in a large circle around the fire. One of them pulled Joseph into the line beside him and motioned that he should imitate the others. Each man sang his own tune as he stomped his way around the fire, but Joseph had no sense of what they were saying.

At first he kept pace with the group, just to avoid being pushed along. But the children outside the circle began to wave at him, inviting him by their motions to stamp his feet with the rhythm. It felt strange, but he gradually joined them in the movement, dancing awkwardly to the rhythm of the drum.

My father would frown if he saw this, Joseph thought. The children clapped their hands at his progress, and he realized they were celebrating his arrival as a captive.

Tamaqua, who had accompanied Joseph from Custaloga's Village to Presque Isle and back, came alongside Joseph. "*Nar wiscumpton*," he said to Joseph.

Joseph wrinkled his brow.

Tamaqua said it again. "*Nar wiscumpton*."

This time Joseph mouthed the words, not knowing what they meant.

Tamaqua's face lit up. He motioned for Joseph to do it repeatedly, in rhythm with the dance.

As he chanted the words, Joseph began to imitate the young men dancing in the circle, waving his arms in rhythm with the drum. He soon caught on to the rhythm and forgot for a moment that he was a complete stranger. *This is almost like running in place*, Joseph told himself. *I should be able to do it as fast as the others*. The children laughed and clapped as he passed by. Touching Sky flashed him a wide smile, as did Runs Free.

Joseph was worn out by the time the drummer stopped. Despite the chill in the air and his bare legs, he had managed to work up a sweat. But when he stood still for a time, and felt the cold on his legs, he stepped closer to the fire. Touching Sky came up to him and offered him a piece of corn cake sweetened with syrup.

Joseph stuffed the food into his mouth without saying anything. It was nothing like *Mam*'s cooking. He was famished, though, and grateful for food of any kind.

When people began to retire to their wigwams, Tamaqua took Joseph by the arm and led him to a wigwam. It was a small home with a dim fire that made little pretense of pushing away the darkness. After his eyes got adjusted to the dim light, Joseph could see a wide shelf that hung some three feet above the floor along one wall, with blankets and hides lying on top. Tamaqua motioned for Joseph to lie on it and then tied his hands in front of him.

After Tamaqua left, Joseph lay there in wonder. There was no lock on the door. It was the first time in weeks that he'd had such an opportunity. *If I stay awake until everyone else is asleep, I could escape. I wonder what they'd do if they caught me.*

His heart beat faster as he recalled the morning of the attack, with the bodies of his mother and Jakey sprawled on the ground. *They'd likely kill me. They've probably got guards posted outside by the fire, waiting to put a tomahawk into my skull. I'd better stick around here for a few days before I try to get away.*

Although he was tired from the day's march and the dance, sleep was elusive. He thought about his friends back home at the Northkill and wondered what they'd say if they saw him now. There'd be plenty of stories to tell once he got home. He thought about the friendly woman who called herself Touching Sky. *I wonder what she has in mind. Does she want to be my new mother? Or will she use me like a slave?*

He'd show her soon enough that no one could take the place of his real mother, whom her people had murdered in cold blood. Someday he'd get revenge.

He thought of Runs Free. She was almost the same age as Franey. Cute too. But it was her people who had killed his little sister.

He remembered the night of the apple *Schnitzing*, the social gathering to prepare apples for drying, when he had bested the other boys in a race. He remembered how his mother's face beamed with happiness when he crossed the finish line. If only he'd known that the Indians were in the woods that night, they could have escaped to the fort. They could have avoided the attack.

Joseph's anger rose as he thought of his father. Why had *Dat* stopped him from shooting at the war party? Perhaps if he'd shot at them, the whole family would be alive today. With that in mind, he fell into a troubled sleep.

-3-

December 1757

A wave of worry washed over Touching Sky as she stole a last look at Joseph before she went to bed. Perhaps she had trusted him too soon to be safe. Curled up hound-like on a mat on the floor with his eyes open, he gave no sign that he saw her.

In her eagerness to find a son to take Suckameek's place, she hadn't thought through how she'd deal with an angry captive in her home. She'd seen smoldering fury in the young captive's eyes as Tamaqua left the wigwam to go home. Perhaps she should have asked him to stay with her yet another night. Or perhaps they should have kept Joseph in the guardhouse longer. But she'd wanted so much to have the boy do tasks for her that she'd begged to take him in right away.

Since Joseph had more freedom with his hands tied in front of him rather than in the back, he could be more dangerous. What if he found the knife she used to skin game and prepare meals? He'd seen her use it and might have taken note where she kept it. Even with his hands tied in front of him, he could handle a weapon.

She waited until she heard Joseph settle into steady breathing and then she slipped quietly to the other side of the room. From deep familiarity as much as from the dim light, she found the knife without making a sound and carried it back to her bed.

There were nearly thirty captives in the small village now. That didn't count the ones that the village had decided to kill because they refused to cooperate. It was too much trouble to keep captives who were dangerous or who were likely to escape. That is, unless they could be sold to the French for ransom.

The villagers who'd recently taken custody of captives would have good advice for her regarding the best time to stop tying Joseph's hands at night, or when to let him be trusted with tools like knives and axes. Perhaps more advice than she wanted. She didn't care to hear another word from Walks Proud or Tom Lions, who stood ready to mock her if the boy escaped or harmed her family.

She was sure that it would be love, not force, that would win over Joseph's loyalty to her family. But until his anger subsided and he proved his willingness to cooperate with assigned tasks, she'd need to watch him closely. She couldn't take a chance that he would harm her or Runs Free. Nothing could be worse than to lose her only child or see her harmed in some way.

Maybe she could ask her nephew, Tamaqua's son, Miquon, to help keep an eye on Joseph for her.

She shifted onto her left side so that she could watch him. The knife was secure under her blanket. She could reach it at a moment's notice.

The next morning, Joseph woke to see sunlight streaming through the open doorway. Touching Sky was squatting on the dirt floor next to a pot that simmered on the open fire. The smoke from the cooking fire drifted upward and out of the smoke hole in the middle of the roof.

Joseph pretended to be asleep, taking in the dimly lit room with his eyes almost closed. The oval wigwam was made of a gridwork of saplings covered with bark. It had no window, but the sunlight shown around the edges of the reed mat that served as a door. Braided husks of corn and dried plants hung suspended from wooden crosspieces near the roof. A shelf was mounted on the wall above the ledge that served as his bed.

Joseph's eye was drawn to Touching Sky as she rose gracefully from her squatting position without the use of her hands.

She tore a few leaves from a dried plant that hung from the ceiling and then squatted back down to crumble them into the pot. Mam *could never squat down like that and get up again without using her hands,* Joseph thought. *Of course,* Mam *was a lot bigger than Touching Sky.* He glanced around the room again. *I guess she's used to it. There are no chairs to sit on around here.*

Touching Sky caught Joseph's eye and smiled at him as she pantomimed breakfast.

Joseph scowled. But he was hungry. And if he were going to escape, he would need to eat in order to build up enough strength to get back home.

Over the next few weeks, Joseph tried to make sense of his situation. He was stuck with three women in the wigwam—Touching Sky, who seemed to be a little younger than *Mam,* Runs Free, about Franey's age, and Silver Sage, whose black hair was threaded with strands of gray. Was she a relative of Touching Sky? If not, why was she living in the same house? They chattered all day and often glanced in his direction, but most of their words were just noise to him. *They could be talking about me and I wouldn't even know it.*

Touching Sky rarely let him out of her sight, and when she did, someone else was always close by. It was December, what the Delaware referred to as "the month of the clouded moon," and every day that slipped by seemed to lower his chances of getting away before winter set in. There would be no escape without being noticed.

One day Touching Sky handed him two large gourds and motioned for him to fill them. Joseph headed for the creek, hoping to be by himself. It was not to be. Runs Free came trailing along.

I'm just a slave, Joseph said to himself. *Touching Sky makes me carry water, gather firewood, and carry out ashes.* Although his wrists were no longer bound—Touching Sky had untied them two weeks earlier—they were still marked and red.

He stood at the edge of the creek and watched the swirls where the water dashed against the rocks. The splashing sound was a balm to his soul, reminding him of the times he'd played back home in the Northkill Creek not far from their cabin.

He dipped the two gourds into the cool water and carried them back to the wigwam. Joseph set them onto the ground near the cooking fire and looked at Touching Sky.

She nodded her head as though approving, and then motioned for him to follow her. With Runs Free dancing at her side, she walked to Tamaqua's home. Joseph tried to make sense of the connection between Tamaqua and Touching Sky. They stood close together as they conversed, displaying an easy familiarity that spoke of a kinship with each other. Perhaps they were siblings. It helped make sense of the times he'd seen them together.

Tamaqua brought an ax out of his wigwam and handed it to her. She nodded her thanks and walked back toward her home. Joseph followed after, wondering what it meant. He soon learned. She wanted him to add to their woodpile.

Joseph took the ax and started chopping. At least this was familiar ground; *Dat* had often made him chop wood back home. It might help him rebuild the upper-body muscle he'd lost during the weeks of walking on the trails with his hands tied. He'd need all the muscle he could get if he got into a fight with an Indian.

Although he hated to be told what to do, he soon settled into an easy rhythm. About the time he had broken into a sweat in the cool air, he examined the blade of his ax.

Dat would say it's time to sharpen this, he observed. *I wonder if they have a stone to sharpen it.*

He carried the ax to Touching Sky and showed her the dull edge. She shrugged her shoulders as though to say she didn't understand. Using his hands, he demonstrated the motions he would've used back home to sharpen the ax. Soon she nodded in recognition, and brought out a fine-grained stone.

Joseph rubbed the stone along the ax's edge until he noticed that it was getting sharper. He didn't care how long it took as long as the edge got sharp.

As Joseph sat cross-legged with the ax on his lap, Runs Free watched from a distance. The longer Joseph worked, the closer she moved in to watch. *She's curious, just like Franey was,* Joseph thought.

Finally she asked him a question in the Delaware language.

Joseph guessed at her meaning. "I'm sharpening this ax," he said in Swiss-German. "It will make it easier to chop firewood."

Runs Free pointed to the ax. "*Temahican,*" she said. She pointed at the stone. "*Kinhikan.*"

Joseph nodded and kept rubbing the stone against the edge.

Runs Free repeated the words. "*Temahican,*" she said again as she pointed at the ax. She pointed at the stone again—"*kinhikan.*" She motioned for Joseph to speak.

He pronounced the words as best he could, not sure they'd sound right.

Runs Free laughed and clapped her hands. "*Lenhaksen,*" she said as she reached down and touched the footwear Joseph had been given on the trail. The moccasins were nearly worn out; a small hole was showing in the sole.

Joseph stopped working on the ax. He repeated the words she had spoken as clearly as he could. It was hard to imitate the sounds exactly; it was like talking with his mouth full of food. Why did it have to be so hard?

Runs Free repeated a few German words she had picked up from him. She said each one like a question, pausing after each word.

Joseph knit his brow for a moment as he tried to comprehend the words. Much as he hated being a captive, he didn't want to disappoint the little girl who reminded him so much of Franey. She didn't seem to mind that he was a captive, and she spent more time with him than anyone else in the village.

Joseph pointed to each of the things she had named to him, and spoke them back to her in German—*axt, stein, mokassin*—pointing to each one in turn.

Runs Free repeated them all in such passable German that Joseph nodded his head in affirmation.

If Runs Free learns to speak German, he thought, *I won't have to work so hard to understand the Delaware language. I can't understand all of the sounds they use, much less the words.*

He continued burnishing his ax. When he was satisfied with the edge, he went back to chopping wood with Runs Free observing nearby. She seemed as happy that Joseph was learning the Delaware language as he was that she was learning German.

The next morning when Joseph woke up, he wasn't sure what to do with his time. Back home, he'd worked alongside *Dat* or *Mam* every day, except on Sundays. On long winter evenings, *Dat* would take a break from farm chores and carve figures out of wood.

Maybe I could try that, Joseph thought. *At least it will give me something to do.* Runs Free was still sleeping and Touching Sky and Silver Sage were outside the wigwam talking to friends, so he rummaged around in Touching Sky's basket until he found a knife. Outside, he looked for the right tree and found a good-sized maple sapling only a stone's throw away. Joseph sliced off a section the size of his thumb from one of the lower-hanging branches and then sat down under the maple, thinking hard.

What could he make? Maybe something to remind him of his home at the Northkill. A cow? A hog? No, that would be too complicated. Maybe the log cabin where he'd grown up. That shouldn't be too difficult.

Sitting on the ground in the morning sunlight, he soon got engrossed in the task, shaping the small piece of wood into a miniature cabin. As he carved the outline of the front door, it brought back memories. How many times had he whipped open that door and slammed it behind him, racing down to the path to the creek or barn?

"Joseph, you don't have to slam the door when you go out," Mam would say when he returned. *"It makes the windows rattle. Why do you have to be in such a hurry?"*

He'd usually shrug his shoulders and mumble something about needing to stretch his legs. *Mam* was a large woman who ran out of breath when she walked. How could she have understood the pent-up energy that stirred up inside him, pressing for release in a good race?

Joseph incised small lines to show the windows in the cabin. As he carved the one that marked the upstairs bedroom where he'd slept, he recalled the times he'd watched the full moon outside his window rise above the walnut trees. So many memories! Engrossed in the work, he drifted back into time, until the sudden chatter of a squirrel brought him back to the present. The sun was high in the sky now, warming the crisp autumn air.

He rose, stretched his aching muscles and brushed off the wood shavings. Joseph looked at his carving. *Not half-bad.* Dat *would be proud that I'm learning to carve.* He went to the wigwam and hid the little wooden cabin under the bearskin where he slept each night, then put Touching Sky's knife back where he had found it. Just as he stepped back outside, Runs Free came skipping up. She said something in her own language and tugged on Joseph's arm.

Joseph gave her a puzzled look, so she repeated her words, showing him an iron hoop and pointing to the stick. She mimed rolling the hoop.

He nodded. "Okay, Runs Free, I'm all yours!"

She grinned and grabbed his hand, pulling him along until they were in the village clearing. There she tossed the hoop out front of her and chased it with a stick. The hoop rolled until it hit a clump of tall grass.

She handed him the hoop and said something in Delaware. It seemed as if she wanted him to try rolling it.

Joseph studied the hoop. *Looks like it came from a wooden keg*, he thought. *They must have gotten it from a trader.*

He tossed the hoop in front of him and started to chase it. It wobbled and fell. He tried again. This time, he kept it going with his stick. Runs Free ran beside him, cheering as he made the hoop roll all the way to the clearing before it hit a rock and fell over.

Runs Free picked up the hoop and set it on its edge. It was obvious that she wanted to give it another try.

Joseph watched as Runs Free tried to keep the hoop going. *Franey would have liked this game*, he thought to himself.

By this time, several villagers had gathered to watch. One of them, a young father, held his little girl up on his shoulders. The girl sat watching the game, giggling from her vantage point up high.

Runs Free pointed to the little girl and said something to Joseph in Delaware. He shook his head, not understanding. She repeated her words, tugging at Joseph's arm. It seemed that she wanted him to lift her onto his shoulders.

What would the villagers think of such a thing? thought Joseph. Runs Free seemed too big to be carried that way. She persisted, and reluctantly, he hoisted her up and set her on his shoulders. Her legs dangled onto his chest. He held her hands to help her balance. It felt familiar, since he'd seen his father carry Franey that way.

Runs Free jiggled with excitement. She babbled something in Delaware, and it seemed like she wanted to go for a ride. She waved at the villagers, who laughed at the sight. Joseph didn't understand her words, but he understood the kicks she was giving his chest. He bounced on the balls of his feet as he began to walk, imitating the sounds and motions of a horse as he had often seen his father do with Franey.

Runs Free got into the act, bouncing on his shoulders and pretending to be a rider. She wiggled her right hand out of

Joseph's and waved at Touching Sky, who had followed the sound of laughter to the scene.

Touching Sky smiled and waved. She said something to Runs Free. It must have been something about holding on tightly, because Runs Free reached down to grasp Joseph's scalp lock.

"Ouch," Joseph said. "Don't pull on my hair or I'll make you get down."

He said the words in German, but Runs Free heard his tone and relaxed her grip.

As Joseph marched around the village with Runs Free bouncing on his shoulders, other children begged their fathers to do the same with them. Before long there were a dozen men carrying boys and girls in a line that snaked between the dwellings. Older children ran alongside, clapping their hands and yelling encouragement. Runs Free directed the line, shouting instructions to Joseph and pointing in the direction she wanted him to go. *She loves attention, just like Franey.*

Before long, as the other children started chasing hoops, Runs Free signaled that she wanted to join them. The two of them chased the hoop until Runs Free was tired and hungry.

I don't mind playing games with Runs Free, Joseph thought as they headed back to the wigwam to eat. *She helps people trust me. Maybe they won't suspect that I'm planning to run away from here as soon as the winter is over.*

-4-

The wind whipped through the trees as Joseph headed for the creek clutching three large gourds. As usual, Runs Free tagged along behind when he left the wigwam.

I could dash away into the woods and Runs Free wouldn't be able to keep up with me, Joseph thought. *This might be my last chance to get away from here before it gets really cold.*

He glanced up at the gray sky laced with wispy clouds racing by. *I'd need a good blanket though. And I'd need to take some food with me.*

Runs Free trotted alongside to keep up with Joseph's long strides. "Here," Joseph said as he extended a gourd to her, "you carry this one." Although he spoke to her in German, she seemed to understand. Her quick smile told Joseph she didn't mind being asked to help.

Fallen leaves, thick on the path, swirled in the breeze as Joseph and Runs Free neared the creek. Joseph slowed his pace and breathed deeply of the autumn air. He closed his eyes for a moment and felt himself back home, walking down the path to the Northkill Creek, where *Dat* kept his muskrat traps in the wintertime.

Runs Free tugged at this arm.

He realized that he'd stopped walking, lost in the reverie of a different time and place. *I've got to get back home*, Joseph thought as he nodded to Runs Free. He walked to the mouth of Deer Creek where it joined with the much larger French Creek, then knelt down to dip from the smaller of the two streams. The water seemed clearer and better to drink. *This is not nearly as good as our spring back home*, Joseph thought, remembering that *Dat* had said it was one of the reasons for choosing the wooded tract called Ipswich. *Dat* said it was named by William Penn after an English town.

If I can get back home, I'll never complain again about having to get water for Mam, he thought, forgetting for a moment that she was dead. She seemed plenty alive and real in his dreams at night. At times he heard her laughing or scolding at the thoughts dancing inside his head. *Can* Mam *really be gone?*

Joseph watched as Runs Free squatted down and filled the gourd. *She is lucky to have a mother,* Joseph thought. *I wonder if she realizes that her people killed mine.* He swallowed the bile that rose in his throat. He motioned roughly for Runs Free to follow him back to the village.

Just as he started back, a young woman passed him on her way to the creek. She looked to be his age or a little older, with dark brown hair drawn together and tied back with a yellow ribbon. Her dark brown eyes met his for a moment as the bark basket she was carrying brushed against one of his heavy gourds. Water sloshed onto his leg.

He hesitated for a moment, and then turned to follow her to the creek. He set down the gourds on the side of the path to keep them from spilling. She looked like another captive. His heart was racing. Might she understand German? He would try.

"*Guten Tag,*" he said.

"*Guten Tag,*" she replied, with a hint of a smile playing around the edge of her lips. When her eyes met his, they seemed filled with pain. Joseph remembered his *Mam*'s eyes had looked that way as she talked about the killing and scalping of their neighbors—the Reichards and Meyers—earlier that summer.

"*Ich bin der Yoseph* (I am Joseph)," he said, hope rising in his heart. "*Vas is deinen Nomen* (What is your name)?"

"Elizabeth," she continued in German, "or Lizzie for short." She spoke better German than Joseph, who preferred the Swiss dialect that he'd imbibed with his mother's milk.

"That's my mother's name," Joseph said.

"They never use my name here among the Indians. They call me Summer Rain. I've been a captive here since . . ." Her voice trailed away as the wind tugged on the blanket that she had wrapped around her shoulders.

Joseph thought he understood. How could one keep track of time without clocks or calendars? Only because *Dat* had collected a little stone in his pocket each day had he been able to keep track of the twenty-one days on the trail from their Northkill home to the fort at Presque Isle. It seemed as though there had been a couple of full moons since then, but Joseph couldn't be sure. One thing was certain; winter was just around the corner. If he was going to escape from the village, he'd need to do it soon, before snow blocked the paths that led home.

"They call me Swift Foot. That's because I outran them when they chased me during the attack."

"I saw you race Tom Lions when you first came here."

For a moment, Joseph thought he saw a little light in her eyes. "Where are you from?" he asked.

"My family settled next to the Susquehanna, near Fort Harris," she said. "The Indians killed my folks and took me as a captive." She wiped the corners of her eyes with her blanket as she spoke.

Joseph swallowed hard. "They killed my mother, and one brother and sister too, and took *Dat* and me and my brother Christian captive. I don't know where *Dat* and Christian are. One of these days I'm going to find them."

Summer Rain cast a worried glance at Runs Free as Joseph spoke. "My mother used to say that the little stalks of corn have big ears," she said.

It was a proverb *Mam* used when she feared that six-year-old Franey was eavesdropping. Joseph realized it might be risky to talk to Summer Rain with Runs Free listening in, even if she didn't understand German.

"Have you ever thought of running—" He was interrupted by a shout. He looked up to see Touching Sky huffing down the path. She looked worried. What was she so bothered about?

Joseph wheeled and picked up his gourds. Touching Sky spoke sharply to Runs Free and snatched the gourd from her hand. She motioned for Joseph to go ahead of her.

Joseph sighed. *Now what have I done? She can't be that upset about my taking a little extra time to get the water.* He thought for a moment. *Maybe she doesn't want me talking to Summer Rain.*

Touching Sky followed Joseph as he walked back to the village carrying the water. Why had he been talking to that white captive?

When they got back to the wigwam, Touching Sky took the gourds from Joseph's arms and set them down on a mat in the wigwam. She shooed him outside with her hand.

"You stay here," she said to Runs Free, who had started to follow Joseph outside.

Runs Free stepped back inside.

"Now tell me," Touching Sky said to Runs Free, "what were Swift Foot and that girl doing at the creek?"

Runs Free shrugged her shoulders. "Nothing. Just getting water."

"What did they say to each other?"

"I don't know."

"What do you mean, you don't know? Weren't you listening?"

"I couldn't understand them. They talked some other language."

Touching Sky sighed. "That's what I was afraid of. Who knows what they are saying to each other? They could be making plans to run away from here, for all we know."

"They would freeze to death in this weather."

"True, but they might be desperate."

Touching Sky squatted down and took Runs Free's chin in her hand. She looked hard into her eyes. "Daughter, you must tell me if you ever see Swift Foot with that girl again. Or any other white captive. Do you promise?"

"Yes, Mama."

Touching Sky took a deep breath as Runs Free wiped her nose with her blanket and went outside.

Touching Sky waited for a moment and then walked over to where Silver Sage squatted by her cooking pot. The stately widow woman was not only her aunt—she was also her confidante, her best friend, and her wisest counselor.

"Aunt," she said with her hands on her hips, "I sent Swift Foot to fetch water this morning, and then found him talking to a young white woman in German. What should I do?"

Silver Sage picked up a long wooden spoon and stirred the stew as Touching Sky waited. "What are you worried about?"

"You know what I'm worried about. If we let them talk to each other in German, they might be conspiring against us. We've gotten so many new captives lately that it could be dangerous."

Silver Sage nodded. "There are nearly thirty captives. That's a fourth of our village." She paused. "Perhaps Swift Foot has no ill intent. He may be attracted to that young woman. She is pretty—and he is coming into manhood."

"It's not good for whites to be together. It will keep them from becoming Indian."

Silver Sage nodded as she stirred her stew, which was bubbling. She held out a spoonful for Touching Sky to taste. Touching Sky blew on it and took a bite. "Mmm. That's delicious."

"Just remember that children most long for stew when you forbid them to taste it," Silver Sage said. She looked at Touching Sky out of the corner of her eye.

Touching Sky went to the door and looked out at Joseph. He was standing at the edge of the woods with Runs Free at his side. He was pointing into the woods, as though explaining something. What might he be telling her?

Touching Sky sighed. Although six moons had passed since Joseph had arrived, and the cold winter was nearly over, Joseph hadn't learned to fit into her family the way she had hoped. She pulled down the basket of herbs and spices that hung from the ceiling of her wigwam. She prided herself in being a good cook, but Joseph didn't seem to like her food. How different from her son, Suckameek, who had always eaten her fare with a glad heart. She could see him now, sitting cross-legged next to the cooking fire with a wooden plate in his hands, downing generous portions of stew and corn cakes.

She closed her eyes to savor the memory of a gentle and obedient son, the kind every mother would want: one who not only enjoyed her food but thanked her for it!

"Mother," he'd said to her on the day he left on that fateful trip to Kittanning, *"You're the best cook in the village. My friends are jealous. That's why they like to come here to eat."*

Her chest swelled as she remembered that several of her son's friends had spent more time eating in her wigwam than Suckameek did at theirs.

She set the basket of herbs on the table and looked at what she had. What would make Joseph happy? She looked toward the far end of the wigwam. "Aunt! I have a question for you."

Silver Sage laid down the mat she was mending and came over to Touching Sky. "You look sad," she said.

"I wish Swift Foot would eat my food," Touching Sky said.

"I think he eats pretty well," Silver Sage said. "He keeps growing. He's as tall as I am. Besides, he likes your cooking better than mine. Runs Free told me that he misses the bread and butter his white mother made for him. If I lived with the white man and had to eat their food every day, I'd miss our food just like he misses his."

Touching Sky arched her eyebrows. "So would I." Suddenly she felt sorry for the boy. He must miss his mother badly. "Maybe I should bake him some corn cakes. I think the white man makes those too. I haven't made those since Suckameek died." Her voice choked on the words.

She reached up to tear several ears of corn from a braided cluster of husks. She wrung the dry kernels off the ears and tossed them into her mortar to grind.

Silver Sage spoke. "Maybe there are other ways besides food that could help Swift Foot feel at home here."

"I'm sure that when the boys start playing games and running, he'll feel at home."

"The weather will soon be warm enough now. Couldn't you let him go hunting or fishing?"

Touching Sky frowned. "I'm afraid he'll run away. He seems wild and unsettled."

Silver Sage cocked her ear toward the door. "I can hear him playing outside with Runs Free. They seem to be enjoying themselves. Isn't that a good sign that he's adjusting?"

"Maybe. But I'm afraid he's waiting for warmer weather to escape, like the man who tried to run away last year." Touching Sky paused to remember that Walks Proud had tracked down the captive, who then was burned to death.

Touching Sky pounded the pestle into the grain, avoiding Silver Sage's eyes. "How could I face the village if Swift Foot ran away and never came back? Or if he ran away and got caught and then had to be killed? Walks Proud and Tom Lions would mock me to my grave. Custaloga would never let me have another captive. Runs Free would grieve—she already loves Swift Foot like a brother."

"You can't hold him forever. He won't be fully Indian until he has the freedom to come and go as he wishes. Remember that your children are not your own but are lent to you by the Creator." Silver Sage spoke so quietly that Touching Sky stopped her grinding to make sure she could hear every word.

She pulled out the pestle to see if there were any stubborn kernels left unground and then jammed it back into the mortar. "Swift Foot doesn't realize he owes his very life to me. If Tom Lions would have had his way, he'd be dead. I wish the boy would show some appreciation for what I've done for him."

"Does he know that you saved his life?"

"I doubt it. Maybe I should tell him. I got him as a son to replace the one I lost, and all I've had so far is trouble. I wonder if he'll ever come to love me like a son loves his mother." Touching Sky poured the ground corn into a mixing bowl and crumbled in a few herbs.

Silver Sage shrugged her shoulders. "He's only been here a few moons. You need to give him more time. Feed him some good corn cakes with maple syrup. I have a little bit of sugar left in a gourd I can give you."

Touching Sky nodded. "Thank you. I'll try to think of other things that I can do for him as well." She sighed. "I need patience! But it's hard when you want to show love to someone and he doesn't love you in return." Her eyes were moist.

As she put the corn cakes on to bake over the fire, Touching Sky heard Runs Free's laughter. She went to the door. Runs Free and Joseph were chasing a hoop together. Both of them had a stick and Joseph only hit the hoop when Runs Free couldn't keep it rolling. *My son never helped her with the hoop that way,* Touching Sky observed. *I guess she's a little older now. That's why he lets her do it.*

The pair was still playing with the hoop when Touching Sky called them in to taste the corn cakes. She lifted them from the baking surface, so hot that she nearly burned her hands. She cut one of the cakes with a knife and poured a generous serving of maple syrup on it before handing it to Joseph. After blowing on it to cool it, he gulped it down in two bites. The expression on his face gave her no satisfaction, but the speed that he consumed the corn cakes was thanks enough.

She upended the gourd with the syrup and let the last drops fall onto another cake as Joseph looked on. This time, he didn't wait for her to hand it to him, but picked it up and blew on it, then ate it. His face was expressionless. Then he turned to go outside again.

Runs Free gulped down a cake as well and followed Joseph outside. In a few moments, the sound of laughter drifted back into the wigwam.

Touching Sky took up the empty gourd and gave it back to Silver Sage. "It worked," she said. "He ate those cakes right up. I hope the sap drips heavy from the trees this year. It could make the difference between having a happy captive who might become like a son . . . or not."

-5-

April 1758

Now that the long winter had passed, Joseph found that the memories of his family were growing dimmer. But his resolve to escape was still firm. With the coming of spring and the scattering of warriors from the village, Joseph's hopes for an escape gained ground against the desperation that hung like a cloud in his soul. Would he ever be free from Touching Sky's dominant hand? Would he ever get back to his beloved home? It was warm enough now that he could make the journey back to the Northkill without fear of freezing to death.

Over the winter, Joseph had made many adjustments to Indian life. Now he could understand the rudiments of the Delaware language. Although he still didn't like the food, it didn't bother him as much. His breechcloth and leggings seemed normal to him now.

But he would never become one of them. Never.

Joseph sauntered through the village, hoping to catch sight of Summer Rain. If he was lucky, he might get to talk to her without rousing anyone else's attention. He walked along the backs of the wigwams, looking into the tops of trees as though watching the birds as they flitted through the greening leaves.

He stopped for a moment as he neared the wigwam where Summer Rain lived, thrilled with what he saw. She was walking toward the woods from the little hut in the back of the wigwam. Just as she disappeared in the woods, he moved to stand at the place where she was sure to return. He looked up into a large maple whose leaves had sprouted to about half the size they would be when mature. *Mam* always said that meant it was time to plant the first things in the garden.

Soon Summer Rain came into view. "*Guten Tag,*" Joseph said, not caring what Touching Sky would say if she saw them together. "Do you want to take a little walk in the woods with me?"

Summer Rain glanced quickly toward the wigwam where she lived. "I don't see anyone, so we should be safe." Together they took the path that headed into the woods.

Now that they were alone, Joseph felt unaccountably awkward. He cleared his throat. "It's been a hard winter," he said in German, hoping to start a conversation.

She nodded, answering him in German. "I can't stand it here. I miss my family. I want to be back with my family around the fireplace in a warm cabin, not in these cold wigwams." She looked as though she was about to cry.

"Me too," Joseph said.

"The Indians watch me all the time. I can never get out of their sight."

"How did you get away today?"

"They think I'm in the hut."

"Oh, the one in back of the wigwam?"

She nodded.

Joseph paused. Dare he ask Summer Rain the question that had been stirring in his mind for months? He ventured out, choosing his words with care. "What are those huts for?"

The color in Summer Rain's cheeks and neck took on a pinkish hue. "It's a place for women to go when they can't be in the wigwam."

"I thought it was just for women," Joseph said. "But only Touching Sky goes there, never Silver Sage or Runs Free. She usually stays in there for a few days, so Silver Sage does the cooking for us. The food is never as good as when Touching Sky cooks."

"I hate staying in the hut all by myself. And it's cold in the wintertime."

"How often do you they make you stay in the hut?"

"Just when . . ." Summer Rain paused and her cheeks flushed again. "You know, about once per moon." She looked down to the ground as though to study the fern that was sending out its curling shoots near her feet.

"Oh, I see." Actually, Joseph didn't see. What did the moon have to do with it? But the way that Summer Rain shifted her shoulders told him not to ask more questions. He decided to change the subject.

"I'm thinking about running away," Joseph said.

Summer Rain looked around before she spoke, and even then she lowered her voice. "That's very dangerous. If they find you in the woods, they'll kill you. Or bring you back here and torture you to death."

"Sometimes I think I'd rather die than stay here," Joseph told her. "I've got to get away."

"I'm not going to take the chance," Summer Rain said. "I'm waiting for the British to win this war and come to rescue us." She paused, considering. "It might take a few years."

"I don't want to wait that long." They both fell quiet for a few moments, thinking.

Summer Rain spoke again. "Have you ever seen what they do to people who make trouble?"

Joseph shivered. "I saw a man run the gauntlet when we were at a large island in the Susquehanna River. They really beat him up." He could still hear the man's shrieks. He blocked the image and sounds out of his mind.

"You didn't have to run the gauntlet yourself?"

"No, *Dat* gave the chief some peaches and he spared him, along with me and my brother."

"You mean he just happened to have peaches in his pocket?" Summer Rain stared at Joseph in disbelief.

"No, *Dat* planned it that way. Before we left the house when it was on fire, *Dat* crammed dried peaches in his pocket. He asked us to do it too so we'd have extra food."

Summer Rain's eyes were wet. "You're lucky your *Dat* planned ahead that way. They made me run the gauntlet here at Custaloga's Town. They nearly broke my arm." She pulled back the blanket that covered her arms, and held it out it for Joseph to see. A scar ran across her upper arm.

"That's awful."

"It hurt bad. But not as bad as what they did to the older man who tried to run away." She paused, and swallowed hard. "They burned him to death."

Joseph sucked in his breath.

"They made us watch. He screamed for mercy. You could smell his flesh burning. They didn't care. They just laughed and put more wood on the fire."

Tears trickled down Summer Rain's face. Joseph put a hand on her shoulder.

"So you're not going to run away with me?"

"No, we'd surely be caught."

Just then, Joseph heard Runs Free calling. "Swift Foot, where are you?"

"I've got to go back to the hut," Summer Rain said as she started toward the edge of the woods. "Don't tell anyone that I talked to you."

Joseph quickly left the path and walked along Deer Creek. The next time Runs Free shouted for him, he yelled back. "I'm over here."

He sat on the bank of the creek and chewed on a stem of grass. *What am I going to do now?* he asked himself. Summer Rain would be no help. Her spirit was broken. He was on his own. He felt the ray of hope he had nurtured all winter begin to dim.

Might there be another white captive—a brave man perhaps—who could join him in an escape? He needed someone who knew the paths through the woods better than he did. If he left now, he'd have to follow all of the main paths, with no one but enemies to ask if he lost his way. All the forts were manned by the French, who were just as dangerous as the Indians.

What was he to do? Was he going to be stuck here forever? Would he never be free?

Half a moon later, while Joseph was chopping wood, he heard the sound of warriors firing their guns at the edge of the village. Several warriors from within the village fired their guns in return.

Joseph gathered up the firewood he had cut and carried it back to the wigwam. Surely there must be captives. He wanted to see them arrive.

A party of ten warriors came into the village, led by Tom Lions, who waved a scalp at the end of a pole. Two tongues dangled from his belt.

There were four captives—two young men, a young woman, and a little girl. All of them appeared to be younger than Joseph. All four of the captives had their hands bound behind their backs. They looked frustrated and angry. All but the little girl. She just looked exhausted.

The captive who walked just in front of Tamaqua caught Joseph's eye as they passed. He was taller than anyone else in the party, with a heavy thatch of blond hair. *I'll bet he's Swiss*, Joseph thought. The young man glanced at Joseph and their eyes met for a moment before he yanked at the hemp ropes that bound him and slowed his walk. Surely he had noticed that Joseph was white, despite his Indian clothing.

Joseph followed the warriors and watched as the villagers quickly grabbed weapons and took their places in two lines to form a gauntlet. Soon dozens of men, women, and children stood waiting in two lines with axes, clubs, switches, brooms, and heavy sticks. Touching Sky appeared, carrying a large stick that she kept in her house. Joseph looked at her, the woman who made his meals and slept in the same wigwam with him. *Surely she wouldn't* . . . Runs Free joined them, carrying a small tree branch.

Joseph tried not to stare at the captives. He heard Touching Sky laugh. The hideous paint on the warriors' faces added to the nightmarish feeling of the scene.

The chief motioned for the tall young captive to go first. The young man cursed and started off running between the two rows of people toward a pole perhaps fifteen paces away. No one blocked the young man's way, but Tamaqua picked up sand and threw it into his face. He slowed, trying to wipe the grit out of his eyes. As he did, Touching Sky tripped him by thrusting a stick between his legs. A young warrior grabbed the young man's long hair as he struggled to regain his feet. Meanwhile, Tamaqua rained blows on him.

Joseph looked away. The memories of his own capture brought bile to his throat. *How could Touching Sky, who seemed so gentle in the wigwam, act this way toward a captive?*

When Joseph looked up again, the young man was back on his feet, pushing his way through the gauntlet by flailing his arms in front of his face. He staggered to the end of the line and fell onto his knees, grasping the end post with both hands. After he caught his breath, he staggered to his feet and held his hands against his left ribs. Pain was written on his face. Blood ran down his nose from a cut on his forehead. He wiped the blood off his face with his tattered shirt.

The little girl was next. As she entered the gauntlet, Joseph could no longer watch. He took deep, ragged breaths, blocking her screams by holding his hands over his ears. How could this be happening? How could the village deliberately inflict harm on their captives and then expect them to feel good about being adopted into Indian families? Did they hope to instill such fear that the captives would submit to whatever happened? No wonder Summer Rain was afraid to run away.

The time seemed endless. Joseph watched the captives being led away, bloody and defeated. The little girl was crying. He looked around but couldn't see Runs Free or Touching Sky. *I hate them! I never want to see them again!*

Depressed and sick at heart, he went into the woods and stayed until the sun dropped low in the sky. He could not dispel the sounds and images from his mind.

It grew dark. Joseph knew he must go back to the wigwam. He could see the smoke of the cooking fires curling into the sky. Tentatively, he entered the wigwam. Touching Sky was calmly stirring something over the fire, and something smelled good. Despite his bitterness, he was hungry. Runs Free looked up and smiled at him—she was halfway through her dinner.

Joseph sat on the floor in his accustomed place and Touching Sky held out a bowl of bear meat mixed with corn. He took a few bites and then gagged. Despite his hunger, he couldn't eat. He handed the bowl back to Touching Sky.

Touching Sky looked at him with concern.

"Swift Foot, what is wrong with you? Don't you like my food?"

Joseph looked at her for a long moment, and then the words burst forth with the words he was learning in Delaware. "Why do you make captives run the gauntlet? How could you hit a little girl with your sticks? She was as innocent as Runs Free."

Touching Sky's face hardened. "The gauntlet is a way of testing captives to see how brave they are. If they shrink back or beg for mercy, they will be severely punished as they run through."

"But what if they are weak or old? And what if they are small, like the girl?"

"We do not try to kill or maim anyone who cooperates, and we will be considerate if the captive is weak or young," she said. "Didn't you notice—the little girl was barely touched. She mostly screamed out of fear."

Joseph thought about this. He remembered the bloody wounds of the younger man. "But who would want to adopt a captive who has been handicapped by running the gauntlet?"

"Captives must be taught to fear us," she said. "When we make them run the gauntlet, we teach them to be afraid of what could happen, so they will not try to escape." She looked searchingly into his eyes.

Joseph was silent. Touching Sky returned to tending her food.

Joseph stared at the ground. Runs Free jabbered about something she had done with friends that afternoon, down by the creek. He heard her voice but didn't take in the words.

How long must he endure this? *I want to go home.*

-6-

It was late spring in the village, the season of the year the Delaware called *seekun*. The snow had melted, joining with spring rains to swell the streams that flowed into French Creek. Each day Grandfather Sun lingered longer in the sky, warming Mother Earth with his powerful rays, preparing the soil for the spring planting.

Touching Sky picked up her small hoe made of bone and walked toward her garden plot on the edge of the village. She squatted down to feel the warming earth and scooped up a handful of the dark brown dirt. She held it up to her nose. The odor of the crumbly, pungent loam filled her nostrils.

She moved to the edge of the plot and squatted down to hoe, coaxing the soil into hillocks, ready for the corn. *Swift Foot should be doing this*, she said to herself. She formed another small mound, then dropped her hoe and walked back toward the wigwam.

Joseph was playing a game with Runs Free, chasing her hoop with a stick.

"Swift Foot," she said as she motioned toward the garden, "come help me hoe the garden." She saw the look of disappointment on his face. "There will be time to play later."

Joseph stopped chasing the hoop and let it roll on its own until it collapsed near her cooking fire. He shuffled toward Touching Sky with Runs Free close behind.

Runs Free asked, "Can I help too?"

"Of course, little one," Touching Sky said. Together, the three walked toward the garden.

By the time they got to the plot where Touching Sky had begun hoeing, several other women and young girls were working. Touching Sky picked up her hoe and showed Joseph how to use it, but his attention seemed drawn toward one of the young girls.

"That's Summer Rain," Runs Free said to her mother. "She's the one who talked German to Swift Foot."

Joseph glared at Runs Free and then turned to Touching Sky. "What do you want me to do?"

Despite his reluctant tone, Touching Sky was pleased with how clearly he'd said the words in the Delaware tongue. "I want you to make little hills like this with the hoe," she said, pointing to the ones she'd just finished.

Joseph picked up the hoe and began to work.

Touching Sky watched him for a few moments and then moved to pull up some of the weeds in the seedbed. "You can help me," she said to Runs Free. "The soil is nice and moist, so you can yank them out easily. Here, watch me."

Touching Sky breathed deeply of the moist air as she pulled weeds, moving to the edge of her plot. As she neared the end, she nearly bumped into Summer Rain, who was hoeing in the next plot. Touching Sky studied her, taking care not to stare. Summer Rain worked methodically, chopping up the soft earth. *This one is a good worker,* Touching Sky thought.

Summer Rain straightened up and swept back a strand of dark hair that escaped her ribbon. She wiped her brow, then fingered the long earrings that graced her ears. She looked briefly at Touching Sky. Her nose was long and thin in the manner of whites, not short and pushed back like Touching Sky's people. But she had the Delawares' dark brown eyes.

Touching Sky glanced over at Joseph, who had stopped hoeing. He was watching Summer Rain, following her every move with admiration.

Touching Sky watched with amusement as well as alarm. *What might be going on between those two?* Her mind flitted to the memory of her son, Suckameek, at about Joseph's age, starting to notice the young women in the village. *Ah, well.*

She bent down to resume weeding. The small plants swam in her eyes as she remembered the young woman who had captured her son's heart. She was a member of the Turtle clan whom he surely would have married if he had returned from the battle at Kittanning. Perhaps she'd even have a grandchild by now, a little one to hold in her arms and love. If only Suckameek had not died, everything would be so much better.

Love was a wonderful thing, as long as it drew together the right people. Surely Joseph must be lonely for someone who spoke his language and reminded him of home. But it wasn't right for Joseph to be enamored with Summer Rain. Not now, while he was pushing against Delaware ways. On the other hand, Summer Rain seemed to have adjusted to life in the village. Might she draw him to love her people, who loved and cared for the earth without taking possession of it like the white man?

Joseph didn't mind working in the garden. It was ten times better than being cooped up in the wigwam in the dead of winter with only a smoky fire to keep the family warm. How often he'd awakened at night in the cold wigwam, shaking from bad dreams about the attack on their farm in the Northkill, or crying because he missed his family more than he had ever thought possible. He'd tried to ignore his homesickness during the day. Now that the weather had improved, nearly everyone was outside. While the women planted gardens, the boys who were Joseph's age went hunting or played games.

Although Joseph didn't join them, he enjoyed watching. But he longed to test his skills against theirs.

One afternoon when he, Touching Sky, and Runs Free left their work in the garden to watch, he was especially restless. At first, Joseph thought he'd be content to stand on the side as several young boys lined up for a race. His heart beat faster as he watched them take off running. *I could run faster than that*, he thought as the fleet-footed boys raced to a tree and back. They ran naked except for breechcloths, pumping their arms with their locks of black hair streaming behind them.

Suddenly Joseph felt the urge to compete against the others. He looked at Touching Sky, hoping for a clue that it would be okay. She smiled and waved him into the contest.

Joseph strode up to the mark in the grass that served as a starting line.

"Yahoo!" several of the boys yelled as they took up the challenge. They pointed toward the tree, gesturing to show that the runners would have to touch it and then return.

Someone yelled "Go," and the group was off. Joseph slipped on the grass and almost fell as he leaped off the line, so he trailed in the rear as the runners took off.

I'm going to catch up, he thought as he heard Runs Free yell encouragement. By the time he reached the tree, he was only a step behind the frontrunner. By the time the runners were halfway back to the starting line, he was out in front, and he easily finished a stride ahead of the rest.

He waved at Runs Free, who was jumping up and down as she cheered and shouted his name. Several boys motioned to Joseph with their hands, challenging him to a longer race. "To the tall tree and back," they said in Delaware.

I think I know which tree they're talking about, Joseph thought. After seven months in captivity, he'd learned a lot of Delaware words, but it was easy to miss people's meaning when they got excited.

By the time the runners lined up at the mark, the crowd of spectators had swelled by half. Joseph breathed in deep gulps, anticipating a hard run.

As soon as the runners were off, Joseph's mood turned sober. This would not be an easy race; he could barely keep up. He could see now that they were headed toward a large, tall pine on the very edge of the clearing. He got there a stride behind two others, and kept his place as they touched the tree and headed back.

The spectators shouted and a man pounded on his drums as the group came running back. By the time they were halfway, Joseph was neck and neck with the leader. His chest ached as he neared the finish line, but he put on a burst of speed that thrust him to the front by half a stride.

Whew! He bent over double, breathing hard but smiling broadly. The sound of drums celebrated his win. He looked at Touching Sky, who was smiling too.

That was the end of the footraces, but there were lots of other games. Joseph played alongside the boys his age all afternoon—chasing hoops, wrestling in the grass, and swimming in the cold water of the stream nearby.

I could do this every day, he thought. *It's a lot more fun than work.*

A group of boys beckoned him to join in a wrestling match. He watched two of the boys as they wrestled on the grass, each straining to pin the other down. He flexed his muscles, remembering the time he'd wrestled his older brother Jakey to the ground. *I bet they're no stronger than Jakey. If I got him down, I should be able to wrestle them.*

Within a short time, he was in a match, struggling to pin down another boy. It was more difficult than he had imagined. Joseph had hardly gotten started when his head was pinned to the grass. A sharp stone was cutting into his ear.

Joseph felt a flash of anger. This was too much like having his hands tied as a captive. His heart pounded and his legs trembled as he got up off the ground.

His face burned. Joseph took a deep breath and sauntered across the clearing as nonchalantly as he could muster. He needed to clear his head.

Joseph sat on a stump at the edge of the woods and pondered what had happened. Why was he so upset by a minor defeat, particularly after the spontaneous joy of winning the race?

It wasn't a disgrace to be defeated in an informal match. That had often happened when he wrestled his older brother. Something else was at stake, it seemed: a hatred for being dominated by one of the people who had murdered three members of his family. How could he live among them in peace? He felt like walking away and never coming back.

Touching Sky was coming toward him. *She must be worried that I'm going to do something foolish or run away.* He stood up. Without the Delaware words to convey his feelings, he would simply need to swallow them. *Perhaps I should avoid wrestling matches.*

By midafternoon, Joseph's anger had cooled enough that he competed in the hoops. Back home in the Northkill it had been a game for small boys. Here it was a contest of speed as well as coordination. The hoops didn't roll easily in the tall grass, so it took constant vigilance to keep them moving toward the goal with a stick.

Joseph won, just as he had in the footrace, earning a wide smile from Touching Sky. Her warm look dissipated Joseph's knot of anger that remained from the early part of the day. Perhaps she liked being a winner as much as he did.

"Ho . . . ho!"

Joseph heard the greeting as he finished eating a corn cake next to the cooking fire. He looked up as Touching Sky swung open the covering of the door. Her nephew Miquon stood there, smiling. He was dressed in a calico shirt, breechcloth, and leather leggings, with a knife in his belt. He also carried a fishnet made of wood fibers and woven with strands of hemp.

"Can Swift Foot go fishing with me today?" he asked.

Joseph's heart leaped. Here was a chance to get away. *I can explore some ways to escape from the village.*

Touching Sky searched Joseph's face, as if to gauge how much he could be trusted. "How far will you go?" Her voice was pitched a little higher than usual.

"Not far. Just up the creek a little ways. I have cornmeal to eat if we are hungry." Miquon pointed to a leather pouch that dangled from his waist.

Touching Sky nodded. "Here, take this basket with you. I could use some fish. And clams too. Be sure to be back before the sun goes down."

Joseph jumped up and pulled on his leggings.

"You won't need your leggings to go fishing, will you?" Touching Sky asked.

"We may go through some heavy bushes or thorns in the woods," Miquon replied. "It might be good to take them."

Touching Sky scooped a handful of corn from her woven basket and poured it into a leather pouch. She handed it to Joseph along with one of the uneaten corn cakes. "In case you get hungry," she said.

Joseph nodded but said nothing as she handed him the basket in which to place the fish.

"I want to go along," Runs Free said.

"No." Joseph was thrilled at the opportunity to truly get away with Miquon, and he didn't want Runs Free to spoil it for them.

Runs Free stuck out her bottom lip and pouted. "I want to fish too."

Touching Sky put her hand on Runs Free's shoulder. "No, you stay here. You'll have other times when you can play with Swift Foot. I need you to help me make corn cakes."

Runs Free began to cry. "I don't want to make corn cakes!"

Joseph hastily left the wigwam to the sounds of wails and forced himself not to look back. *Little girls. What a nuisance.* Miquon looked at him and shrugged. His expression said it all.

Joseph had seen Miquon around the village but had never spent any time with him. *I wonder why he wants to go fishing—with me.* Joseph was intrigued. It had been a long time since he'd enjoyed doing something with a boy his own age. He realized for the first time how lonely he was for a friend.

Miquon led the way toward the large creek forks at the edge of the village. A number of others were fishing there, so Miquon continued to a place further upstream.

Joseph breathed deeply. The spring air was fresh and smelled clean, like *Mam's* laundry used to smell on wash day, with just a tinge of smoke from the village cooking fires. He heard the call of the *memedhakemo*, the turtledove, which sounded just like the slender-tailed bird that perched in the oak tree near his bedroom window back home. It was as though it was beckoning him to follow it on swift wings to the Northkill, where he had first grown to love its plaintive cry. Now it echoed the song of lament in Joseph's heart, a desperate wish to be free.

Miquon pressed forward on the trail, pushing to the place where the creek widened into a sunny cattail swamp. Two ducks flapped noisily out of the water. Back home, Joseph would have had a rifle to shoot the ducks. Would he ever win that privilege here? Did Touching Sky even own a rifle? He'd never seen one, and she probably couldn't afford to buy one.

Miquon finally found a spot that satisfied him. It was far enough upstream that Joseph could no longer smell smoke, even though it drifted lazily in their direction. It was the farthest that Joseph had been away from the wigwam since being brought from Presque Isle.

Miquon sat on the bank of the creek and put his net in the water. Joseph knelt beside him and watched.

"Don't we need bait?" Joseph asked.

"Maybe. But I might be able to catch a crayfish without it. Here, flip up that rock for me."

Miquon's net was so poorly made that Joseph didn't expect him to catch anything, but he reached down and nudged the rock, which was about a foot under the water.

Miquon made a quick move with his net. He swept up a small crayfish. "I got it!" He reached into the net and grabbed the crayfish by its arched shell. "Here, you hold it." He handed it to Joseph, who watched its frantic legs wave in the air as Miquon pulled a piece of hemp string from his pouch.

Joseph watched Miquon tie the heavy string around the crayfish's body. Miquon gently dropped it back into the water after tying the free end to a sturdy cattail growing in the shallow water at the edge of the creek. Together they watched the creature tug hard against the rope. Then it disappeared into the murkiness.

"We'll pull it out later," Miquon said.

Joseph hoped Touching Sky wouldn't cook the crayfish for a meal. *Mam* had never cooked crawdads to eat. They were like bugs—big, muddy bugs.

Would he ever learn to do without the food *Mam* served at home every day—bread and butter, milk and cream, or sugar and salt? The only food he really liked in the village was the corn cakes that Touching Sky made. If only they could have more maple syrup on them! But there were few sweets.

"Let me dig some worms," Joseph said. "That will help us catch some fish." He walked a little ways into the woods, looking for a fertile spot near a rotten log, the most likely place to find some sort of bait. It would also be a place where he could be alone. Here he could dream about a time to run away.

He picked up a stick and dug up a soft place at the edge of a rotten log. The log had seemingly birthed a row of saplings. They sprung like piglets at a sow's side in the pen back home. Joseph smiled to think of it.

It turned his mind to bacon, something he hadn't tasted for more than eight moons. *Mam* knew there was nothing like the aroma of frying bacon and mush wafting up the stairs to lure Joseph and his brothers out of bed. That was especially true in the wintertime, when the nighttime frost etched exquisite patterns on the window panes and glistened in the first rays of the morning sun and when the bedroom he shared with his brothers was freezing cold.

Thinking of *Mam*'s food brought back memories of three family meals each day with everyone seated on chairs at a table. He missed not only the sumptuous fare but also the banter with his brothers. Here at Custaloga's Town, no one used a table or chairs, and they only ate twice a day.

He'd just dug out first grubs from under the log when Miquon sauntered up to him. "Find anything?"

"A few grubs and a cricket."

"That will do. I have a fishhook." Miquon held out the curved bone at the end of a hemp line, motioning for Joseph to thread the bait onto it.

Joseph jabbed the cricket onto the hook and followed Miquon with the grub worms in his hand. He watched as Miquon threw the line into the water. It landed with a quiet *plunk*. They both stretched out on the bank and sat in companionable silence. Miquon, Joseph was discovering, wasn't big on words. But he was easy to be with.

The water flowed by. This was the wide creek where he'd paddled the bateau up from Fort Machault as a captive, such a short time ago. If only he could find a canoe or a dugout, he could float back down at night with little effort. Or lacking a boat, he could follow the creek to the fort. From there, he could retrace his steps back home.

It was *Dat* who'd paid the most attention to where they had been on the trail, and even he had lost his bearings. The safest way to find his way back home was to find a friendly Indian guide, a settler, or a British soldier. Maybe if he became Miquon's friend, Miquon would help him.

He looked at Miquon, who was quietly chewing on a grass stem. *No,* thought Joseph, *I can't do that.* He'd be punished severely for betraying Touching Sky's trust.

He'd have to take the chance at finding a British soldier. But the truth of his situation weighed heavily on his mind; if he were to leave the village to head downstream today, he'd be a hundred times more likely to run into a hostile Indian than a friendly soldier.

His reverie was interrupted by Miquon's shout: "I've got one!" Joseph glanced up to see Miquon yank a catfish the length of his hand out of the water. Miquon gutted it with the knife that hung at his side and tossed it into the large basket.

Joseph threaded a grub worm onto the hook and went back to daydreaming as Miquon fished. The day passed quickly. When the sun was high in the sky, they ate dried corn in the shade of a large cottonwood that hung over the creek.

"Touching Sky should be happy with our catch," Joseph said as he carried the crayfish and several catfish back to the wigwam. To Joseph's relief, Miquon insisted on taking the crayfish home for his mother, leaving Joseph the two catfish.

Touching Sky fried the fish for supper. The meal was the next best thing to having corn cakes. Joseph felt a flicker of hope—things were definitely improving on the food front.

The best chance I have of escaping from here is to gain Touching Sky's trust to go fishing and hunting by myself, Joseph thought as he ate. *Then I can go a long ways before they miss me. Maybe I can do that before the snows falls this year. I could live at my brother John's house or with my sister Barbara's family, and eat bacon all winter long.*

He fell asleep that night thinking of home.

-7-

July 1758

The sun was peeping over the horizon when Miquon showed up at Joseph's wigwam. Since their first fishing trip, Miquon and Joseph had fished and hiked together, and they were well on their way to becoming friends. On one outing, Miquon had told him about a cliff that overlooked a valley, where you could see for a long distance.

"This would be a great day to go to those big rocks I told you about," Miquon said. "We will be able to see a long way in this clear sunshine." He had a bag strapped over his shoulder with food for two days, and he carried a hatchet in his belt.

Joseph nodded eagerly.

They headed into the woods. The sun beamed shafts of light through the leaves, splotching patches onto the forest floor. Joseph listened to the sounds of a woodpecker just off to the left. The hammering stopped and a flash of black, white, and red crossed the path ahead of them.

If Joseph were home on the farm today, he would surely be working in the field, likely cleaning up rocks to clear the field for plowing and planting. It was far more fun to be hiking in the woods, enjoying the warm spring day. But . . . home. The air was warm enough now that he wouldn't need to worry about freezing. This trip might be his chance to escape. He didn't dare speak of his desire, even to Miquon.

Joseph and Miquon strode along at a leisurely pace, taking in the sights around them and listening to the birds in the trees. Joseph paid particular attention to signs along the trail. If he were ever to escape and find his way home, he would need to become familiar with the art of tracking in the woods.

Joseph was thinking so hard he almost stepped on a rattlesnake sunning itself on the path. He jumped backwards, nearly knocking Miquon down. Both boys moved away from the snake.

"Let me kill it," Joseph whispered to Miquon. "I'll club it to death."

"No!" Miquon grabbed Joseph's shoulder.

"Why not? We can use the skin to make a belt."

"We do not kill rattlesnakes. They are our brothers." Miquon stepped between Joseph and the rattler, which slithered off the side of the path.

Joseph stared in disbelief. "You call them brothers? Are you serious? They can kill people."

"Not if we treat them as friends."

Joseph shrugged his shoulders. He would never learn to think like an Indian.

The two boys had walked for some time when they stopped at a small stream for a drink. After satisfying his thirst, Joseph sat down on a fallen log for a brief rest. As he glanced back along at the path where they had come, he saw something move on the path.

It was Runs Free! She slipped behind a large oak tree as he gazed in her direction.

Joseph motioned to Miquon, who rolled his eyes. Then he walked to where Runs Free was hiding. She wore only her moccasins and a thin blanket. She stood very still.

"Runs Free," Joseph said angrily, "what are you doing here?"

She shrunk back against the tree. "I want to see the big rocks."

Joseph sighed. "You're not dressed to walk in the woods. And besides, you won't be able to keep up with us."

"I can keep up! I can! I can! I can! I kept up so far—"

"We weren't walking very fast."

"I can run to keep up."

"She needs to go back," Miquon said.

Runs Free began to cry. "I don't know the way back."

Joseph shrugged his shoulders and looked at Miquon. "Must we take her back to the village?"

Runs Free shook her head. "I want to go with you."

Miquon thought for a moment.

"Does your mother know where you are?"

"Yes, I told her I was coming with you."

Joseph wondered. Would Touching Sky have given Runs Free permission to accompany them into the deep woods without leggings? He looked at Miquon.

"Okay," Miquon said with a sigh. "You can come along. But we won't be able to go as far as I had intended."

Runs Free scrubbed the tears from her face. "Thank you. I'll be very good."

Miquon took the lead as they continued their journey, with Joseph and Runs Free following behind. They walked for a long while with scant conversation. Chipmunks and squirrels scampered on the forest floor while birds flitted overhead. It was a perfect day to be in the woods.

When they stopped to eat, Joseph couldn't help but admire Runs Free's stamina. She hadn't complained once about the pace. She didn't ask for a bite of his dried corn. He took one look at her hungry face and felt sorry for her. He offered her a generous helping.

Her eyes flashed appreciation as she stuffed the corn into her mouth. Trustingly, she curled up next to Joseph. Despite his frustration, he put his arm around her shoulders. She snuggled up to him and closed her eyes.

Miquon and Joseph sat silently and let her sleep for a while before waking her up and continuing the hike. It was early afternoon when they came to a steep slope covered with large boulders. "Is this the place we're looking for?" Joseph asked.

"No, it's farther on, but this place is somewhat like it. It will be fun to climb up on these rocks." Miquon started to scramble up the slope.

"Wait for me," Runs Free called.

"Don't worry," Miquon said as he climbed ahead. "We'll wait for you at the top." Joseph scrambled after Miquon, at times jumping from one boulder to another on his way to the top.

They were far ahead when they heard a plaintive cry from Runs Free. "Help! Don't leave me behind!"

"Just take your time."

"Swift Foot! I'm afraid. I need you."

"I'll go help her," Miquon said. "You can stay here."

Joseph sat on a large boulder and watched as Miquon made his way back down the hill, leaping from one large rock to another.

"Look out!"

Joseph sucked in his breath as Miquon dislodged a large boulder, sending it tumbling down the slope. Miquon lost his balance and tumbled down the slope toward Runs Free, who was toiling up toward the ridge.

"Get out of the way," Joseph shouted to Runs Free as the boulder bounced toward her.

She screamed and threw herself to one side. Joseph watched in horror as the boulder smashed into her leg.

Suddenly, everything was quiet. Then he heard a whimper.

Joseph picked his way down the slope to the spot where Runs Free lay. Miquon was on his feet. He headed toward Runs Free, clutching his elbow.

Joseph got to Runs Free first. She lay on the ground, holding her leg. She was crying with pain.

Joseph's face blanched. Her foot was twisted to an odd angle, and blood seeped from the wound. He glimpsed white and shuddered. *Bone. Her ankle is mangled.*

Joseph reached down to examine Runs Free's injuries. She looked at him with pain in her eyes. "Swift Foot, it hurts!"

Joseph gently touched her leg and Runs Free screamed.

"It's okay. It's okay," Joseph said, but he knew it wasn't. *What can I do?* "We have to stop the bleeding," he said to Miquon.

Miquon nodded. His clothes were ripped from his fall, and his arm was bloody.

Joseph took off his linen shirt. "Runs Free, this might hurt. You must be brave," he told her. She gritted her teeth and nodded, her face wet with tears. Joseph ripped up his shirt into strips. He wrapped several of the strips around the place where the bone came through the skin, trying to stop the bleeding. Despite her assurances, Runs Free screamed again. Joseph shuddered, but Miquon leaned over and soothed the little girl.

He turned to Joseph. "We need to find a plant for her to chew on to stop the pain. "

Joseph picked up Runs Free and cradled her in his arms. "I will carry her for the first part of the trip back," he said. "See if you can find the plant we need."

Miquon set off in search. Joseph gently picked his way among the rocks. *If only Touching Sky were here,* Joseph thought, *she'd help us. But we're a long way from home.*

Runs Free moaned.

"Don't worry. Touching Sky and Silver Sage will know what to do," Joseph said.

Joseph made his way along the trail. Not long after, Miquon appeared, clutching some plants. "Chew on these, Runs Free," he said.

She obediently opened her mouth and chewed, then gagged. Miquon spoke to her rapidly, crooning words in Delaware Joseph had not learned. Whatever he said caused Runs Free to keep chewing, despite making an anguished face at the taste.

We've got to take Runs Free back to the village, Joseph thought. The sun was high in the sky now, and the air was warm. Sweat glistened on his skin as he walked. His arms ached. He would not be able to keep going this way.

"Miquon, please stop. I have to take a rest," Joseph said. He set Runs Free on the ground as gently as he could. Despite his care, Runs Free was crying with pain. "What else can we do?" Joseph asked in desperation. "Why isn't the plant helping?"

"Maybe we can make some kind of litter to carry her in," Miquon suggested. "We could both carry her that way."

"That sounds like a good idea," Joseph said. "We could cut saplings for the sides and use vines to stretch across them."

It didn't take long to chop down a thin sapling and cut it into two carrying poles. Joseph's hands trembled as he and Miquon laid the two poles onto the ground and wove honey-suckle vines between them. He ran the small vines under one side and over the other until they had a litter as long as he was tall. Every few moments, he glanced over toward Runs Free, who lay groaning on the forest floor. Her face was pale and blood oozed from her ankle. He would need to wrap it again.

"We've got to hurry," Joseph said. What would Touching Sky do if Runs Free bled to death before they got home? Surely she'd blame him for not taking care of her. Would the village treat him like a murderer and burn him at the stake?

And he loved the little girl! He hadn't realized it before. But seeing her follow him—and now, depend on him—brought all his feelings to the surface. Runs Free was like a little sister. She couldn't replace Franey, but he cared about her.

He rushed to gather several small pine boughs to make the litter softer. Joseph and Miquon gently laid Runs Free on it. Then he and Miquon picked up the two ends of the litter and continued the trek toward home.

Runs Free gripped the sides with her hands as the litter tipped a bit from side to side, whitening her small knuckles. What if she passed out?

"Wait," Joseph said. "We'll have to tie her onto the litter or she'll fall off." Miquon paused as they laid the litter onto the ground and Joseph bound Runs Free onto the litter with his tumpline, the strap used to carry a deer.

If my father were here, Joseph thought, *he would probably ask God for help*. With that, he began to whisper the words of the most familiar prayer he knew: "Our Father, who art in heaven, hallowed be thy name. Thy kingdom come, thy will be done, on earth as it is in heaven."

He watched Runs Free as he prayed, hoping to see the lines of pain on her face soften. It seemed that she relaxed ever so slightly as they walked along. Was it the plants? Or the prayer? It didn't matter—he just wanted her to be released from the pain.

The rest of the trip back was a blur for Joseph. After stopping twice for brief rests, they got back to the village in late afternoon. They had barely entered the village clearing when they met Touching Sky. She was tending the garden not far from the edge of the woods. She ran toward them.

Miquon and Joseph laid the litter on the ground. Runs Free no longer seemed conscious. Joseph began, "We were a long way from home when we saw her following us—"

Touching Sky motioned for him to be quiet. She loosened the tumpline and bent over Runs Free's body, and then unwrapped the makeshift bandage to scan the wound.

"This is very serious," she said. "Miquon, run to fetch Silver Sage."

Miquon set off without a word.

Joseph looked at Touching Sky. Would she blame him? What would happen to him?

Touching Sky put a hand on Joseph's shoulder. "Swift Foot, my son, I need you to be brave and to live up to your name now. We will need to find a shaman with special powers to set this bone back in place. There is a man named Black Elk in the Shawnee village to the north of here who might be able to help."

"I can run to fetch him. How far is it?"

"Maybe two days. Tamaqua can tell you the way. But first, you must help me carry her to the wigwam." Touching Sky's face was etched with worry.

Joseph was silent as they carried the litter into the wigwam and lifted Runs Free into her bed.

"Before you run to fetch the shaman," Touching Sky said, "you must put some dried corn into your pouch and some tobacco and beads to give to him. Here, let me rub some of this bear oil on your skin to keep away the gnats and mosquitos."

Joseph stood quietly as she smeared the oil onto his face and arms. When he'd first come to the village, he'd hated the smell. Now he'd come to tolerate it. And today, he didn't care. All he wanted was for Runs Free to be okay.

As Touching Sky put the lid back on the vessel, Joseph shoved a hatchet into his belt and swung the strap of his bag around his shoulder.

Worry lines creased Touching Sky's face as she poured a generous amount of corn into the bag. She glanced at Runs Free, who was moaning in her bed. "Please hurry," she said to Joseph. Her voice softened to a whisper as she turned her back on Runs Free. "No one in this village will be able to straighten out her foot."

At that moment, Silver Sage entered the wigwam and gasped. She squatted down by Runs Free and began examining the ankle.

Touching Sky motioned to Joseph. "Run, Swift Foot! Run!"

Joseph ran. First he headed for Tamaqua's home to get directions. And then he loped along the trail that headed north out of the village. Up to now, he'd always run for enjoyment or for sport, but this was different. If he didn't find the help Runs Free needed, she might never walk again. *What if Runs Free dies?* He didn't dare dwell on the thought.

He wondered why Touching Sky hadn't suggested that Miquon go with him. Wasn't she worried that he'd run away? Or was she so desperate for help that she was willing to take a chance?

He took care to notice the marks along the trail as he ran, pushing aside the worries that he might lose his way. His new family was depending on him, so he would have to pay attention to the woods like never before. He simply couldn't afford to go off on the wrong path.

Already tired from the strain of carrying the litter, Joseph soon slowed to a rapid walk. By the time the sun was setting, he was so tired that he knew he'd need to stop for the night. Not long after he got a drink from a creek, he laid down on a bed of pine needles and fell asleep.

He woke up with the first rays of the early morning sun and pressed on his way. After another day on the trail, Joseph knew he should be close. Had he missed it? It seemed like he should have arrived.

The sun was setting. He heard the sounds of the village before he saw it, and then smelled smoke. His shoulders sagged in relief.

Joseph walked quickly toward several men who were sitting around a small fire. "I am looking for a healer named Black Elk," Joseph said.

"I am he," a man said calmly. "What is it that you need?"

"I am Swift Foot, from Custaloga's Town," Joseph said, suddenly aware that his white features might pose a barrier to his mission. "My sister, a niece of the chief, has been badly hurt. A boulder crushed her leg and broke her ankle, so that the bone is sticking through the skin. My mother, Touching Sky, said that you may be able to set the bone for us."

"You are asking a hard thing," Black Elk replied. "How long has it been since this happened?"

"This is the second day," Joseph said. "I ran as fast as I could, stopping only to sleep last night." He held out a pouch of tobacco. "Can you come with me?"

"I have been to Custaloga's Town," the shaman said. "He is a wise chief. After you and I have slept, I will accompany you early in the morning. But now, you must join us for food."

Joseph's stomach growled as Black Elk handed him a plate. He had just sat down to eat when he noticed a white boy with blue eyes sitting opposite him in the circle. When Joseph looked into the boy's eyes, the boy winked at him. Joseph's heart leaped. *It's Christian!*

Joseph stifled the impulse to speak as he glanced at his brother, whom he hadn't seen since they had been separated at Fort Presque Isle nine moons earlier. He yearned to be near to Christian, to put his arm around him and hear how he was doing. Maybe they could run away together. But if the villagers found out they were brothers, they might ruin their plans to escape.

Christian's head was shaved except for the scalp lock, which hung down to his shoulders. His blond hair was much darker now, as was his face. *I wonder what he uses to darken his skin?*

Joseph pretended to be interested in the story that Black Elk was telling, but his mind was buzzing with questions about his brother. How had Christian adjusted to life as a captive? Might they escape together?

The men passed a pipe around the circle as Black Elk droned on with his story. Joseph took a dutiful puff as it came by. *I must find a way to speak to Christian alone,* he thought. *Without anyone else finding out.*

The crickets in the nearby woods chirped in chorus as the men exchanged tales. The fire had dimmed to a glow of embers when the men got up to go to bed for the night. Joseph stepped forward as casually as he could manage. He whispered to Christian in Swiss-German as they lingered near the fire. "After everyone else is asleep, let's meet by the creek where the canoes are tied."

Christian nodded. "I'll meet you there."

When Black Elk invited Joseph into his wigwam a few moments later, Joseph said: "Thank you, but the sky is so beautiful tonight that I shall prefer to sleep outside. I'll be ready to leave as early in the morning as you wish."

"I shall rise with Grandfather Sun. If you're not up when I'm ready to leave, I shall wake you."

"Good." Joseph found a patch of grass near the creek that would serve as his bed, but he had no interest in sleep. This was the chance he had dreamed about for months. If Christian was willing, they could plan a way to escape together.

The moment the idea crossed Joseph's mind, he thought of Runs Free, moaning in pain with a bone sticking out of her ankle. *How could I leave her behind?* Joseph wondered. *Touching Sky would be grieved. But Black Elk could find the way without me. This might be my only chance to escape!*

The waxing moon had risen above the trees when Christian walked up to where Joseph rested. Joseph leaped up and embraced his brother in a long hug. The two of them gazed into each other's faces in the moonlight.

A dog barked nearby.

"Let's sit by the creek," Christian whispered in the language of their childhood. "I don't want anyone to know we're brothers."

Without further words, they sat down by the creek's edge. Moonbeams shone on the water as it flowed lazily around a small bend.

"I am so glad you are here," Christian said as they sat down on the creek bank. "I was afraid I'd never see you again." His voice quivered.

"Me too. I wondered if you were still alive." Joseph's voice was husky. He reached over and put his hand on Christian's shoulder.

"How have they treated you here?" Joseph asked. "You're looking good."

"I take care of an old man with no family," Christian said. "He's really quite friendly, and he treats me like a son. How about you?"

"I live with a widow named Touching Sky and her little daughter, Runs Free. They expect me to do chores around the house. I hunt and fish as well."

"Are they decent to you?" Christian asked.

"Good enough. But I've been trying to figure out a way to go back home." Joseph looked down at the ground as he spoke.

"I did too, at first. But not now."

Joseph startled. "Why not?"

"A few days ago an old Seneca warrior came through our village. He claimed that he killed *Dat* when he escaped from Buckaloons with another man not long ago."

The words cut like a knife. "No, it can't be."

"Yes, he claimed he surprised them at a campfire after sundown."

Joseph searched Christian's eyes in the moonlight. "Do you believe him?'

"I'm not sure. But they told me if they ever caught me trying to escape, they'd kill me."

Joseph shivered in the nighttime air. "They've killed captives in my village too. That's why I haven't tried to run away."

Christian grimaced. "They won't kill a rattlesnake, but they can be very cruel to people."

Joseph's heart was racing. Now he was an orphan. Would he still want to go home if *Dat* wasn't there? Or *Mam*, or Jakey, or Franey? It wouldn't really be a family anymore. Except for Barbara and John, with their families.

Christian broke into his reverie. "Sometimes I wonder if the old warrior wasn't just bragging. Maybe he didn't kill *Dat* at all. Or maybe it was someone else."

Joseph took a deep breath. "So *Dat* might still be alive?"

"There's a small chance."

"I hope so."

The two brothers sat quietly for a time before Joseph told Christian about Touching Sky and Runs Free, the little sister who reminded him so much of Franey. He talked about Summer Rain and other white captives he'd met. Christian told him about the old man he lived with and the adjustments he'd made to Shawnee life. They stayed away from further talk about *Dat* or the attack that had taken them away from their childhood home.

The moon was high in the sky when Joseph stood up. This wasn't the time to escape—not without Christian. He had made up his mind. "I've got to sleep tonight," he said. "I'm leaving early in the morning to go back to my village. Let's hope we see each other again. Maybe by then the Indians will trust us more, and we can go on a long hunting trip, all the way back to the Northkill."

"Especially if we find out that *Dat* got back home alive," Christian said.

"*Jah.*" Joseph's voice choked as he threw his arms around Christian. If only they could know for sure.

The sun had just peeked over the horizon when Joseph and Black Elk left for Custaloga's Town. Joseph swallowed hard as he turned away from the village where his younger brother still slept. He took a deep breath and tried to convince himself that he would see Christian again soon, that someday they would escape together. When they arrived at the end of the second day, Joseph took the shaman directly to the wigwam. Touching Sky was sitting by Runs Free's bed, stroking her forehead. She looked up with relief when they came in.

"At last!" she said to Black Elk. "My daughter is not doing well. Please help us." With that, she handed the man a generous helping of tobacco.

Joseph slumped against the side of the wigwam. *Is there any hope?*

Joseph watched Black Elk labor over Runs Free's ankle. Touching Sky and Silver Sage had worked the bone inside the skin, but it was not set properly. Black Elk gave the young girl a stick to bite on as he probed her ankle and moved the bone around inside. With Touching Sky's help, he prepared a potion for the injured girl to drink, and then put some ointment on her ankle and wrapped it with strips of linen.

Joseph expected to hear Runs Free scream. She was either too exhausted or somewhere past pain. He only heard her whimpers.

Black Elk stood, then left the wigwam. Joseph followed him out. As he watched, Black Elk raised his hands to the sky and prayed to the great Creator to heal the girl. Joseph stood close by, listening to the shaman's incantations and wondering what some of the words meant.

Was the shaman praying to the same God as the Amish? *Dat* had always said the Indians were idolaters who prayed to false gods, so those prayers would do no good. If only the shaman would know the true God, Runs Free would have a better chance to get well.

Would she ever walk again?

-8-

Touching Sky stepped outside the wigwam. Joseph and Runs Free were throwing a ball back and forth in the shade of a large maple tree. A smile came to her lips as she watched. It had been two moons since the little girl's injury, and Touching Sky was amazed at how quickly she'd gotten used to hopping around on her good foot.

"You throw the ball funny, just like the girls back home," Joseph said to Runs Free. "And you need to learn to catch better." He threw the ball far to the side, making her rush to reach it. She hopped on her good leg, but not fast enough to catch it.

"I wish you wouldn't tease her that way," Touching Sky said to Joseph.

Joseph shrugged his shoulders but said nothing.

"Take me on your shoulders," Runs Free said to Joseph, reaching up her arms in expectation.

Touching Sky watched as Joseph hoisted her onto his shoulders. Runs Free giggled and waved as they walked away. Nothing seemed to make her happier than riding on Joseph's shoulders, especially now that she had a bad foot.

Touching Sky felt a wave of emotion as she watched the two of them head for the creek. *Swift Foot really does care about her*, she thought. *He seems less angry now, and more willing to fit into our family.*

She thought for a few moments. What could she do to make Swift Foot feel more like a part of Indian life? *Maybe I should do something nice for him, like make him a medicine bundle.*

Not long after, when Joseph returned with Runs Free still on his shoulders, she asked, "Would you like me to make a medicine bundle for you?"

Joseph looked surprised. "Would it be like the one you wear?"

"Yes. It could be bigger or smaller. Or have different decorations."

Joseph lifted Runs Free off his shoulders and set her on the ground. He straightened. "What would I put in it?"

"Things that mean something special to you. No two people put the same things in their bundles. But everyone carries tobacco and something that connects them with the spirit helpers. Some call it a spirit bag."

Joseph nodded, and she thought he seemed eager. "Yes, I would like to have a bundle of my own."

Touching Sky was pleased. That afternoon, she cut a circle out of a tanned deer hide. She punched holes around the perimeter and used a sinew thread to gather the leather into the shape of a bag. Working with the leather, she arranged several rows of porcupine quills, dyed red, into a pattern designed for the front of the bag.

It took all afternoon to sew the quills onto the leather. When she was finished, she smiled. It was lovely—well worth the time it took to make it.

When Joseph ate his breakfast the next morning, she handed him the bag. She noticed the gleam in his eye as he accepted the gift.

"Does this mean I'm grown up now?" he asked.

"No, it just means that the next time something really bad happens, like when Runs Free got hurt, you'll have something with you that can help."

Joseph hung the medicine bundle around his neck and started toward Miquon's home. He was eager to show off his new possession. Miquon had been given his own bag nearly a moon earlier.

Joseph looked back to see Runs Free trailing him. "You can't come with me," Joseph said as he motioned her toward home.

"I want to see what's in your new bag," she said.

"You already saw it. You watched your mother make it."

"I didn't look inside it since it was finished."

"All that's in it is a little cabin that I carved."

"I want to see it now!"

Joseph rolled his eyes. "Okay," he said. "Then you'll need to go back to the wigwam." With that, he knelt down, unloosed the drawstring, and opened it wide for her to see.

"What's that?" she asked when she looked inside. "That's not a house."

Joseph scowled and looked into the bag. Runs Free was right. In the bottom of the bag was a small claw, about the size of a talon on a crow's foot.

"I didn't put that in there," he said. "I didn't see it before."

"I think Mama put that in there as a spirit helper," Runs Free said. "I want to give you this." She opened her right hand to reveal a purple wampum bead on her open palm. "This is the only bead I have," she said as she dropped it into the bag. "It will remind you of me whenever you see it."

"Thank you," Joseph said. "Now please go back to the wigwam."

Runs Free wrinkled her nose and turned back.

I don't need a wampum bead to remind me of Runs Free, Joseph thought. *She trails me everywhere I go.* He groaned, then smiled despite himself.

In a few moments, Joseph was at Miquon's home, and they compared their new medicine bundles. Joseph's was a little bigger, with more decorations.

"I don't know what to put in it," Joseph said. "I've never looked into anyone else's bundle, so I don't know what people carry in it."

"It's a very personal thing," Miquon said. "Once I looked into my father's bag, and he whacked my side so hard with a stick that it gave me a bruise."

"What did you see?" Joseph asked.

"A tiny bow and a miniature war club. That's because my father is a warrior. And he had some tobacco too. Oh yes, and a little wooden carving."

Joseph nodded. "I'm going to gather some sassafras root and put a little piece in there and also some—" He stopped midsentence and grinned. "I guess we're supposed to keep this a secret, right? So maybe I shouldn't tell you."

Miquon scowled and shrugged his shoulders. "It's okay to tell friends. Why should we keep secrets from each other?"

"Okay, then, I'll tell you. I made a wooden carving of our house back at the Northkill, just so I don't forget what it looked like before it got burned down."

Miquon stared at him for a moment. "Are you still thinking about that place?"

Joseph swallowed hard. What was he to say? He would never forget his home, but he was less inclined to risk his life for an escape these days. Truth be told, memories of his life in the Northkill were becoming less and less clear. Sometimes he thought of his family only once or twice a day. He had not seen any of them but Christian in ten moons.

"I'll never see it again," he said to Miquon. "That's why I made a reminder of it."

Miquon raised his eyebrows. "If I were you, I'd want to forget the house where I used to live, not have a reminder hanging around my neck." He picked up a hoop.

Joseph shrugged. "I thought it might be good to remember where I came from."

That night, as Joseph was crawling into bed, he took the bundle off his neck and laid it on the floor beside him. But just as he laid it down, he heard Runs Free stir in her bed. *I better not lay it on the floor,* he said to himself. *I don't want Runs Free to think she can play with it.* He picked up the little bundle and laid it on his bed, next to the wall.

As Joseph lay awake, he smelled the familiar scent of smoke that hung lightly in the night air. He wrapped the blanket around him, as much for comfort as to ward off the slight evening chill. There was a slight rustle. Touching Sky was climbing on the nearby sleeping platform.

Now that he'd lived for some months in Touching Sky's wigwam, the smoke that wound upward from the fire in the center of the room reminded him of the taste of good food, like the aroma of *Mam*'s kettles on the fireplace back home in the Northkill. Touching Sky's cooking was definitely better than when he had first come. Or had he gotten used to it? Her various recipes for corn no longer tasted like the same bland mixture; he could tell when she used different herbs for seasoning and he didn't always long to add salt.

What he missed most about *Mam*'s cooking were the cakes and pudding that she'd served on special days. He was learning to do without baked sweets, since the village had no cows or milk. *Touching Sky is a good cook*, Joseph admitted to himself. *Not as good as* Mam *was, but good enough that I look forward to the meals.*

Joseph gradually drifted off to sleep. He did not wake again until the first rays of the sun showed through the smoke hole in the roof. He lay with his eyes closed, reluctant to step across the threshold from sleep to wakefulness. In his dream, he had been eating one of his favorite meals, cooked by Touching Sky. *This is the best dream I've had since I came to the village*, he thought. *It's the first time I wasn't hit by someone or being yelled at*. He opened his eyes and looked at the few live embers that remained in the fire. *It must be morning.*

What stood out the most in the dream was that he had been speaking to Touching Sky in her native language. The whole dream had taken place in Delaware rather than Swiss-German, as it always had before.

Dat's parting plea that he not forget German had seemed foolish at the time. How could he forget the language he'd known from birth? Now it seemed likely; there were few good opportunities to speak German, even with Runs Free, who seemed to have lost all interest as soon as he learned to speak to her in Delaware. And even though his native language had seemed infinitely better suited to explain the world, mixing even a few German words with Delaware expressions brought looks of disdain onto people's faces.

Dreaming in a new tongue mirrored the change that was taking place inside; he often found himself thinking in Delaware, rather than German. It was certainly more efficient than translating everything into Delaware when he wanted to speak, often with words that had no good match in his mother tongue. Was this a simple change issuing from common sense in his head, or had it arisen from a conversion in his heart? Was he learning, deep inside, to think like the Delaware? Was that what had worried *Dat*? How could he stop it from happening?

When Joseph got up the next morning, he reached for his new medicine bundle and pulled out the carved likeness of his childhood home. He rolled it around in his hands, taking care to keep it out of Touching Sky's sight. *I wonder if Dat ever got back home. Did the neighbors clean up the rubble after the fire*? If he ever went home, he didn't think he could bear to see a pile of ashes where his childhood home had once stood.

"How do you like your new medicine bundle?" Touching Sky asked Joseph after he got dressed.

"I really like the red quills," he said.

"Runs Free says that you have a carving of a little house from your home in the Northkill," she said.

"It's none of her business what I carry in my bag," Joseph said through clenched jaws. He glared at the little girl, who quickly slipped out the door.

"I just want to know what it means to you."

Joseph refused to meet her eyes. "It's a reminder of the house I used to live in," he said.

"Maybe it can remind you that white people keep pushing us away and building new homes on land that still belongs to us," Touching Sky said heatedly.

Joseph looked up at her.

"They cut down the trees, set up farms with fences around them to keep in their animals, and then threaten to shoot us if we come to hunt in the places that have been ours for generations."

Joseph burned at Touching Sky's words. It was like *Mam*, who had scolded him for so many things—slamming the door too hard, being too noisy when Franey was napping, or not paying attention to the preacher in church. He had always needed to swallow the words that rose up in his defense. *Dat* was often nearby, ready to use a switch to enforce *Mam*'s will.

Yet Touching Sky was scolding him for actions that *Mam* and *Dat* had never taught him to be wrong: clearing land, farming, building fences. But hadn't the Indians killed his family? Burned his home? How could he explain that the white people he knew best—the Amish at the Northkill—wouldn't harm anyone? They tried to follow the saying of Jesus that they should love even their enemies.

Yet this didn't seem to be the time and place to explain it, especially when Touching Sky was so upset. Looking at her face, he felt a flicker of shame. They were silent for a moment.

"I'm sorry," Joseph said. "My people—the Amish—believe that people should not kill each other but live at peace with everyone." He turned away from the heat of Touching Sky's anger, hoping to rearrange his jumbled thoughts. He wanted to leave, to find a retreat from Touching Sky's accusations against his people. Touching Sky turned away.

He left the wigwam and walked slowly toward the creek. As he sat on the bank and watched the water flow by, he fingered the medicine bundle that hung around his neck. Without opening the bundle, he felt the hard edges of the little cabin inside. He opened the bag and took out the wooden carving, turning it over in his hands as he mulled over Touching Sky's harsh words.

In the past months, he'd heard Tamaqua complaining about reports of land-hungry settlers who had built log houses in the Ohio territories, brashly pushing beyond the

boundary lines that the British had drawn after painful negotiations with the Indians. A tear ran down his cheek, and he
swiped at it with his bare arm.

Joseph stood up with the little carving in his hand. And
then, with fierce determination, he threw the little house far
out into the water. It disappeared under the surface and then
bobbed up again.

He watched it float downstream until it was out of sight.

PART II

-9-

Shortly after the sun rose, Touching Sky headed for her brother Tamaqua's wigwam. She found him outside, stretching his hands to the heavens. She politely waited for him to finish his prayers.

"Good morning, sister," he said.

"Good morning, brother." Touching Sky smiled, then looked serious. "Brother, I need you to mentor my son Swift Foot. He has a lot of promise, but he has much to learn about our Indian ways."

Tamaqua nodded. "He could become a great hunter. He is quick. And I've noticed he has sharp vision when walking in the forest."

"Will you agree to be his teacher?"

Tamaqua hesitated. "What would you like me to teach him?"

"Everything he needs to know in order to be a true Indian. I want him to take the place of Suckameek. So teach him everything that he would have known."

Tamaqua tapped his foot as he thought. "That will not be easy, since Swift Foot is far behind." He was quiet for a few moments.

Touching Sky forced herself not to speak—not to present a list of arguments.

Finally, Tamaqua spoke. "I shall do my best." Touching Sky let out a breath of relief.

"Will you agree not to interfere with my training, even if you judge it too severe?" Tamaqua looked at her.

Touching Sky had not anticipated such a question. "Yes," she said, after a short pause. "Teach him as you will. Just don't be too hard on the boy. I don't want him to run back to his home among the whites. He seems to be adjusting to our life here."

Tamaqua nodded. "I shall seek the guidance of the Great Spirit and the help of the lesser ones."

Joseph followed Tamaqua and Miquon as they walked into the woods. It was Joseph's first formal lesson in Indian hunting, and he could learn alongside Miquon, who was already quite accomplished, under Tamaqua's tutelage.

Joseph was carrying Tamaqua's rifle. It was the first time he'd carried a gun since his capture more than ten moons ago. Surely it was a sign of Tamaqua's trust.

"You must learn to hunt like an Indian," Tamaqua said, motioning for Joseph to catch up. "The white man would easily starve to death if he was left to hunt for his food."

That might be true, Joseph thought. If he were left alone in the woods, he would dread nothing more than death by starvation.

"The white man blunders along in the woods," Tamaqua said as the path narrowed and they came to a heavy thicket. "He doesn't notice the many signs of game around him." He turned to Miquon. "Show Swift Foot how we would trace game here."

Miquon stopped for a moment and then pointed to a tuft of hair caught on a small branch. "It looks like a deer went by here not long ago." He walked forward a few steps and squatted down to examine a telltale track on the ground. "And here I can see that a dwarf passed by within the last day or so."

Joseph wrinkled his brow. "How can you tell it was a dwarf?"

"You can easily tell by soles of his moccasins. Indians never leave tracks like that."

Tamaqua nodded and led them further up the path.

"Have you ever met a dwarf?" Joseph asked Miquon, who strode along just in front of him.

"No, but one of the old men in our village saw one as a child. It fed him when he was lost in the woods."

Joseph struggled to not seem skeptical. "What do they look like?"

"They dress like hunters, but wear green clothing," Miquon said, "and they always use the bow and arrows. They never use muskets or rifles like humans."

Joseph paused, taking this in. *Does he actually think . . . ? Dwarfs?* The unspoken thoughts surely showed on his face. "Where do they live?"

"Mostly in the deep woods or in the rocks at the tops of the hills, but they sometimes follow the paths."

"Where did you learn about them?"

Miquon turned and frowned. "What do you mean—learn about them? I've always known about them, just like I've known about the great Creator."

They came to a fork in the woods, and Tamaqua headed off to the left. "The white man loses his way because he pays no attention," he said to Joseph. "Take notice of the tall tree where the path divides. Do you see anything unusual about it?"

Joseph stopped and stared at it and then at the trees around it. "No, it looks like the others."

Tamaqua shook his head and pointed to a small growth of bark where two branches of the tree forked apart from each other. "You can tell that a spirit lives in the fork of that tree," he said. "It guards the fork of this path, so we shall leave it a little tobacco for its kindness." With that, he pulled a pinch of tobacco from the bundle around his neck and placed it in the tree fork.

Joseph's eyes widened. *Dat* would have considered that a form of idolatry—not to mention a waste of tobacco.

As they walked along, a black squirrel scampered across the path and up a tree. Joseph swung his rifle toward the animal.

"Stop!" Miquon said. "We do not shoot black squirrels. The Creator left those for the dwarfs to eat."

Tamaqua nodded. "The dwarfs like the hearts of black squirrels the best. That's why we call them *wematekanis*—'we eat hearts.'"

Joseph's mind was whirling. "If you were starving," he asked Miquon, "would you not kill a black squirrel and eat it?"

Tamaqua overheard the question and stopped walking. "I would not kill a black squirrel without leaving its heart for the dwarfs to eat. And perhaps a pinch of tobacco. Otherwise they might take revenge on us."

"How would they know who did it?" Joseph asked.

Tamaqua looked at Joseph sternly. "They just know those things. They are likely watching us now, knowing that we are talking about them."

Joseph finally had enough. "My father told me that dwarfs are make-believe."

Tamaqua shook his head. "That is why the white man can never live in the woods. He does not understand the spirits in the forest. If he says unkind things about the dwarfs, they may take away his mind."

Whoa! Joseph wondered if he was dreaming. *They really believe in* dwarfs? But he asked respectfully: "How can they do that?"

"Many years ago, one of our hunters offended the little people," Tamaqua said. "He cursed the dwarfs because he thought they had driven the deer and the bear from that part of the woods. He was very hungry so he was not thinking clearly.

"The dwarfs took away his mind so that he could not remember who he was," Tamaqua continued. "He could not remember his way back home, so he wandered about in the woods until one of our hunters found him."

"How did he keep from starving to death?" Joseph asked.

"He ate grass and berries, but he was very thin. He could not even speak or remember his name. He could not talk or do any work. Ever since that time, we are careful not to offend the spirits."

Joseph sat thinking, his mind bursting with questions. If the man could not talk, how did the villagers know what had happened to him? How were they so sure that dwarfs had been the cause of the problem? He tried not to let his face reveal his skepticism.

"Son, you will never be a successful hunter unless you learn about the dwarfs," Tamaqua said to Joseph as they rose to their feet. "They will tell the deer and the bear about your ignorance and show them where to hide, so that you will never be able to shoot them as game."

Tamaqua picked up his rifle and his pack-strap—a soft, woven belt decorated with figures—and led the way deeper into the woods. It was afternoon when they first spied a deer bounding through the woods not far from the path.

"Now we shall follow him," Tamaqua said. Joseph's stomach growled as they followed the deer's track. He was hungry. Venison would taste so good!

At first it was easy to follow the deer's trail, even for Joseph, who had learned some tracking when he hunted with his father. But at times, only Tamaqua could tell the places where the animal had crossed rocky ground or leaped over a rivulet.

It was late afternoon when they saw the deer at some distance away, grazing on tufts of greening grass where the sunlight pushed its way through the trees. Tamaqua put his finger to his lips and motioned for Miquon and Joseph to stay where they were. He turned and moved silently toward the deer, slipping behind trees and bushes to hide his advance.

A shot rang out. Joseph and Miquon ran to see the deer up close.

"The spirit of that oak tree gave me success!" Tamaqua said. "He hid me from the deer's sight." They moved in closer. The deer was still.

Joseph knelt down and stroked the deer's hide as the light faded in its eyes. It was a beautiful creature, and part of him hated to see it die. If only there was a way to find meat without killing game, he'd gladly do it.

Tamaqua tossed down some tobacco by the deer's nose and quickly gutted it as the boys watched. He bound the legs to the body with his pack-strap and hoisted it onto his shoulders. Then he put the strap around the front of his forehead. The deer was ready for the long journey back to the village.

"You carry my gun," he said to Joseph. "Later, I'll have both you and Miquon take a turn carrying the deer."

Joseph rested the gun on his shoulder as he followed Tamaqua, watching with admiration as the man carried the heavy animal alone.

"What do the figures on the belt mean?" he asked Miquon.

"You have to ask my father," Miquon replied.

Tamaqua overheard and turned around. "The figures on the belt please and flatter the spirit of the dead deer," Tamaqua answered. "They help it feel better about the way we have bound up its body with the strap."

Sometime later, they came back to the fork in the path where Tamaqua had put the pinch of tobacco. "Swift Foot, this is the place where you carry the deer," Tamaqua said. "Show us your strength." With that, he lifted the deer off his own back and laid it on Joseph's, then put the strap around the front of Joseph's forehead.

"You set the pace," Tamaqua said. "And we'll follow."

Joseph felt the tug of the heavy weight. He had never carried anything with a strap around his forehead. They had only gone a little way when his neck began to hurt. He said nothing but wondered how long he could keep going.

How could Tamaqua carry it so far? he wondered. His admiration for his mentor was growing. He gripped the strap with his hands to relieve the burden on his neck.

It's going to be a long trip home.

In the autumn, Joseph accompanied Tamaqua on one of their now frequent hunting trips in the woods. Miquon stayed back to help one of the villagers gather new bark for a wigwam.

Joseph and Tamaqua walked a long way without seeing much game. It was late when Tamaqua called a halt.

"Let's stop here," Tamaqua said, pointing to an open dry spot. "It will be a safe and comfortable place." They dropped their packs. "We'll stay overnight and then head back in the morning."

Joseph began collecting a handful of sticks to make a fire, one of them a young green oak branch. Tamaqua stopped him. "We cannot use this branch," Tamaqua said. "It will burn readily enough, but it will throw sparks to a great distance and perhaps burn holes in our blanket."

"I am sorry," Joseph said, embarrassed. He tossed the branch aside.

"More than once when I have traveled with white men," Tamaqua said, "I have seen them choose green branches of oak, walnut, cherry, or chestnut to put on a fire. They do not seem to understand that unless the wood is dry, it can throw sparks. In dry weather—as we have now—it could set leaves on fire."

"That would be very dangerous," Joseph said, nodding.

"I have observed that white men are very clever when it comes to making things—like guns and kettles—but some of them do not seem to understand the most simple things, such as making fires. They seem to think that any wood will do, whether it is dry, wet, or half-rotten. Then they have a smoky fire." Tamaqua looked disgusted. "Because they are impatient, they will hang a kettle or a pot over a newly kindled fire, before it has finished smoking. Worse yet, they may not even take notice of which way the wind is blowing. They suffer all night with smoke blowing over them." Tamaqua shook his head as he spoke, as though incredulous at such stupidity.

I can't help it if white people aren't smart about fires, Joseph thought. But he kept his face impassive.

Tamaqua continued, "My brother told me of a foolish white man who did not even bother to look up to see what was above him when he made camp. When the wind rose that night, it brought down a large dead branch that had been hanging there in plain sight. It fell on his gun and broke the stock. He was fortunate that it did not fall on his chest and kill him."

Joseph chuckled. "It serves him right for not paying attention."

Tamaqua smirked as he held up his hunting knife. "Do you see this knife?"

Joseph nodded.

Tamaqua waved the knife as he spoke. "I found this lying in the woods where a group of white men had camped not long before. I also found some flints and a couple of bullets. It seems as though the white men are always losing things or leaving them behind. Do they not value what they have?" He looked at Joseph inquiringly.

Joseph shrugged. What could he say? Was Tamaqua implying that he was still living like a white man?

Tamaqua must have perceived Joseph's uncertainty. "I think better of you, my son. You are learning that if you do not pay attention in the woods, it can cost you plenty—even your life. You are becoming one of us."

"Yes, I have much to learn about the woods. Sometimes I fear getting lost. And I have not learned to track game like you."

Tamaqua nodded. "I have never seen a white man who can find his way through the woods without an Indian guide. They walk in circles because they cannot tell directions. Or they walk right into danger, because they are blind to the signs of wild beasts or an enemy. Even great Indians can get lost in the woods, but that is rare."

"I am amazed that you can tell your way through the woods," Joseph said with admiration showing on his face. "I would have lost the path more than once."

"You can learn too," Tamaqua said, "if you give yourself to the task. You have learned many things in a short time.

Someday you will teach others." He put his hand on Joseph's arm as he spoke, an affectionate smile lighting his face.

Joseph's face glowed with the rare compliment. He reached out with his stick to stir the fire, which burned bright and warm with only a small wisp of smoke. He was proud to be an Indian. Not like the whites back home who blundered along in the woods.

-10-

The late spring rains and the warmth of early summer were good for the garden. Touching Sky was hoeing around the new shoots of corn when she saw Joseph approach. She put down the hoe and wiped her forehead, glad for an excuse to rest.

"I carved this spirit doll for you," he said.

Touching Sky rubbed the smooth surface of the doll for a moment. "Thank you," she said. Her voice trembled a little. She swallowed. "Have I ever told you that my husband was a good carver of wood? Maybe you've seen some of his carvings around the wigwam."

Joseph nodded. "I knew you liked carved things. But I didn't know he made them."

Runs Free came hopping up. "Do you like it, Mama? I watched him make it. I kept it a secret."

"I like it very much. I shall keep it in my bag."

Runs Free beckoned Joseph to play, and they went off together.

Touching Sky stood silently for a while. *It is time to formally adopt Swift Foot. He has shown himself to be a true son. And it will make Runs Free very happy.*

When she finished hoeing, Touching Sky went to speak to Tamaqua.

"Swift Foot is learning well, Sister," he said. "It may be time for you to adopt him. But I have a few more things to say to him about the differences between his race and ours. Otherwise, the village may destine him to be a slave or worse."

Touching Sky shrank back at the truth of his words. Several recent captives had not proven to be suitable for adoption. They had been killed or sold as slaves. It must never happen to Joseph. When she got back to the wigwam, she spoke to Silver Sage. "Aunt, I am thinking of adopting Swift Foot. Do you think it is the right time?"

Silver Sage took her broom and swept some twigs from the dirt floor into the fire. "Perhaps. Have you heard from your spirit guide?"

"No, but I feel an inner longing. I want for him to have that longing too. How can I know?"

Silver Sage thought for a moment. "Remember, our grandmother used to say, 'Ask a question from your heart and you will be answered from the heart.'"

The matter weighed heavily on Touching Sky's mind all afternoon. *I wonder what Swift Foot will say.* She tried to imagine Joseph's response as she removed a few slabs of bark from the side of the wigwam and hung woven reed mats in their place to let the breeze flow through. *It seems as though Swift Foot is feeling at home here, and he loves Runs Free.*

That evening, she brought up the matter to Joseph as she offered him a plate of food. "Swift Foot, it is time that you become a full Indian. I would like to adopt you into my family and clan as soon as Custaloga returns to the village from Fort Duquesne. That would be less than a moon away."

Joseph was quiet. "Must I decide right now?"

Touching Sky smiled. "No, you may think about it for a few days."

"Thank you." Joseph sat in the open air eating his food.

Her thoughts raced as she stirred the pot. *What will I do if he says no? Maybe I should have waited a little longer.* She swept back a wisp of hair and tried not to look worried.

Joseph brought his plate to her for another serving of food. He seemed to be thinking about what it would be like to be adopted. "Do I need to do anything?" he asked.

Touching Sky smiled. "We have an adoption ritual. You'll be honored with a blessing by the chief and receive gifts from the family. It will be a special occasion."

"Would you think of me as a white son or a red one?"

"You'll be a white son with a red heart. And if you marry an Indian woman someday, your children will be fully red."

"Will I need to believe in your religion like you do, and pray to the spirits?"

She paused, searching the expression on his face. "No," she said slowly. "At least not until you understand it better."

Joseph's visage seemed to relax. The two of them lapsed into silence for a time, broken only by the scraping sounds of Joseph's spoon against his wooden bowl.

"Tamaqua has a few things that he wants to say to you before you would be adopted," Touching Sky said.

"About what?" Joseph asked, a note of uncertainty in his voice.

"Oh, just some things that will help you understand our people. I'll invite him to come here tomorrow to talk to you about it." *I should have waited to speak about Tamaqua until Swift Foot said yes. What if Tamaqua frightens him away from being adopted?*

It took more time than usual for Touching Sky to fall asleep that night. Had she said the right thing about the need for Joseph to believe in spirits? How could he be successful as an Indian without fully embracing the Delaware way of understanding? She couldn't shake her worries. She woke up twice thinking about what she was going to do if Tamaqua's advice turned Joseph away from her. *I must not lose him.*

The next morning, when she heard Tamaqua approaching, she took him aside where Joseph couldn't hear. "Brother, please speak kindly to Swift Foot and do not make him stumble on the journey to becoming my son."

Tamaqua nodded. He invited Joseph and Silver Sage to join Touching Sky to sit around the fire as he spoke. "Joseph, you should know that Chief Custaloga is at a large council fire with other Indian tribes and the white men," he said. "They are trying to find a solution to the problem of the white man in Ohio territory."

Joseph nodded. "Touching Sky speaks often about this problem."

Tamaqua continued. "Long ago, when she and I were young, our family lived close to the *keekachtanemin,* which the white man calls the Blue Mountains. We hunted in the woods and fished in the creeks. But our enemies, the Iroquois, made a treaty with the white men and sold our land to them. We thought that we could keep fishing and hunting in those lands, but the white men put up fences and forbade us to hunt there.

"Finally, they forced us to move away toward the setting sun. They promised that we could freely use these lands, but now there are forts and trading posts and settlers. That is why we are fighting the white man. We want the settlers to stay out of the Ohio valley."

"Why did the Iroquois sell the land away from you?" Joseph asked. "Are they not your cousins?"

"The Iroquois insist that they are our uncles, and that they can tell us what to do. They want to subdue us and control us, so they call us women."

"Women? Why?"

"It is their way of saying that we are weaker than they. They do not want us to negotiate directly with the white man. But now Chief Custaloga is at the council fire with a wampum belt. We hope that the white man will agree to move out of this territory. If you are to become a member of our tribe, you must understand these things."

Touching Sky nodded. It was good for Joseph to understand that the Iroquois often acted as enemies of the Delaware.

"The white man is always eager to get more land," Tamaqua said. "He never seems to have enough. About ten summers ago, the Penn brothers persuaded us to let the white man have the ground a man could walk around in a day. But they ran instead of walking, so they got much more land than they deserved."

Touching Sky studied Joseph's face as he listened, but he showed no emotion. *I wonder how Swift Foot's parents got the land for their farm.*

"The British built forts on our territory," Tamaqua continued. "Now the settlers are moving here. They have broken their promise. We want all but the traders to move back east of the Alleghenies."

Touching Sky nodded. Surely Joseph must understand that the Indians needed a place to call their own—without fear that the Iroquois would trade it away.

"We take captives because the white man's numbers are growing and ours are shrinking. They have killed many of us in battles. Others have died from their diseases, especially smallpox." Tamaqua shuddered. "It's a fearsome plague that has killed many of our people. That's how my mother died."

"*Dat* told us that on the ship that brought them from the Old Country, many of the children died of smallpox," Joseph said. "They had to bury them at sea."

"The white man should never have brought that disease to us," Touching Sky said. "Our spirits have been overpowered by it."

"The white man also brought us his rum," Tamaqua said with a look of disdain on his face. "Although our people long for the taste of it, it is destroying us. Many of us cannot handle the white man's drink."

Touching Sky felt Tamaqua's eyes on her as he spoke of rum. Why must he bring it up now? The village hadn't had any rum for many moons. Besides, Joseph had heard enough to recognize the grievances they had against his people. Now he could help to make things right by joining her family and clan. She gave Tamaqua a look that indicated he had said enough.

Tamaqua turned to leave. "You will make a wonderful son for Touching Sky," he said to Joseph as he headed toward the door.

Over the next few days, Touching Sky watched Joseph closely. What was he going to say about adoption? What if he said no? Must she warn him that if he chose not to be adopted, the village elders might kill him or sell him to another village?

One morning after Joseph had finished off several corn cakes and dried berries, he met her eyes in a way that told her the answer.

"I'm ready to be adopted," he told Touching Sky. "I have come to like it here."

Touching Sky flashed her brightest smile. "That's good," she said. "We'll do it as soon as Custaloga returns."

He is coming to understand my people. Perhaps my cooking helped.

At the time of the full moon, Chief Custaloga returned to the village to lead the adoption ceremony. Joseph was nervous as the chief led the village to the edge of the French Creek. *Why are we going to the creek?*

After quieting the people with his raised hand, the chief made a short speech. "We have gathered to welcome one of our white captives into the Delaware tribe. After he is cleansed of all his white ways, he will be adopted by Touching Sky, a strong woman of the Wolf clan." When he was finished speaking, he motioned Joseph over to three young women. They led him by the hand to the bank of the creek, stripped off his breechcloth, and pulled him into the water up to their waists. Joseph drew a deep breath as they plunged him under the water and scrubbed his skin with the stones from the creek bottom. *What are they doing to me?* The scrubbing left pink scratches on his arms and legs.

It was not like the ritual washing of baptism that brought young people into the Amish church back home. *Dat* had explained to the family that unlike their Dunkard Brethren neighbors, who insisted on baptizing their converts in a running stream, it was sufficient to be baptized with a little water poured on the head.

Joseph's older brother Jakey had been baptized in the spring of the year when the Indians attacked. Joseph had watched Bishop Hertzler pour water in the cupped hands of the deacon, who released it onto Jakey's head as he knelt on the floor in front of the gathered assembly. The bishop made clear that baptism was not a "putting away of the filth of the flesh, but the answer of a good conscience toward God." And then he reached down and gave Jakey the "right hand of fellowship," bade him "rise to new life," and greeted him with the holy kiss. It was a warm adoption into the church fellowship, something Joseph had anticipated for himself.

That was then. This was now. Joseph was jerked back to the present as the three women, laughing with glee at his embarrassment, led him back toward the creek bank. *I want my breechcloth.* The leather hide, once awkward and bulky between his legs, now brought comfort and security. At soon as he donned it, Touching Sky led him toward the lodge, which served as a council house. Several members of her family stood waiting for Joseph with new clothes.

Silver Sage held out a ruffled shirt. "You'll look good in this."

Joseph pushed his arms into the sleeves and fastened the buttons in the front. He realized that he hadn't worn a shirt for months.

Touching Sky's eyes glistened as she handed him a pair of leggings decorated with ribbons and beads. "I made these for Suckameek," she said. "He hardly got to wear them."

Tamaqua stepped forward with a skunk pouch. "Now that you're a real Indian, you'll need this."

Joseph opened the pouch. There was tobacco and dry sumac leaves to be mixed with the tobacco—as well as a flint and steel to help start fires. He sat cross-legged and admired the sparks that sprayed out when he struck the flint against the steel.

Chief Custaloga stepped up with a rifle and held it out to Joseph. "We seized this weapon in a recent raid against the settlers," he said. "I wanted you to have it. I trust that you will become a great hunter and a brave warrior among us."

Joseph reached out to receive the gift. "Thank you," he said, pushing the words past the lump that formed in his throat.

While he was seated in the midst of all his gifts, other guests and clan members came into the council house, dressed and painted as though for a dance. They took their seats in silence.

Chief Custaloga lit a pipe and puffed on it, and then passed the pipe to the next one in the circle. Each one took a puff and passed it on in silence.

When the pipe came around to Joseph, seated opposite the chief, he took it into his hand. *You can't do anything around here without tobacco*, he thought. He gave a small puff on the pipe and handed it to Tamaqua, seated next to him.

When the pipe came back around to Custaloga, he looked at Joseph. "You are Swift Foot, a true Delaware," he said. "Today at the creek, every drop of white blood was washed out of your veins. Now you are taken into the Delaware tribe, an ancient and notable nation. You are being received into a great family, with all seriousness and solemnity in the place of a young man lost in battle. After what was done today, you have become one of us by ancient law and custom. My son, you have nothing to fear; we are now under the same obligation to you as we are to those born among us. We will love, support, and defend you. Therefore, consider yourself to be part of the Wolf clan."

Joseph's pulse quickened at the smiles and nods around the circle. Was he ready for this? It was wonderful to be accepted by the Indians, but was he giving up the hope of running away with Christian? Would he ever see his birth family again?

Everyone remained seated except Runs Free, who came limping up to him. "You are now my big brother," she said. She gave him a hug and then tugged at his arm. "Come, let's go outside to play."

Joseph glanced at Touching Sky, who smiled and nodded. He fastened his skunk pouch to his belt and led Runs Free outside. The air was warm with a slight breeze.

"Let's race," she said. She started to hop on her good leg and waved for Joseph to follow.

Joseph laughed and hopped after her on one foot. Did she really think she could beat him in a footrace?

As Runs Free bounced in and out among the small homes, giggling and waving her arms, Joseph thought of Franey. He thought of her less often now, and with less pain. She had always loved to run, especially when he chased her in a game of tag. Joseph came to realize that chasing Franey wasn't about racing but about having fun together. Perhaps that was true for Runs Free as well.

As Joseph hopped around the back of a hut in pursuit of his new sister, several men stood outside their huts with broad smiles.

"Go, Runs Free," they shouted as they watched Joseph give pursuit. She threw off the blanket she had worn over her shoulders, weaving among the dwellings with two long black braids bouncing against her bare back.

Joseph picked up the blanket and continued to give pursuit. Silver Sage laughed and waved as they ran by the council house. Joseph nearly tagged Runs Free twice, reaching out and then falling to the ground on purpose. The game finally ended when Runs Free hopped up to Silver Sage with Joseph two steps behind. She clung to her legs and chanted, "You can't get me now."

"Oh yes I can." Joseph threw the blanket around Runs Free and swept her up in his arms. He strode back to the wigwam and lowered her next to the small pit where Touching Sky was pouring popcorn kernels into a pot over the outside cooking fire. He put an arm around Runs Free's shoulder as they sat there in silence, waiting for the corn to pop.

He was warmed as much by her presence as the heat that rose from the flames. Having a little sister again was beginning to heal the hole in his heart.

Just then Touching Sky stepped up with a small knife in her hand. "Swift Foot," she said, "I want you to have this knife. It's the one that my husband used to carve wooden things for me. The Creator has given you a gift of carving, and I want you to use it."

Joseph looked deeply into her dark brown eyes. They reflected joy as well as pain.

"Thank you," he said. "I admire some of the things he carved for you."

She nodded. "Yes, the mortar and pestle, several spoons . . ." Her voice broke.

"What was your husband's name?" Joseph asked.

A shadow crossed her face. "Now that he is gone, we do not speak his name out loud lest he think we are calling him from his rest." Her voice dropped to a whisper. "But I will tell you. We called him Tamahican."

"Will you still call me Swift Foot now that I'm adopted? Miquon said you might change my name."

"Maybe someday, if you find a spirit helper, you will get a spirit name. Now you are Swift Foot, a true Delaware. But you must never call yourself Joseph. That is a white man's name."

"Tom Lions has a white man's name," Joseph said with a frown.

"That's not his spirit name," Touching Sky said.

"What's his real name?"

"I don't know it. He has not revealed it to me."

"Is Tom Lions his nickname?"

"No, it's a real name, just not his spirit name."

Joseph was even more confused. "I don't understand. How can you have more than one real name?"

"We give names to our babies sometime in the first year or two. That is the name by which the spirits know you. We don't speak those names aloud to our enemies, because they could use them to overpower us."

Joseph looked perplexed. "Is Touching Sky your spirit name?"

"No. I was given that name when I was your age."

"What is your spirit name?"

Touching Sky paused and then said quietly. "We do not have a custom of asking people their spirit names."

Joseph's face flushed slightly. He looked away.

Touching Sky regarded him tenderly. "Because you are now my son, I will tell you my spirit name, but you must not tell it to others."

Joseph nodded.

"When I was a child, my mother would take me to the creek. I was never afraid of the water, even when I was very small. So they called me *Winkpie*: She Likes Water. It is my spirit name."

"That is a lovely name," Joseph said. "Why do they call you Touching Sky now?"

"I suppose because my parents saw me watch the clouds and point to the sky. Or they saw me praying with my hands to the sky. I always feel closer to the Creator that way."

Joseph paused. "So do you have any other names besides She Likes Water and Touching Sky?"

She smiled and shook her head. "No. But there are some people in our village who have three or four names. Especially men. They may get a new name on a vision quest, or perhaps if they earn a special honor as warriors."

Joseph was confused.

"Some of our bravest warriors have been given a name of honor," she said. "Like Tamaqua. His honorary warrior name is Brave Heart."

"I never heard him use that name."

"He is a humble man. He will not introduce himself that way. He will wait for others to use that name if they want him to tell about his exploits."

The two of them slipped into silence for a few moments, and then Joseph said, "I have one more question. Are people ever named after their fathers or mothers? Or how do you know if people are related to each other?" He paused, remembering. "All of my brothers and sisters had the same last name—Hochstetler. That is, until my sister got married. And then she took her husband's last name."

Touching Sky laughed. "That is the way of white people. They are used to carrying their father's name. That is not how it is among the Delaware. We know who our uncles and aunts and nephews and cousins are. We do not need surnames like white people to tell us whether or not we are related."

"How can I find out Tom Lions's spirit name?"

"You could ask him, but I doubt he would tell. He is afraid of you."

Joseph's eyes widened. "What do you mean, he is afraid of me? He is very cruel to me. I think he hates me."

Touching Sky nodded. "He hates you because he is afraid. When Tom was a little boy, his father, Lame Deer, was killed by a white man who thought he'd stolen his horse. Lame Deer was walking on a path near the man's farm down by the Susquehanna. He just happened to be in the wrong place at the wrong time. When he denied that he'd taken the horse and pulled out his tomahawk, the man called him a liar and shot him."

"Why would he do that?"

"White men don't believe Indians."

Joseph sat wordless as Touching Sky continued. "Tom saw it happen. He escaped into the woods and ran to a nearby Indian village. Tom loved his father very much. We found out later that a Seneca warrior had stolen the horse. Now Tom hates Senecas as well as white settlers. That's why he treats you so badly."

Joseph swallowed hard. "Do you mean Walks Proud is not Tom's real father?"

Touching Sky nodded. "That's right. He is Tom's uncle. They took him into their home after Lame Deer was killed."

"I wish . . ." Joseph started to speak but thought the better of it.

"Perhaps you wish you could make Tom stop hating you."

Joseph nodded.

"Revenge is as sweet to the heart as maple syrup is to the tongue," Touching Sky said. "It repays the debt we owe to those who were treated unjustly."

Joseph reached into the bowl for the last handful of popcorn. A thought appeared on the surface of his consciousness. *Now that I'm an Indian, could I get revenge on Tom for murdering my family?*

-11-

The day after the adoption, Touching Sky imagined Joseph becoming a great hunter, supplying deer and bear to the village. *It is time for Swift Foot to find a spirit helper*, she thought as she headed back to the wigwam. *He will need more help than Tamaqua or I can give.*

"Swift Foot," Touching Sky said to him that afternoon when he and Miquon returned from the creek with several large fish, "it is time for you to seek for a spirit helper."

His brow furrowed. "Why?"

"You are becoming a man, and you will be hunting in the woods by yourself. You will need protection by a guardian spirit. Has Tamaqua not spoken to you about the need for spirits to help you hunt?"

"He told me about dwarfs and spirits in trees," Joseph said. "What does that have to do with a guardian spirit?"

Touching Sky shook her head in wonder. How could white captives be so ignorant of the spirit world? How did they expect the forest to release its game without deference to the spirits who lived there?

"You cannot become a great hunter without the help of the spirits. Now that you have become one of us, you must learn our ways."

Joseph shrugged. "How can I find a guardian spirit?"

"You must go into the woods alone, with no food or water. There you must pray for a vision and see who comes to help."

Joseph wasn't sure about the idea, but he wanted to be accepted. "If I must, I will go."

"Tomorrow you must take a bath in the sweat lodge to purify yourself. You must fast for one day. Then you'll go into the woods for several days. While you are there, you won't eat or drink."

Joseph looked horrified. "I might starve to death."

Touching Sky stifled a smile. She couldn't blame him for worrying about food. Like Suckameek, he could eat and eat and eat—and still be hungry. But in order to become the man she envisioned, he would have to learn self-control through fasting. How could she encourage him so he would be brave and not afraid? She thought a moment, then spoke.

"If you cry out to the Great Spirit, he will have mercy on you by sending a guardian spirit to comfort you. When Custaloga went on a quest, a little bear came to comfort him. The bear promised to guide him through life and protect him from wolves, which he feared. That is why we sometimes call him Little Bear."

She could see Joseph still looked uncertain.

"What if I have no vision or no one comes to help me?"

"You must trust the Great Spirit to have pity on you."

The next morning Touching Sky called on Tamaqua to help her prepare the sweat lodge for Joseph's ritual bath. She laid twelve round stones in her outside cooking fire and sent Joseph to the creek for water. When the stones were too hot to touch with her bare hands, Joseph and Touching Sky picked them up with sticks and piled them in the tent she'd help to erect—a wooden framework covered with leather skins.

"It's ready for you now," she said to Joseph. "Just pour the water on the stones when you're ready for the steam."

She watched as Joseph crawled through the tent flap. *I hope he takes this seriously.* Sweat baths were such a regular part of village life that it was hard to believe that Joseph's people never used them. What did they do when they got sick? Or needed to purify themselves?

Joseph pulled the tent flap snugly against the opening and took off his breechcloth. Steam rose into his face as he poured water onto the rocks. He sat down cross-legged in the middle of the tent and inhaled the steam. Sweat oozed from his pores and dripped from his forehead.

After the steam dissipated and began to cool down, he pushed the flap aside and dashed out of the opening. He ran toward the creek and dived into the water. The cold water shocked his skin and made his heart beat faster. He rubbed himself all over with his hands and then swam to the bank.

Joseph retrieved his breechcloth and dried off by the fire, trying to imagine what kind of vision he might receive in the woods. He went to bed that night without eating or drinking anything. When he woke up, his stomach was growling.

He waved goodbye to Touching Sky and headed into the woods with a knife in his belt and his medicine bundle around his neck. The sun was rising. He marked his path with care so he'd be able to find his way back. He saw no one as he strolled along, but a few animals scurried away and a deer looked at him with watchful eyes from a distance.

When the sun had risen to its zenith, Joseph stopped and sat down on a log. His tongue was dry from thirst and his pulse thumped in his temples. Although it was the season for berries, none were in sight. He spotted a vine that wound its way up the side of a large oak tree, so he cut it with his knife and drank the sap.

The warmth of the sunshine made him sleepy, so he raked together a few leaves for a cushion against the hard ground and laid down to rest.

When he opened his eyes, the sun had dropped toward the horizon. He sat up and looked around. A crow cawed some distance away.

Joseph got up and stretched, then walked toward the crow, just to see how close he could get without frightening it away. By keeping the trunks of the trees between him and the crow, he got quite close before the crow flew off. It landed close by.

Joseph stood and stared at it for a time before he walked toward it again. This time, the crow flew away before he could get close, and then landed. Joseph doggedly followed it. The crow cawed loudly at times, as though in protest of being stalked. Several times, Joseph was close to touching the crow before it flew away.

To follow the crow was a pleasant pastime that took Joseph's attention away from the gnawing in his stomach. Finally, he tired of the game and sat down cross-legged on the ground. It was late afternoon, and the air was growing cool. *A fire—that's what I need!* He found sticks and dead leaves, struck steel against flint, and sighed as the sparks ignited the kindling.

He watched the fire for a long time, mesmerized by the way it consumed the wood. He kept adding sticks.

Finally Joseph's eyes grew tired, and he lay down beside the fire. As he lay half-awake in the settling darkness, a scene from his childhood flashed before his eyes.

He was playing outside the house as darkness fell. *Dat* was reading the evening prayers with the rest of the family gathered round when Joseph finally came into the house. *Dat* kept reading but gave Joseph such a reproving look that he felt deeply shamed.

As *Dat* recited the Lord's Prayer, Joseph rehearsed his excuse for being tardy. *Dat* said nothing, but ever after, Joseph was careful to be on time for evening devotions. The words of the familiar prayer still evoked the shame he had felt at being late.

Now, as Joseph stared into the fire, he felt ashamed. He hadn't thought of the Lord's Prayer very often, and he had to concentrate just to remember all of the words. The German words seemed less familiar. He had to struggle to remember them. They came to him in snatches. Especially the part about temptation. He tried to translate it into the Delaware language, but couldn't think of the right words.

In a way, he was relieved that Touching Sky's family never recited prayers together as his family had done back home. *Dat* had always had the family kneel for the reading of a prayer from *Die Ernsthafte Christenpflicht*, an Anabaptist prayer book.

Since he'd never found much joy in the nightly ritual, he didn't miss it now. On the other hand, he felt a longing for the times when *Dat* made spontaneous mention of the family's concerns, along with the written prayers from the book. Like the time when Joseph had twisted his ankle and couldn't run. The swelling had gone down soon after *Dat* prayed for him. At such times, it was reassuring to have *Dat* close by, an embodiment of the infinitely more powerful *Vater im Himmel* they addressed in their prayers.

As Joseph drifted off toward sleep, he imagined he saw a glimpse of the great *Vater*, a white-haired man seated on a throne, stroking his long white beard with one hand and holding a scepter in the other. In his mind, he watched as angels dressed in white surrounded the throne, their hands folded in front and their wings spread out behind.

Joseph wondered why the Delaware never referred to God as Father. They always addressed their prayers to the Great Spirit or any number of lesser spirits, something that *Dat* had never taught the family to do.

He lay in the nether world between sleep and wakefulness, watching the smoke curl from the fire. *I think I just had a vision. I saw God and an angel.* Maybe it was the *Vater* who had reminded him of the Lord's Prayer. Or maybe it was the Great Spirit offering to be a father to him. Was the Great Spirit offering to protect him from temptation?

He certainly was tempted to eat something. His thoughts were jumbled and the fire swam before his eyes. Why had he agreed to this needless fasting, a torture of body and soul? Why hadn't he slipped some dried corn into his bag?

His tongue stuck to the sides of his mouth. Maybe he could just slip over to the little creek he'd seen that day and relieve his parched throat. Surely a few sips of the cool water wouldn't hurt. He'd already had some sap from the vine.

Joseph slept fitfully. When daylight came, Joseph's stomach cried out for food. He tried to ignore his hunger, but it wouldn't go away. He got up and walked around. His legs felt weak. He spotted the same crow he had seen the day before, or so it seemed, this time not far from where he had slept. The crow did not fly away at first, but perched overhead and cawed noisily at him. When it finally flew off, Joseph noticed a feather floating to the ground. He walked over and picked it up. It was a black pinion feather. He stroked it as he carried it back to the campfire.

The day passed slowly. Joseph's stomach felt tight, and he had a piercing pain behind his eyes. *Water. I will never take water for granted again.*

That night he saw the crow in his dream, cawing as always. This time, it seemed to be speaking to him. "I gave you a feather," it said in his dream. "If you carry it with you, you will be safe from danger."

"It is a very nice feather," Joseph said.

"It is the best that I have to give," the crow rasped.

"I will take good care of it," Joseph said solemnly. "I will not let anyone harm it."

Joseph watched the crow. Perhaps it was to be his guardian spirit. *I'll tell Touching Sky how it stayed close by and gave me a feather.* What else might a guardian spirit do?

After another day of fasting in the woods, Joseph's stomach ceased its growling but his head continued to pound. The trees swam before his eyes when he stood up, so he passed most of the day sitting still.

He had just fallen into a swoon when a large flock of crows landed in the trees above him. He gazed at them in fright. Did they mean to harm him? Or protect him? He tried to pray the Lord's Prayer but the words got jumbled in his mind, except for "deliver us from evil." He repeated the phrase several times, first in German and then in Delaware. Something to push the fear away.

Suddenly a flame flickered inside his head. It burned steadily, a comforting light that pushed back the darkness in his mind. It began to dawn on Joseph that this was what he had been looking for. The soothing light steadied him, and suddenly he felt clear-minded and strong.

So this is what Touching Sky meant by a guardian spirit!

Joseph reached for the black feather in his medicine bundle and twirled it between his fingers. Within a few moments, he fell asleep.

The next morning, a streak of sunlight pierced the overhead shade and shone into Joseph's face. He sat up and rubbed his eyes. *Did I dream all of that?* No, it was too real. Content that he'd seen a vision, Joseph set out for home, following the markers he'd left along the way. He gripped the black feather as he walked.

He smelled the smoke of cooking fires and heard children laughing. He was home. He stepped into the wigwam and Touching Sky's face lit up.

"Swift Foot!" she said. She handed him a gourd full of water. Joseph drank it dry and held out the gourd for more.

"Slowly, my son, slowly. You don't want to make yourself sick."

Joseph obediently took a deep breath and then sipped the next gourd full of water.

"Did you have a vision," she asked. "What did you see?"

"Yes," he replied, feigning more confidence than he felt. "Brother Crow spoke to me. He gave me this black feather. He said it would guide and protect me." He handed the feather to her, and she stroked it thoughtfully.

"This feather is a very good sign," she said. "You must always keep it with you."

"A large flock of crows roosted nearby while I was sleeping."

"That means they are looking out for you. How fortunate you are that they can warn you of danger or show the way when you're unsure."

Joseph reached out for the cracked corn Touching Sky offered. He chewed it slowly, savoring it. He hadn't remembered that dried corn tasted so good.

He mused as he ate. The Great Creator, the one his family called *Vater*, had sent the crow, he thought. It gave him comfort to know that he had not been alone.

-12-

Joseph gathered up an armload of sticks for the fire. He carried it behind the wigwam and dumped it onto the woodpile. Just as he was about to return into the forest for another load, Miquon called to him.

"Swift Foot! Come, let's play ball," he said. He tossed the deerskin ball to Joseph, who caught it and threw it back.

"I have to finish gathering wood first," Joseph said.

"Can't you do it later this afternoon? Why must you do it now?" Miquon asked impatiently.

"Touching Sky said I must gather enough wood for the next week. She's going to cook more than usual." He hesitated. "If you help me, I can get it done sooner."

Miquon scowled. "Carrying wood is women's work. Touching Sky should do it herself."

Joseph thought about this. *Touching Sky has always made me carry her wood.* He asked Miquon, "Don't you have to carry wood at your house?"

"No, my mother always does it. Men don't carry wood."

"Then why does Touching Sky make me do it?" Joseph asked.

"Because you were a captive and she could make you do whatever she wanted. But now that you're adopted, you could quit doing it for her." Miquon juggled the ball back and forth in his hands as he spoke.

Joseph's mind whirled. Back home in the Northkill, *Mam* had never chopped wood. It was a man's job, and the boys had helped *Dat* as soon as they were old enough to carry a few pieces. *I wonder what else I'm doing here that is supposed to be women's work.*

"Tell me," Joseph said. "How am I supposed to know what is man's work and what is women's work around here? I need to know so I can tell Touching Sky I'm not going to do it anymore."

Miquon began backtracking. "Touching Sky has treated you well, Joseph. Better than some of the other white captives were treated. Look at Thitpan. You can be grateful you didn't end up in her home. She yells at the captive she adopted and knocks him around with her stick."

Joseph shivered. He had heard Thitpan yell once too many times. *Maybe I better not complain about Touching Sky.*

"I still want to know if I'm doing women's work."

Miquon tossed him the ball. "Gardening. Real men don't garden."

"What? When I've hoed the garden or pulled weeds for Touching Sky, there are often men or boys helping."

"I bet they were white captives. Right?"

Joseph paused. Perhaps it was true. He couldn't remember seeing Indian men help in the garden.

"I never thought about that," he said. "What about cooking? Some Indian men cook."

Miquon shook his head. "Not much. Touching Sky taught you to cook a few things so you won't starve in the woods someday. But women do most of the cooking. "

That's the same way we did it back in the Northkill, Joseph thought to himself. Dat *never cooked, and he stayed out of* Mam*'s way when she was preparing food.*

"My mother always grows the food in the garden—corn, squash, beans—and she gathers roots, nuts, and berries in the woods," Miquon told him.

"But I've seen you help gather nuts."

"Yes, men can help gather nuts, but not usually roots or berries."

Joseph was exasperated. "Who decided that?"

"I don't know. It's just the way it is," Miquon said. By this time, the two boys were at the edge of the woods. Miquon picked up sticks while Joseph chopped a fallen sapling into pieces. They bundled the wood together and headed back to Touching Sky's woodpile.

"My father does all the hunting," Miquon continued. "But as soon as he brings the game to the front door of the home, it belongs to Mother. She can do anything with it that she wants, no matter what kind of animal it is. Sometimes she gives most of it away to her friends, or to widows who need it."

Joseph nodded. "I remember once when your mother gave Touching Sky a deer." *Touching Sky doesn't have anyone to hunt for her except me.*

"Sometimes the women go along on the hunt when it's a long way from home," Miquon said. "Once when I was a little boy, my father killed two deer in the woods. My mother carried the smaller one with a pack strap and Dad carried the bigger one."

"Really?" Joseph asked. "Your mother is not a big woman." He thought about Miquon's mother, who was slender and girlish and so much different from *Mam*, who had been comfortably plump and well-padded. He couldn't imagine his *Mam* trying to haul a deer out of the woods.

Miquon was obviously proud of his mother. "She's little, but she's strong. And she knows how to tan the hides. Dad never works with the hides. He makes things with wood, with stone, with bones, or sometimes with copper."

Joseph thought of *Dat*, whose features were beginning to fade, like the faces of other family members back home. Was he still alive? Or dead, as the old Indian had bragged to Christian? He felt a rush of homesickness as he thought about the way *Dat* had worked so well with his hands. "My father used to carve wood."

Miquon looked interested. "What kind of carving did he do?"

"Mostly little farm animals for my sister Franey to play with—a cow, a horse, a pig, a little sheep." Joseph stopped. It all came rushing back. Franey, his *Dat* carving by the fire. He had blocked it out for a long time.

"Did she wear them around her neck?"

Joseph was puzzled. "No, she played with them. Why would she wear them around her neck?"

"As spirit helpers, or charms."

Joseph could barely contain his scorn. *We didn't believe in charms.* "These were just toys—little farm animals like the ones we had on the farm."

"What are farm animals?"

Joseph's jaw dropped. *Doesn't Miquon know what a farm animal is?* "They're animals you keep on the farm. You know—cows, pigs, sheep, horses . . ."

Miquon looked defensive. "A few of our people have horses, but I've never been on a farm. What does a sheep look like?"

Joseph's mind whirled. How could he describe something as simple as a sheep? "A sheep is a lot like a big dog," he said, "but it has wool. Wool is like long curly hair, but it's soft. My *Mam* made clothes out of it."

Miquon leaned forward to listen, so Joseph went on. "Cows are a lot like horses, except that they give milk. *Mam* used milk and cream to make things like butter or cheese. She used it for making bread too."

"What do butter and cheese taste like?" Miquon asked. "I've never eaten such a thing."

Joseph was at a loss. How do you describe butter and cheese to someone who doesn't even know what a cow is? He thought hard for a few moments, then gave up. "I don't know how to describe it," he said. "Maybe someday you'll visit a farm and then you can taste it for yourself."

By this time, they had made another trip into the woods and were headed back to the wigwam, each with an armload of wood. They dumped the wood onto the pile.

Joseph straightened up and brushed the dirt from his hands. "That should make Touching Sky happy. Now I can leave this women's work and play ball with you."

Miquon laughed. "Someday when you get married, your wife can do all of the women's work for you. If you get a good wife like my mother, she can sew mats from fibers, or work with skins and husks or clay. Or she can sew clothes with leather and make them look special with porcupine quills, deer hair embroidery, or feathers."

Joseph's thoughts were jumbled as he and Miquon ran toward the open field at the middle of the village. *Married? Who would I marry here?* It seemed more likely that he'd get married to someone like Summer Rain than to an Indian girl. Someone for whom he didn't have to explain things like milk and sheep. But—married? He was far too young.

Over the next few days, Miquon's words echoed in Joseph's mind: "Someday when you get married . . ." Joseph wasn't interested in getting married. It wasn't that he didn't notice some of the young girls in the village. Like Spring Flower, who had a bubbly laugh, or Quick Bird, who had a way of drawing his eyes toward her by swinging her hips as she walked. Most often, his thoughts went to the few times he'd been with Summer Rain.

At first, Touching Sky had been upset to find him talking with her. Lately, she hadn't seemed as worried. Now that Touching Sky had adopted him, would she mind if he spent time with Summer Rain? Or would she expect that he'd marry an Indian girl?

The corn tassels were turning brown, and it was almost harvesttime. Joseph didn't enjoy working in the garden, but if it were a way to meet Summer Rain, he would look forward to it.

"Isn't it about time to harvest the corn?" he asked Touching Sky, who was pulling down a basket from its hook in the ceiling.

"Yes." She gave him her broadest smile. "I'm so glad you noticed. I was just about to ask you to help me pick it."

Joseph followed Touching Sky to the garden, where several women were at work. Grandfather Sun warmed Mother Earth and shone bright on the vines of the squash that wrapped their long arms around the stalks of corn. Touching Sky moved toward a row of corn and examined one of the ears. She split the thick husk with her fingers to reveal the pearly kernels underneath. She ran the edge of her thumbnail against a row of plump kernels.

"Perfect," she said to Joseph. "Let's start picking in this row of hills." A hill, Joseph knew, was a small mound of corn planted in a cluster. She handed Joseph a basket.

Joseph followed Touching Sky, holding the basket for her as she stripped each ear from its stalk. By the time they walked to the end of a row and back, the basket was heaped full.

"Empty the basket onto that mat at the end of the field," Touching Sky said. "We will husk the corn when we are finished picking."

Summer Rain walked up just as Joseph was about to dump the basket onto the mat under a spreading oak. She emptied her basket onto a mat next to his. For a brief moment, it seemed, they were alone.

"Do you like it here?" he asked in a low voice to keep others from hearing his native German. "Are you feeling more at home here since we last talked?"

"Not really," Summer Rain said softly. "But I'm getting used to it."

Joseph glanced back at the corn patch, where Touching Sky waved impatiently from the end of the corn patch.

"I must go," Joseph said, turning back to where Touching Sky waited. He held the basket for Touching Sky as she quickly stripped ears of corn from the stalks.

The last time he'd spoken to Summer Rain, he'd been planning to run away. Did she know that now he was planning to stay? Although he thought less and less about his Amish life these days, speaking to Summer Rain in German transported him back to the summertime at the Northkill. He could hear *Mam* calling him to a dinner table set with dishes and utensils, groaning under a load of vegetables, meat, bread, and desserts. He would pull up a chair and devour succulent sweet corn, boiled in a kettle and slathered with butter. Then he would banter with his brothers until *Dat* said it was time to return to the field.

He felt again the admiration of the young women at the apple *Schnitzing* on the night before the Indian attack. The girls had giggled and whispered to each other as the boys bobbed for apples. Joseph's heart ached at the memories, at once so distant and yet so close that a few words in German brought them rushing back like leaves driven before the wind. It had been a long time since he'd felt that pain. Most of it he'd pushed deep down, along with his anger.

After dumping two more baskets of corn onto the pile, Joseph sat down with Touching Sky in the shade of the tree. Together, they began to husk the corn. The process felt comfortingly familiar, since he and his brothers had often helped *Mam* with this task.

Joseph had only husked a few ears when Summer Rain and her Indian captor squatted on a mat nearby. Joseph stole a glance at her as she started to work. He noticed her long supple fingers as she peeled back the husks and brushed the silk off the juicy corn. Twice when he glanced at her, their eyes met. He wanted desperately to speak to her in their shared language but didn't dare.

"This is the best corn we've had in several seasons," Touching Sky said to the Indian woman who was working next to them.

"Yes," the woman answered. "I am glad that I have Summer Rain to help me."

"Summer Rain is a lovely name," Touching Sky said. "She is a good helper for you."

Joseph's heart leaped. Perhaps Touching Sky might not mind if he spent time with her. But what would Summer Rain's captor think?

Joseph's mouth watered as he thought about eating fresh corn on the cob, but Touching Sky said they would dry most of it. After they had husked a few of the ears, she showed him how to tie the rest of them together, weaving the husks into a long braid.

Joseph felt awkward as he tried to weave the dry husks. Summer Rain made it look so simple. *She gets lots of practice braiding her hair*, he thought as he watched her work. *Just like* Mam.

"My son," Touching Sky said to Joseph, "I want you to carry all of these ears up to the wigwam." She piled the corn into her largest basket as she spoke. Joseph glanced at Summer Rain as he picked up the basket and hoisted it onto his shoulders. He winked in response to her shy smile.

With this kind of company, he didn't mind working in the garden. Not at all.

More than a moon passed after the corn harvest. Now Joseph could see his breath in the air each morning and found himself drawn to the cooking fires in the chilly evenings. The bare trees seemed to shiver in the cold winds that blew through the village.

It was not long into the changing of the seasons that Tamaqua came to Touching Sky's wigwam. Joseph looked up and greeted him, then went back to eating a bowl of stew Touching Sky had prepared for him. He wore a blanket over his bare shoulders, but even so, he shivered in the crisp morning air.

Tamaqua squatted next to him and looked at the goose bumps on Joseph's arms. "If you truly want to become an Indian, you will need to learn to endure the hardness of cold weather," Tamaqua told him.

Joseph started at the thought. He had never liked the harshness of winter in the Northkill, and it was even worse facing it with only a wigwam for protection against the elements. Tamaqua seemed to read his mind.

"The white man is very soft," Tamaqua said. "He builds log houses with fireplaces and wears heavy clothing." He punched Joseph playfully on the arm. "You must learn to live with cold weather like we do."

How am I going to do that? Joseph wondered. His puzzlement must have showed.

"We are going to sit in the creek each day to teach your body to stand the cold," he replied. "We'll start this morning."

Joseph shrank back at the thought but said nothing as he finished his breakfast. He didn't want Tamaqua to think he was a weakling.

The wind was cutting as Tamaqua led him to the creek. *I can't do this,* thought Joseph. Tamaqua tossed off all his clothing and motioned for Joseph to do the same. Naked, they waded into the cold water. Tamaqua led Joseph to a place where the water came well above his knees and then sat down. Only his head showed above the surface. His face was stoic. He motioned for Joseph to do the same.

The shock to Joseph's system almost made him cry out. Determined, he gritted his teeth and was silent. He and Tamaqua sat close to each other in the swift-flowing stream.

This is strange, Joseph thought, Mam *would tell me I'll catch my death of cold.* His teeth began to chatter in the chilly water.

"You'll soon learn to stand it," Tamaqua said without any show of sympathy. "We're going to do this every day until you can easily endure it, even if we have to chop ice from the surface."

At least he's doing it along with me, Joseph thought. *He's not expecting me to do something that won't do himself.*

"You have much to learn before you will be a true Indian," Tamaqua said. "Until the white man came, our people did not drink whiskey or rum. Since the traders came and sold us rum in exchange for pelts, we have not been the same. There are people in our village who would sell everything they have in order to get rum. The white man is to blame for this."

"Your people would not need to buy strong drink, would they?" Joseph asked, remembering the way that *Dat* reasoned. His voice was uneven as he spoke and he struggled to control his chattering teeth.

"That is true," Tamaqua replied, "but the white man has found ways to fool our people. Many of us who should know better have gotten caught in this problem. Even Touching Sky."

Joseph's eyes widened. He'd never seen Touching Sky touch strong drink. But then, he'd never seen rum in the village.

"The white man also curses and swears—something that our people never do. They use the name of the white man's God, cursing one another or trying to impress one another. Our people would never speak that way of the Great Creator, or of the spirits."

"The Bible taught my people not to swear," Joseph replied. He tried to focus on the conversation rather than on the fact he could no longer feel his feet. "My father never swore, and he taught me never to use the name of the Lord in vain. We do not even swear an oath, because we believe it to be wrong."

"Then your father must be different than the white soldiers and traders I have met," Tamaqua said.

"I promise never to disrespect you by swearing," Joseph said, hoping to talk about something else. *Will this never end? Now I can't feel my legs!*

"Yes, I have seen you show respect to the elders as well as Touching Sky," Tamaqua said. "You are learning quickly."

After what seemed like a long time, Tamaqua stood up in the water. "That will be enough for today," he said as he made his way toward the bank. "We'll come back tomorrow."

Joseph tried to stand, but his legs were numb and collapsed underneath him. Resolutely, he used his arms to leverage himself to a standing position, hoping Tamaqua wouldn't notice. *Tomorrow?* He blanched at the thought. He put on his breechcloth and wrapped a blanket around him, grateful for a few warm rays from the sun as they walked back into the village. Feeling returned to his body in sharp pains up and down his legs and feet.

Would this really make him tougher? It seemed more likely to kill him!

-13-

October 1758

"Thanks for helping Swift Foot become a true Delaware," Touching Sky to Tamaqua as he led Joseph back from the creek. "He will grow stronger as he learns to stand the cold."

Tamaqua glanced at Joseph, who was drying himself by the fire. "I don't think he's very happy about it," he said softly, so Joseph wouldn't hear.

Touching Sky nodded agreement. "Not now, but later he will be. Nor does he understand our religion. Now that he is adopted, he should be a part of the Big House ceremony."

Tamaqua raised his eyebrows. "I don't think Swift Foot will like that any better than sitting in cold water."

"But this is a good year for him to learn, since our clan will do the preparation," Touching Sky countered.

"I'll do my best to draw him in." Tamaqua moved toward the door. "I'm looking forward to wearing the bear costume this year, but I think it needs a little repair."

"I can stitch it for you if you wish," Touching Sky said. He nodded and waved his hand in farewell.

Tamaqua will make a good Misinghalikun, she thought. *He'll help Joseph understand our sacred worship.* She reached for the basket that held the red-and-black mask Tamaqua would wear along with his costume. The *Misinghalikun* was a living mask, the guardian of all the wild animals in the forest.

"What's the Big House ceremony?" Joseph asked as Touching Sky put fresh paint on the mask.

"It's a time of celebration during the month of October. We worship in the Big House for eleven nights in a row."

"Will I have to do something?" Joseph's voice was low.

"Yes, you must help me get the Big House ready and then come to the meetings each night. You will hunt deer with other young men on the sixth day of the ceremony. If you bring back plenty of meat, we will have a feast."

"Will Miquon be there?" Joseph asked.

"Of course. Everybody in the village will come, and others from villages nearby."

Swift Foot has to come, Touching Sky thought. How could she excuse his absence at such an important occasion? There'd be no better way for him to become a part of the Delaware religion than to worship in the Big House and hear men share about visions they'd seen. And perhaps, if Silver Sage shared on the night when women were allowed to speak, Joseph would be inspired by her vision story.

The next day, Touching Sky and several other members of the clan began to prepare the Big House for the annual ceremony. She asked Joseph to help her take down the bark doors on the two ends of the house. "We must let the breeze flow through," she said. After they were finished, she asked Joseph to cut down the tall, dry grasses along the sides of the building. Runs Free came alongside and piled them into a large basket.

Next, Touching Sky swept the dirt floor and scooped up the ashes from the two fire pits inside the Big House. Joseph carried them to the gully at the edge of the village. Touching Sky watched as Runs Free hopped alongside Joseph. *I'm so glad they love each other,* she thought.

When the Big House was clean, the three of them brought in baskets of new grass and spread it on the floor along the walls where people would sit. Touching Sky took a deep breath, reveling in the familiar scent.

She looked around at the wooden faces carved on the poles around the perimeter. *We'll need to repaint those faces,* she thought. *We can't have a meeting until they are properly painted.*

Touching Sky turned to Joseph. "We'll need to gather enough logs to last for eleven nights in two fires. Why not ask Miquon to help you?"

She glanced at Tamaqua and a cousin, who were setting up the supports for the large kettle they would use to cook hominy for the feast. If the spirit helpers assisted Joseph and the other young men to get a deer, the village would have a great feast. Her mouth watered to think about it.

Touching Sky wondered if Joseph would ever learn to worship like an Indian. She'd never heard him speak about his need for spirit helpers. What did the white men do in their houses of worship if not speak about their visions? The white captives, including Joseph, never talked about rituals of worship.

I'm going to ask Swift Foot about it, she said to herself as she watched Tamaqua show Joseph how to repair the rack on which the food for the meals was to be stacked. Another man fixed the bark on the outside wall. *I hope Swift Foot will be honest with me.*

When evening fell, Touching Sky squatted next to Joseph as he sat on the floor near the fire inside the wigwam. She pulled the bear costume onto her lap to stitch a ripped seam, and Joseph worked on a new carving. "Swift Foot," she said, "what kind of Big House did you have back home? How often did you go there?"

"We had no Big House."

"No place where everyone could gather to worship the Great Creator?" Touching Sky was amazed.

Joseph tried to explain. "We worshiped in each other's homes."

"Didn't you have a big ceremony where the whole tribe could meet?"

Joseph thoughtfully worked with his knife for a while before he spoke. "Twice a year, we gathered in an all-day meeting called the Big Church. Bishop Jake was in charge. We shared communion with each other and washed each other's feet as an act of humility."

Touching Sky thought about that. *They washed each other's feet? The ways of the white man are strange.* "Then you won't mind coming to the Big House?" Hope edged her voice as she spoke.

Joseph put down the carving. "I'll come the first night, but I won't promise to come to the rest of them."

"I'm sure you'll enjoy it." Touching Sky wished she was as sure as she sounded when she said it aloud. But why wouldn't he? There would be storytelling, singing, and dancing—all of which any true Delaware would enjoy. And that's what Joseph was bound to become, now that he was part of her family. She'd see to it, whether he liked it or not.

Joseph stood with arms crossed as Tamaqua put on his bear costume and fastened the face mask in place. Tamaqua bent down to let Runs Free stroke the wiry fur, and Tamaqua let out a loud roar. Joseph laughed as Runs Free stepped back with a frightened look. To a child, Tamaqua really did look like a bear, especially with the bear's ears sticking up on top of his head.

Joseph tried to imagine Bishop Jake back home donning a costume to call the faithful together for the biannual communion service. As a young boy, Joseph had never been excited about going to the solemn church service that lasted all day. The preachers told stories from Scripture, from the time of creation to the death and resurrection of Jesus as their Savior. *If a man in a bear costume told the stories, it would certainly have livened things up!* Joseph thought.

He stepped to the door to watch Tamaqua jumping and waving his arms as he ran through the village, shouting: "Come to the Big House ceremony!" When several children appeared at a doorway, Tamaqua roared and chased after them. They squealed, their excitement tinged with fright. Dogs barked and ran after him.

That evening, Joseph trudged toward the Big House along with Runs Free and Touching Sky. He'd never seen his adopted mother so dressed up, even for a dance. Like the other women, she had painted a round red spot on each cheek. Her hair was tied behind her neck with an ornament made of slate. Her skirt and leggings had wide borders of embroidery, and her moccasins were covered with dyed porcupine quills worked into fancy patterns.

Touching Sky's cape was made of thousands of soft turkey-breast feathers. Each feather was fastened to a finely woven net, laying smooth and even. A string of shell and bright copper beads adorned her neck, and a string of beads hung from her ears.

The sun was setting as people arrived at the Big House for worship. *Maybe it will be like a dance and I can see Summer Rain. I wonder what she'll think of this.*

Everyone entered the door at the east end of the building. In the church services back home, no one paid much attention to north, south, east, or west. But it really mattered to the Delaware, Joseph realized. They spoke of these directions as though they were people—grandparents—who brought things to them.

Joseph paused inside the door to let his eyes adjust to the darkness. Two fires staved off the evening chill, each about halfway between the center supporting pole and the opposite end of the building. Smoke from the fire floated upward and drifted out of the smoke hole.

He studied the carved wooden faces that decorated the sides of the ten posts that supported the walls—three posts on each long wall and two on the wall at both ends. Two other faces stared from atop the east and west sides of the center pole. The grim faces were painted red on the right half and black on the left.

No one back home would want to worship in a place with ugly faces like that, Joseph thought. Then he remembered. The ugly faces were there to scare away the evil spirits, a constant worry in his adopted village. Would he ever learn to fear them the way Touching Sky did? How could she believe they were real? Although the preachers back home spoke about the devil who enticed people into hell, they said next to nothing about evil spirits. They did mention angels, who served as messengers from God.

Joseph pushed the evil faces to the back of his mind when he saw Summer Rain seated along a wall, wearing a skirt embroidered with colorful quills. She looked lovely.

Touching Sky tugged at Joseph's arm. "You'll sit with our clan," she said as she headed for the north end of the building. "The Turtle are over there, and the Turkey over there," she said as she motioned to the different sides of the building.

The men, women, and children from each clan sat or squatted together on the loose grass. What a difference from the way the congregation sat back home in the Northkill, where the men and women sat on chairs in separate parts of the room to worship! Joseph sat cross-legged next to Touching Sky, while Runs Free snuggled into his lap.

Walks Proud lifted his head to quiet the people and the room fell silent. He began to speak.

"We have gathered to give thanks for the many ways in which the Great Creator has helped us in the year gone by," he said. "We have found abundance in the field as well as the forest, so that we have food to eat, clothing to wear, and wigwams to keep us warm in the cold."

Joseph looked at Touching Sky. She squeezed his hand.

"Let us then be thankful," Walks Proud continued, "showing our gratefulness to the Great Spirit with body and soul in the nights ahead. And now, let us pray."

Joseph bowed his head to pray in the manner of the people back home, quite sure that Walks Proud was praying to a different Creator than to one to whom Joseph had been taught to address his prayers. Just then Runs Free poked him and pointed to a small group of people entering the Big House with Chief Custaloga in the lead.

"Uncle Custaloga is here," she whispered to Joseph. He looked up to see the chief wearing a bearskin cap with several eagle feathers attached to it. He stood in silence as Walks

Proud finished his prayer of thanks, and then he led the small processional around the room to the sound of a drum.

"Who are they?" Joseph asked Touching Sky.

"They are the heads of the Turtle and the Turkey clans," she said, "along with the assistant chiefs of the clans. And the three war leaders are behind them."

Behind these leaders came Tamaqua and two other men carrying long poles, followed by three women. "Those are the helpers," Touching Sky said. "They will sweep the floors and bring in the food at the proper time."

The procession marched around the room several times, and then the chief stopped and waited for the persons in the processional to take their seats among their various clans. The six helpers sat or squatted at the end of the building by themselves. There were three women on one side of the entrance door and three men on the right.

When everyone was seated, Chief Custaloga spoke. "We are thankful that so many of us are alive to meet together here once more, and that we are ready to hold our ceremonies in good faith. Now we shall meet here twelve nights in succession to pray to *Kishelemukonk* (our Creator), who has directed us to worship in this way."

The chief pointed at the six helpers seated at the end of the house. "Our attendants must keep everything here in good order and try to bring peace if there is trouble. They will haul wood and build fires, cook and sweep out the Big House. When they sweep, they must sweep both sides of the fire twelve times, which sweeps a road to heaven. Women in their menses must not enter this house."

Joseph started at the chief's words about women. *I wonder if that has something to do with their being in the hut.*

"We come here to pray for *Kishelemukonk* to have mercy on us in the year to come and to give us everything to make us happy. We are thankful to the East because we feel good in the morning when we awake, and see the bright light coming from the East, and when the Sun goes down in the West we feel good and glad we are well; then we are thankful to the West. And we are thankful to the North, because when the cold winds come we are glad to have lived to see the leaves fall again; and to the South, for when the south wind blows and everything is coming up in the spring, we are glad to live to see the grass growing and everything green again.

"When we eat and drink and look around, we know it is *Kishelemukonk* that makes us feel good that way. He gives us the purest thoughts that can be had. We should pray to him every morning."

Touching Sky does that. So does Tamaqua.

"Man has a spirit," Custaloga continued, "and the body seems to be a coat for that spirit. We should take care of our spirits, so as to reach heaven and be admitted to *Kishelemukonk's* dwelling. We must all prepare for this meeting, so that *Kishelemukonk* will look upon us and grant what we ask. When we reach that place, we shall not have to do anything or worry about anything, only live a happy life. When we arrive we shall see our fathers, mothers, children, and sisters there. Everything looks more beautiful there than here, everything looks new, and the waters and fruits are lovely."

If he's talking about the same heaven that's in the Bible, Mam *and Jakey and Franey are there. Maybe* Dat, *if that Indian killed him. I wonder if they can see me down here?* Joseph turned toward Touching Sky, who was leaning forward, following the chief's words with rapt attention. *She's probably thinking of Tamahican and Suckameek.*

The chief extended his hands toward the people as he spoke. "No sun shines there, but a light much brighter than the sun; *Kishelemukonk* makes it brighter by his power. All people who die here, young or old, will be of the same age there; and those who are injured, crippled, or made blind will look as good as the rest of them. It is nothing but the flesh that is injured: the spirit is as good as ever."

I remember Bishop Jake saying that heaven won't need the light of the sun, because God will be there, Joseph thought. *It's in the book of Revelation.*

After a few more words, Custaloga picked up a turtle shell rattle and began to march around the room, shaking it. Several men rose from their seats and followed him as he marched, stepping to the rhythm of the deer-hide drum in the center of the room.

Joseph was startled as Touching Sky got up and joined the chief, followed by Silver Sage and a number of other women. They formed a new circle of dancers, just a little to the side of the men, dancing where the floor was dirt, rather than where the grasses had been spread. Runs Free stood up and clapped to the rhythm.

Runs Free tugged at Joseph's arm as the dancers followed the chief in a figure-eight pattern, circling the fires and the center post. "Get up, Swift Foot," she whispered.

Joseph sighed and stood up, dutifully clapping his hands to the rhythm of the drum. It wasn't that he didn't like the rhythm; it was just that he couldn't make sense of the words that Custaloga was chanting, even at the times when the dancers stopped and the chief chanted his vision alone.

When the chief was finished, Touching Sky and the other dancers returned to their seats. Joseph sat down again. He listened to Touching Sky's rapid breathing as two of the helpers, a man and a woman, used turkey wings as brooms to smooth out the tracks of the dancers. Everyone fell silent as Custaloga handed the turtle rattle to the next person on the perimeter. Joseph watched as the people passed it counterclockwise around the circle, each holding it carefully so as not to make a sound unless they intended to speak.

And then a man in the circle shook the rattle, and the drummer began to drum. The man with the rattle in his hand got up and began to dance in the circle, just as the chief had done. Men and women followed in two circles, dancing their way around the fire. *Is this going to go on all night?* Joseph thought as he listened to the volunteer chant his vision.

Joseph stumbled back to his wigwam just as the first rays of the sun lightened the eastern sky. *This is worse than the Big Church back home. They won't even let you go to sleep.* At least back home *Dat* had let him doze off during the worship service, with its earnest chant and droning sermons. Here, they'd woken him up three times, making him listen to the long recitations about vision helpers.

I don't think I'll ever believe like the Delaware.

-14-

It was late November, and Touching Sky felt an urgency to sew winter clothing for the family. One day while Joseph was gathering firewood, she chose six beaver skins from the pelts that Tamaqua had trapped. She laid them out on the floor of the wigwam and cut them to fit against each other to form a large skin Joseph could throw over his left shoulder. Touching Sky arranged the grain of the fur in a way that would let the rain and snow run off easily.

Over the next several days, she sewed the skins, punching holes with a small awl and then threading sinew through the holes to stitch them together. The day she finished the sewing, she called to Joseph. He was talking quietly outside the wigwam with Miquon.

"Swift Foot, come in and try on your new winter robe," she said.

Joseph lifted the flap in the doorway and stepped inside. Touching Sky motioned for him to stand still in front of her as she hung the new robe on his left shoulder, wrapping it under his right arm, and overlapping it in the front.

Joseph shook his head. "It feels strange," he said. "How will I keep it from falling off?"

Touching Sky dismissed his frustration. "You can hold it together with your left hand, from the inside."

Joseph shrugged and grasped the folds of the robe with his left land. "You mean my right hand won't be covered?" he asked. "How will I keep it warm?"

"I'll make a sleeve for you," Touching Sky said as she lifted the skins off Joseph's shoulder. *My poor white boy*, she thought to herself. *He has always worn thin coats in the wintertime. He doesn't know how to stay warm as an Indian.*

Joseph went back outside as Touching Sky tossed the robe onto the floor and proceeded to make a sleeve for his right arm. Using an otter pelt that Tamaqua had trapped, she cut the skin so that it would reach from his shoulder to his wrist. With an awl, she pushed holes through the skin and stitched it together with sinew, and then fastened two strips of leather to the upper end, which he could use as a tie around his neck to keep the sleeve in place.

Again, she called for Joseph, who grimaced as she had him try on the sleeve, together with the robe. He looked dour as he put on the winter clothing, but Touching Sky was pleased. "You look good in your new clothes," she said. "Now all I need to make for you is a pair of leggings and some winter moccasins."

The next day, she worked on the leggings made of deerskin and cut to fit around his legs from his crotch to his ankles. She folded them into a sleeve and bored holes along the edge he would wear to the outside, joining them with strips of sinew at short intervals. On the bottom half of the leggings, she cut a series of fringes as decoration. When both of the pieces were sewn, she stitched a pair of leather thongs on the top that Joseph could tie to his breechcloth belt.

Touching Sky watched as Joseph tried them on. *At least he didn't frown this time*, she thought as he examined his new clothing.

Over the next two days, she finished a pair of moccasins that were large enough for his growing feet, even when they were wrapped with rabbit skins to stave off the winter cold.

Joseph put his winter wear to immediate use the next morning. Overnight, a foot of snow had fallen. The wind from the north howled and shook the wigwam. "This will be a good day to try out your new outfit," Touching Sky told Joseph as he threw off the covers and scrambled out of bed.

Joseph frowned and reached for the new clothing. Touching Sky helped him put on the robe, with the longest parts draping down below his knees. She fastened the robe in front with a piece of leather. After he pushed his arm into the otter-skin sleeve, she helped him fasten it up with a strap around his neck.

Finally, Joseph wrapped his feet with two rabbit furs and shoved them into the new moccasins, which fit tightly against his leggings. Touching Sky looked at him, proud of her handiwork. She was quite pleased. Her adopted son looked every inch an Indian.

Well, except for his green eyes. And his brown hair.

Joseph stepped outside into the winter cold, blinking against the bright light. He forged a path through the deep snow by pushing it aside with his moccasins. The cold air stung his nose.

If I were home, he thought, Dat *would be clearing a path to the barn with a shovel so we could feed the animals and milk the cow. There's no good reason to clear the snow here.* He rarely thought about the Northkill anymore, but the snowfall brought back memories in a rush.

Just then Miquon trudged by, carrying a large kettle "I'm going to get water at the creek," he said. "It's women's work, but because of the snow, I'm getting it for my mother."

Maybe there is a reason to clear the snow after all, Joseph thought. He hated getting water. But Miquon was his friend.

"Wait," Joseph said to Miquon. "I'll go with you. But first let me get something to carry water for Touching Sky."

He stepped into the wigwam and picked up a kettle. "I'm getting water," he said.

Touching Sky flashed him a smile as he grabbed the pot with his free hand and hurried to catch up with Miquon. Together they made a path through the heavy snow, pressing their way to the creek.

The winter air rustled the last oak leaves clinging to the trees as Joseph and Miquon slogged through the snow on their way to the water. Joseph felt strange in his new outfit. It was so different from anything he'd worn back home! He was mostly warm, although the right side of his neck felt the sting of a few flakes of snow that dropped from the leaden skies.

Joseph and Miquon arrived at the creek together, gazing at the water that rushed between heavy banks of snow. They broke through the thin layer of ice near the bank. Both boys filled their kettles to the brim.

"Do you think Tamaqua will make me sit in the creek today?" Joseph asked. He shivered as he said it.

"He might. I've seen him do it when it was snowing like this. Sometimes he has to chop the ice with his tomahawk."

"I hope we don't do it today," Joseph said. "Getting water in freezing weather is bad enough."

"Don't tell him that," Miquon said, "or he'll likely make you do it."

"Oh, I could easily stand it," Joseph said, hoping he hadn't given the impression that he was soft. "It's just that I don't feel like getting into the water today."

Miquon nodded. "I won't mention it." With the kettle sloshing water at his side, he headed back up the path toward the village, with Joseph close behind.

Joseph realized for the first time that he didn't mind his new clothes. He actually felt warm.

Touching Sky was pleased with the way that Joseph adapted to his new winter clothes. Not just his clothes, but her food as well. He still seemed reluctant to accept her religion, but he would surely adapt over time.

The following fall, two soldiers in red uniforms with white trim strode past Touching Sky's wigwam. A pair of Indians led the way to the center of the village. On their shoulders the soldiers carried long rifles with knives fastened at the ends of the barrel. Short knives hung from their belts.

Who are they? Touching Sky wondered. Their uniforms were different from the French soldiers who had come by a few summers ago, back when the war troubles began.

Chief Custaloga greeted the men, who followed him to the council house.

"You stay in the wigwam. I don't want these Yengwes to see you," Touching Sky said to Joseph. She often used this term of derision for the British. As she left the wigwam to head for the council house, she told Runs Free, "You stay inside with Joseph. You can play with your dolls, but don't go outside."

The white soldiers sat with a circle of the elders, smoking the ceremonial pipe and talking. They spoke in the strange tongue of the great British lord, who reigned from far away over the waters that carried men in large boats with sails. One of the Indians interpreted for them.

"We have come to strengthen the chain of friendship," Touching Sky heard the interpreter say, "and to make sure that your people are not lured into war by the French."

Custaloga nodded. "We have resolved that none of our people will fight against your people anymore." He held up two belts of wampum. "We will send these to you if we see a threat arising from the French."

"We are well pleased," the older of the two men responded through the interpreter.

Touching Sky breathed a sigh of relief. So the war was nearly over. Custaloga had forged a treaty with the British. The tribe, once loyal to the French king, had switched its allegiance.

"I hope that means our warriors can once again hunt game in the woods, rather than fighting the white man," Custaloga continued. "What gifts will you give to pay us back for all that we have lost?"

Their conversation went on late into the night. Over the next two days, the men walked through the village and made marks on papers they carried in their hands. Touching Sky shrank back when they walked around the back of her dwelling.

"Swift Foot, you stay hidden," she said to him as they sat inside the wigwam. "Who knows what those men are looking for or what they are writing down? Perhaps they are counting the captives among us so that they can bring their army and take them away from us."

She thought for a moment. "No good thing has ever come from the white man's writing. They write things down on paper when we talk with them about our lands, and then they tell us that the paper says the land belongs to them."

Joseph was sitting cross-legged on the floor. She squatted down beside him.

"The white man must have no memory or other way to learn. Their god gave them a great book to help them do what is right. We Delaware can tell what is right by learning from the world around us and by listening to our elders. We don't need paper."

Joseph thought about trying to explain the Bible. He opened his mouth, but then closed it with a snap. *Touching Sky is right,* he thought. *Who needs paper when you can learn from the natural world?*

After the men left, Touching Sky went to the council house to speak to Custaloga about their mission. "Who were those men?" she asked. "Why did you let them spy on us for so long?"

"They are both officers in the British army, Patterson and Hutchins by name," he said.

"They must have poor eyes," Touching Sky said. "They crowded up close to you and nearly stepped on your moccasins."

Custaloga gave a slight smile. "Yes, and they must have thought we are hard of hearing. For they talked loudly, even when they were very near to us."

Touching Sky frowned. "And one starts talking before the other is finished. Or both speak at the same time. They must be quite impatient."

"I fear you are right. But we must learn to overlook their faults. These men are on the way from Fort Pitt to Presque Isle, taking inventory of the forts that the French have left behind. They were not spying; they were strengthening the chain of friendship by coming to know our people. Why would we not show them hospitality?"

Touching Sky stamped her foot. "The chain of friendship may soon be wrapped around our necks, so that they can drag us away from this place," Touching Sky said. "Or they may come and take our captives and claim them as their own."

"I have told them more than once that the captives among us are like family," Custaloga told her comfortingly. "We will never let them go."

Despite his reassuring words, a snake of suspicion wrapped itself around Touching Sky's chest. She felt as if she couldn't breathe. "If they ever come back for Swift Foot," she said, "you shall bear the blame."

Custaloga looked at her solemnly but said nothing.

Touching Sky left, thinking deeply. She walked back to her wigwam, her hands trembling—just as they had on the day she was told of her son's death.

-15-

August 1760

Touching Sky and Runs Free were harvesting squash in the garden when Silver Sage waved from the edge of the cornfield. "Come," she said. "A white trader just showed up, and Custaloga says he has brought some goods for clothing."

Touching Sky waved back. "I'm coming," she said and turned to Runs Free. "Let's go. I hope I'll be able to get a new blanket for you. Your old one looks like a rag."

Touching Sky and Runs Free joined Silver Sage and other villagers assembling near the lodge where Custaloga stood with a couple of men beside two packhorses. He introduced the British trader, whose name was George Croghan.

"You have come with a message from the white chief," Custaloga said. "Tell us what you have to say."

The trader nodded and spoke. "His Majesty's general who is now at Pittsburgh has sent me to announce that it is necessary for his Majesty's service to open the communication from Pittsburgh to Presque Isle and to establish a post there."

It would be very convenient to have a post close by, Touching Sky thought. *We have needed to travel much too far to get to Fort Pitt.*

But Croghan's next words brought her up short. "We desire that you will assist any troops that may at any time be passing by your settlements. His Majesty assures all nations of Indians that by this belt of wampum, they will have his protection as long as you behave well. You may be sure that the general will render any of your people any services in his power for the establishing a lasting peace and friendship with all nations."

Touching Sky frowned. The man sounded so pompous! It frightened her to think of British troops marching through the area. It wouldn't be long before they would take over all the forts. Soon they would claim all of Indian country.

Her eyes narrowed as she watched Custaloga receive the wampum belt. Custaloga held the belt across his open palms and said to Croghan: "Our people desire to live at peace with you. We will welcome your troops to travel our paths—as long as no settlers move into our region. Only traders will be allowed to live here."

Touching Sky nodded approval. The troops could be present to keep the peace, but not to make way for white settlements.

After the exchange of wampum was complete, Custaloga and Croghan took their place in the circle of elders to smoke the calumet pipe they used to mark treaties with neighboring peoples. Custaloga took a large pinch of tobacco from his pouch and dropped it into the cup of the pipe. He lit the tobacco with a glowing stick from the fire. Then, he took several long puffs before handing it to Tamaqua, who was sitting cross-legged in the circle next to him.

Touching Sky stood at the edge of the council house, watching as the pipe made its way around the circle. The men puffed the pipe with impassive faces, in keeping with the solemnity of the occasion.

When the decorated pipe had made its way around the circle, Croghan took up the pipe to conclude the agreement. After several puffs, he handed the pipe back to Chief Custaloga and said, "Now that we have made our treaty of peace, I have gifts from the general to clothe the women and children."

These were the words that Touching Sky had been waiting for. She watched with eagerness as Croghan and the elders rose from the council circle. As Croghan walked toward his packhorses to unload his cargo, Touching Sky joined several other women from the village. Together, they laid out a row of reed mats on the ground.

Croghan began with a gift for Custaloga's wife—a large scarlet blanket, along with a pair of scarlet hose and garters. Touching Sky envied her sister-in-law mostly for the garters, which were hard to find.

"It appears there is no rum," Touching Sky overheard Custaloga say to Walks Proud as Croghan and his helpers carried the goods from the horses. That was sure to be a disappointment. Rum helped to ease the pain of negotiations. It also put the white man at an advantage in the exchange, as he had a better tolerance for liquor.

The villagers crowded around as they distributed the gifts on the mats. Touching Sky scanned the range of goods. She reached down to finger the stroud cloth, a cheaply woven wool with a white edge. There was also the linsey-woolsey cloth fabric, useful for making clothing or blankets.

"Look at these," she said to Silver Sage as she pointed to some decorative lace, tinsel, and nonsopretties, a decorative braid for clothing. Other women crowded in around Touching Sky to make their choice of colors for the brightly dyed fabric. Touching Sky rubbed her hand over the mazarine blue cloth, and then laid it next to the deep red before comparing it to the yellow and multicolored fabric. Nothing pleased her as much as the blue, so she chose a piece of the colorful fabric, along with some thread. She also chose a piece of linsey-woolsey cloth to make a shirt for Joseph, and a small red blanket for Runs Free. She held the new fabric close to her chest, dreaming about the new blouse she would make for herself to wear during the Big House celebration. She reached over and squeezed Runs Free's arm, and threw the new blanket over her shoulders.

After all of the fabric was gone, Croghan distributed the decorative tape and tinsel. With scissors in hand, he cut off portions for each woman, dropping the trimmings into their outstretched hands.

When all of the goods were distributed, Touching Sky and Silver Sage carried their clothing and blankets back to the wigwam. "We got some nice things," Silver Sage said.

"You always see the bright side," Touching Sky said. "I was thinking that these gifts aren't as good as the ones that the French used to bring us. It's been several winters since we received any gifts, and there was no rum or powder. The British are stingy."

Silver Sage thought for a moment. "Perhaps. But we must still be grateful. My mother used to say, 'If you see no reason for giving thanks, the fault lies in yourself.'"

The two women stepped into the dimly lit wigwam. "I *am* grateful for all of this clothing," Touching Sky said. "I just know that Custaloga sometimes feels that white men only give us gifts to appease us or entice us into their wars. They give gifts to us with one hand and take away our land with the other. Which is worth more: this clothing or the hunting lands that we've enjoyed for generations?"

Silver Sage nodded. "The words you speak are both hard and true. But today, I shall be thankful that I have a blanket without holes in it, and I shall begin sewing up my new blouse tomorrow."

Touching Sky took a deep breath. "And I shall start sewing a new shirt for Swift Foot, who has been a gift to me. Even if the white man comes to take away our land, I have my son."

Touching Sky was about to sew Joseph's new shirt when Runs Free poked her head through the door flap. "Mama, some new people just arrived! At the creek."

Touching Sky laid down her fabric and stepped outside. Runs Free hopped next to her as they walked toward the creek, where a man and a woman were pulling canoes out of the water. Her heart leaped when she recognized her young cousin.

"Tender Foot," she said, reaching out her arms in welcome. "Are you well? Where have you come from?" Tender Foot was from the Wolf clan, and she had grown up in the same village as Touching Sky.

"Cousin, we are well and in good health," the woman replied. "But we left our home in Wyalusing to strangers. The white man came from the east and claimed our village. We left quickly, not knowing if we would ever see our home again." Her face was full of grief.

Touching Sky looked at her cousin more closely. Tender Foot's blanket was ragged and full of holes, and she looked exhausted. "Let me help carry your things. We have plenty of room for you to spread your mats. I'm sure you are hungry. Let's eat something, and then we'll get you settled."

She turned to Joseph, who stood nearby. "Son, this is my cousin Tender Foot. Please help them carry their things to the wigwam."

"And this is my husband, Black Fish," Tender Foot said, pointing to the man who was lifting a large basket out of their canoe.

Joseph nodded and took the basket from Black Fish. Touching Sky led the group back toward their home, each carrying something. Runs Free hopped alongside Joseph with a gourd in each hand.

Touching Sky's anger rose as they walked. The white man was stealing land everywhere! "I am so sorry to hear that you have lost your land to the white man, dear cousin."

Tender Foot's eyes grew dark. "They claimed our land by a treaty we knew nothing about. They say our cousins—the Iroquois—have granted it to them. I am inclined to believe it."

"The Iroquois have given away too much of our land," Touching Sky said. "They gave away the places where my father once hunted. We must find a way to stop them."

"This is a beautiful place for a village," Black Fish said. "I hope you never lose it."

Touching Sky nodded. "Our village has doubled in size over the past winter. You can see there are many new wigwams."

"Where are the people coming from?" Tender Foot asked.

"There are many, like you, who have fled here for safety. And we have taken more captives." She glanced at Joseph as she spoke.

"We do not want to be a burden to you," Black Fish said.

"No, no," Touching Sky said, shaking her head with vigor. "You will not be a burden to us at all. My dear son, Swift Foot, is a good hunter and fisherman. He will supply us with food and help you to build a wigwam close to mine." As she spoke, she noticed that Tender Foot's blouse was worn thin and torn under the sleeve. She needed a new shirt worse than Joseph did. Especially at this time of year, when Grandfather Sun scorched the earth, he could do without. Joseph would understand. It was she, not he, who worried about his clothing.

"You are very kind," Tender Foot said.

"It is only our duty," Touching Sky replied. "Here you will find a haven from the selfishness of the white man."

She hoped she'd taught Joseph enough about hospitality that he'd give up his bed without complaining. There would be more work ahead. Tender Foot and Black Fish would need a wigwam.

Winter came a few moons after Tender Foot and Black Fish came to the village. Joseph was grateful that he'd helped them build a wigwam. It was much too crowded for everyone to live in Touching Sky's wigwam.

Nevertheless, Tender Foot often came by to play games with Touching Sky and Silver Sage in the evening. Although Joseph seldom dreamed of *Mam* these days, he always thought of her when he watched the three women bet on dice and other games of chance. He couldn't imagine *Mam* ever gambling away her household goods. Twice he watched Touching Sky gamble away all of her spoons.

"Don't worry," Touching Sky said to him and Runs Free when they had to eat with their fingers. "I'll win them back." Sure enough, she won them back, and more. For a time, Runs Free got to wear a pair of earrings that Touching Sky won in a game of dice. It was all done in fun and shortened the long evenings on the days when Grandfather Sun went to bed early and got up late.

It seemed to Joseph that Touching Sky easily gave away anything she had, even gifts given her by friends. Not like *Mam*, who had always guarded her possessions with care. It seemed that every time Touching Sky gave away something, she soon received something in return. It was fun to watch the expression on her face when she received even the smallest gift.

It was even more fun for Joseph to listen to the stories on winter evenings in the lodge. Villagers crowded around a fire to listen to the stories of their people—tales of creation, of war, and village life in years gone by.

Joseph was particularly drawn to a storyteller from another village who told stories each evening for several days. Each winter, the man traveled from village to village, telling stories in exchange for food.

"Why doesn't the storyteller come in the summertime, when it would be much easier to travel?" Joseph asked Tamaqua one evening after the man finished his tale. "Then we could sit outside to listen."

Tamaqua laughed. "That is something every Delaware child knows. In the summertime, there are many little creatures who might overhear the stories, such as snakes and bugs. If they don't like what is said about them, they might try to punish the storyteller. Or they might repeat them to a spirit helper who would come to their aid. In the wintertime, these little creatures are asleep so they don't make trouble."

Joseph shook his head in bewilderment. Would he ever understand the Delaware world?

Tamaqua took a puff on his pipe, breathing deeply of the smoke and then blowing a stream into the air. It wafted lazily through the vent hole in the roof, along with the smoke that rose from the fire in the middle of the room. Joseph pulled the blanket around his shoulders as he sat cross-legged in the circle.

"Swift Foot, tell the villagers how you got your name," Tamaqua said.

Joseph glanced at Touching Sky, who was sitting on the outer edge of the circle. Had she put Tamaqua up to this?

"It was given to me by the people at a village on the Great Island in the Susquehanna," he said.

"How did it happen?"

"I was traveling with the war party and we stopped at a village. There they took away my shoes and gave me moccasins to wear for the first time. And they painted my face. That's when they called me 'Swift Foot' for the first time."

"But why did they call you Swift Foot? Did they see you run fast?"

"Yes, when they came to my father's farm, I outran the warriors. I suppose that's when they first saw that I was a fast runner. And when I first visited this village, I won a race."

Several of the men nodded to each other. "We remember."

"What was your name before we called you 'Swift Foot'?" Tamaqua gently prodded Joseph. "What did your father and mother name you as a boy?"

Joseph glanced at Touching Sky and hesitated. She nodded to him to go ahead. "Joseph," he said.

"Why did your parents give you that name?" Black Fish asked. "What does it mean?"

"I don't know what it means. The white man doesn't always know the meaning of a name. But it comes from the Bible, the white man's book, which tells of a man named Joseph."

There was silence for a few moments, as the villagers sat, thinking.

"Tell us, was he a good man? What did he do?"

"Yes, he was a good man." Joseph's mind flew back to the stories his mother had told him and the other children as they were growing up. He remembered a sermon that Bishop Jake had preached, likening Joseph to Jesus. He'd never listened to sermons—he usually daydreamed while the bishop was speaking—but he had paid attention that Sunday because of his name.

"Tell us why he was a good man."

Joseph thought about how to summarize the story he had heard so many times. "Joseph was a man who could interpret dreams. Because of that gift, he was able to save his people from starvation."

Tamaqua nodded approval. "Interpreting dreams is a very special gift. Tell us the story of Joseph's dreams from the beginning. We want to know how he saved his people."

Joseph was flattered by the opportunity to share a story that none of the others knew. "When Joseph was a boy," he began, "he was born to a man who was the head of his tribe. The man's name was Jacob; but he was also called Israel. He created a new nation."

Joseph saw Touching Sky's face light up on the other side of the circle. Encouraged, he continued. "Joseph was a favored son. Jacob loved him so much that he gave him a special coat, which made his brothers jealous. He also had dreams."

"Tell us about the dreams," the men said. "What did he see?"

"Joseph had two dreams that made his brothers very angry. In the first dream, he saw his family tying stalks of grain together in the field and stacking them into bundles. When Joseph's bundle stood up, the other bundles bowed down to it."

Walks Proud nodded. "That means the boy will rule over his brothers," he said.

Joseph nodded as he continued, "In the second dream, the sun and the moon and eleven stars bowed down to the boy Joseph. This made the brothers so angry! They were so angry that they sold Joseph into slavery in a foreign country.

But they lied to their father, Jacob, telling him that Joseph had been killed by a wild animal."

The men looked somber as they listened. To sell your own brother! Truly, it was unthinkable. And to lie to one's father was a grave offense. They leaned forward to hear more.

"Joseph became a slave to a man named Potiphar, a chief who served Pharaoh, the king of Egypt. Although Joseph lived a just life, he was wrongly accused of trying to sleep with Potiphar's wife—something that was unacceptable in that country—and was thrown into prison. While in prison, he was able to interpret two difficult dreams of the Pharaoh's servants."

Joseph glanced at Summer Rain, who squatted on the far side of the fire. She looked lost in memory. Perhaps she knew the story as well.

"After seven years in prison, Pharaoh called upon Joseph to interpret a dream that even the wisest men in the kingdom couldn't understand. He interpreted the dream to mean that there would be seven years of good crops in the country, followed by seven years of famine. He counseled the Pharaoh to store the grain during the years of plenty, so that they would not starve during the famine. The Pharaoh was so impressed by Joseph's wisdom that he put him in charge of the storehouses. This made it possible for him to feed his own family when they were starving."

The men and women in the circle leaned forward with rapt attention. "Do you mean he fed the brothers who sold him into slavery?" Tamaqua asked.

"Yes," Joseph said, remembering that *Dat* had always emphasized that part of the story. "He forgave them and gave them a place to live where there was plenty of food. And he was reunited with his father, the one who counted him as a favorite son."

Tamaqua shook his head in wonder. "I would have killed the brothers for their treachery."

Joseph answered, "Joseph believed that the Great Spirit had led him to Egypt, since he saved not only his father's family, but many other people as well." Joseph's voice broke and he fought back tears as he thought of his own father, Jacob, and his brother John, whom he hadn't seen for three winters. He composed himself and began again. "Joseph buried his father in the land of his birth, and then he returned to Egypt."

He stopped again, overcome with emotion. It was difficult to keep the story of his own separation from his family apart from the biblical story. He sat quietly, too embarrassed to look into the eyes of his listeners.

After a few moments, Tamaqua spoke. "That is a wonderful story," he said. "Your father must have loved you very much to give you the name Joseph. Perhaps he thought you would someday lead your people with dreams. Now that you have a red heart, perhaps your dreams can show the way for us."

Joseph tried to swallow the lump in his throat. He got up and left the lodge, stepping into the cold night air. They must not see him cry.

The waxing moon shone bright, accenting the starry sky. Why had he agreed to tell that story? Now he would be marked as one who could not keep his emotions under control.

The Bible story about Joseph had never meant much to him as a child. But now, the story had deep meaning. For the first time, he noticed Jacob's tears of anguish and heard the cries of lament when Joseph was reported dead. He took notice of Jacob's eagerness to travel to Egypt to see his son, who had been reported dead. It made him wonder what *Dat* must be feeling about Joseph's own absence, since he too had been jerked away from him and taken to a foreign place. Was *Dat* still alive?

To whom could he speak about these deep feelings? *Perhaps Summer Rain*, Joseph thought. *She might understand.*

❖

The next morning, Touching Sky couldn't get the biblical story of Joseph and his father out of her mind. She was so occupied with her thoughts she nearly missed a rung on the narrow ladder as she lowered herself into the underground pit where she and Silver Sage keep food for the winter. She fished around for the onions in the dim light, and then made her way out to the top.

Silver Sage stood nearby as Touching Sky emerged from the pit. She offered her a hand. "That was a very interesting story that Swift Foot told us last night," she said. "I had never heard the story of Joseph from the white man's book."

Touching Sky shrugged and took a deep breath. "I remember the Moravians telling that story when I was a child," she said. "I liked the part about the dreams, and how they came true."

Silver Sage looked intently at Touching Sky. "Is something wrong? You look worried."

Touching Sky frowned. "Yes, I'm worried that the story will get Swift Foot thinking about his family. Maybe he'll dream about going back home to see them again."

Silver Sage nodded slowly. "That's possible. We had better remind him of the white man's evil ways. He is Delaware now."

Touching Sky drew in her breath and blew it out slowly. "Yes, I'll do that this evening."

All day long, Touching Sky rehearsed what she might say to Joseph. Now that he had been in the village for several winters, he might be ready to learn just how badly the white man had treated her people. She saw her chance when Runs Free huddled next to Joseph by the fire after the evening meal.

"I enjoyed your story from the great book last evening," she said to Joseph.

Runs Free snuggled a little closer to him. "Me too," she said. "You're a good storyteller."

"The white people say that God gave the great book to them," she said, "and they want us to believe it. We would likely have done so, if we had seen them practice what they pretend to believe."

Joseph flushed at the accusation. It didn't fit *Dat*, who had always seemed sincere in following the Bible. He remained silent.

"Some of the white men hold the great book in one hand and in the other, they hold murderous weapons—guns, knives, and swords—to kill us. And they kill other white men too, even those who believe in the book."

Touching Sky had Joseph's attention now, and she intended to keep it. "We know that the Great Spirit gave the book to the white man, who needs to be told what to do. He is naturally disposed to wickedness and needs something to show him what is right and what is wrong. We Delaware have no need for the book, since the Great Spirit has engraved his ways upon our hearts."

Touching Sky looked up at Silver Sage, who overheard the conversation and stepped into the light of the fire. "When the white men came to this land," Touching Sky continued, "we believed that the Great Spirit had brought them to us for an important purpose. Our fathers welcomed them into our company and shared our land with them. When they cultivated the land to raise food for themselves, we realized that the Great Manitou had made them good farmers.

"But now, we realize our mistake. We have learned that the white man can never be content with enough land to raise food for their families. Now they want to take over the whole country of the Ohio and beyond. They want to push us out."

Silver Sage spoke. "Many of the white men are thieves. They not only steal from the Indians, but they also steal from each other. I have heard that they put locks on their doors to protect their goods from their own people. Have you ever seen us put locks on one of our doors?"

"No," Joseph replied. "But I have noticed that when people leave their homes for a time, they put something like a chunk of wood against the door to keep it closed."

"You have observed well," Touching Sky said. "We put something on the outside to show that no one is at home. But we do not fear that anyone will break into our homes and steal our things. No one would enter a home that had something in front of the door, even though it could easily be removed. I have not once heard of anyone stealing something from the home of another in this village."

Runs Free came over to Joseph and put her arm around his neck. "Mama," she said, "that's not the way that Swift Foot is. He has never stolen anything from anyone."

"I'm speaking of white men who want us to believe the great book. I don't want Swift Foot to follow their ways."

Joseph shrugged. "I don't want to be that way either. Now I am red at heart."

Touching Sky went on. "Why do white men strive so hard to get rich? Why do they store up things that they cannot carry with them into the next world? Do they fear that the Great Spirit will not take care of them?" She looked sharply at Joseph as though she expected a response.

"Let me get some more wood," Joseph said. Was he stalling for time? He got up from his place and pulled sticks from a small pile just inside the door of the wigwam. He tossed several pieces onto the fire and sat down again by Runs Free.

Touching Sky continued, "We Indians know that there is enough in this world to live upon, especially since we share with one another. We don't need to build big barns the way white men do, because we believe that the Great Spirit will supply everything that we need. When we die, we only need to take with us sufficient food to carry us from here to the world of spirits."

"I'm never going to build a barn for myself," Joseph said. "I'm glad I don't have to work on my father's farm anymore. I'll do just enough hunting and fishing to keep us supplied with food." Then he smiled at Runs Free. "And play games the rest of the time."

Everyone laughed, and the tension was broken.

"That's a good idea," Touching Sky said. "Let's play a game of dice." It was good to hear Joseph say that he liked hunting and fishing in the village better than working in the fields back in the Northkill. She could only hope that he'd feel that way for the rest of his life.

-16-

July 1761

Touching Sky could hardly believe her good luck. Rum—a full keg! Custaloga came striding into the village with the fiery liquid at twilight.

Touching Sky followed the chief toward the council house, where excited villagers gathered around. What had he given to the traders in exchange for such abundance?

Custaloga held up his hand to call for calm. "We had the good fortune to come upon a shipment of supplies being sent by bateau up the waters that flow by our village. We asked the man in the bateau to stop and give account of his intentions. When he refused to cooperate, we gave him a lesson—with blows!" He smiled. "And then we took his rum!"

A chorus of whoops rang out. Custaloga nodded to acknowledge the affirmation. He continued, "Tonight we shall celebrate this good fortune. Because we have been blessed with such quantity, all shall be able to taste of the rum!"

Shouts, cheers, and dancing broke out. Everyone gathered around the fire that burned in the center of the clearing outside the council house.

Touching Sky quickly ran back to her wigwam. It had been a long time since she'd imbibed of the white man's spirits, a sure way to rid herself of the worries that plagued her each day. This was the time to celebrate.

"Let's get ready!" she said to Runs Free, who stood at the door of the wigwam. "We're going to have a dance and taste the white man's spirits."

Runs Free's face lit up with glee. She headed for the wigwam, where she and Touching Sky got dressed for the occasion. First, Touching Sky brushed back their hair with the comb she'd made of bone and put a touch of bear grease on it.

She tied it in the back with a piece of the mazarine blue cloth she had gotten from the trader the summer before. And then she rummaged through a basket to find a ring of bells to fasten around her ankles and some trinkets to tie onto each arm. She was fastening her long earrings when Joseph stepped through the door.

"What's all the excitement about?" he asked, setting down a basket of fish. "People are shouting and throwing wood onto the council fire as though the warriors just took a dozen scalps."

Touching Sky smiled. "The chief has a keg of the white man's spirits, so we're going to have a dance to celebrate. You should put on some paint for the occasion."

"I'm hungry. I was hoping to have some of this fish to eat."

"First get yourself painted for the party. We can cook the fish at the dance."

"I want some bells for my ankles," Runs Free whined. "My friends all wear them."

"Maybe Silver Sage will loan you some bells," Touching Sky said. "I don't have any others." Runs Free nodded and went to look for Silver Sage. She returned a few moments later, prancing across the dirt floor to tingle the bells and announce the success of her mission. Touching Sky sighed. *You would never know she's lame—listen to those bells ring!* "You look beautiful," she said.

Runs Free smiled for a moment in the firelight, and then a cloud crossed her face. "I won't be able to dance as well as the other girls."

Touching Sky swallowed hard. It was the truth. Runs Free would never be able to dance as she should. If her daughter felt sad now, how much more keenly she'd feel it when she came to be a woman. *What young man will want a woman who can't dance?* She shook her head to clear out those thoughts. Tonight, all sadness and disappointment would be banished. They had rum!

Joseph watched them. He looked unsure of what he was supposed to do.

"Swift Foot, you can't go to the celebration without putting on some paint," Touching Sky said. "Here, I'll put some on for you." She pulled open the seal on a storage gourd and daubed red paint on Joseph's face and arms as he stood, patiently as always. He'd never shown much enthusiasm for painting himself, but he didn't seem to mind if she did it for him.

That will change, she said to herself, *as soon as he starts noticing a girl. At least that's the way that it was with Suckameek.*

Touching Sky looked into the basket that Joseph had brought in and counted five fish, all gutted and ready. "I'll cook these at the celebration," she said to Joseph. "You can have all you want to eat and we'll share the rest."

Joseph's appetite was more ravenous than Suckameek's had ever been; he'd grown to be taller than anyone in the village. He loved fresh fish more than anything else she prepared. Thank goodness he was an excellent fisherman! Miquon had taught him well.

Silver Sage had just baked corn cakes. She stacked them in a basket and joined the others for the short walk to the village center.

Touching Sky and the other women gathered around the fire. She soon had the fish frying on some hot coals. Runs Free joined the children who ran and played in the clearing, stopping now and then to sample bites of food.

The men began to pound the drums. Some shook rattles. Others sang. Touching Sky joined the ring of dancers who circled the fire, stepping to the rhythm and whooping with the joy of the moment. She motioned Runs Free into the dance and watched with shining eyes as the girl pranced in the circle, hopping on her good leg and waving her damaged foot high, rattling the bells on her ankles in chorus with the shouts of the warriors. She admired her daughter's pluck; her unwillingness to be sidelined might help her live a normal life.

Custaloga stood beside the keg of rum not far from the fire, with Tamaqua nearby to help guard the precious drink. Villagers crowded round with small gourds and wooden cups, waiting for the men to ladle out their portions.

When Touching Sky handed her wooden cup to Custaloga, Runs Free crowded in beside her. "Can I have some too, Uncle?" She held out a small gourd.

Custaloga glanced at Touching Sky, who nodded. He poured some rum into the small container before filling it nearly to the top with water. "Don't spill it," he said as he handed it to her.

Touching Sky couldn't help but notice the shadow that flitted across Tamaqua's brow as he watched Runs Free take a long sip. Why should Tamaqua worry himself with Runs Free having a little spirit water? He had always been the strict one in the family. But shouldn't the young girl have at least an evening of relief from the burden of her handicap?

"Don't drink it all at once like water," she told Runs Free. "You'll enjoy it more if you sip it a little at a time."

What good fortune, Touching Sky thought to herself as they walked back to watch the circle of dancers, villagers of all ages taking their turns in the circle between times of eating and drinking next to the fire. *My husband would have enjoyed this.*

"It burns a little, Mama," Runs Free said as she took another sip of the drink. "But it also tastes a little like maple syrup."

"It makes you feel better than maple syrup," Touching Sky said. "You'll soon forget all your troubles." She walked over to the place where Silver Sage was seated on the ground with a few other women, playing a game of dice.

"Join us." Silver Sage beckoned with her hand, so Touching Sky squatted in the circle with a wooden bowl in the middle.

She watched the game as she sipped on her drink, laughing out loud at the amusing comments the women made as they threw dice into the bowl. She soon joined in the tossing of the dice, placing small bets on the way they would fall. Her luck seemed better than usual. She soon collected two sets of ear-rings and a stroud cloth.

The dance seemed less orderly now, with the revelers twirl-ing and twisting in an uneven line. The drummers hammered out a syncopated rhythm that Touching Sky suspected came partly by design and partly by the good effect of the rum. She looked up to see Runs Free hopping on her good leg, laughing with glee and weaving among the tipsy dancers.

Touching Sky went to get another container of spirits and got a bit more for Runs Free as well. She went back to her game, aware that some of the shouts of the warriors had turned from hoots to angry threats.

"Bring me the whites from Fort Pitt," one of them shouted with garbled speech, "and I'll smash their skulls like this." He slashed his tomahawk into the painted post near the edge of the fire.

"Yes!" another whooped as he brandished his knife. "I'll eat their hearts and throw their brains to the dogs."

"If any white man comes to this village," shouted the first, "I'll roast him alive."

Tom Lions is drunk, Touching Sky thought as she took an-other sip of the sweet spirits and made another bet. *I hope he doesn't take it out on Swift Foot.*

The edges of the dice were a little wavy now, and it was hard to distinguish between the colors. What was wrong with her eyes? She finished her second draught of the sweet drink and leaned forward to concentrate on the game.

Several of the children took on a game of chase, and Runs Free giggled with glee as she hopped by the place where Touching Sky was playing. She tripped over the gambling bowl, sending the dice flying into the darkness. She pulled herself up and started running again, this time hopping to-ward the fire.

Tom Lions stumbled along not far behind her. "Where's Swift Foot?" he mumbled. "Let me give him what he deserves." Blood trickled from a cut on his hand from where he'd nicked himself from falling. "Runs Free will tell me where Swift Foot is hiding!" He slurred the words as he rubbed the blood onto his breechcloth.

Touching Sky tried to stand up and walk toward the warrior. Tom needed to be quiet—to shut up! Swift Foot was her son.

Her legs were as weak and unsure as a rotten log. She swayed, then stumbled on a heavy tuft of grass and fell forward. Her face hit the ground just as she heard Runs Free scream.

It was the last thing she remembered before everything went black.

"Ho!"

Touching Sky woke up when she heard Tamaqua lift the flap of her wigwam and step inside. Her head throbbed with the rhythm of her heart. She groaned as she reached up to rub a tender spot on the side of her forehead. She sat up on her bed and glanced toward her daughter's bed. "Where's Runs Free?" *Ohhhh. My head!*

"She's resting in our wigwam," Tamaqua said. "She had a rough night."

Touching Sky groaned again and held the side of her face. "What happened?"

"She got hurt last night. It's best she stay with our family for a day or two."

When the truth of Tamaqua's words sunk into Touching Sky's confused thoughts, she stood up. "Oh no! My little girl."

The room seemed bright. Too bright. She groaned and splashed water from a bark pitcher onto her face. "Is she hurt badly?" she asked, shaking her head as though to jostle her thoughts into better order.

"Bad enough, but we're taking care of her. When you're feeling better yourself, you can come see her. She's been asking for you."

"I want to see her right away." She wobbled toward the door.

"Here, let me take your arm," Tamaqua said.

The two of them walked slowly toward his wigwam as he explained what had happened.

"When Tom Lions got drunk, he started looking for Swift Foot. I saw trouble coming, so I told Swift Foot to go into the woods to avoid a confrontation."

Touching Sky got quiet. She clenched her fist. "I will kill Tom if he touched Runs Free or Swift Foot," she said.

"Calm down," Tamaqua said, grasping her arm. "Let me finish my story."

"The children were chasing each other. Runs Free was unsteady on her lame foot, so she tripped on a log and fell into the fire. Tom Lions yanked her out of the fire but was too drunk to put out the flames. I grabbed a blanket and put out the flames with it."

"Tom Lions saved Runs Free from the fire?"

"Yes, she was lucky that he was close by. She lost the hair on the back of her head and her neck got burned a little, but I think she's going to be okay. She was lucky the fire was burning low at the time. It was mostly embers."

"Oh, my child, my child," Touching Sky wailed, quickening her steps toward Tamaqua's home. "How can I thank you enough for saving her?"

"Just be glad that Custaloga asked me to guard the keg and watch for strangers so that I didn't have any of that fire water in me when this happened."

"What shall I say to Tom?" Touching Sky asked, her head still throbbing.

"It's hard to know what to say. He was threatening to harm your son, but he saved your daughter."

Touching Sky's head spun as she tried to make sense of it.

"I doubt he'll remember anything that happened," Tamaqua said. "He'll probably wake up with a whopping headache."

She slipped through the door at Tamaqua's wigwam and stumbled over to Runs Free, who was sitting up on a mat on the floor. "Oh my little one," she said, squatting on the floor and holding the girl's head in her hand. The smell of singed hair filled her nose as she stroked the top of her daughter's head.

"Ouch," Runs Free said. "It hurts when you rub my hair."

"I'm so sorry, honey," said Touching Sky. "The boys shouldn't have been chasing you."

"We were having fun." Runs Free snuggled into her mother's lap. "I couldn't see straight and I felt like I was floating. It felt good, mostly, except when I tried to run."

"That was the rum, honey. That's what it does to you. You feel good, as long as you don't drink too much, like I did. I have a terrible headache." *More than terrible*, she thought to herself.

"I'm sorry you're not feeling well, Mama. I'm going to be okay. Aunt put some salve on my neck, which makes it feel better."

Just then Joseph sat up on the mat that had served as his bed. Apparently he'd stayed in Tamaqua's wigwam to be safe from Tom Lions. "How's Runs Free?" he asked.

"It may take a little time," Touching Sky said. "But she's going to be all right."

The next day, Joseph pondered what had happened. He was relieved that Tom had yanked Runs Free out of the fire, but he was angry that he'd tried to harm him. *There must be some way to get back at him for his drunken threats. Maybe I could put a curse on him, or use a charm to keep him away from me.* Joseph recalled hearing Touching Sky talk about the charm she carried in her purse. Did she still have it? Might it work on Tom Lions?

Joseph glanced up in the bright afternoon sunlight at the sound of laughter. Touching Sky and a group of women were heading toward the creek to bathe. This would be the moment to sneak a look inside her bag. He moved as nonchalantly as possible toward the wigwam.

He paused to let his eyes adjust to the dark room. He looked around for the bag, which didn't seem to be where she usually kept it on the flat platform she called her bed. He lifted the blanket. It was not there. He looked on the floor underneath the bed. Nothing.

Could Touching Sky have taken it with her? No, he was sure she hadn't carried the bag with her to the creek. Might it be hanging on the peg under her clothing? He lifted up the woolen blanket. *Yes! There it was.*

Quickly, he scanned the area around the wigwam. No one was around. He turned the buckskin leather bag over in his hand, rubbing his fingers over the beads that decorated the flap, and then flipped it open. Feeling around inside, he pulled out a familiar string of beads he'd often seen her wear. He took out the string and placed it on the bed. Next he pulled out two pairs of earrings. These looked familiar too. He laid them next to the beads.

Surely she must keep something else besides jewelry in her purse! He looked again. He could see several small leaves of tobacco inside. They crumbled as he laid them on the bed next to the jewelry. He kept looking. Next he pulled out a glass bead. What was it for? He didn't know how to find out—he couldn't ask Touching Sky, or she'd know he'd been looking in her bag.

There were more items in the bag—a few sprigs of an herb, a brass mirror, two needles, some black thread, and a white feather. *Is it from a goose?* He placed them alongside the other items. No charm. Why had he bothered to look?

But wait. There was something on the very bottom of the bag—a folded piece of paper. He pulled out the paper and then laid the purse on the bed. He unfolded the sheet with care. It was about the size of a page from the *Ausbund*, the hymnbook that Joseph had used at church services back home. Had the sheet been taken out of a book?

No, surely not, because the message was handwritten in German. The ink had faded with age. Joseph moved closer to the door for light. The script was barely legible.

It was the first time he'd held a piece of paper in his hand since the attack.

Joseph murmured the first sentence aloud. *"Unser Vater in dem Himmel! Dein Name werde geheiligt."*

He paused as he pondered what he had just read. *Could it be . . . ?* He read the next two sentences. *"Dein Reich komme. Dein Wille geschehe auf Erden wie im Himmel."* What was Touching Sky doing with a German copy of the Lord's Prayer in her bag?

Or was it really the Lord's Prayer? *"Denn dein ist das Reich und die Kraft und die Herrlichkeit in Ewigkeit. Amen."*

He swallowed deeply and closed his eyes. Suddenly, in his thoughts, he was transported back to his childhood home, listening to *Dat* praying the Lord's Prayer before bidding the family good night. There was *Mam*, sitting on the chair next to *Dat*, her eyes squeezed shut in silent devotion, holding Franey on her lap. He saw his brother Jakey in the circle too, next to Christian.

He stood there with the paper in his hand, his heart beating swiftly. Four summers back, the prayer had been a daily bedtime ritual, an unwelcome interruption of his free time. Now it seemed distant, strange, and out of place.

He read the words again in his mother tongue, noticing their meaning in a completely new way. As he mouthed the words, he recalled the moment at Fort Presque Isle when he was about to be separated from his father and brought to Custaloga's Town. The words, spoken softly to him and his brother Christian at the time, came thundering back as reminder of his neglect: "Sons, if you are taken so far away and are kept so long that you forget the German language, do not forget your names. And say the Lord's Prayer every day."

He cringed with the realization that he had neglected to follow his father's advice. How often had he prayed the prayer? Only a few times after coming to the village.

He stood there for a time, lost in thought. Tears filled his eyes. He angrily wiped them away. Where had Touching Sky gotten a copy of the prayer? Why would she carry it in her bag? Could she read it? What would she think of him if she knew he had gone through her things?

Joseph was still standing with the paper in his hand when he heard the women returning from the creek. He folded up the paper and stuffed it back into the bag. He jammed the other things back inside it, closed the flap and hung the bag on the hook.

Just in time. Touching Sky came through the door.

"I'm going outside now," he mumbled.

Touching Sky remained silent as Joseph left. *Were those tears on his face?* What had moved him so?

She looked around the room. Everything seemed in order. But then she noticed a needle lying on the bed. Had Joseph been trying to sew something? How had he found the needle?

She lifted her bag off the hook and looked inside. Things were not in order as she usually kept them.

Why was Swift Foot rummaging around in my bag? She looked over everything carefully. The tobacco leaves were crumbled, but nothing seemed to be missing except the needle. She unfolded the paper, now crinkled into the bottom of her purse. She looked over the words. There was a small spot where it looked wet. Even though she'd carried it in her bag for years, she hadn't looked at the paper since Suckameek's birth. It was a good luck charm, a reminder of a better past, when her people lived at peace with the white man near Nazareth, in the eastern end of the province.

She could still hear the kindly voice of the Moravian missionary who had given her the paper. She'd vowed at the time that she would learn German and go to the Moravian school, but since then everything had changed.

Apparently the paper meant something to Joseph. How could she have imagined anything like this happening?

She hung her bag on the hook and began to grind corn for the evening meal. She pounded harder than usual with her pestle. *What shall I say to my son?*

She poured the cornmeal into the boiling water and then added deer meat and savory leaves from a dried plant that hung from the ceiling. When the meal was ready, she called out the door: "Swift Foot, please come to eat."

Joseph came to the cooking fire. He hung his head and avoided her eyes as he sat on the ground next to the fire. Touching Sky handed him a dish of squash and beans. She spooned some of the food onto her own plate and squatted down next to Joseph.

After a few bites, she said, "My son, you were looking in my bag."

Joseph nodded. His face was red, and not from the fire.

"You must have been curious about what I keep in there."

"Yes."

"Did you find anything you didn't expect to see?"

"Yes."

There was a silence. Touching Sky waited for Joseph to say more. When he didn't, she continued. "What did you see that surprised you?"

Joseph spoke slowly. "The paper with the prayer on it."

"I suppose you're wondering where it came from."

"Yes." For the first time, Joseph met Touching Sky's gaze.

"A Moravian missionary gave it to me, many years ago, when our family lived near Nazareth."

Joseph put down his spoon. "Where is that?"

"Near the forks of the Delaware River. Some of my people once worshiped the white man's God and believed in Jesus. Some joined the German-speaking Moravians missions at Gnadenhütten and Meniolagomekah, north of Philadelphia.

"One day when I was visiting there, a missionary gave me a copy of this prayer. I learned a few words of German but never enough to read the whole prayer." Touching Sky fell silent for a moment as she worked up her courage. "Would you read it to me?"

Joseph was surprised. "Do you mean now?"

"As soon as you are finished eating."

He hesitated and then ate the last few bites that were left in his bowl. He set the bowl on the ground and asked: "Where is the paper? I mean, where is the prayer?"

"In the same place you found it before."

"Do you mean—"

"Yes, you may get it now."

Joseph took the bag off the hook and dug out the worn piece of paper. He sat down cross-legged beside Touching Sky, unfolded the paper, and began to read: "*Unser Vater in dem Himmel! Dein Name werde geheiligt* (Our Father who art in heaven, hallowed be thy name)." He paused for a moment to look at Touching Sky, who nodded, so he moved on through to the end, following the paths of the words with his forefinger.

After he had finished reading, Touching Sky said, "Now tell me what it means in my language."

Joseph frowned. "I know what all of these words mean, but I don't know how to say them all in Delaware."

"Please try. Tell me the words that you know."

Joseph began, "*Ki Wetochemelenk, talli epian Awossagame, Machendasutsch Ktellewunsowagan . . .*" He spoke with hesitation, drawing from the shallow creek of his new vocabulary, trying to match the river of ideas that flowed in his mother tongue. He looked into Touching Sky's face. What was she thinking?

Touching Sky gave a faint smile and nodded. "Keep going."

Joseph translated the next few sentences, but he paused when he came to the words "*Und vergib uns unsere Schuld, wie wir unseren Schuldigern vergeben* (and forgive us our

debts as we forgive our debtors)." How did one speak of trespasses in the Delaware tongue? Or forgiveness?

He read the words aloud in German, and then he said: "I
don't know how to say it in Delaware."

Touching Sky shrugged, "Then go ahead and read the rest."

Joseph slogged his way through to the end of the prayer, not
satisfied that he had rendered it correctly. He hoped he had
paid for the transgression of snooping in Touching Sky's bag.

"Thank you," she said. "I have always wondered how the
white man wanted my people to pray. Now I know." She took
the paper from Joseph's hand, folded it back up, and put it
back into her bag.

That night, as Joseph drifted off to sleep, he recited the
entire prayer in German in his mind. As he came to the end
of the prayer, a calmness settled into his lungs. Perhaps *Dat*
had had a reason for telling him to pray it every day. It seemed
so out of place in the Indian village, at least when he said it
in German. Perhaps someday he would learn to recite it in
Delaware, especially if it was useful to Touching Sky or others
in the village.

-17-

March 1762

Joseph whittled at the elderberry stick. It would make a good spout for collecting maple tree sap. Grandfather Sun shone brightly each day, enticing the trees to push out their buds despite the frosty nights. *I can't wait to taste that syrup.* Ever since he'd first helped *Dat* and *Mam* harvest the sugary sap back home, he'd looked forward to this season of the year.

Joseph eyed the small pile of spouts he'd made. *Twelve should be enough, at least for today.* He gathered up the spouts and tossed them into a basket. He stepped outside the wigwam onto the thin white blanket Brother Snow had sent during the night. His leggings and the cape that Touching Sky had made would keep him warm.

Touching Sky and Runs Free joined him to trudge into the woods with baskets and collection buckets in hand. They soon came to a stand of sugar maples, and Joseph began slashing the bark to gather the sap. The year before he had tried to do it *Dat's* way, by boring a small hole into the side of the tree. But Touching Sky insisted on the Indian way, so he cut two grooves into the bark that came together like two forks into one path.

"I want to taste it," Runs Free said as the first drop of sap dripped off the end of the spout.

"It won't be good until we boil it," Touching Sky said as she put a collection bucket under the spout.

It was midday when Touching Sky and Runs Free went back to the wigwam. Joseph had two spouts left, so he walked a little way farther, looking around for more sugar trees. *I could use a red maple if there aren't any sugar maples here.*

A crow cawed. As he looked around, he saw a large pine tree with unusual markings. His heart beat faster as he examined the tree. *Those claw marks look fresh. A bear!* The marks went all the way up to a large hole in the side of the trunk. Several small branches near the hole were broken off. Joseph looked around the base of the tree. There were no tracks except for his own.

There must be a bear up inside that tree. He recalled that Tamaqua had said she bears would sometimes climb into trees to have their cubs. *How can I get it out of there?*

He examined the woods around him so he could easily find the spot again. Then he hiked back to Tamaqua's wigwam.

"It sounds like a bear all right," Tamaqua said when he heard the story. "If it's a big one, it would be worth taking down that tree."

"Can't we just lure it out?"

Tamaqua shook his head. "Not at this time of year, unless we can smoke it out."

He couldn't believe his ears. "You mean we'd cut down the tree just to get that bear? It's a huge tree." It would take three men just to reach around the pine. If he were to chop at it by himself, it would take days.

"Of course," Tamaqua answered. "We'll all work together. Meat has been scarce this winter."

"Okay. I'll show you where it is."

After Joseph told Touching Sky and Runs Free about his find, he led them, along with Tamaqua, toward the site. His heart was pounding. Shooting a bear would make everyone proud of him.

When they got to the place, Tamaqua gazed up the trunk. "There's a good chance there's a bear up there," he said. "Those tracks up the side look fairly fresh, and I don't see evidence of it being on the ground lately."

"Okay," said Joseph, "let's take it down." He leaned his rifle against a nearby tree and whacked at the bark of the pine with the ax he'd brought along. Tamaqua chopped at the opposite side.

"I'll go for more help," Touching Sky said as she headed back to the village. She soon returned with Silver Sage and Miquon. They took turns all afternoon, while Runs Free gathered up the chips in a basket and dumped them onto a pile.

More people joined the next day and the next, men and women chopping with tomahawks, hatchets, and axes. Joseph only took brief times to rest. *This will be my bear. But what if there's nothing in the hole*? Joseph pushed away the thought and kept working.

In the early afternoon, the large tree began to tilt toward one side. "It looks like it's going to fall in the direction we want," Joseph said. He picked up his rifle and checked it with care. It looked ready to fire. He leaned it against the side of another tree close by where he could snatch it at a moment's notice.

Joseph delivered the final blows to the trunk and shouted, "Everyone stand back!" His head thrummed with excitement as the huge tree creaked and began to fall. The tree crashed to the ground, ripping the branches off another tree as it fell. And then all was still.

Joseph seized his gun.

Tamaqua followed with a bow and arrow. "I'll back you up."

Joseph took a step toward the opening. *I've got to be ready. I can't afford to miss.* He had only taken a few steps when a large bear pushed her way out of the hole and lumbered toward him. His hands trembled as he lifted the gun to his shoulder and aimed.

The bear reared up just as Joseph pulled the trigger. The bear stayed suspended for a moment and then fell at Joseph's feet. He whipped out the knife from his belt and stuck her in the neck.

The only sound was the crow, which cawed several times in succession. Then the hunting party erupted in shouts. "You got her!" Tamaqua whooped. "You must have hit her in the heart."

Joseph wiped the sweat from his forehead as Runs Free hopped up to give Joseph a hug. "I'm proud of you," she said.

Touching Sky waited for a few moments and then came up to the bear. She took the bear's head in her hands, stroking and kissing it several times.

"You are our relation and grandmother," she whispered. "Please pardon us for taking away your life."

The bear was too large to drag back to the wigwam, so Joseph skinned it on the spot. Touching Sky and Silver Sage cut off the fat, which in some places was six inches deep. They gathered it into baskets so large that two women could barely carry them. Next they loaded up the flesh, which gave four people all they could carry. Joseph dragged the heavy hide with the head still attached, leaving a trail of blood behind him as he trudged through the light snow on the ground.

When he reached the lodge, he hung the hide on a scaffold, with the bear's head facing forward. Touching Sky poured a pile of tobacco near the bear's nose. Silver Sage and several other women adorned the bear's head with trinkets—wristbands, armbands, and belts of wampum.

Runs Free clapped her hands as she hopped around the lodge. "My brother is a real hunter," she said. "I can't wait to eat the meat."

Joseph watched with a wide smile. *It was worth chopping down that tree and skinning the bear. I'm part of the tribe now.*

The next day Touching Sky declared a feast to honor the spirit of the bear. Silver Sage helped her boil some of the meat in a kettle. Others swept and cleaned the lodge, and put a new blanket under the bear's head.

Joseph's chest swelled as Summer Rain and several girls her age joined the feast. Several times when he glanced at her, she was looking his way with a smile.

When the lodge was ready, Tamaqua lit tobacco in two pipes. He took one for himself and handed the other to Joseph. He stepped up and blew smoke into one of the bear's nostrils and invited Joseph to puff into the other.

"Why are we doing this?" Joseph asked. "The bear's not going to be able to smell that tobacco."

"This will take away her anger at you for killing her."

"But she's dead. She can't hurt me."

Tamaqua looked at him askance. "Of course she can hurt you. Her spirit lives on. She can haunt you."

Joseph shrugged his shoulders and blew into the bear's nostrils. It seemed harmless enough.

Tamaqua addressed the bear. "You are a beautiful bear. Please pardon us for waking you up and taking your life. We regret that we must kill our friends in this way. But we cannot live without your help, for we would starve to death. Do not take revenge on us. We wish the best for your offspring. May they prosper and grow in the forest."

What would Dat *say if he saw me now?* Joseph wondered. *He'd be proud of me.* Yes, proud of his getting a bear. But he'd frown to see the way his adopted people talked to plants and animals.

"They're idolaters." That's what *Dat* would say.

But why does it hurt to speak to the spirits if there are none? Joseph wondered. If spirits did exist, they could lash out in curses and death if they weren't appeased.

Tamaqua soon finished the ritual, and Touching Sky began to serve the bear meat.

Joseph took a large helping. *This meal is as sweet as maple syrup.*

"I'd like to make a necklace out of the bear's claws," Joseph said to Miquon as he watched Touching Sky and Silver Sage melt down the bear's fat in kettles over the fire. The smell of the fat rendering on the fire reminded Joseph of summertime, when everyone wore bear oil to keep mosquitos and gnats at bay.

"My father will show you how to make a necklace of the claws," Miquon said.

Good, Joseph thought. He didn't like to admit it, but he was beginning to worry about what girls thought of him, and he knew that they would like such a necklace.

Joseph stepped up to help Touching Sky pour the hot oil into the skins of porcupines they had sewn into vessels. The oil filled six skins.

"You are a great hunter," Touching Sky said. "We haven't gotten such a big bear for a long time. Are you going to make a necklace like Walks Proud wears?"

"Yes," Joseph said with a gleam in his eye. "Miquon said Uncle Tamaqua will show me how to do it. I'm going to ask him now." He motioned for Miquon and the two of them headed for the lodge.

"It won't be hard to make since you're a carver," Tamaqua told Joseph when he asked about the necklace. "But it will take time." He took a sharp knife and cut the claws from one of the bear's four paws and scraped off the flesh.

"Now you do it," he said, handing the knife to Joseph. He observed as Joseph cut off the rest of the claws and trimmed each one.

"We'll use an awl to bore a hole in the large end of each claw," Tamaqua said. He picked up one of the claws and started to bore the hole. "When you're all done, you can string them on a leather thong."

"I'll do the rest of them," Joseph said.

Over the next several days, when he wasn't carrying maple syrup for Touching Sky, Joseph used the awl to make holes in the bear claws. When he had drilled all the holes, he strung them onto a leather thong and hung them around his neck.

"How do you like it?" he asked Touching Sky when he was finished. She was stirring a kettle of syrup over the fire.

She paused to look. "You look great," she said. "Now I'll have trouble keeping the girls away from you."

Joseph's face felt warm. If it made that much of a difference, he'd be sure to wear his new necklace all the time.

-18-

Joseph was wearing his bear claw necklace when Miquon came by his home more than a moon later.

"We're going to play *Pahsaheman* today," Miquon said with a wide smile lighting his face. "I'm collecting trinkets for the prizes that we'll give to the winners." He opened a bag and showed some tin bells to Touching Sky. "Do you want to put some trinkets into the pool?"

Joseph watched her reach into a bag and hand two tin figures to Miquon. Why were they given as prizes for betting and games? What enduring value lay under their cheap shininess?

His thoughts were interrupted by Miquon, who was leaving. "We'll start the game when Grandfather Sun has moved past the center of the sky." With that, he left and headed toward the next home.

Joseph looked at Touching Sky. "Will you play this time?" He recalled that she'd been in the hut the previous spring and hadn't played at all, although the season for the game lasted until midsummer.

"Sure. I love to play."

Since the game involved running, Joseph looked forward to the yearly contest in the spring of the year. It was unlike anything back home in the Northkill, since the Indian men always played against the women. Mam *would never have gotten involved in a game where she played against* Dat.

The sun had just passed its zenith when the players began moving toward the clearing on the west side of the village. Joseph watched as several men pounded two wooden stakes about a man's arm span apart into the ground at each end of the large grassy field. The length of the field appeared to

Joseph to be about the distance between the house and barn back home at the Northkill.

Soon the men began to gather on one end of the field and the women on the other. Miquon waved at Joseph, "Come on, let's play."

Joseph trotted over to the men's side, recalling the first time he'd witnessed the game. At first it didn't seem fair to pit the women against the men, but he soon learned that the rules evened out the disparities. The women were allowed to carry the ball or throw it with their hands, while the men could only hit it or kick it. If a man caught a ball in the air, he had to drop it onto the ground.

Joseph walked toward the men and boys, who were stretching vigorously in preparation for the game. Some pretended to kick the ball to each other, while others jumped and waved their arms or raced each other on the side of the field. Miquon started toward the chief, who was standing near the goalpost with the *Pahsahikan*—an oblong deerskin stuffed with deer hair—in his hand.

The chief smiled at Joseph and handed him the ball. Joseph squeezed it in his hands. The deerskin was soft, yet stuffed so tight that it could easily be kicked. It was longer than Joseph's hand but shorter than his foot.

Joseph gave the *Pahsahikan* back to the chief, who then moved toward the center of the playing field. He motioned to an elderly man, who nodded and began to pray. "Thank you, Great Spirit, for the beauty of this spring day. We give you thanks that you have allowed us to live to play this game again after a hard winter. We ask that in your mercy you might allow us to play again in future seasons."

When the old man finished praying, he walked to the edge of the field. The chief crouched and tossed the ball high into the air and then quickly stepped back. As the ball came down, a tall man jumped high and batted the ball toward the men's goal on the women's end of the field. A young man caught the ball, dropped it to the ground, and kicked it toward Miquon.

Miquon deftly maneuvered it toward Joseph, who had run toward the side of the field in anticipation.

Just as the ball landed in front of Joseph, Summer Rain dived to the ground and grabbed it with her hands. She rolled over quickly and handed it to another young woman who had a red band in her hair. The girl tucked it under her arms and ran toward the opposite goal.

Joseph watched, amazed, as Summer Rain bounced up from the ground and ran down the field in front of him. This was Summer Rain? The girl who had been so reserved, so proper in her conversations? Now she was shouting like a warrior.

Several men, with Miquon and Tom Lions in the lead, grabbed the woman with the red hair band and wrested the ball away from her. Tom tossed it to the ground and kicked it to the side, where another woman pounced on it. Several other women surrounded her as she jumped to her feet. Together they pushed their way forward until Tom punched the ball hard enough that it popped out of the woman's hand, near the center of the field.

Joseph had just run up to the ball when the young woman with the red hair band shoved him sideways, making space for another woman to grab the ball. His face flushed. *Hey! Not fair.*

The woman quickly handed the ball to another woman, who passed it to another. A group of five women pushed forward together with the ball wedged somewhere among them. The women's team shouted and cheered as the group advanced through the goalposts. A man beat his drum while the children on the edge of the field clapped their hands.

Both teams paused to rest for a moment while the scorekeeper took one of his twelve sticks and laid it on the side for the women's score. The team that had the most sticks on their side when the twelve sticks were gone would win the game.

When the ball was back in play, Miquon kicked the ball toward Joseph, who quickly kicked it toward the side of the field where a young boy stood waiting. The boy kicked it toward the goal, where it was intercepted by a group of women who pushed it back toward their goal.

The women's teammates shouted as they moved forward. Tom Lions was quick, however, and knocked the ball out of the carrier's hands.

The ball switched back and forth from one team's control to the other. Once, when the ball came within a few steps of the women's goal, Joseph was able to kick it to Miquon, who kicked it to the center of the field.

The men scored their first goal when Tom Lions got the ball at the edge of the field, kicking it along in front of him with no one else close by. He kicked it past a group of women defenders to Miquon, who kicked it in to the goal. The drummer beat his drum.

Joseph stopped to catch his breath. Although he had kicked the ball several times, he had yet to really help his team advance it. The field was so crowded with players that someone else usually ended up being closer to the action.

The women's team scored again after a fierce contest in which two of them wrestled Miquon to the ground and grabbed the ball. One of them handed it to a tottery old woman who tucked the ball under her arm and pressed toward the goal surrounded by several strong young women. Tom yanked one of the young women by the arm, but no one touched the old woman until she stepped over the goal line. The women's team erupted in a chorus of shouts. The old man beat his drum with vigor. Joseph looked up to see Runs Free shouting from the side of the field.

Joseph shook his head. *That's not fair either! No one would tackle that old woman.*

His body glistened with sweat as the old woman handed the ball to Tom Lions, who kicked it to Miquon. In turn, Miquon kicked it to Walks Proud, who quickly kicked it toward Tamaqua, who kicked it to Joseph.

Joseph kicked the ball down the field, where one of the women caught it and began to run it back. When a group of men blocked her way, she quickly tossed it over their heads toward another woman, but Joseph intercepted it. Just as he pulled the ball out of the air, two young women tackled him, grabbing him by his arms and yanking him back. He clung to the ball as the women sought to wrestle it from his hands. A woman jerked his legs out from underneath him. He fell backwards onto his right elbow and the ball popped from his hands. *Oomph!* The wind was knocked out of him. Another young woman grabbed the ball and tossed it to another woman.

If only I could carry the ball, Joseph thought as he jumped up from the ground. *I could outrun them all.* He ran toward the woman who had the ball. Just as he got within reach, Tom Lions came alongside and jammed his elbow into Joseph's ribs.

Joseph gasped for air as Tom lunged ahead, whacking at the ball in the woman's hands. The ball squirted off to the side not far from Joseph. He leaped forward to kick it, but Tom was there first, flicking the ball to Miquon with the side of his foot. Miquon kicked it far down the field, where several other men maneuvered it into the goal with their feet. The team cheered to the sounds of rapid drumming.

Joseph's face flushed hot at Tom's malicious actions. Didn't he realize they were on the same team?

As the game wore on, Joseph determined to get back at Tom. But how? *Maybe I can elbow him hard. Or trip him when he has the ball.* No, that would be too obvious, and Tom would surely come back in revenge. It would be better to show him up by playing better.

It was harder than it looked. It seemed that every time Joseph got near the center of the action, the field was too crowded to kick the ball very far. Tom seemed to get lucky; several times someone kicked the ball to him when he had the space to kick it a long ways toward the goal.

Once when Tom got the ball near the goal, he scored a point for the men's team by kicking it past the women's team and through the goalposts. The team cheered—all but Joseph, whose bitterness deepened.

Joseph grew tired as the game wore on, with the women's side gaining ground. The women finally won the game, 7–5. Their team cheered as the men brought out the victor's prize—a bag of trinkets. They doled out the gifts to the winners, beginning with the three women who had scored one or more goals. One of them was the girl with the red hair band.

None of the women claimed the gifts as they were being distributed. They handed them around to each other until everyone had something in their hands.

Joseph took another look at the young woman with the red hair band as she fastened a little bell to her ankle. He watched enthralled as she made it tinkle by doing a few dance steps. In the heat of the game, he hadn't noticed how pretty she was. Then she laughed. *I love her laugh!* Joseph shook himself when he realized he had been standing and staring.

"Who's that woman with the red hair band?" he whispered to Miquon as he wiped the sweat off his face.

"That's Nunschetto. She's a good player, isn't she?"

"She sure is. How can someone so good-looking be so rough on the field?"

Miquon laughed. "You have a lot to learn about Indian women."

That evening, Joseph moped as he waited for Touching Sky to serve the meal. He was thinking about the game and his disappointment that he didn't get to score or even be recognized as a good player.

"How did you like the game today?" Touching Sky asked as she ladled out some soup for him.

"I was surprised by how well the women play, especially some of the ones my age."

She laughed. "Our women are as tough as the men."

Joseph scowled. "Tom Lions pushes me around."

Touching Sky paused. "Tom is one of our best players. Don't compare yourself to him or you'll come up short. And we both know he's someone to stay away from."

"But . . ." Joseph's voice drifted off as he thought the better of his objection and lapsed into silence. Tom Lions was a problem that just wouldn't go away.

As Joseph ate his soup, Runs Free came to sit beside him. "I think you are a great *Pahsaheman* player," she said, snuggling up next to him. "I think you are better than anyone else, even Tom Lions."

"I saw you cheering," Joseph said. "If you didn't have a bad foot, you'd be a great player too."

"At least I can throw," she said, taking a bite of soup. "How about if we practice throwing the ball as soon as we're finished eating?"

"Sure. If you can find a ball, I'll throw it back and forth with you."

As Joseph played ball with Runs Free that evening, he kept thinking of the young woman with the red hair band. Nunschetto. She was even prettier than Summer Rain, although she looked a couple of years younger. And she was a great *Pahsaheman* player, too. How unlike the women back at the Northkill, who would never have played in such a rough game!

"Swift Foot!" Runs Free's voice pulled him back to the present.

"Yes?"

"Can you get the ball? I threw it right past you."

Joseph brought himself back to the present. "I'm sorry. I must have been thinking of something else."

He turned to pick up the ball and threw it to back to Runs Free. How he wished he could be tossing it with Nunschetto.

He must find a way to see her again.

❖

Joseph woke up the next morning with Nunschetto on his mind. How might he get to spend time with her? He could ask Miquon. He pulled on his clothing and started to head out the door when Touching Sky waved her wooden spoon at him.

"Swift Foot?"

"Yes?"

"Don't you want to eat something before you go out? This corn cake will be ready before long."

"I'll be back in a little while. I'm going to see Miquon."

"He might not be up yet," Touching Sky said as she braided her long hair.

Joseph shrugged his shoulders and headed out the door. He had to admit it was unusual for him not to eat. He was always hungry in the morning, so Touching Sky usually had something ready for him.

When Joseph got to Miquon's wigwam, he was still in bed. Joseph stepped inside the wigwam and waited for him to get dressed.

"What's your hurry?" Miquon asked.

"Oh, nothing," Joseph said, suddenly embarrassed that he'd skipped his routine just to ask about Nunschetto. "I just woke up early and thought it would be a good day to go fishing."

Joseph ate a few bites of breakfast with Miquon before the two of them took a net and two poles to the creek. They settled down in companionable silence, and for a while, the only sounds were the wind in the trees and the birds chattering nearby.

Joseph waited until they'd caught their first fish before he brought up the matter foremost on his mind. "The girls really surprised me yesterday. I didn't think they'd be such good players."

Miquon smirked as though he knew where Joseph was leading the conversation. "Nunschetto is pretty impressive, isn't she?"

Joseph nodded. "I'd like to get to know her better, but I don't know how."

"Just go to dances and spend time with her and her friends. If you try to spend time alone with her, her mother might notice. If you want to be alone with someone, you have to marry her."

"Marry her!" Joseph and Miquon looked at each other and burst out laughing.

As Joseph and Miquon dragged their net through the water, Joseph's mind drifted back to the way that his nineteen-year-old brother Jakey had gotten to know his sweetheart. Neither his parents nor hers had seemed to mind them being together alone, but the couple didn't show affection in public. Maybe that's how it was here too.

"I know there'll be a dance tonight," Miquon said, picking up the conversation where they'd left off. "You can see Nunschetto there."

The two boys chattered on, making plans for the dance. "You should have an earring," Miquon said to Joseph. "I don't think you'll get Nunschetto's attention without it."

"Really?" Joseph's mind flew back to *Dat*'s admonition that neither women nor men should wear jewelry but dress plainly instead. "How would I go about it? Must I get a hole in my ear?"

"Of course. I'll make it for you with my father's awl."

Joseph drew in his breath. "Maybe tomorrow."

That evening, Joseph and Miquon sat by the fire and watched as the young women danced around the circle. Joseph's eye was drawn to the way that Nunschetto's skin glowed in the light of the fire. She smiled at him when she passed, her eyes sparkling with life. Joseph watched enthralled as she danced, her feet moving to the rhythm of the rattles and the drum. She swayed with the music, tossing her dark hair this way and that. She beat out the rhythm with both hands and feet, tinkling the bells fastened to her ankles.

Joseph glanced at the other young women in the circle, but his gaze kept coming back to the girl with the graceful steps and the swinging hips.

"What family is Nunschetto from?" he asked Miquon.

"She is the daughter of Walks Proud. And he really *is* proud of her. Look at him now as he watches his daughter dance."

Joseph's heart sank as he glanced over at Walks Proud, who was gazing at the beautiful young woman. "So Tom Lions is her adopted brother?"

"Yes, haven't you heard him brag about her?"

Joseph scowled. "No. Tom doesn't deserve to be part of her family. She's much too beautiful for him."

Miquon shrugged but said nothing.

When the music stopped, Nunschetto and the other dancers moved toward the fire. Joseph couldn't help but stare at her. Why hadn't he noticed her before the *Pahsaheman* game? She squatted gracefully on the ground with her long wrap skirt draped over her knees. He caught her eye and smiled as she fingered the beads on her necklace. She flashed him a wide smile in return.

Joseph's heart beat faster. He must find a way to talk to her alone.

When it was his turn to dance, Joseph danced with more gusto than usual. He tried not to look at Nunschetto too often, but each time he did, he caught her eye. *She must like me. Maybe I can talk to her after the dance.*

It was late when the dance ended. As people went back to their homes, Joseph walked casually toward Nunschetto in the soft glow of the fire. He was a few steps away when Tom Lions stepped between them, his face drawn and hard. His look alone told Joseph not to get any closer.

"I hope you're not trying to talk to my sister," Tom said.

Joseph glanced past him toward Nunschetto, who looked away.

"No," Joseph said, "I was just going back to my house."

"You're a liar," Tom said. "I saw you watching her all night. I want you to leave her alone." Tom took a step closer, his eyes flashing.

Joseph swallowed hard and stepped back. What was he to say to this protective older brother?

Just then Miquon, who was standing just behind Joseph, tugged at his arm. "Come, Swift Foot, let's go."

"I could lay Tom out with my fists," Joseph muttered to Miquon as they went back to the wigwam.

Miquon shook his head. "You won't win with Tom," he said. Joseph groaned.

That night, Joseph lay awake, thinking. He felt his chest tighten as he tried to imagine a way to get past Tom to be alone with Nunschetto. Her hair was so shiny in the firelight. Her lips were so full. Her eyes—*oh . . . her eyes are so beautiful.*

He fell asleep, dreaming about Nunschetto. He was in the woods, holding her hand and looking deeply into her eyes. Her eyebrows lifted as he spoke to her, and a few loose strands of her dark hair stirred in the slight breeze. He stepped closer, his arms clasped around her waist as he bent to touch her lips with his.

Just then an arrow smacked into the tree above him and he heard a shout. *It's Tom!* He grabbed Nunschetto and swept her deeper into the woods.

Joseph woke up with his heart pounding. How dare Tom ruin his dreams? How could he get Tom to stop bothering him?

Just then, Joseph remembered *Dat*'s voice, entreating him not to try to get back at Tom when he was harassing them as a guard on the captive trail. He bristled as he thought about his father. What did *Dat* know about revenge or Indian ways? What good had his pacifist ways done for their family? Nothing. That's why Joseph had no family—none now but Touching Sky and Runs Free.

Joseph fell back into a fitful sleep. He wasn't sure which bothered him the most: that he couldn't get close to Nunschetto or that he couldn't figure out a way to get back at Tom for trying to keep them apart.

The trees were fully leafed out and the air was warm in the late-spring sun when the village gathered for outdoor games. After three years of winning races with his own age group, Joseph was confident that he was the fastest runner in the village. Even faster than Tom Lions, who'd won the year before.

Joseph looked forward to showing off his speed. Most of the village would be out to watch, and he would surely get to see Nunschetto. It had been several days since the dance, but every detail about Nunschetto was still fresh in his mind. Maybe he could find a way to meet her alone in the woods, free from Tom's watchful eyes.

The men ran races in several heats, starting with the young boys. Several young white captives joined in the races, but none could outrun the Indians.

Joseph scanned the crowd but didn't see Nunschetto. Had Tom made her stay home?

When it was Joseph's turn to race, he moved eagerly toward the starting line. Miquon was in the race, as were three other men their age. Just as he crouched down to start, Joseph noticed Nunschetto standing at the sidelines, looking in his direction.

He was still looking at her when someone shouted the signal and the other runners leaped off the starting line. *Oh no!* He was off to a late start. But by the time they passed the place where Nunschetto stood, Joseph had caught up. She flashed an admiring smile at him, and he held her gaze for a moment as he passed by. He crossed the finish line two steps out front. Nunschetto clapped and cheered.

Joseph made his way back to the starting line. He tried to walk as nonchalantly as possible, glancing at Nunschetto only for a moment as he passed the place she was standing. Again, she met his gaze and smiled.

Joseph raced two more times and won, proud that Nunschetto was watching. He thought the races were all finished for the day when Tom Lions came swaggering up to him. "Let's race," he said, "so we can see who's the fastest."

"If you like," Joseph replied, trying hard not to show his excitement at the chance to prove his speed. Revenge would be sweet.

"Does anyone want to join us?" Tom asked as they stood at the starting line.

Joseph looked around at the stony-faced men and then at Miquon, who shook his head. This would be a contest between only two runners. And he was determined to win.

"Get ready," the starter shouted. Joseph crouched down beside Tom, waiting to leap off the line at the signal. But when the starter shouted "Go!" Tom was already a step off the line.

That's not fair, Joseph protested inside as he jumped off the line and strained to catch up. When would Tom stop cheating and taking advantage of him? Just then, Joseph spied Nunschetto at the side of the racecourse, looking in his direction. His new earrings swung wildly as he put down his head and ran. He noticed the onlookers remained quiet rather than cheering loudly as usual. The two of them ran side by side for most of the course, but Tom led by a half step as they crossed the finish line.

Joseph's heart was pounding from exertion as well as anger. "If only he hadn't gotten a head start," Joseph muttered under his breath, "I would have won the race. I hope the people say something about his cheating."

This time Joseph kept head down as he passed Nunschetto, not wanting her to see the disappointment and anger in his eyes. He was going to win the next year, even if Tom cheated again. Then Nunschetto could see for herself that he was faster than her brother.

The next morning, Touching Sky studied Joseph's sour expression as she stirred the fire to life. When their eyes met, he looked away.

"Did you sleep well?" she asked, hoping he would tell her what was troubling him.

"Why do you ask?"

"You look a little tired."

"I'm not tired. I'm mad at Tom Lions."

Touching Sky stood next to him. "I saw you butting heads with him after the dance the other night. What was that about?" She had no doubt what had happened but wanted to hear Joseph tell it.

"Nothing, really. He's always got it in for me."

"I thought things were getting better between you. Maybe you should just stay out of his way."

"He acts as though he owns the whole world. And he hates me."

Touching Sky pressed a little harder. "Did you want something he doesn't want you to have?"

Joseph looked down, embarrassed to meet her eyes. "I was just going to say something to Nunschetto. Miquon says she is his sister."

Aha, thought Touching Sky. She paused for a moment to think. Nunschetto was a beautiful girl. But Tom Lions was trouble.

"Tom's very protective of Nunschetto. He wouldn't let her marry a white man, even if he was adopted." Touching Sky looked at Joseph sympathetically.

"I just wanted to say a few words to her. She is a lovely dancer," Joseph mumbled.

"I saw you watching her." Touching Sky spoke gently.

"Really?" Joseph asked.

Touching Sky nodded. "It was very obvious. Be careful, Swift Foot."

"You mean I can't talk to her like I talk to any of the other young women?" He half-turned away from Touching Sky so she wouldn't see his dismay.

"Probably not. Tom will watch you like a hawk, and so will her father, Walks Proud."

"You mean we can't get off by ourselves for even a little bit?"

"Not without Walks Proud's permission, since she'll soon be of marriageable age."

Touching Sky lapsed into silence. *Swift Foot will need to learn that some of the things we most want in life don't come by pushing harder.*

-19-

"Miquon says there's no place like the corn dance to get to know the girls," Joseph said to Touching Sky as he daubed paint onto his face and spread it out with his fingers. "Would you mind if I borrow your little brass mirror so I can see how this paint looks?"

"Of course." She took her bag from the hook and pulled out the small mirror. She smiled as she watched Joseph look over the front and sides of his head.

Touching Sky pulled out a container of bear grease and removed the lid before handing it to Joseph. "The paint looks good. You might want to put a little of this grease on your hair, though."

Joseph didn't usually pay much attention to his appearance, but tonight it was different. Ever since he'd met Nunschetto at the *Pahsaheman* game, he'd worried about whether or not he was making a good impression on her. He wasn't the best dancer, but at least he could look his best. He fumbled with the long silver earrings he'd gotten from the trading post, making sure they were hanging just right.

He paused for a moment to watch Runs Free comb her hair. Her straight black tresses had grown back in the year since she'd fallen in the fire, but they were still too short to tie back the way she'd done before. Her hair was long enough, though, to hide the burn scar on the back of her neck.

Runs Free walked at Joseph's side as they headed for the clearing where the dance would be. It was a hot summer evening, with only the slightest breeze stirring the trees.

When Joseph arrived at the dance site, Summer Rain was there, her long brown hair braided and pinned on top of her head. It was good to have her as a friend, Joseph determined.

She could give him advice about getting to know the other girls. Summer Rain was like an old pair of moccasins—comfortable and predictable. Whenever he thought of Nunschetto, his breath came faster and blood rushed into his head, like the time he had tracked his first deer through the thick woods.

Joseph sauntered over to Miquon, who wore a deer-hair crest in his hair. "You're looking good," Joseph said to Miquon, smacking him on the arm. Miquon ducked and punched him in the side.

"You're looking pretty good yourself. You really put on the paint this time."

"This is a big occasion. There should be lots of tasty food and some great dancing." Joseph pointed toward the grill that several women had set up over a fire, where a piece of venison was roasting. "Don't you love that smell?"

Joseph and Miquon walked around the clearing, savoring the smoky scent of grilled meat. They watched women stir kettles of food. The first green kernels were appearing on the ears of corn in the field, and it was time to celebrate the corn spirit.

Joseph found Nunschetto squatting by her cooking fire. He motioned to Miquon to follow him, and sauntered over to speak with the young woman. What Joseph noticed most was her dark brown eyes. The name Nunschetto, he had learned, meant "doe." *How appropriate. Her eyes remind me of a doe in the spring.* The dimples on her plump cheeks complemented her broad flat nose. *I wouldn't mind kissing that nose,* he thought. *Whoa!* He shook his head to clear his thoughts.

"That looks really good," he said to Nunschetto, who was stirring a bubbling pot.

"Do you want a taste?" she asked.

"Sure," Joseph said.

Nunschetto dipped two large spoonfuls of the mixture onto a wooden plate. "You can both have a bite," she said, glancing at Miquon as she handed the plate to Joseph.

Joseph scooped the corn mixture into his mouth with his finger, and smacked his lips.

"You want more?" Nunschetto looked at him and smiled.

"Sure!" He handed the plate back to Nunschetto, who ladled two more large spoonfuls of corn onto the plate. Her eyes glowed as she handed it back to Joseph. "I'm glad you like it."

In that moment, Joseph saw the face of his mother in the kitchen back home in the Northkill. He felt the warmth of the fire in the hearth as *Mam* handed a plate of corn mush to *Dat*, her eyes twinkling with the pleasure of a cook whose food was appreciated. Perhaps Nunschetto would be that kind of a wife.

He stopped himself short. Was he really thinking about marrying an Indian girl? Only five winters earlier, he wouldn't have dreamed of such a thing. Now it was a distinct possibility, since both of them were nearly of marriageable age.

He wondered what *Mam* would think. She'd never know, of course. Unless—could she see him from heaven? But John and Barbara—and maybe *Dat* if he was still living—might find out someday. Would they think less of him? Would they accept his wife as part of the family?

Joseph stood transfixed as thoughts whirled through his head while Nunschetto stirred the bubbling mixture. He drank in every detail. Her cheeks were painted with two large red dots, accenting her dimples when she smiled. Her hair was tied back with a piece of yellow cloth. He looked at her feet, shod with moccasins that had porcupine quills carefully stitched onto the leather. The moccasins were unusually intricate, even to Joseph's untutored eyes.

"Did you make your moccasins?" he asked. "They look really nice."

"Yes, I like to decorate my clothing."

So she's handy with a needle too. Her blouse was sewn with perfect lines, and her leather skirt was decorated with a border of porcupine quills dyed red and blue. *An artist.*

"It must have taken you a long time to make the border on your skirt," Joseph said.

"It's fun, so I don't mind if it takes a while. I do it for other people too."

Like Mam, Joseph thought. Her hands were always busy with the needle when she wasn't gardening or cooking.

Joseph would have liked to ask for another taste of the corn, but Miquon poked him in the ribs. "The drums are starting to play. Let's go see what's happening over there."

"We might be back later for some more of that food," Joseph said to Nunschetto as they walked away. He scowled at Miquon. "Why did you poke me like that?" he asked as they moved out of earshot for Nunschetto.

"Didn't you see Tom Lions glaring at you?" Miquon asked. "You know he doesn't want you hanging around with his sister."

"Why should he care if I just talk to her? She's the prettiest girl in the village."

Miquon shook his head. "No, she's not. Autumn Leaves is prettier."

Joseph laughed. "You only think so because you like her. Why don't you just marry her?"

Miquon smiled. "Don't tell anyone, but I'm planning to ask her very soon."

"Really?" Joseph raised his eyebrows. "How are you going to do it? You can teach me if it works."

"So you can ask Nunschetto?"

Joseph nodded. "If I can push Tom Lions away from her."

Joseph was astounded at his own words. It seemed strange to be thinking of getting married to Nunschetto before he'd spent much time alone with her, but that's the way the Delaware did it. And she was constantly on his mind. *Why not?*

"Good luck! Besides, if you want to marry Nunschetto, you'll need to learn how to play the flute," Miquon said.

Joseph looked at him. "The flute? Why would I have to do that? I'm not even musical."

A smile played around the edge of Miquon's mouth. "The flute song tells her that you love her and want to marry her."

Joseph let out a sigh. *Another thing I have to learn.* "Will you play the flute for Autumn Leaves?"

"Of course. Every girl expects it. And then, if she likes the music and is open to marriage, you have to bring her gifts. Her parents will decide if they are good enough."

This is more than I bargained for. The music was getting louder, and Joseph had to raise his voice to be heard over it. "What kind of gifts will you give to Autumn Leaves?"

Miquon pushed out his chest. "I'll give her meat and furs to prove that I'm a good hunter. She already knows that. But I have to prove it to her family."

Joseph was perplexed. "What if they're not convinced? Does the family decide whether or not she can marry you?" He tried to remember how marriage proposals happened back home in the Northkill. Had *Dat* and *Mam* given their permission to Christian Stutzman to marry his sister Barbara?

Miquon said something, but Joseph couldn't catch it over the sound of the drums. He motioned for him to repeat it.

"I said 'yes.' Since Autumn Leaves is from the Turkey clan, they'll have a clan council to help the family decide. My Turtle clan gets along well with the Turkey clan, so I'm not worried about that."

Joseph was silent for a moment. "I'm sure Nunschetto likes me. But her brother Tom hates me. He has poisoned his whole clan against me." *I must find a way to put him in his place.*

"What did Autumn Leaves say when you played the flute for her last night?" Joseph asked Miquon as they looked for clams in the creek several days later.

"Of course she said yes to my proposal," Miquon said as he tossed a clam into the basket. "She said she liked my music very much."

"What did her parents say?"

"They'll have a clan meeting today to decide on the marriage, so I'm getting my gifts together. My cousin Little Wolf is going to deliver some of these clams this afternoon, along with the furs I've been collecting. And some of my uncles from the Turtle clan are bringing gifts as well."

"Aren't you worried her family might say no?"

"A little. One of her uncles will probably say my gifts aren't worth enough. He always brags that the Turkey clan brings the best gifts."

"Is that true?"

"No. He just wants to make me bring lots of gifts."

"Would it help if I give you one of my wooden carvings?"

Miquon's face brightened. "I would like that very much. I know Autumn Leaves loves wooden things."

"I'll give one to you. And I'll help you fill this whole basket with clams."

That afternoon, Joseph helped Miquon's cousin carry Miquon's gifts to the wigwam where Autumn Leaves lived. They carried a collection of furs, shell beads, and blankets, along with a carving that Joseph had made of a beaver. When they arrived at Autumn Leaves's home, her mother came to the door.

"Welcome," she said. "Miquon said that you would be coming." She pointed to several mats on the ground. "You can lay the gifts right there, where our family can look them over. We will send a message to Miquon's family before sundown."

Joseph walked to Miquon's home and told him what they had done. Miquon seemed nervous in a way that Joseph hadn't seen before. Maybe he really was worried that Autumn Leaves's family might refuse the gifts and the marriage arrangement.

About sundown, Miquon came running to the door of Touching Sky's wigwam. "The family said yes, and we are getting married after two sleeps. Autumn Leaves needs that much time to get her clothing ready."

Two days later, Joseph accompanied Miquon to the small clearing near the wigwam where Autumn Leaves lived. He watched with a measure of envy as Miquon waited for Autumn Leaves to emerge from her home. Miquon's face was painted for the occasion, with two red streaks that ran from the top of his ears across his eyebrows and then down the front of his nose. He wore a new linen shirt and a new pair of leggings decorated with porcupine quills.

Joseph stood beside Miquon and watched as Autumn Leaves came out of the wigwam and walked toward them with a wooden bowl. She was dressed in deerskin, with decorative fringes on the edges of her skirt, leggings, and cape. Quillwork graced the rim of her cape and skirt as well as the flaps of her moccasins. Her hair was tied back with a yellow ribbon, and she wore a beaded necklace.

Miquon stepped forward to take Autumn Leaves's hand, and then sat with her on a new mat that Miquon's mother had woven for the occasion. A gentle breeze stirred the clump of tall grass that lay behind the couple.

Joseph sat down nearby, eager to learn what a wedding was like in the village. Although several young couples had been married since he'd come as a captive, he'd never paid much attention. Now that he was losing his best friend to marriage—and he was in love himself—he wanted to learn how this was done.

Miquon and Autumn Leaves sat opposite each other on the mat, eating out of the same bowl. Joseph leaned over to Touching Sky, who was squatting nearby. "When will the ceremony start?" he asked.

Touching Sky knit her brow. "There will be no ceremony. Now that Miquon and Autumn Leaves have eaten out of the same bowl, they are married."

Joseph was puzzled. "I thought maybe Tamaqua or Chief Custaloga would make a speech or that we'd all go to the Big House for the wedding."

Touching Sky laughed. "You are still thinking like a white man."

Joseph shook his head. How could a couple be married just by eating together? He remembered the time when his sister Barbara got married. There was a long service, when the bishop preached a sermon and then pulled out a black book and read vows for the couple to repeat to each other. There were witnesses who stood nearby, confirming the promises that had been made, binding the two together for life.

It was so different here. There was no book and there were few words. What would hold this couple together?

A few moments later, a small procession of Autumn Leaves's kinfolk marched up to the couple, carrying presents. Miquon and Autumn Leaves got up from the mat to receive the gifts. Joseph took careful notice of what they received—a bowl, a spoon, a pot, a basket, a string of corn, a sack of dried meat, and a skin bag full of bear grease. It was all they would need to furnish a small new wigwam, which Miquon was hoping to build after they'd lived with Autumn Leaves's parents for a season.

Joseph imagined himself in Miquon's place, standing next to Nunschetto. In his mind's eye, he saw Tamaqua, Touching Sky, Silver Sage, and Miquon all standing in a line, waiting to give them gifts. He could see Nunschetto's wedding outfit, quilled with the skill of an artist, and hear her soft laughter as she received each gift.

I hope it happens very soon.

-20-

Summer 1762

Touching Sky tossed a piece of venison into the iron kettle that boiled on her cooking fire and then threw in a bit of sage. She must not disappoint her brother Custaloga, who always liked the savory hint of sage in his food. Too many times over the past few summers he had been away from the village when the Wolf clan gathered. This was a chance to celebrate.

She left the pot, picked up a basket, and headed for the garden to pick a fresh squash that was growing among the corn stalks. She surveyed the crops, happy for the healthy appearance of the corn, squash, and beans. The tall stalks of corn were about to tassel.

If only she could keep the worms from infesting the squash, this would yield a good crop. She bent down to examine several squash and then selected one that looked ripe. She tossed a bit of tobacco beside the root of the vine and then gently tugged the squash away from the stem. She put it into her basket, along with a handful of leaves from the vine.

When she returned to her cooking fire, she spooned some bear grease into an iron skillet and set it over some hot coals. She peeled the squash and then cut it into chunks. She tossed them into the pot and covered them with the large squash leaves. *I must not let this get too hot or else my squash will burn.* When she had first learned to cook, Custaloga had teased her about the many times she'd burned the food. She smiled. *Not anymore.*

As the clan gathered at Touching Sky's home in the early evening, each of the women brought food to share. Touching Sky rolled her eyes as Custaloga looked over each of the dishes in turn. Did he think it was his business as chief to examine each one for any faults? Or was he choosing his favorites? She couldn't be sure.

The children crowded around, anticipating the best meal they'd had in several moons. The summer crops were coming in, and there would be enough food for all.

Touching Sky called everyone to attention and lifted her hands upward. "Great Creator of all," she prayed, "we give thanks on this glad day for all that you have made for our enjoyment. We thank you for the gifts of the good earth—the Corn Mother and her sisters, for the plants and herbs, and for the spirit helpers, which assist us on this journey of life. We thank you for this clan and the prosperity we enjoy." With that, she dropped her hands and looked at the dozen or so children who crowded close to the food dishes. Runs Free pushed up with the others, clamoring for a taste.

"You'll need to wait until all the men are served," she said, smacking the hand of a young boy who was dipping his finger into one of the hot dishes.

Several mothers stepped up with ladles and began to serve the food. Silver Sage arrived and began to help. Touching Sky's face softened as she watched the children's faces. There was no better time than when a clan gathered to enjoy good food and conversation together.

After everyone was served, Touching Sky sat down next to Custaloga. "I heard that the whites are calling for a council fire," she said. "What do they want this time?"

Custaloga frowned. "Governor James Hamilton is calling a treaty conference in Lancaster. The British insist that we return the captives among us."

Touching Sky's face darkened. "They mustn't try to take Swift Foot away from me. I will die before I allow him to leave my home."

Custaloga nodded. "We told the British agent at Fort Pitt that most of the captives among us do not want to return. They have become part of our families."

Touching Sky took a bite of her food, but it stuck in her throat. "Tell the governor that Swift Foot and the other captives have become red at heart." Her voice rose as she spoke.

"We've told them that already. And I'm not planning to attend the conference."

Touching Sky frowned. "How can you stay away? You're the chief."

"The governor sent an invitation to King Beaver but not to me. So he will go with thirty of our people and eighteen white captives, mostly women and children."

"How can you trust King Beaver to speak for us? Why not send Walks Proud to speak for our village?" Touching Sky abandoned all pretense of eating. *Surely they would not take Swift Foot from me now?*

Custaloga scraped the last bite of corn stew from his plate and rose for a second helping. When he sat down again, Touching Sky continued as if he hadn't left. "How will you decide which captives to return? Surely you will not take them from their families who have adopted them."

"We will first return the children who have not been with us long, especially the ones whose families are begging the government for their return. We have also decided to allow any captive who wants to return to do so."

Touching Sky breathed a deep sigh. Joseph had now been with them for five winters. Although she'd heard him say that he'd never return to the Northkill settlement, he might be forced to go if King Beaver agreed to the governor's demands.

"I agree that someone from our village should go to the council fire," Custaloga said. "Walks Proud would be a good ambassador to lead the delegation and to receive the gifts from the governor on behalf of our people. We are desperately in need of gunpowder and lead."

Touching Sky nodded. "Walks Proud would speak well for our people. And he would never agree to return Swift Foot to his family. He was the one who captured Swift Foot for me, and he will not allow him to return to the whites unless I say so."

Custaloga nodded. "I will speak to him."

Touching Sky had intended to take a second helping, but her stomach churned.

I will never let anyone take Swift Foot from me.

More than a moon later, Touching Sky was gathering herbs at the edge of the clearing when Walks Proud returned from the conference. Joseph was chasing a hoop with Runs Free in the bright August sunshine.

Touching Sky picked up her basket and stood to watch as Walks Proud, whom Custaloga had appointed as his ambassador, made his way to the clearing in the center of the village. He and a small party of fellow delegates strode by with purpose, reflecting the gravity of their mission.

"Where did they come from?" Runs Free asked.

Touching Sky took a deep breath. "Walks Proud was our ambassador at a council fire with the white man. Come, let's see what happened at the conference." She fell in line behind the group, with Runs Free hopping alongside. Joseph followed after. Did he realize that the outcome of the conference could alter his future? Probably not. She had done her best to keep any talk about the conference away from him.

Silver Sage and other neighbors joined the knot of people moving toward the council house. Touching Sky sidled over to stand near Chief Custaloga as he stepped forward to welcome Walks Proud and the others back into the village. "Is everything well?" the chief asked.

"Yes," the ambassador replied. "We are all well."

"Then we shall eat food together," the chief said. "And when we have eaten, you shall tell us the story of your journey."

Touching Sky joined the circle of women who prepared the meal. Joseph sat with the men as they ate, while Touching Sky and the other women gathered in a different circle.

After everyone had finished eating, Custaloga called for a meeting in the council house. He seated the ambassador in the center of the circle and asked him to speak about his venture.

"We have been to the city of Lancaster near the Conestoga," the ambassador began. "The governor of Pennsylvania, a man named Hamilton, was the chief at the conference. Christian Frederick Post was the translator who helped with the negotiations."

Touching Sky felt a small sense of relief. Post was a Moravian missionary, and the most honest white man she knew.

"The governor was quite upset that our chief was not there," Walks Proud said, looking at Custaloga. "He had expected all of the heads from the invited tribes."

"I did not receive a proper invitation," Custaloga said. "He should not expect me to attend unless he treats me with respect."

"That is what I told him. But he would not admit his wrong."

"Which of the tribes were there?" Custaloga asked.

"Besides us Delawares, there were Shawnee, Twightwees, Wanaghtanies, Tuscarora, and Kickapoo," he said. "Many of their chiefs made speeches, and several belts of wampum were exchanged."

Touching Sky held her breath.

"What did the governor say?" Custaloga asked.

"He said he wanted to brighten the chain of friendship between the province and our people. But in the end, he made a very hard speech against us. He said we have not kept the promise we made at the recent treaty conferences to return all of the captives among us."

"We always keep our word," Custaloga said. "It is the English who make promises and then promptly forget what they have sworn to do."

Touching Sky nodded. She glanced over at Joseph, who gazed intently at the ambassador as he continued. "The white man cannot understand that our former captives have become part of us, our very own people. They are demanding that we return the ones whom they call their own flesh and blood."

Touching Sky clenched her jaw. *But they have become* our *flesh and blood. The governor must not be allowed to take Swift Foot away from me.*

"We have given up the people who were most willing to go," Custaloga said. "Did the governor not receive the twenty captives we brought to the conference? Did he not show gratefulness that we gave them up?"

Walks Proud nodded. "He said he was grateful for this small beginning, but there will be no peace until we have re-turned all captives taken in the war. He was not moved by the tears that were shed at the parting of the captives from us. They even bound one of them with ropes to keep her from coming back. The governor's heart is hard toward our people and the captives who have become one with us."

Touching Sky shivered with fear as she glanced at Joseph. What was he thinking? She felt hollow inside as the ambassador finished his report.

She waited until Runs Free tugged on Joseph's arm and the two of them headed back to her wigwam. Now she'd have a chance to speak to Walks Proud. She stood by him until he acknowledged her.

"I hope you made no promises to return Swift Foot to his people," she said. She could feel tears beginning to start, but she resolutely steeled herself to show no emotion. "If they truly want him to be free, he should be free to stay with us, as he wishes."

"I made no promises regarding captives, but I spoke to Swift Foot's father."

Touching Sky sucked in her breath. "I thought he was dead."

"No. I am sure he was Swift Foot's father, since I helped capture him on his farm. You might recognize him too; he was here when Swift Foot beat Tom Lions in a race."

A knot formed in Touching Sky's stomach. "What did the man say?"

"He said he needs his son on the farm to help with his crops. He sent me a gift to give to him."

Walks Proud reached into the bag that was dangling from his belt and pulled out a bundle of cloth. He unwrapped the bundle to reveal two shirts. "He said these were made by his daughter. One is for Chief Custaloga. The other is for Swift Foot."

He proffered one of the shirts to the chief, who had been listening nearby. The chief smiled as he reached out his hand to receive it. Touching Sky knew he would be happy to wear it. He often wore white man's clothing for special occasions.

Walks Proud stretched out his hand to give the second shirt to Touching Sky.

She took it with a frown. "I don't think Swift Foot should wear this shirt," she said. "He does not need to be reminded of his white family."

Walks Proud shrugged. "You may decide what to do with it."

Touching Sky turned to Custaloga. "If the father knows that Swift Foot is in this village, he will surely tell the governor. How can we keep the white chief from taking him from us?"

Custaloga reached out to touch her shoulder. "We will never force Swift Foot to go home."

She felt some relief at the chief's promise. But would he have the will or the power to enforce it?

She tucked the linen shirt into her basket and headed back to her wigwam. She would look for a place to hide the shirt where Joseph wouldn't find it. *He must not find out that his father is still alive.*

Touching Sky had gone only a few steps when a tall man who had accompanied Walks Proud stepped into her path. She'd remembered him as a guest from the Delaware village just upstream on French Creek.

"I wonder if Swift Foot recognized me today," the man said. "If he did, he didn't show it. I was part of the war party that took him captive. I killed and scalped his little sister."

Touching Sky glanced at the man's large scar. "I remember you were here when the war party brought the captives by on the way to the fort. It's a wonder Swift Foot didn't say something."

The man nodded. "Is he doing well here? Apparently he doesn't want to go home."

"It took him a while to adopt Indian ways, but now he's decided that he's going to stay here for life."

"Then perhaps you can tell him something that happened at the treaty conference."

Touching Sky leaned forward. "What was that?"

"I met Swift Foot's father, whom we called Fruit Grower. He must have recognized me. Near the end of the conference, he gave me a small basket of peaches. When he handed them to me, he said, 'God bless you.' He is a humble man."

"What did he mean by the peaches?"

"The man grows peaches and other fruits on his farm. We picked some when we attacked the farm. When he was a captive on the trail, he gave dried peaches to the chief at the great island, so they spared him and his sons from running the gauntlet."

"Do you think he was trying to make peace with you?"

"Yes, so I thanked him and wished him peace. And then I tied a little string of wampum around his wrist. He said 'thank you' and turned away. I doubt I'll ever see him again. I hadn't expected to meet his son today."

Touching Sky grimaced. "Thanks for telling me that you met Swift Foot's father. Please don't tell Swift Foot about it, or that his sister sewed a shirt for him. It might draw him back to the Northkill."

The man nodded. "I suppose that's why his sister made it."

With that, Touching Sky turned and walked back to her wigwam.

Joseph was chasing a hoop with Runs Free, who was hopping along on one leg. It warmed her heart to see him playing with her, despite the girl's handicap. Or perhaps because of it. He never spoke of her injury, but she wondered if he felt responsible in some way for not preventing the accident that had crippled her.

Her throat tightened as she watched them play. Joseph would surely want to know that she'd met the man who'd killed his little sister, and that his father had offered the man a gift of peaches. *Should I tell him?*

It was a fleeting thought. She pushed it aside with the cold realization that it could turn Joseph's heart toward his father's home just as the shirt surely would have. She couldn't bear the thought of losing her adopted son. What would Runs Free do without Joseph?

And what would I do without my son?

-21-

Hardly a day went by when Touching Sky didn't think of the shirt that she'd kept from Joseph, hidden away in a basket that hung from the ceiling in her wigwam. Her conscience nagged her, especially since the shirt he wore each day was getting ragged.

But why should she encourage a bond between Joseph and his father, whom he called *Dat*? The treaty conference in Lancaster had ended like most such events; after her people made reluctant concessions, the white man demanded even more. Custaloga spoke often about the difficulties of dealing with the British.

Touching Sky took heart when the prophet Neolin paid a visit to the village. The young man spoke of reviving the old ways, a time when her people were free from the influence of the white man. The prophet told of powerful visions he'd seen of the Master of Life, imparting a message that burned like fire in his bones. The spirits blew so powerfully around this enlightened one that they could make a tent shake.

On the very day the young prophet from the great lakes came to town, Custaloga brought him to Touching Sky for a visit. Joseph was away from the wigwam, fishing.

She looked up from grinding corn as they approached. Her heart stirred. How had she earned the opportunity to speak with their esteemed guest?

"Brother Neolin," Custaloga said as they came up to her, "this is my sister, Touching Sky. She lives with our aunt, Silver Sage, who is a wise woman and a name-giver who sees visions. I wanted them to meet you."

The prophet bowed to both of them and said, "I am blessed to meet you, for dreams and visions are needed to sustain our people."

"We must thank the Great Creator and all of his spirit helpers," Touching Sky replied. "I have been told that you have seen the Master of Life. Please sit down by my fire and tell me how this came about." She studied the young man as he sat down cross-legged on the mat next to her. She marveled at his youth, surely less than thirty summers in age. He was tall and strong; his muscles bulged against the bands he wore on his upper arms. Silver earrings dangled from circles cut in the lobes of his ears, and a silver ring hung from his nose.

With a distant look in his eyes, the prophet said: "One evening five winters ago, when the spirits were speaking to me, I fell into a dream. In my dream, I was hunting game. I walked for eight days on a trail, carrying my rifle, ammunition, and trade kettle, camping each night along the way. On the eighth evening, as I set up camp, three wide roads opened before me. I started out walking on two of the roads in turn, but they only led to a huge fire.

"But when I took the third road, I journeyed for a full day until I came to a mountain of marvelous whiteness. As the road disappeared before me, a Delaware woman dressed in a radiant garment appeared to me. She told me that if I wished to go up the mountain, I would have to leave everything behind."

Touching Sky leaned in closer to listen as the prophet gestured with his hands. She glanced at Silver Sage, who nodded encouragement.

"So I laid down my hunting equipment and all of my clothing, as the woman directed me. After washing myself in a stream that flowed from the mountain, I climbed to the top of the mountain, as I had been told. When I arrived at the top, I set out for one of the three villages at some distance away. When I arrived at the gate, a handsome man dressed in white opened it for me. He welcomed me in and led me to the Creator, the Master of Life."

Touching Sky gasped. It was hard to fathom.

At this the prophet paused and took a few puffs on the pipe that Custaloga had offered to him. The smoke rose in rings in the warm, late-summer air.

Touching Sky rose, then squatted to stir the corn that was cooking in the kettle over the fire. "May I offer you some food?" she asked the prophet. He nodded and she dipped several large spoonfuls onto a plate. "And then I want to know what the Master of Life told you," she said as she handed the steaming food to him.

"Thank you," he said as he took the plate from her hand. Touching Sky filled another plate and handed it to Custaloga, who had been listening intently to the young prophet's story.

Touching Sky stood nearby as her guests ate in silence, marveling at the power of the prophet's dream. To be ushered into the presence of the Great Creator was too wonderful to imagine. What had the prophet been told in paradise?

When the prophet was finished eating, he took up his story again. "The Master of Life told me that he hates the occupation of our land by the whites, and he admonishes us to stop relying on the Europeans for the goods we need. He loves our people, but he hates some of the things that we do. He wants us to put away drunkenness, adultery, polygamy, and fighting with our fellow Indians. As punishment for our disobedience in trusting the whites, the Creator has taken away the game we need for food." The prophet paused and took several more puffs on the pipe.

Touching Sky thought of the shirt hidden in the basket. What would the prophet say about keeping it, since a white man had made it?

"What did the Creator say we should do about the whites?" Custaloga asked.

The prophet blew another puff of smoke. "The Creator said, 'As to those who come to trouble your lands, make war upon them and drive them out. I do not love them at all.'"

"How would the Creator want us to deal with the British?" Custaloga asked.

"We are to drive them back to the sea. They have polluted our land, killed us with their diseases, and driven the game from our hunting grounds."

Touching Sky wished Joseph could hear the prophet speak. "Did the Creator say anything else?" she asked.

"Yes, he gave me a paper on which was written a prayer for Indians to use. I was embarrassed, because I am not able to read. He forbade me to speak to anyone until I had delivered the prayer to my village chief, who can read. After that, I went back down the mountain, picked up my possessions, and went back to my home village. I did not speak to anyone until I had given the prayer to Netawatwees, our beloved chief. We have memorized the prayer as the Creator requested. We repeat it morning and night."

Touching Sky thought of the written prayer in her bag. She was about to show the prophet her copy of the prayer when she thought better of it. Instead, she poked at the embers on the fire with a stick. Would he ask her to get rid of it, or perhaps burn it?

"The rest of the village must meet the prophet too," Custaloga said as he got up.

Silver Sage nodded. "I want to hear all that he has to say."

Touching Sky dipped some boiled corn for herself and Silver Sage from the kettle on the fire. The prophet's words echoed in her ears.

Joseph was on his way home with a small catch of fish when he saw the villagers gathering at the lodge. He glanced inside the wigwam. Touching Sky was gone. He set the basket of fish on a ledge and headed for the lodge.

He found a comfortable place to sit on the ground with the rest of the villagers. Nunschetto was only a few steps away, but he didn't dare sit next to her. He was trying to catch her eye when conversations ceased and Custaloga welcomed the prophet, inviting him to give his message to the people.

"I was at home alone by a fire," the prophet explained. "I was deeply concerned about our people's evil ways. Then the Great Spirit showed me the avenue by which he intended Indians to enter heaven. He has sent me to tell my people that their evil deeds have offended him and how we might regain his good favor."

Joseph glanced at Nunschetto, who leaned forward to watch the young prophet unroll a piece of deerskin with markings on it.

"I need someone to hold this open for me," he said. Tom Lions jumped to his feet and helped stretch out the tanned leather to reveal a crude map. The deerskin was a square about two hand spans in width and length, with a smaller square in the center.

"In the beginning, the Great Manitou put us here," the prophet declared, pointing to a spot on the left side of the map with the figure of a plump turkey. "It was a place of calm and plenty. He intended that we, the original people, take this avenue to enter heaven when we die. But the white man came and blocked the way. Now, the Great Spirit has opened up a different avenue for us, but it is far more difficult to enter." He pointed to the lower right hand corner of the deerskin.

Joseph followed the prophet's finger, pointing to the various lines he had drawn on the map. "It is much more dangerous to go this way," the prophet declared, tracing out the lines of a deep ditch. "Not only must we leap this gulf, but an evil spirit keeps watch as we pass. Whenever an Indian comes by, he grabs hold of him and carries him away and never lets him go again. He lives there in misery and poverty, because the parched ground does not bring forth much fruit."

The prophet looked emotional as he pointed to the figure of a starving deer.

"The Great Spirit wanted us to live here on this side," the prophet continued. "It is a place to hunt and fish to our heart's content. But we have offended the Manitou by allowing the people who are different from us to take over our land. We have welcomed them among us and received them as our own. We have brought this trouble on ourselves."

Joseph squirmed in his seat. Had the prophet noticed his green eyes and light-colored skin?

"The Master of Life told me that we must no longer allow the English to live among us. What have they brought to us? Some of you will say that the Europeans have brought us guns, knives, kettles, and cloth. It is true that they have brought us things that we depend on every day. But they have made us their slaves by their trade. They have brought us rum, poison, sickness, and death."

Tom Lions nodded vigorously as he handed the deerskin back to the prophet.

"The Master of Life says that we do not need all the things the white man has. We must give them up, as I will show you. We must take up the bow and arrows again. We must stop drinking the strangers' deadly spirit water, and we must not listen to their missionaries."

The prophet shouted and danced as he spoke. "If we do these things, the Great Spirit will give us success. He will strengthen us to take up arms and conquer our enemies." He brandished a tomahawk in his right hand. "We will drive the white people away and recover the passage to the heavenly places that he has taken from us." He jumped up and down in rhythmic dance, his staccato voice accenting his words. Several young warriors danced in rhythm with him, waving tomahawks and knives.

Suddenly, the prophet dropped his voice to a loud whisper. "And now, my friends, to help you remember these solemn warnings from the Great Spirit, I will make you maps like this one." He beckoned to Tom to hold it up again. "For the price of one buckskin or two doeskins, I will draw a map for you."

Joseph stepped to the back of the lodge as people crowded around to see the map up close. Would the prophet's words against the white man lead to war? How else would people show their obedience to the Great Manitou's warnings?

When the crowd thinned out and people began to return to their homes, Joseph ventured up close to see the map for himself. Touching Sky walked over to stand beside him.

"I'd like to have him make me a map like this one," she said to Joseph. "Can you get a deer hide for me?"

"Yes," he said, turning to go. "I will go tomorrow if I can find powder for my gun."

Touching Sky walked beside him as they headed for the wigwam. "I saw doubt in your face when the prophet was speaking. Do you not want to heed his words?"

Joseph let the worry seep into his words. "Why does the prophet hate the white man so?" he asked. "Even though I am now a true son of yours, I do not like the way he speaks of the whites."

Touching Sky patted his arm reassuringly. "He does not hate all white men," Touching Sky said. "Mostly he hates the British. They wish to wipe our people from the face of Mother Earth like I sweep the crumbs of cornbread from my dish."

"But what can we do?" Joseph asked. "They have taken all of the forts from the French with their powerful guns. Now they say we must go to the forts to trade. They have cut off our supply of ammunition, so that we will starve to death if we don't bow to their ways." Joseph paused. "I haven't had much luck hunting lately."

"Perhaps if you learn to use a bow and arrows, the spirits will send deer into your path," Touching Sky said.

Joseph straightened his shoulders. "I am willing to try."

"Unless you find more game, we will have a desperate winter. It will force our women to rely on the men at Fort Pitt for food. I fear that too many of them have already been snared by those lonely soldiers' lures and traded their bodies for corn and venison." She snorted. "I would die before I would lie with a white man on his blanket."

Joseph still looked concerned. "But I don't even have a bow," Joseph said. "Where can I get one?"

"You must make your own," Touching Sky said, "just as my father did when I was young. My brother Tamaqua will help you."

"Does he know how to make arrows too?"

"Of course. My father made such good arrows that he was called Straight Arrow. Tamaqua learned from him."

Joseph stopped. "I will speak to Tamaqua right now," he said.

Joseph headed for Tamaqua's home, intrigued by the possibility of making his own bow and arrows. He worried about the possible effect of the prophet's angry appeal, but it would only be to the good if he could learn to shoot game without relying on the diminishing ammunition supply from the British.

"Ho," Joseph called as he stepped up to the door of the wigwam.

"Come join us, Nephew," Tamaqua said, pointing to the pot his wife was stirring over the fire. "Have some stew."

Joseph dipped some food onto a plate and sat down beside Tamaqua. The light from the flames danced in Tamaqua's earrings as he ate.

"The prophet told us we should hunt with bow and arrows rather than the white man's guns," Joseph said, "so I was wondering if you could help me make a bow. Touching Sky says that your father made bows and arrows."

"That is true. But I have not made one since I was your age."

"Can you help me?"

Tamaqua nodded. "Yes, I will. And I will teach Miquon as well."

"Why don't our people make bows and arrows anymore?" Joseph asked.

"The white man's gun reaches farther."

Joseph leaned forward. "Why then does the prophet insist that we go back to the old ways? Does he believe we can drive the white man out of our land with bow and arrows?"

Tamaqua paused for a moment to get more stew. "No, the prophet knows that we cannot win with bow and arrows alone. But we must heed his warning not to depend on the white man for everything. Already the British are making it hard to get ammunition. The traders no longer come to our villages. We have to go to the forts to get our wares."

"Have you ever fought in battle with bow and arrows?"

"Yes, I learned alongside my father. He could shoot ten arrows in the time it took the enemy to load his gun."

Joseph's eyes widened. "Why then do you not use bow and arrows today?"

"We have been charmed by the white man. But that must change. Tomorrow we will hunt for wood to make bows and arrows for you and Miquon."

The sun was rising above the trees the next morning when Joseph and Miquon followed Tamaqua into the forest. The woods were alive with the color and sound of migratory birds charming their mates with song.

"What kind of wood do we need?" Joseph asked.

"My father always used a hickory tree for a bow and then some ash sprouts for arrows," Tamaqua said. Joseph kept alert as they walked, hoping to be the first to spot the ash or hickory.

"There's a hickory tree," Joseph said not long after, pointing off to the side of the path.

The tree appeared to be about three hand spans in circumference with no branches near the ground. "It's just the right size," Tamaqua said. He threw a bit of tobacco at the base of the tree and said, "Tree, I am giving you tobacco. Give us some of your wood to make a bow. May the bow be strong and throw its arrows straight and true."

Joseph watched carefully as Tamaqua took the hatchet from his belt and hacked a ring not far above the base of the trunk. He cut another grooved ring a little ways above his head and connected the rings by cutting two parallel vertical grooves with his knife.

"Now, my nephew," he said as he handed Joseph the knife, "keep cutting these grooves until they are about two finger widths deep."

Joseph took the knife and deepened the parallel grooves until Miquon stepped up to have a try. The two boys took turns until the grooves were deep enough. And then, using a rock as a hammer and the hatchet as a wedge, Tamaqua pried the long piece of wood out of the tree.

"This will be the bow stave," he said, as he thanked the tree and tossed it a little more tobacco. "Now let's find some wood for arrows."

They soon found an ash tree with a group of shoots sprouting near the trunk. They cut the straightest ones—each at least an arm's reach in length—and then Joseph wrapped them into a bundle with a hemp rope.

"Can we start carving the bow today?" Joseph asked.

"No, the wood for both the bow and the arrows will need to season for several moons in the wigwam."

Joseph dropped his head. "I had hoped I could hunt with it right away."

"All good things take time," Tamaqua said. "You can hang this wood in your wigwam to dry. I'll help you carve it as soon as the sap runs in the maple trees this spring."

"Thank you," Joseph said as he carried the wood in his arms. Touching Sky would be proud of him.

❖

Touching Sky sighed as she thought about the Great Manitou's call for her people to return to the old ways. She remembered the first time she had met a European, a pale-faced man who came to their village, trading pots and pans for furs. As a little girl, she'd watched her grandmother bargain for their household's first iron kettle. It was so much easier to cook with an iron kettle than with clay pots, which could not stand the heat of a fire. Surely the prophet didn't expect them to go back to the practice of heating up stones in the fire to throw into clay pots to warm up their food.

And what about the white man's clothing? She fingered the blanket she wore over her shoulders. Would she be willing to give up the bright colors and bold patterns the European traders brought? Surely the prophet wouldn't expect them to wear only clothing made from animal skin, as her grandmother had done. Or do without the beads on her moccasins and the silver bells she wore as anklets.

She glanced around the cabin, making a mental note of the wares she'd gotten from traders. There was the ornamented comb she used to brush her hair, and the iron hoe, ax, and tomahawk. Yes, and there was the strike-a-light she used to start her fires. Would she be willing to give up all of these things, as the prophet exhorted them to do?

Nevertheless, she thought, w*e are so fortunate that the prophet visited us. He will make the way for us to overcome the domination of the white man.*

She turned to face the afternoon sun. Lifting her arms, she prayed: "Thank you, Great Creator, for all you have made for us to enjoy. You have given us the forests and all its creatures. Yet we have done wrong and squandered what you have given. We have allowed ourselves to be pushed away from our homeland by our uncles, the Iroquois. We have accepted the ways of the white man, trading away the pelts of our beloved friends—the deer, the beaver, and the bear, for things we do not need. Worst of all, we have allowed the white man to steal our goods by giving us spirit water to drink, which brings us ruin instead of joy."

Touching Sky turned at the slight sound of a footstep behind her. It was Silver Sage, heading toward the creek with two gourds. "I have been thinking about what the prophet told us," she said to Silver Sage. "I am hopeful that we will follow his teaching."

"He had many good things to say," Silver Sage replied. "Come with me to get water, and tell me what you believe the Great Spirit would have us to do."

Touching Sky nodded and walked with Silver Sage to the creek. Grandfather Sun's light filtered through the heavy leaves of the boughs that hung over the trail, patching the dusty path with odd-shaped blotches. The day was getting hot, so they decided to bathe before returning with the water.

When they reached the creek, both women tossed the blankets off their backs and the moccasins off their feet. Naked, they waded into the water until it covered their hips. Touching Sky squatted down on the rocky creek bottom, the water just under her chin. "I've often wished we could go back to our original land," she said. "I've never thought it would be possible. But if we follow the message of the prophet, perhaps we can drive the white man back to the sea."

Silver Sage lowered herself into the water to squat alongside Touching Sky. "My heart yearns with yours to go back to the place of my birth on the far side of the Delaware River, but"—she paused and splashed some water over her graying hair—"it does not seem possible. The white man has become too strong."

Touching Sky nodded. "Perhaps it is because we have done wrong and offended the spirits. Perhaps if we confess our wrongs, as the prophet declares, the Thunder Beings will help us. If the spirits of the forest and the skies would join with us against the white man, we could drive him into the sea."

They enjoyed the cool water for a while, not speaking. After a while, Silver Sage asked, "Have you ever told Swift Foot that you once played in the woods where he grew up?"

Touching Sky shook her head.

"Why not?"

Touching Sky dunked her head under the water for a moment and then shook the water out of her hair before she replied. "I have often wished that I could return to the places where my father once hunted. But I have not mentioned it to Swift Foot because I want him to forget his childhood home. And I would be afraid to accompany him there."

"Why?"

"That is a foolish question. Surely you know that it would be dangerous for Swift Foot or me to visit the Northkill. If his family is still alive, they would murder me on the spot."

"Perhaps not. Walks Proud says they are peace-loving people. "

Touching Sky vigorously shook her head. "The only way I would return to the Northkill is if our people drive the white man out." She stood up, wrung the water from her hair, and then moved toward the bank of the creek. She dried herself by running her hands over her body. Then, she pushed her feet into her moccasins before tossing the blanket over her shoulders.

Silver Sage dried off, then picked up her gourds and filled them with water. The two women walked the dusty path back to their home in silence.

How can Silver Sage think that I could go back to the place of Swift Foot's birth? Touching Sky thought to herself as she neared their wigwam. *I would be throwing my life into the hands of white men who I have never met.* Her jaws clenched at the thought.

Joseph was waiting near the wigwam when Touching Sky and Silver Sage approached. "I'm going hunting," he said. "I'd like to get a deer."

Touching Sky's face lit up. "Good. I'll be able to get a map from the prophet if you are successful in the hunt, my son." She reached for a comb to run through her wet, tangled hair.

Joseph was such a loyal son. But he mustn't know about the hidden shirt. He mustn't know that she had dreamed of someday returning to the Northkill, where she had played as a child.

PART III

-22-

Touching Sky thought about the prophet's warnings as the winter came and went. Now she noticed every time she used something—a blanket, a pot—that the white man had provided for the villagers. Surely the prophet was right. They should no longer depend on the white man's traded goods for their sustenance.

She was pleased at the way that Joseph responded, carving his own bow and arrows with Tamaqua's help. It carried her back in spirit to the time when she'd begged her father to let her string and shoot an arrow.

"Why can't you teach me like you taught Custaloga?"

"Hunting is for men, not girls," her father had replied.

"Can't I try? Just once?" she begged. Straight Arrow put the bow into her hand and helped her string the arrow. "You must keep your eye on the target. Now, pull the string."

"It pulls too hard," Touching Sky whined.

"Let me help you." He stretched his strong arms around her back and pulled the string taut for her. "Now let it go."

Her heart thudded as the arrow whistled away and pierced the mark.

"Let me do it again!"

She stood for a moment, lost in remembrance, then shook herself back to the present. Just outside the wigwam, Joseph practiced shooting his new arrows. She smiled to see Runs Free beg in the same way. Her heart leaped as she watched Joseph indulge Runs Free without complaining.

She stood there basking in the warmth of the sunshine as Custaloga strode up from the creek with a guest at his side. The tall Indian wore feathers dyed red in his hair, and a small braid hung from the crown of his head in front of each ear.

"We are pleased to have Pontiac, Chief of the Ottawa, as our guest," Custaloga said. "He has come to recruit warriors for an alliance against the whites."

Touching Sky waved to Joseph to join her in the lodge. Together, they sat down on a blanket and waited to hear from the chief.

After Custaloga introduced his guest, Pontiac stood in the center of the circle and raised a red-stained tomahawk. "My dear Delaware cousins," he said, raising his strong voice to reach the edges of the crowd, "I am here as a friend. The white man is our enemy. He tells us with smooth words and wampum belts that he wants to make peace, but we all know that he is lying."

Several warriors whooped with approval.

The visiting chief's face was etched with anger. "The white man wants only to claim our land. He has broken every treaty that he has made with us. Look into the matter and you will see. When the French pushed their way into the valleys of the Ohio and the Alleghenies, Tanacharison spoke for the confederacy of Six Nations, solemnly warning them three times to leave these lands. We have relied on the solemn promises of the English to leave the areas west of the Alleghenies as soon as the French were driven out."

Touching Sky listened intently.

Pontiac continued, "Ten summers ago, Governor Hamilton clearly declared in a treaty with the Six Nations that they have title to the lands on the River Ohio. This has never been denied by the English crown or the settlers who dwell in these lands. Why then are the English occupying the forts along the Ohio?"

"Because they have broken their promises!" Walks Proud shouted as he jumped to his feet waving his tomahawk.

"Yes, yes!" shouted another.

Touching Sky's face grew hot. The chief's speech stirred up anger as though he was waving his hand in front of a nest of hornets.

"Didn't your people join with the Shawnees to make a peace treaty with Frederick Christian Post in the council at Easton after Fort Duquesne fell to the British? And did not your own chief, Custaloga, along with King Beaver and the other chiefs at Kuskuskies, make it clear that you expected the English to return to the east of the Alleghenies?"

"That is true!" Walks Proud shouted. "The British are like children, who change their minds when it is convenient to them."

Touching Sky saw Runs Free and two of her friends looking on from the edges of the group with somber faces. Pontiac was right; the white man had not kept his promise to leave their hunting lands. He must be driven out of the forts that had sprung up over the past few summers.

She noticed Joseph shift on the blanket. *I wonder how he feels about all this talk about the white man. I'm glad he gave up white ways to join our people.*

"There were many other treaty councils," Pontiac continued, "but I must mention the council fire held by Governor Hamilton in Lancaster last summer. More than five hundred of our brothers from many tribes were there."

But not Custaloga, Touching Sky thought. *He didn't get a proper request. That's when Swift Foot's father sent him a shirt.*

Pontiac was shouting now. "Have our people ever forgotten a promise or a treaty?" Pontiac's voice rose as he leaned forward, stretching out both hands to the assembly.

Several onlookers stood and shouted. "No. No, we have not."

Pontiac gestured with his hands. "Our beloved homes and hunting grounds have been taken from us by force and fraud, and we shall not stand for it. We must rise and drive the white man back into the salty water from which they came!"

"Yes, yes," several warriors echoed. "Drive them back into the sea!"

Pontiac continued, "I have heard that Prophet Neolin recently spoke in your town." He shook his finger for emphasis.

"You must listen to his voice and join our alliance to push the white man away. *Together* our various tribes can do what we could never do *alone*." With that, Pontiac wiped the sweat off from his brow and sat down.

Custaloga rose and cleared his throat. "Chief Pontiac has spoken the truth about the grave offenses our enemies have committed against us. We could speak of more, for the English have become very stingy. They once gave us gifts for guiding them through the woods, or keeping peace among our tribes. Now they give us next to nothing. And they don't give us enough powder to hunt game. How do they expect us to live?"

"We will not be treated this way," Walks Proud shouted.

"Then join our alliance," Pontiac said. "The Shawnee and the Seneca of the Six Nations are joining with my people in this effort. We plan to strike all of the English forts along the Ohio on the same day, so that the enemy will not be able to send warnings or reinforcements to each other."

He looked at Custaloga. "Can we count on your people to join us?"

Custaloga looked solemnly at the gathered group. "We will decide in a few days."

That evening, Joseph pondered Pontiac's invitation as he shot arrows at targets until it was too dark to see. Would the village join the alliance against the British? If so, should he march on the warpath with them?

No one in Custaloga's Town had asked Joseph the question directly, but he knew it was sure to come. Would he show his loyalty to his adopted tribe by going out to fight with them? Or not?

On the one hand, his answer had to be yes. How could he stay in the village while his friends gave their lives to save the land that had been theirs for as long as anyone could remember? How could he claim to have a red heart if he refused to attack the white man who had wronged them so deeply?

Joseph eyed the night sky as he thought. *Christian used to talk about the stars,* he reflected, gazing at what might be a constellation. *He probably has Indian names for them now.*

Thinking about Christian made him wonder if his brother's Shawnee village was going to join Pontiac's forces. If they did, would Christian join as a warrior? His brother had taken up a gun with him on that fateful night when the Indians burned down the family cabin, but he had never argued with *Dat* about guns the way Joseph had.

What if the Pontiac's war party was sent to attack his family and friends at the Northkill? Bile rose in his throat as he recalled the whooping of the warriors who swept onto their homestead after Tom Lions spied their family and shouted the alarm. He shrunk back at the thought of his little nieces running for cover like Franey had done, only to be killed, and have her scalp sold like a pelt. He could never join an attack against his home community.

Dear God, I hope they don't force me to choose between my two families.

Joseph sat quietly by the fire outside the wigwam, watching the stars twinkle in the sky. He wondered what Touching Sky was thinking about Pontiac's appeal.

Touching Sky squatted down next to him. "Do you remember the time when you looked into my bag and found the copy of the German prayer?" she asked.

Joseph's face flushed. "Yes." It was first time she had mentioned it since the day it happened. Why would she bring it up now?

"At the time, you weren't able to translate all of the words into our language."

"That's when I was just learning to speak Delaware."

"Would you be able to read the entire prayer now?" she asked.

"I can try."

"I'll get it now." When Touching Sky went inside to get the paper from her bag, Silver Sage and Runs Free followed her back out and joined them by the fire. Joseph read the prayer aloud, straining to see the fading words in the flickering light of the fire. He translated each phrase from German into Delaware as best he could.

Touching Sky leaned forward as Joseph came to the words in the middle of the prayer: "*Woak miwelendammauwineen ntschannauchsowagannena, elgiqui niluna miwelendammau-wenk nik tschetschanilawequengik* (And forgive us our trespasses, as we forgive those who trespass against us)."

"What does that mean?" Silver Sage asked.

"I guess it's asking the great God—*Patamauwoss*—to forgive us for the wrongs we have done, in the same way we forgive the people who have wronged us."

Touching Sky nodded slowly. "That's what I once heard a Moravian missionary say."

Joseph wrinkled his brow. "My father always said we cannot expect God to forgive us if we do not forgive others for the way they have wronged us. He even taught us to love our enemies."

"That's impossible," Touching Sky said. "Who would ever love their enemies?"

Joseph's stomach tightened. "My father tried to. He was so opposed to war that he wouldn't let us take up arms. He wouldn't take up a weapon against other people, even to save the life of our family."

Touching Sky raised her voice. "What do you mean? He fought against my people!"

Joseph shook his head vigorously. "No, he did not."

"Do you mean to say that when the war party attacked your cabin, he didn't fight to save the family? Of course he did!"

"No! When my brother and I picked up guns to shoot, my father said, 'Joseph, put your gun down.' If only he would have let me shoot, I could have driven them away." Joseph's mouth went dry as he thought of Pontiac's appeal to attack the whites.

"Do you wish your father had allowed you to kill Walks Proud or another warrior in the war party?" Silver Sage asked.

"I didn't know any of the warriors then."

"But we did. If all the settlers were peacemakers like him, we wouldn't be out killing them."

Joseph's faced burned. "But Delawares are warriors at heart. How could you respect a man who didn't fight to protect his family?"

"We have peace chiefs as well as war chiefs. Perhaps your father is a peace chief."

Joseph swallowed hard. He had never seen his father's refusal to shoot as a mark of honor. He had never thought of him as a peace chief.

"What would your father do if Tom Lions treated him the way he's treating you?" Silver Sage asked, looking directly at Joseph.

Joseph's heart pounded. *Why are they asking me these questions?* He reached out and stirred the fire with a stick. He remembered *Dat*'s warning against trying to get even with Tom. What was he to say?

Silver Sage looked at him expectantly.

Joseph cleared his throat. "Well, my father would probably try to forgive him. That's what he believes is right." Sweat trickled down his brow as he stared into the fire. "But why are you asking about my father? I don't even know if he's alive." His voice was laced with anger.

"I was just wondering what you were taught," Silver Sage said in her most soothing voice. "The wisdom we are taught as children is like a trail through a heavy forest."

Joseph took a deep breath. He wasn't about to forgive Tom Lions for all that he'd done to him. But maybe *Dat* had been right, arguing that the white man shouldn't shoot the Indians. Now that Joseph was an Indian who might decide to attack a settler's farm, he'd prefer to encounter an Amish man with principles of nonresistance over one who thought the only good Indian was a dead one.

-23-

Joseph went to bed later than usual that night, worried about the decision that he would need to make about joining Pontiac's war against the British. If he decided not to go, Tom Lions was sure to taunt him in front of the village elders. He began to sweat. What was he going to say if Tom pushed him?

Maybe he should fight Tom, and show the village once and for all that he could beat him at his own game. Joseph turned over in bed and tried to put Tom out of his mind.

A few moments later, Joseph heard the cawing of a crow on the roof of wigwam. *What's going on? Crows don't caw at night.*

Just then Joseph heard excited shouts as warriors ran past the wigwam in the direction of the creek. They were shouting a war cry, whooping and calling the village to arms. "The British are coming!" they shouted as they ran. "Our scouts have seen them."

Just then, Miquon burst into the wigwam. "Come, Swift Foot," he urged. "Our village will soon be overrun by the white man!"

Joseph hurried to get dressed. There was no time to put on war paint or go through other rituals of preparation. The enemy was at hand. He fastened his breechcloth in place, pushed his feet into moccasins, and hung his medicine bundle around his neck. Fear tightened his throat. He tied a supply bag to his waist, grabbed his musket and a powder horn, and ran to join the warriors who were shouting the alarm.

Joseph had barely gotten to the creek when he saw a vast army approaching from the other side. The blue-clad soldiers came by the hundreds, marching in step with the drummer in front. Cavalry followed close behind. Joseph could hear the mounts neighing in anticipation. Far to the rear, other horses pulled wagons filled with supplies. Custaloga's village would be no match for this horde.

Custaloga's warriors quickly slipped into the woods on the sides of the village, priming their weapons and waiting for the soldiers to come within firing distance. Joseph joined Miquon at a wooded place close to the creek, crouching on the ground and waiting for the chance to shoot.

To Joseph's great surprise, Custaloga marched to the creek waving a white piece of linen in his hand. Was he going to surrender?

Custaloga stood at the edge of the creek and paused. An army officer and two other soldiers crossed the creek in a bateau, then disembarked. They solemnly lined up in front of Custaloga. There was silence.

How strange, Joseph thought, as he watched the proceedings. *How will he keep his honor if he surrenders without a fight?*

The village warriors who had been hiding in the woods came out with their weapons lowered, wondering at the scene unfolding before them. They watched as Custaloga reached out to shake the hand of the officer in charge, and hand him a string of wampum.

Just then, Joseph awoke, his body soaked with sweat.

It was a dream!

He turned to glance toward Touching Sky in the dim light. He saw her get up and then slip out the door.

An owl hooted in the night air. What time of night was it? He turned his back to the room and curled up on the bearskin rug that padded his bed. No need to wake up now.

He lay motionless as Touching Sky returned. He listened as she rustled the covers and got back into her bed. He was still awake when she began to snore softly.

The dream was still vivid in Joseph's mind the next morning. What was he to make of it? Should he tell Touching Sky? Or would she laugh at him?

As Touching Sky stirred the fire to life, Joseph sat cross-legged and watched her for a few moments. Then he spoke. "Last night I had a dream." He paused to watch the expression on her face.

She glanced at him, the corners of her eyes crinkling with interest. "Dreams are good. What did the spirits have to say to you?"

"I saw an army coming toward us. I think the soldiers were British."

Touching Sky looked at him with concern. "Where did this take place?"

"Down by the creek. There were hundreds of soldiers about to cross the water to attack our village. Our chief raised a white flag. He shook hands with the officer and gave him a string of wampum. No one fired a shot."

Touching Sky did not speak. She simply nodded her head and poured some corn into the boiling water in the kettle.

"What do you think it means?" Joseph asked.

"I do not know. It would not be Custaloga's way to make peace before trying to defend the village. Perhaps you should share your dream with Tamaqua. He is wise at discerning the meaning of dreams."

"Perhaps he'll think I'm afraid to fight."

"No, Joseph. Everyone knows that you are very brave since you killed that bear. Tamaqua will not make fun of you. He will decide whether or not you should share your dream with the chief."

Later that day, Joseph shared his dream with Tamaqua and Miquon. He cleared his throat as he began recounting the way that Miquon had burst into his home to warn him of the army's approach and how the warriors had rushed out to defend the village.

Tamaqua listened in silence until Joseph was finished and then asked, "How did you feel as the dream was being revealed to you?"

"I felt terror in my heart as it was happening, and then a strange peace when the battle ended before it began. It is not what I had expected."

Tamaqua hesitated and then said, "I believe the dream is a warning from the spirits that a powerful enemy is approaching. You must share your dream with the chief. I will go with you."

That evening Tamaqua accompanied Joseph as he shared his dream with the village elders. They listened in silence just as Tamaqua had done, and then they pondered the meaning of the dream. After sharing around the circle, they agreed with Tamaqua's interpretation. The spirits were telling the village that an enemy would soon come to attack the village, too powerful for them to resist.

"We may need to leave this place," said the chief after listening to the elders speak. "Many of the villages where our people once lived have already been abandoned. The Long Knives surprised us at Kittanning a few summers ago, and we stand in greater danger now that they have driven out the French. If we cannot drive the Long Knives out of Fort Pitt soon, we will need to move our homes farther toward the setting sun."

Joseph knew the story of Kittanning well. How many times had he heard Touching Sky recount how Suckameek had died in that surprise attack? But ever since the prophet had come to town, Joseph had known there would eventually be more war with the whites. The question was not whether, but when.

And then he'd be forced to make a decision about whether or not to join the warring party. Was he white, like his birth family? Or red, like his adopted Delaware?

Two days later, the village gathered to see which warriors would accept Chief Pontiac's invitation to take the white man's forts and drive their people out of the Ohio territories.

Each warrior would decide for himself whether or not to join the new war effort.

As soon as the dance began, Joseph was inundated with sound and color as the village sang war songs and went through ritual ceremonies. Several drummers sat near the edges of the lodge, leaving room for warriors to pass in front of them. As the drummers beat out the rhythm, warriors danced around a colorful pole planted in the middle of the room.

Joseph knew the wooden post stood for the enemy. Warriors took turns brandishing their weapons and then enthusiastically attacking the pole. Their facial expressions, their murderous weapons, along with the ferocity of their actions and bodies bedaubed with paint, struck terror in his soul.

He edged back to the entrance of the lodge as a young warrior screamed and attacked the post with his tomahawk, splitting off a corner. Joseph's stomach clenched as the young man drew his knife and pretended to scalp his victim. As he finished his task, he receded into the circle. Another young man screamed as he came forward to strike the post with his knife. He cut slivers off the top of the pole, as though to cut off his victim's ears.

That's when Tom Lions stood up and pointed his finger at Joseph. "Come on and prove you are truly one of us," Tom sneered. "You can't be both red and white. Remember the saying, 'Those who have one foot in the canoe and one foot in the boat are going to fall into the river.'"

Joseph's face flushed as he looked into the fire, not knowing what to say. He moved farther back into the shadows, hoping Tom would leave him alone.

It seemed as though each succeeding warrior tried to outdo the previous one in viciousness and anger, showing the terror they would cause their victims. And then, as the warriors finished their feinting and attacking, they began to sing.

O poor me
Who is going out to fight the enemy

And know not whether I shall return again
To enjoy the embraces of my children
And my wife
O poor creature!

They paused their singing as the drums went on, beating out a rhythm new to Joseph's ears. Many of the warriors were quieter now, as though weighing the consequences of their decision. Joseph knew from earlier conversation that each of the warriors who had danced had committed to join the war. An older man started to sing again, and others took up the tune:

Whose life is not in his own hands,
Who has no power over his own body
But tries to do his duty
For the welfare of his nation.

A few of the warriors tapped their feet in rhythm with the drums as they continued to sing:

O thou Great Spirit above
Take pity on my children
And on my wife
Prevent their mourning on my account
Grant that I may be successful in this attempt
That I may slay my enemy,
And bring home the trophies of war
To my dear family and friends,
That we may rejoice together.

The mournful sound reminded Joseph that some of the men would likely not return from the battle. He could see that the show of bravery was just that—a show. Inside those men felt frightened, and needed courage from above. As he pondered the idea, they took up the strain.

O! take pity on me
Give me strength and courage to meet my enemy,

Suffer me to return again to my children,
To my wife
And to my relations!
Take pity on me and preserve my life
And I will prepare for you a sacrifice.

Only as the song ended did the truth dawn on Joseph. The warrior song was a long prayer to the Great Spirit. It was as true here as in all other important occasions—the Creator loomed large in the Delawares' thoughts.

Dat had always said that Indians had been created by God. They might be idolaters, but they weren't demons or brutes without souls, as some of the settlers described them.

Memories of his father came flooding back. *Dat* said it was wrong to willfully take any man's life, even in war. Joseph would never forget the evening when he rode with the family to Fort Northkill. He'd been up front in the wagon with a gun in his hand, primed and ready to shoot at the sight of an Indian. His sister Barbara was arguing with *Dat*, who insisted that they should never aim their gun at people.

"What's so wrong about using a gun to stop the Indians from coming onto our property?" Joseph had asked.

"The Bible teaches us not to kill," his father said. "You know that."

"But last week you shot a fox that was stealing our chickens. Why wouldn't you shoot at an Indian who came to scalp or steal our children?"

"That's different. Foxes weren't created in the image of God. Indians were."

Joseph's sister Franey spoke up. "What's a scalp?"

"It's when the savages cut a piece of skin off the top of your head with your hair still on it," Joseph said. "It's a war trophy."

Dat gave him a stern look. "Joseph, we don't call the Indians 'savages.' Besides, white people take scalps for bounty too."

When Joseph saw Franey shrink in fear at the talk of scalps, he said, "If Indians try to scalp us, I'm going to shoot them."

"Me too," his brother Jakey agreed.

"That's not the way you were taught," *Dat* said. "If that's the way you boys feel about using your guns, I'll take them away from you."

During the night when the family had taken refuge at Fort Northkill, Joseph woke to the sound of a neighbor cussing the Indians and swearing to kill any that came within his sight. "The only good Indian is a dead Indian," the man said. "I'm glad the Gov'nor put a price on their heads. Lets them know they ain't welcome 'round here." The man turned to *Dat* and said, "You Amish folks don't use guns, do you?"

Joseph couldn't stand the man's arrogance. "Sure, we have guns," he said. "My *Dat* is the best shot in the neighborhood."

"But not against our fellow men," *Dat* said.

Joseph's stomach clenched as the man scowled at his father. "Not even against them murderin' savages?" The man's neck was red and his voice shook with anger.

Now as Joseph observed the war dance, he trembled to recall his fear that day, and the terror of the early morning months later when the Indians attacked the family farm. Suddenly it all seemed clear. He could never join an attack on the Northkill, encountering the raw hatred of the settlers against the Indians. For that matter, he wasn't ready to join the warriors in an attack against anyone made in the image of the Great Creator, whether white or red.

-24-

August 1763

Joseph and Touching Sky stood at the doorway of their wigwam, watching as the warriors marched out to battle. One group headed north to Venango and other one south toward Fort Pitt. The leader of both groups carried a bundle of sticks as reminders from Chief Pontiac of the day on which they were to attack. Each day, they'd get rid of one stick. On the day they ran out of sticks, they were to join with warriors from other tribes to launch a surprise attack on a dozen British forts.

Joseph bade goodbye to Miquon and Tamaqua, who headed off in separate directions. Touching Sky was glum as she watched them go.

"Do you wish I would have gone along?" Joseph asked.

She hesitated. "No, you could only be an apprentice anyway, and we need some fresh game." She added, "You'll be safer here too."

Joseph knew she missed Suckameek most at times like this, a poignant reminder of the savagery of war. He reached out and touched her arm.

"Let's pray that the Great Spirit protects them," he said, "and that they return alive." He meant Miquon when he said it, not Tom Lions, who leered at him with contempt as the contingent to Fort Pitt marched by.

Touching Sky nodded. She wiped a few tears from her face with her blanket.

Two moons went by. Then a messenger arrived from Custaloga. "We've captured all but two of the forts," he said.

"Thank the Great Spirit," Joseph said, thinking of Miquon. "Did we lose anyone from our village?"

"No," he said. "But we were not able to take Fort Pitt, so we have put it under siege. Now Colonel Bouquet is on the way to the fort from Carlisle with a large army. Custaloga is planning for an ambush."

Joseph turned to Touching Sky. "Might this be the fulfillment of the dream I had several months ago?"

"I hope not. The Delaware chiefs are much better than the British in the woods. Several summers ago, they won a great victory over General Braddock."

"Was that the time when Tamaqua captured a horse?" Joseph asked.

"Yes, the British always have horses that pull wagons or carry heavy packs, and they sometimes flee in the midst of war."

Joseph thought for a moment. "I'm not ready to fight in the battle, but perhaps I could go and capture a runaway horse. If we ever want to travel a distance, Runs Free should have a horse to ride. And it could help us carry supplies." He would like to ride a horse again—something he hadn't done since he'd ridden Blitz back home.

Touching Sky drew in her breath. "Yes, if you must." She looked worried, Joseph thought. But he had to do something.

The next morning Joseph struck out on the path for Fort Pitt. He carried a bow and a quiver of arrows, as well as a small bag for the trip with a rope to lead the horse he hoped to find. He found the warriors gathered for the night, and although they seemed surprised to see him, they helped him get settled. Then he sought out Tamaqua and told him of his plan to help by capturing a horse.

"Your idea about the horse is a good one. They sometimes panic in the heat of battle and break away."

Joseph's eyes brightened. "I will go with you."

The next morning, they accompanied the other warriors, following a path in the direction of the rising sun. The ambush would be on the same road that General Braddock had carved out of the woods some summers earlier. They planned to fall upon the British by surprise at a place called Bushy Run.

"The scouts say that Colonel Bouquet's army will come by this path about this time tomorrow," Tamaqua said. "We will hide behind these trees and fire at the enemy when Chief Guyasuta of the Seneca gives the signal."

Joseph's heart quickened to think of the battle that was coming.

Shortly after the sun came up the next day, the lead warriors took their place on both sides of the wide path where the enemy was expected to pass. Joseph hung back in the woods, but he could hear the army approaching. Then he saw them. At the front came a dozen woodsmen, chopping down saplings and brush to widen the path. Behind them marched officers on mounts and hundreds of men carrying muskets or rifles with bayonets on their shoulders.

The column was passing through when Guyasuta's shout rang through the woods.

Joseph joined his voice with the bloodcurdling war whoops of his fellow warriors accented by bursts of gunfire. The smoke rose in the summer heat. The convoy halted its march to return fire, and then the soldiers charged the ambush with fixed bayonets.

Joseph followed Tamaqua as the Indians ran into the woods and moved toward the rear of the convoy. There they opened fire, forcing Bouquet's men to move to the top of a hill. His troops encircled his horses and formed a barricade of flour sacks to protect the wounded.

Throughout the day, Guyasuta's warriors attacked the barricade with whoops and shouts accompanied by rapid rifle fire. In the midst of the fray, a horse bolted away from Bouquet's troops and galloped through the woods.

"Go catch that horse," Tamaqua said to Joseph.

Joseph followed the terrified animal. *Just be patient*, he told himself. He remembered the time when Blitz had galloped away from their smoldering barn. *Did he ever come back?*

The horse disappeared from view but Joseph followed its tracks. He walked rapidly, glancing here and there to make sure that there were no British scouts in sight. After a time, he spotted the horse drinking water from a small stream.

"Soo, soo, soo," Joseph called softly, imitating the sounds he'd often heard his father make when calming a frightened animal.

The horse looked up at him and then plunged into the dense woods. *He's probably afraid of me,* Joseph thought, suddenly remembering he was covered with red war paint. *But maybe when he's hungry enough, he'll want some of my corn.*

Night was falling, and the gunfire seemed a long way off when Joseph came upon the horse again. *I'm going to call him Star*, he thought, *because of the white star on his forehead.*

Joseph stood gazing at Star as he grazed the grass in a small clearing. "Soo, soo, soo," Joseph said as he held out some corn in his open palm. Star snorted and backed away at first, and then took a step toward him.

"Soo, soo, soo," Joseph continued. If he waited long enough, he was sure to gain his prize. He took a slow and careful step toward Star, still holding the corn.

Star stepped sideways and tossed his head. Joseph resisted the urge to reach out and grab the horse's bridle.

He stood still as Star sniffed and stretched his neck toward the corn. Finally, the horse took a cautious step toward him. It was followed by another. And another. At last, his long tongue swiped the corn from Joseph's hand. The horse chewed on the corn, keeping his wary eyes fixed on Joseph's face.

Ever so slowly, Joseph reached back into his pouch and got another handful of corn. He held out his open palm toward Star, this time keeping his elbow bent.

Star took another step forward. Just as he took the corn from Joseph's left hand, Joseph grasped the bridle with his right. The horse jerked back, but Joseph held on.

"You'll be all right, Star," Joseph said. "I'll take good care of you. You won't have to carry supplies for the army anymore."

It was nearly dark when Joseph tied Star to a tree with the rope he'd carried in his bag. *I must find Tamaqua to see how the battle is going. Where might he be sleeping?*

He gave an owl call and listened. Sure enough, he heard a response. He moved toward the sound and called again. After a few more exchanges, he knew must be close to Tamaqua. He strained to see in the small slivers of moonlight that filtered through the heavy trees.

"Swift Foot, I'm over here." Tamaqua spoke in a whisper.

"I got the horse," Joseph said. "I tied him close to the stream. How is the battle going?"

"We have punished the enemy severely," Tamaqua said. "They have many dead and more wounded than we do. We shall take up the battle when the sun comes up. They will not be able to escape."

The sun was barely visible on the horizon the next morning when Joseph sneaked to the edge of the clearing where the white army was preparing for the engagement. The soldiers clustered in groups on the perimeter of the hastily assembled camp at the crest of the hill.

Just then Chief Keekyuscung bellowed from behind a large tree near the edge of the clearing. "We shall kill all of you, and carry your scalps back to our villages."

A dozen war whoops from the warriors at his flanks accented his threats, and the rifle fire sounded from all sides as Indians rushed the camp. The army answered with deadly fire and rushed out with bayonets. The Indians stole back into the safety of the woods and reappeared as soon as the army retreated back to camp.

By midmorning, it seemed as though the Indians had the upper hand. The army appeared to be in retreat. Joseph's fellows poured out of the woods and advanced on the beleaguered circle of defenders. The din was deafening as the two warring parties engaged each other, and the smoke from the muskets and rifles of both groups hung heavy in the summer air. Only after Custaloga's men were fully exposed in the clearing did they discover that Colonel Bouquet had tricked them by circling around the back of the hill to attack them from the side.

Joseph hid behind a tree close to the battle and sneaked an occasional look at the confusing scene. He couldn't tell who was winning, just that there were men from both sides lying on the forest floor. His stomach wrenched to see one of the Long Knives drive his bayonet into the chest of a fallen Indian and scalp him with a knife. Soon dozens of warriors fell before the fearsome attack, and the rest ran back into the woods. Joseph fled along with them, retreating to the place where he'd tied Star. After Joseph let the horse drink from the creek, he brought him to the place where Tamaqua was resting in the woods.

"We have lost Chief Keekyuscung," Custaloga said sadly. "And Walks Proud from our village."

Joseph's stomach clenched. *Poor Nunschetto!* How she would grieve her father's death. Now Tom Lions would hate the whites even more.

"We must never again let the white man draw us into the open field," Custaloga said. "Swift Foot, take your horse and tell the warriors at Fort Pitt that the alliance lost sixty men but that we hope to stop Bouquet before he gets there."

The next morning at the break of dawn Joseph led Star through the woods until they were ahead of the army. He mounted the horse and headed toward Fort Pitt. He hadn't ridden a horse since leaving the Northkill, but he was pleased with how comfortable it felt. *I can't wait to show this horse to Runs Free. We can ride it together.*

When Joseph arrived at the fort, he conveyed Custaloga's message to the weary warriors. He told them about the losses and the hope that they'd be able to stop Bouquet's army before they arrived at Fort Pitt.

"The commander of the fort gave us two blankets," one of them said to Joseph.

Joseph was puzzled. "Why would he give us blankets?"

"He's trying to buy peace. We took the blankets, but we're not going to give up the siege."

Joseph looked at the blankets. He thought of Runs Free at home. She could use one of these, as her blanket had become ragged.

"Swift Foot, take one back to the village with you when you go," a warrior said, wiping the sweat from his brow.

"Thank you." *I think Runs Free would like this red one.*

A few days later, Custaloga's scout arrived at Fort Pitt. "We weren't able to stop the colonel," he said. "The army will arrive here tomorrow."

Joseph joined the warriors who gave up the siege and melted back into the woods. Shortly after, he started the trip back to Custaloga's Town with Tamaqua and the other warriors from the village who had suffered defeat. His heart sank as he thought of announcing the death of Walks Proud. *If only it had been Tom instead.* He felt a little guilty at the thought. No one should have to die in a war.

He took a long, deep breath. At least he had two bits of comfort to bring home—Star and a colorful blanket. That should make Touching Sky and Runs Free smile through their tears.

-25-

Touching Sky was working in the garden when Chief Custaloga and the other warriors returned to the village. Her heart beat faster as she saw their grim faces. She put down her hoe and followed them to the lodge. There had been no victory shouts, so there could only be bad news. It wasn't long in coming.

At the center of the village, the warriors laid down their weapons. The villagers crowded around with sad faces. Then, at a word from the chief, there was silence. All eyes were on him as he began to talk.

"We fell upon the Long Knives on the road to Fort Pitt," Chief Custaloga said. "They had hundreds of soldiers in several companies, with horses and wagons carrying bags of flour and other supplies. Our warriors were very brave. We charged the enemy from the edge of the woods, killing and wounding many of them. Finally, darkness fell and we had to wait until morning to continue the battle.

"When morning came, one of the companies of Long Knives made pretense to retreat from the battle. But it was a deception. When we fell upon the retreating army, another battalion fell upon us from the side and overcame us with their guns. We were caught in the clearing, away from the protection of the woods. We were forced to retreat, leaving about sixty of our number dead in the woods. Among the slain was Walks Proud, who fought valiantly."

Touching Sky's mind went numb at the news. Tears poured down her cheeks as she joined others in lament, remembering her own son's death at the hands of the Pennsylvania militia at Kittanning.

Chief Custaloga bowed his head in grief. A chorus of wails surrounded him.

Touching Sky stood close to Wulonquen, who was mourning the loss of her husband, Walks Proud. She watched as Wulonquen slashed at her arms with a knife, mixing her blood with tears of agony and loss. She sliced at her long black hair, cutting it off in clumps and throwing it into the fire.

The acrid odor stung Touching Sky's nostrils as the hair flared up in smoke. The fragile curtain that warded off the painful memory of her son's death was rent. The pain seared her again. She gasped and added her wails to Wulonquen's.

How much longer could they endure such defeats at the hands of the white man? Why had the Great Creator not answered their prayers? How could they ever be safe with Fort Pitt so close by, sending bateaux and supplies up and down French Creek? Would Joseph be the next to go?

Her breath caught at the thought of it.

It was dusk when she walked back to her wigwam. Joseph was standing near the woods, currying his horse.

Runs Free ran toward her. "Mama, Mama, Mama! Look what Swift Foot got for me!"

"I've decided to call him Star," Joseph said. "He's pretty tame. Watch this." He swung Runs Free onto Star's back. She clung to the horse's mane as Joseph led him in a large circle with the rope on his halter.

Touching Sky's face lit up for the first time that day as she watched Runs Free laugh with delight. "Now Runs Free can ride like a chief," Joseph said as he brought the horse to a stop.

"Thank you." The words were hardly sufficient to express the feelings that warred in Touching Sky's soul. How could she celebrate such good news on a day when most of the news was bad?

That evening as the village gathered around the fire, Custaloga spoke. "We will not be defeated by the white man. We shall continue our attacks on the settlements. But it is too dangerous here on the French Creek for our women and children. We must move from this place toward the Muskingum. We shall leave on the day after tomorrow."

Touching Sky's heart sank. Another move to the west would take her farther away from her beloved homeland at the forks of the Delaware River.

As though reading her mind, Custaloga added, "Although we must leave now, we shall surely return to this place. After we have driven the white man into the sea, we shall burn their forts and farms and be free to hunt in all of our former hunting grounds."

The next day, the village began to prepare for the move. Touching Sky picked the vegetables in the garden and brought them in to dry. Custaloga came with several horses from a nearby village and loaded them with food and supplies.

Touching Sky packed some of her household belongings into her pots and pans, and then put them into a large basket that she could carry for a long distance. "And," she reminded herself, "this time we have Star to help us."

The late August sun was hot as Custaloga slowly led the people of the village down to the creek and onto the Venango Path. The warriors followed immediately after the chief, carrying their weapons and other supplies. The older men followed close behind, carrying blankets stuffed with supplies on their backs.

Two of the older men rode horses, as did Runs Free, since they were unable to walk long distances. The older women came next, each carrying as much as they were able. Mothers with children came last, trailed only by a few young warriors with guns at the ready. A few young mothers had babies strapped onto their backs or carried them in blankets.

Touching Sky was somber as she walked along with other older women. Might this be the last time she would live in this village? She thought of the time she'd first moved from her home as a young girl. It had been exciting then, like the yearly move to the hunting grounds. But as the years went by, every move felt sinister, an exile from a beloved home to a place she had not seen. Each move was forced by the white man's greed. Unless the settlers were punished for their misdeeds, they would never stop their push onto Indian lands.

Hadn't Frederick Christian Post, the beloved Moravian missionary, promised the western chiefs that the British would withdraw from Fort Pitt and the Allegheny after they routed the French? Hadn't they signed a peace treaty stating the lands of the Alleghenies would always belong to the Indians? If so, why were they being forced to move even farther west? Who could stop this terrible soldier, the British colonel whose army had made its way to Fort Pitt along the paths that once had belonged only to Indians?

Touching Sky felt a familiar weariness settle into her bones. The defeat at Bushy Run meant they'd need to make more raids into the white settlements to find replacements for the warriors they'd lost. The losses flooded her mind as she set one foot in front of the other.

Joseph walked just behind the warriors in the procession that left the village, carrying a bag of supplies and several gardening tools in his hands. Tom Lions followed with a churlish frown. When Joseph met his gaze, Tom's face warped with hate.

He blames the white man for everything bad that happened in his life, Joseph thought. *Why can't he realize how much he has wronged others?*

Walks Proud's death at Bushy Run had only intensified Tom's surly manner and his desire for revenge. "I'm going to kill any white man that I see along this trail," he boasted in Joseph's hearing. Joseph remained silent. What retort could compensate for Tom's grief and loss? How might his anger intensify Nunschetto's grief for her father's death?

The villagers marched until noon, where they stopped to rest along the banks of a creek. Joseph's muscles ached from carrying supplies. He knelt at the edge of the creek and sipped from his cupped hands. Then, stretching, he sat down and opened the bag at his side and ate several handfuls of dried corn. Other members of the group spread out on the grassy bank. Some napped, while others talked quietly.

Joseph felt well rested when the group resumed their journey. They marched for another long while before stopping at the mouth of a creek to set up camp. That night, as the sun was settling behind the hills, Joseph joined Tamaqua for a short venture into the woods. "I see signs of deer about," Tamaqua said. "The Great Spirit may give us meat to eat before dark."

The two of them walked silently into the woods, following a few fresh signs of deer. They had not ventured far when they spied a young antlered buck, drinking at a rivulet. Joseph motioned to Tamaqua and then held a finger to his lips. He reached into his quiver for an arrow, and then strung it as he moved toward the deer. When he got close enough for a shot, he drew the string and let the arrow fly.

The buck leaped and then fell not far from the creek. Joseph ran to the animal's side with Tamaqua close behind. Joseph pulled his hunting knife out of its sheath and slit the deer's throat.

"We shall have meat to eat tonight," Joseph said as he watched the blood pulse from the deer's neck.

"You have become a good hunter," Tamaqua said as he helped Joseph flip the animal onto its back to remove the entrails. As soon as they were finished, the two of them carried their prize back to the camp, where Touching Sky was tending a fire. Her face brightened.

"Thank you, my son," she said. "We shall all have meat to eat tonight."

❖

As Joseph waited for the venison to roast, he noticed Nunschetto squatting at the outer edge of the group. Her face was illuminated by the light of the fire. *I must find a way to meet her alone tonight*, he thought. All evening, he stole glances at her, drawn by her countenance that glowed in the light of the fire. At long last, she got up from the fire and walked into the woods.

As nonchalantly as he could manage, Joseph got up and stretched. He glanced around to see if Tom Lions was anywhere in sight. Not seeing Tom, he headed into the woods where Nunschetto had disappeared.

He moved as quietly as possible, pressing through the slight undergrowth in the trees. His eyes soon got accustomed to the dim light from the waxing gibbous moon.

There! She was walking back toward the fire. He lengthened his stride to catch up with her. "Nunschetto," he said in a loud whisper. "Don't be afraid. It's Swift Foot. I want to talk to you."

She stood waiting for him to come up to her, the moonlight glinting off her silver necklace. Joseph touched her elbow. "I'm so sorry that your father got killed at Bushy Run," he said. "He was really brave but the battle was fierce."

Nunschetto's face clouded. "He was the best warrior in our village," she said. She paused and glanced toward the clearing. "I'd better get back to my friends. Tom might worry that I got caught by British scouts."

Joseph felt his hackles rise. "I wish he'd let you alone."

"Don't let him bother you. He's just protective, that's all."

Joseph sighed. "He won't even let me talk to you. I've been trying to be alone with you for several moons, and he won't let you out of his sight. I'm lucky I happened to see you go into the woods by yourself."

"Tom is very angry," she said, "so I need to go. I don't want to make things worse." She started toward the clearing.

"Wait." Joseph grasped her arm, surprising himself with his own courage. "Let's meet here in the woods tonight after everyone else is asleep. How about if I give an owl signal about midnight?"

She hesitated. "The scouts will be watching. Look, here comes one now!"

Joseph tugged at her arm. "When can I see you again?"

She hesitated and seemed about to refuse. Then her face changed. "Maybe tomorrow night. About the time everyone is going to sleep."

Joseph's heart pounded. "Is that a promise?"

She nodded as she turned away.

"Good. I'll watch for you to go into the woods and meet you there."

The village marched all of the next day. Joseph did his best to avoid making eye contact with Nunschetto, but his eyes kept straying to her. It seemed like evening would never come.

That night, they made camp. The villagers gathered around the fire, and a drummer beat out a rhythm. Several young women danced to the music. Joseph couldn't take his eyes off Nunschetto as she danced around the campfire in the heavy night air, her long braid bouncing to the rhythm as she swung her head back and forth.

The moon was rising above the trees when the drummer ceased playing and dancers relaxed around the fire. The camp grew quiet as mothers put their children to sleep on blankets laid on beds of fallen leaves.

Joseph's heart pounded as Nunschetto glanced at him just before walking into the woods. He looked up to see Tom Lions bedding down for the night. Had Tom seen Nunschetto look at him?

He went back to the place where he'd left his things and got the blanket that he'd brought from Fort Pitt half a moon earlier. Runs Free had asked him to carry it with his things on the trip. *It will be nice for Nunschetto to have a blanket to sit on while we talk.*

Joseph got up, gave a fake yawn, and carried his blanket into the woods not far from the place he'd seen Nunschetto go. He paused while a large cloud passed under the moon, casting a shadow over the place he was standing. Gradually his eyes adjusted to the darkness as he walked slowly toward the place where he expected her to be.

He soon found her, standing in a patch of moonlight. A breeze rustled the leaves. She was looking around anxiously.

Softly he said her name. "Nunschetto."

She looked up and smiled.

"I'm glad I found you." He reached out and grasped her hand. "Come, let's go a little farther into the woods, where no one will find us."

Joseph carried the blanket over his shoulder as he carefully picked his way through the forest with Nunschetto at his side. Soon they came to a place under some large oaks. "We can sit here," Joseph whispered, as he cleared a spot on the ground with his foot. He spread out the blanket and they sat on it together.

They listened without speaking to the sounds of the night. An owl hooted not far away, and something scratched its way up a nearby tree.

Joseph cleared his throat. "I'm sure you miss your father," he said. "I really miss mine."

"Yes," she said. "He was a good warrior and a good hunter. Our whole family is very sad."

"Touching Sky says that he brought her game to eat after her son was killed."

"Yes, he was very generous."

They sat for a few moments in companionable silence.

"You are the best dancer I've ever seen," Joseph said, squeezing Nunschetto's hand and leaning sideways so that his shoulder touched hers.

"I've always loved to dance."

"You make it look so easy. I can run easily, but it's harder for me to dance."

"You do all right at dancing, but I really like to watch you run. You are a good hunter too."

"Tamaqua taught me well."

They lapsed into silence, their fingers entwined and their moccasins touching.

They both started as an owl swooped down from the tree and flapped away, over their heads. An owl hooted from farther away.

Joseph froze. He could recognize Miquon's owl call anywhere.

"It's Miquon," he whispered. "He must be looking for me. I better see what's going on."

He sat up and gave his own owl call, and a few moments later, Miquon appeared through the trees.

"What's happening?" Joseph asked.

"Tom Lions is out looking for you," Miquon whispered. "If he finds the two of you here, you'll be in big trouble."

Nunschetto stood up and tossed her long braid over her shoulder. "I'm going back," she said in a loud whisper.

"Wait, let me take you," Joseph said. He held onto her hand.

"I'll go ahead of you," Miquon said. "I think I know where Tom is. If I see him, I'll distract him. Just don't let anyone see you together."

Miquon stepped quietly back through the trees and headed for the camp. Joseph took Nunschetto's arm and waited a few moments, then followed behind. He could hear her rapid breathing as they reached the edge of the camp, heading toward the place where Nunschetto's friends lay sleeping close to each other.

Joseph stopped as an owl hooted not far ahead. It was Miquon's call. That meant Tom was near.

Joseph tugged on Nunschetto's sleeve and stepped back. They'd need to circle around and come in from the other side of the camp.

The moon hung high in the sky now, so he avoided the places where the moonlight splashed onto the forest floor. They could see the campfire now, with two guards sitting next to it.

Then, Joseph stepped on a small twig. It cracked loudly enough that one of the guards perked up and shifted the rifle on his lap. He looked around, then relaxed again. Joseph let out his breath. He hadn't realized he'd been holding it until now.

Before long they came to the place where Nunschetto's three friends lay.

"Do you think they're sleeping?" Joseph whispered.

"Don't worry. They won't tell anyone if they see me." She turned toward him. "Good night," she said, and then turned to walk toward her sleeping place.

"Wait." Joseph pulled her close. "I hope we can spend some more time together soon."

"I hope so too."

Joseph's heart was pounding as he watched her lie down beside her friends. *I must find another way to be with her.*

Nunschetto had just pulled the blanket over herself when Tom stepped into the circle of light from the fire with Miquon not far behind him.

Joseph slipped back into the woods and circled around to the place where Miquon had been sleeping. He made sure that Tom was looking in the other direction when he strode to his place and lay down.

We were lucky, he thought to himself. *Miquon is a real friend. He saved me from Tom Lions.*

He gazed at the place where Nunschetto was sleeping with her friends. He rehearsed their short time together, glowing with the memory of her touch. He fought off the fear of what the next days might hold, and soon fell asleep with the thought of Nunschetto's warm hand held firmly in his.

-26-

The August moon had shrunk to a small crescent when Joseph and other villagers arrived at the forks of the Muskingum. Chief Custaloga looked over the area and announced, "We will build our village here."

At last! Joseph thought. He was tired of traveling and longed to call somewhere home again.

"I will make a new wigwam for us to live in," Joseph said to Touching Sky. "If Miquon is willing, we can work together."

Touching Sky's eyes softened. "That would be a good thing for us all. But are you sure that you know how?"

"We can call on Tamaqua if we need him," Joseph said. "I would like to try. Let's choose the place where you want to build it."

Touching Sky led the way toward a large oak. "Let's build it here," she said. "We'll have the shade of the oak in summer and the warmth of the sun in winter."

Joseph agreed. He found Miquon, and together they took axes in hand and headed for the woods. After a patient search, they found a tree trunk, long and slender yet sturdy enough to serve as a ridgepole for Touching Sky's new home.

Joseph had just begun to chop at the base of the tree when Miquon raised his hand and motioned for him to stop. He reached into the bag by his side, got a pinch of tobacco, and cast it at the root of the tree.

"Thank you for giving up your life," he said to the tree, "so that my aunt and my cousin can have shelter." Pointing to the seedlings that sprang up in the tree's shadow, he said, "I can see that already the Creator has blessed you with many children. May they all prosper and grow."

Joseph mumbled something about having forgotten his tobacco and went back to chopping. They took turns at the task until the tree came crashing down. Together they trimmed off the branches. Joseph stepped off the length for the ridgepole. "Let's cut it right here," he said, whacking a mark with his ax. As soon as they had finished cutting off the end of the tree, they hefted it onto their shoulders.

By the time they got back to the place Touching Sky had chosen, the sun was dropping in the western sky.

"This will be a large house," Touching Sky said when they laid the ridgepole on the ground.

"Too big?" asked Joseph.

"No. It will give room for us to share with Silver Sage and others who need it."

The next day, Joseph and Miquon cut two long poles, each with a fork on one end in which to cradle the ridgepole. They dug holes in the ground and set the two poles upright. Then they tamped the ground around the two poles to make them stand strong and true. Touching Sky and Silver Sage helped them lift the ridgepole up to the top of the poles and lay it into the fork at each end. Their look of satisfaction told Joseph that he had done well.

Over the next few days, Joseph and Miquon harvested more than a dozen saplings to serve as vertical poles to form the outline for the four walls of the house. After the poles were ready, they cut long saplings that ran the length of the cabin. They tied them to the vertical poles to form a framework for the walls.

"It really is going to be a big wigwam," Touching Sky commented when she stepped inside the partial structure.

It seems small to me, Joseph thought, leaving the words unspoken. He was remembering the two-story log cabin that *Dat* had built that had several rooms.

"I want to help," Runs Free said to Joseph when he made the poles that formed a grid for the roof. She had now seen twelve winters and despite her bad foot, she was eager to prove her usefulness.

Touching Sky showed Runs Free how to use wood fibers to lash the poles to each other. Joseph and Miquon harvested elm bark to cover the sides and roof. When they had harvested all of the bark that was needed, and soaked it in water to flatten it, Joseph fastened it onto the framework that made up the sides and roof. When he was finished, all of the surfaces were covered except for a hole in the center of the roof and space for a door at each end. Less than a moon had gone by while the wigwam was being built.

Touching Sky looked pleased. "After we have purified it, we can move in. Swift Foot, go to the woods and find some branches of cedar while I get the fire started."

Joseph soon returned with the cedar. He joined Touching Sky and a circle of friends as they gathered around the first fire in her new home.

After the fire had burned down to embers, Touching Sky took a few branches of cedar and tossed them onto the coals. The smoke from the green branches emitted a sweet smell. Touching Sky bathed her face in the smoke and then bade the rest do the same.

Touching Sky's voice was husky with emotion as she raised her hand to pray. She prayed that the new dwelling might withstand any storms that came their way, and that her family might dwell there safely for many years. Never to be displaced by the white man again.

The moon rose. They all slept inside the new wigwam. Joseph felt a sense of pride as he recalled how quickly he had built their new home, and how much Touching Sky liked it. Now he was ready to help Miquon build his home. After that, he would make his own wigwam, where he and Nunschetto could live for a lifetime.

Was there a way to free her from Tom Lions's grip? *If so*, he thought, *I must find it.*

❖

Touching Sky loved her new home, as did Runs Free. But one morning, just half a moon after they'd moved into the wigwam, Runs Free asked to stay in bed after Joseph left to go fishing. "Mama, I don't feel good."

"What seems to be the matter?" Touching Sky bent over and laid her forehead against the girl's brow. It felt hot. "Stick out your tongue," she said.

Touching Sky drew in her breath sharply as she studied the small beads that dotted her daughter's tongue. Her legs grew wobbly, but she tried to stay calm. "Let me get you a cool drink," she said.

Her heart beat fast as she took up a gourd and headed for the water. *It looks like the spotting sickness.* Ten summers earlier, the terrible disease brought by the white man had ravished her village at the forks of the Susquehanna. They'd found no cure for it there, either in the spirit of the plants or the incantations of the medicine man.

What am I to do? Grandfather Sun warmed her face as she headed for the small creek. She reached up to touch her forehead, which suddenly felt hot. *Am I getting sick too?*

She stopped on her walk, laid the gourd on the path, and reached her hands toward the sky. "Oh, Great Creator," she prayed, "do not let my only daughter be taken from me. Point me to a plant in the woods whose spirit can stop this white man's disease from destroying our clan."

She trembled as she picked up the gourd and headed for the water. *I must not leave Runs Free by herself for long.* It had been ten summers now, but she could still feel the pain of her mother's death from the illness. It started out with small spots on her tongue and throat and soon spread over her whole body. When she died half a moon later, her body was covered with the repugnant pocks. *I must keep this from happening to Runs Free. If only I could find a medicine man who could help. If only Black Elk weren't so far away.*

As she approached her wigwam with the water, she noticed Star grazing at the edge of the trees. *When Swift Foot gets back, he can take the horse to find help.*

Runs Free was moaning when Touching Sky stepped into the wigwam. She poured a bit of water onto a piece of an old blanket and laid it on her daughter's brow to cool her fever. "I'm sorry you're not feeling well," she said. "Let me give you a drink."

Runs Free sat up in her bed and took a few swallows, and then lay back down with her face toward the wall. Touching Sky's mouth was dry and her hands trembled as she listened to her moan. *Where is Swift Foot when I need him?*

It was midafternoon when Joseph came back from the river with a kettle of fish. He whistled as he stepped into the wigwam and held out the fish for Touching Sky. She raised a finger to her lips and pointed toward Runs Free's bed.

"What's the matter?" Joseph whispered.

Touching Sky motioned for him to follow her outside. "Runs Free is sick," she said.

"What do you think is wrong with her?"

Touching Sky hesitated. "I'm afraid she has the spotting illness. I want you to go for help."

Joseph took a sharp breath. "Where shall I go?"

"I'd like for you to find Black Elk. He helped Runs Free the last time."

"It would take me half a moon to run to Black Elk's village and walk back with him. And his village might have moved away, like ours."

Touching Sky hesitated. "The people at the Shawnee village just north of here might know how to find Black Elk. You could take the horse."

Joseph's face lit up. "I can try. Anything to help my sister."

"Good. I'll grind some corn for you." Touching Sky picked up her mortar and pestle and carried them outside the hut so that the noise wouldn't bother Runs Free.

Touching Sky pounded out meal while Joseph pulled together a few supplies for the journey. She ground enough to feed Joseph and then put some kernels in a bag for Star, who loved her corn more than the grass that grew unbidden next to the river.

When Joseph was ready to leave, he went to Runs Free's bed and grasped her hand. "I'm going to get help for you," he said. "I hope you feel better soon." His voice was husky as he spoke.

Touching Sky stepped outside to see Joseph off. "Come back as soon as you can," she said, tears rimming her eyes.

"I will," he said as he swung his leg over Star's back. He clucked and the horse started out with a vigorous pace. A crow cawed from a nearby tree and then lit off and flew ahead of them.

Touching Sky stood watching Joseph until he was out of sight. *Will he find Black Elk?*

Touching Sky enlisted Silver Sage to watch Runs Free so that she could go in search of healing plants. Touching Sky walked toward the river seeking calamus roots. Since calamus grew in damp soil, she walked along the edge of the water until she came to a place where the perennial grew in abundance.

She squatted down beside a large plant and with her finger, dug a small hole on the east side of the plant. Then she took a small bit of tobacco from her bag and placed it into the hole. She lit the tobacco in her pipe with the fire she carried in a small pot. She squatted on the ground, puffing smoke into the air and addressing the spirit of the plant.

"Grandfather, I come now for medical treatment. Your granddaughter Runs Free needs your aid. She is giving you a smoke-offering of tobacco. She implores you that she will get well because she, your child, is pitiful. And I myself earnestly pray that you take pity on the sick one. I wish for her to get well forever of that which is causing pain in her body. Only you have the power sufficient to bless and heal her. And now our Grandfather Tobacco, I beg you will take pity on your grandchild and that you will accept this appeal. I am thankful,

Grandfather, also Creator, that you grant our appeal this day for all that we ask. I am thankful, Grandfather."

With that, Touching Sky laid her pipe on the ground and moved to another calamus plant nearby. With a small knife, she dug around the plant until the roots were free. She pulled the plant gently from the ground, thanking the spirit of the plant for releasing it into her hands. After she had dug two other plants in the same manner, she cut off the roots, put them into her bag, and picked up the fire pot to go home.

When she arrived at the wigwam, she tossed the roots into boiling water and then pulled the pot off the fire. She added some dry sassafras root and let the mixture steep for a time. When she was satisfied that it was finished, she poured it into a cup and took it to Runs Free.

"I have some tea for you," she said. She was heartened as Runs Free drank the mixture. *Maybe she is getting better.*

But over the next several days, Runs Free grew worse. In place of the usual giggles and happy laughter, she whimpered and moaned.

"Where is Swift Foot?" Runs Free asked one day, her voice barely above a whisper.

"I hope he'll be back soon," Touching Sky said, bathing her child's forehead with a wet cloth. "You rest." The girl's body was covered with pocks like hardened beads, and Touching Sky nearly retched as she touched them. It felt too familiar, too much like an echo of the death she'd witnessed as her mother was clutched by the dread disease.

She stepped outside to gaze up the path where Joseph had left for the Shawnee village. She was standing there, glassiness in her eyes, when Tamaqua walked toward her.

"How is Runs Free doing?" he asked, his face grave with concern.

"Worse. I hope Swift Foot gets here soon."

Tamaqua took a deep breath. "I suppose you've heard that several other people have gotten spots as well." He looked down as he spoke.

"Who?"

"Turtle Heart, Quick Bird, Nunschetto."

A knife pierced Touching Sky's heart. "Nunschetto?"

Tamaqua nodded. "I just spoke to Wulonquen. She saw the spots for the first time last night."

"Thanks for letting me know," Touching Sky said as she went back to her wigwam. Her head was bowed low as she stumbled along. *That's how it was the last time.* The white man's disease spread throughout the village, dealing out death on the innocent.

She stood outside the wigwam, not wanting to go in. She could barely stand the touch of Runs Free's infested skin or bear the sound of her labored breathing.

She stood there pondering. What if something had happened to Joseph? What if Runs Free died before he arrived? She pushed aside the thought and looked up the path one more time. Her heart leaped. There was Star loping around a bend in the river, with another horse close behind.

She ran to meet Joseph, who waved as they neared. And Black Elk was close behind on another mount.

"I found him, Mother," Joseph said as he dismounted. "Their village moved away from Pennsylvania the same time as ours."

Touching Sky ran to embrace him. "Thank you, my son. You have done well."

The two men tied the horses, and Touching Sky led the way into the wigwam. After she gave Black Elk a helping of tobacco, she held her breath as he stepped up to Runs Free's bed. He studied her appearance and then reached into his bag and pulled out a turtle shell rattle.

Runs Free turned to watch as the healer shook the rattle to the rhythm of a chant. The hint of a smile played on her lips, the first hopeful sign that Touching Sky had seen in several days.

"Thank you, Swift Foot," she whispered.

Black Elk looked at Touching Sky. "Get me some water," he said.

Touching Sky glanced at Joseph. He grabbed a gourd and slipped quickly through the door. She watched him run.

My beloved son! How he loves his sister! I only hope . . . She could not bear to say the words that welled up inside, even to herself.

When Joseph returned, he observed Black Elk as he shook his rattle and chanted the story of the dream-vision he had seen just before sunset some years before. It was the story of finding a guardian spirit during his vision quest. "Oh, Great Creator, grant that the power of these visions may cure your daughter Runs Free."

He prayed on, "Grandfather Fire, may you put forth your healing touch on her. May your spirit cleanse her of this disease. May your spirit enter her body and drive out the evil that is causing these spots." Black Elk stopped to light his pipe. He gently puffed on it and prayed again, "And you, Grandfather Tobacco, let your spirit clean out the evil in Runs Free's lungs."

Joseph recalled that *Dat* had spoken of smallpox on the ship that came from the old country. A number of children had died of the disease and were buried at sea. Was it true, as Touching Sky insisted, that the Delaware had never seen the disease before the white man arrived in the new country? How unfair. *At least I've done what I could. I'm so glad I have Star.*

"Ho, ho."

Joseph started at the voice outside the door. *What is Tom Lions doing here?*

Touching Sky stepped to the door and invited him in. The hair on the back of Joseph's neck rose as Tom stepped inside. What excuse would he give for coming at such a time?

"I'm so sorry to hear that Runs Free is ill," Tom said. "I hope the healer can help her."

Joseph stared at Tom without moving a muscle in his face. Tom went on. "I was wondering if the healer could come to see my mother." He glanced at Joseph. "And Nunschetto. Both have gotten the spotting disease."

Joseph's legs went weak. He opened his mouth to say something, but no words came.

"Of course," Touching Sky said. "Tamaqua told me they were ill. We will do anything we can to help."

Joseph mustered up the strength to speak. "I'll bring Black Elk over very soon."

"Thank you," Tom said, and slipped through the door.

Numbness spread through Joseph's limbs. *Nunschetto can't have smallpox. She just can't.*

Runs Free was resting quietly when Joseph and Black Elk left for Wulonquen's wigwam not long after. Tom Lions greeted them and led them inside, where both Wulonquen and Nunschetto lay ill in bed. Joseph stood as close to Nunschetto's bed as he dared with Tom's eyes on him.

She looked at Joseph with gratefulness in her eyes. "Thanks for bringing the healer," she said.

"I'm so glad I had Star," he said. "Otherwise, it would have taken much longer." He stepped back to make room for Black Elk at Nunschetto's bed.

"You both need to take a sweat bath," Black Elk said after examining Nunschetto and her mother. "Is there a sweat lodge nearby?"

Tom shook his head. "The whole village just moved to this place. People are still building their wigwams."

"Perhaps Swift Foot can help you build one."

Joseph held his breath. *I don't want to work with Tom! But I'll do anything for Nunschetto.*

Tom motioned to Joseph and they stepped outside. "Will you help me?"

"Yes. I want to help your family," Joseph mumbled.

First they gathered twelve saplings, each one long enough that Joseph could just reach their tips when they stood on the ground. Tom pushed them several inches into the damp soil near the river, forming a circle about the size of his outstretched arms.

"I hope Black Elk can help," Joseph said to Tom, partly to break the uncomfortable silence.

"I hope so too," Tom said.

Are those tears in his eyes? Joseph wasn't sure.

Joseph looked down. It was the first time he'd ever seen Tom so vulnerable, instead of the savage who had ransacked Joseph's farm and killed his family. *If he loses Nunschetto and Wulonquen, his whole family will be gone. He helped to kill my family, and my people brought the smallpox that's killing his.* Joseph shook his head at the irony of it.

Joseph wrestled with his own emotions as he helped Tom bend the saplings in pairs from opposite sides of the perimeter, holding the ends in place over the center of the circle as Tom lashed the ends together with a thong. Two of the saplings stood further apart than the others, forming a place to make a door on the south side of the lodge. Joseph said little as they worked, watching Tom's motions and trying not to get in the way.

When the framework was finished, Joseph helped Tom gather twelve hardwood logs and stack them in the center of the fire. Tom lit a fire with his fire pot and then gathered skins and blankets to drape over the saplings. The smoke from the fire puffed out of the door opening.

Silver Sage came to help, arranging a mat of hemp and bark upon which Wulonquen and Nunschetto could lie, in turn. They waited for the fire to burn to a bed of coals. After the coals glowed red hot, Joseph added a few more logs. Then he and Tom carried twelve limestone rocks from the river and laid them on the fire using a long hickory stick—forked at the end—to hold the hot stones.

When everything was ready, Black Elk invited Nunschetto to lie down on the hemp mat and cover herself with a blanket, letting only her face show.

Joseph stood outside the flap of the doorway. He listened as Black Elk poured water on the rocks. They hissed with steam, which filled the lodge and misted out the door.

"Breathe deeply of the steam," Joseph heard Black Elk say to Nunschetto.

I wonder if steam is good for her? Joseph thought. *She already has a fever.*

His mind was numb. He'd often imagined himself at Nunschetto's wigwam, but never under these conditions. *She has to get better. She just has to.*

Joseph sat by the creek, numb with grief. He could hear the wails coming from the village, announcing yet another death. The spotting illness was relentless.

A quarter of a moon had passed since Runs Free's death, and he still wasn't able to cry. He picked up a small stone from the creek bank and turned it over and over in his hands. Why did Runs Free, so young and innocent, have to be the first one to be taken?

Only a few days after Black Elk's arrival, Joseph had come into the wigwam with some fish late in the afternoon to find Touching Sky squatting by Runs Free's body. Touching Sky was rocking back and forth, back and forth, clutching Runs Free's limp hand. The little girl's terribly pocked face was completely lax. It was obvious her spirit had flown.

Frantic with fear and grief, Joseph had run out of the wigwam and found Silver Sage. When they returned together, Touching Sky's shrieks were just beginning. He had fled to Tamaqua.

Tamaqua's face was impassive when he received the news. Then Tamaqua told him Wulonquen had died that morning and that Nunschetto was sure to follow. Joseph didn't remember the next few days—just that Nunschetto had quickly followed the others to the spirit world.

Not long after, three dozen more villagers lay ill and dying. The sickness cast a spell on men, women, and children alike, although only three of the white captives succumbed. Few of the dead had proper funerals for fear that others would be cursed by the powerful spell.

Joseph had stumbled through each day, trying to make sense of what was happening. Now his nerves were raw from the sounds of mourning in the village. Joseph's mind flashed back and forth between Runs Free and Nunschetto. He held his stomach and rocked forward, inundated with waves of nausea and grief.

Both Runs Free and Nunschetto are gone. Can anything be worse than this?

He reached into his medicine bundle and fingered the purple bead Runs Free had given him. Tears came to his eyes as he turned the bead over and over in his hand. *I will never forget you, little one.*

-27-

January 1764

"I wonder what we can do for Touching Sky," Joseph said to Silver Sage one morning not long after the winter solstice. "She hardly talks to me anymore."

"She is ill with grief," Silver Sage said. "She misses Runs Free so much that I fear she's about to starve herself."

Joseph nodded. "If you weren't making the meals, I'd be starving too. Touching Sky hardly cooks anymore either."

"It's difficult to make meals when we have lost so many loved ones. And we don't know who might be next."

Joseph swallowed hard. Although it had been four moons since a villager had last died of the spotting disease, people seemed worried they would get the disease. So far it had claimed only three white captives. Wherever Joseph went in the village, he felt an eye of suspicion on him, as did Summer Rain.

"I wish they wouldn't blame me just because I was born white," Joseph said.

"No," Silver Sage said. "You are not to blame. Touching Sky and I know that."

Joseph sighed. Touching Sky was so consumed by grief that she hadn't stored up food for the winter or patched their winter garments. Losing Runs Free and Nunschetto had taken the edge off his appetite for well over a moon. Today, he felt the first rumble of hunger. His appetite was coming back.

"I'm going fishing," he said. He picked up his net and headed for the creek. He had just sat down on the bank when two white men in Indian garb came striding up the path to the village.

Joseph recognized them as James Sherrick and George Girty, two white outlaws who had been at Custaloga's Town a few summers earlier. "Welcome," Joseph said to the two men. He gathered up his fishing supplies and led them over a dusting of snow to Custaloga's wigwam.

"The white men at Lancaster have committed a grave offense against our people," James said to the chief, who came out to greet them.

Custaloga gave a shout to tell the village that visitors had arrived. He led the men toward the lodge. Joseph followed. Dozens of men and women soon joined them to hear the news. The people huddled close to the fire that burned in the center of the lodge, driving the cold winter air to the edges of the room.

"In the white man's month of December," James said, "an unruly band of white men from Paxtang town murdered all of the Conestogas." His voice was rough with anger. "Not only did the Paxton Boys murder these innocent people, but the Royal Highlanders, who were bound by duty to defend the peaceful Indians, did not raise a finger to help them. These Indian friends of ours have lived in peace on Penn's Manor for many years. They did nothing to provoke this attack."

Joseph saw anger rise in the faces of the crowd. "The men from Paxtang had been plotting to kill the Conestogas for some time," George Girty added. "They hate all Indians, whether they are peaceful or not."

"It was very cold on the morning when this took place," James said. "The men broke in with tomahawks and guns and killed everyone there, except for a little girl whose mother had hidden her under a barrel. They killed the wise old man Shahaise and cut him to pieces in his bed. Shahaise was the one who had met our beloved grandfather William Penn. He had in his possession Penn's deed showing joint white-Indian ownership of the Conestoga land."

Joseph held his breath as the story unfolded. So much hate was unfolding between the whites and the Indians! He could hardly take it in.

"The unruly whites stopped to warm themselves at a Quaker neighbor's home, but they told him nothing of what they had done," James said. "But a little boy went to look at the horses and saw the bloody tomahawks hanging from their saddles. Then he found the gun of his Indian playmate, Christy, and reported it to the neighbors."

George broke in. "Although it was very cold that morning, many of the Conestoga villagers were out peddling their wares—brooms, baskets, and bowls. The authorities gathered the villagers together in the Lancaster workhouse to protect them from the unruly mob."

James pounded the ground with his fist as he spoke. "Alas, it did no good. Half a moon later, during a Christmas service at a nearby church, some fifty of those bloodthirsty Paxtons took the workhouse by force. They killed all fourteen of the remaining Indians, hacked their bodies to pieces, and left them strewn around the prison yard. All of those men pretend to be good Christians. Now they're threatening to go to Philadelphia and kill the Delaware who are under the protection of the Quakers."

Joseph's throat tightened. *There will be vengeance.* His adopted people would not let such an atrocity go unnoticed.

James went on. "Lazarus Stewart, the leader of the Paxton group, is a despicable scoundrel. He told the local magistrate that if he tried to arrest him, he would cut him to pieces and eat his heart. So far the authorities have not arrested anyone. We must do something!"

"We will get revenge for the blood of our cousins, the Conestoga. All whites deserve to die!" Tom Lions shouted. Others murmured their assent.

Tom snarled through clenched teeth, "Did old Shahaise not have the paper on which our Grandfather Penn promised peace with our people as long as the streams flow? Those Christians must pay for their evil deeds." He jumped up and brandished his tomahawk and then sliced it into the side of a sapling. "Who will join me to drive the white man off the land given us by the Creator himself?"

Several men jumped to their feet and waved their tomahawks. Another began to drum a war song.

"I will find others to go with you," James said. "We will tell the Shawnees upriver that the governor has not kept his promise to protect our cousins. His talk is nothing but a string of empty words."

"I will fight with you against the white man," George Girty echoed. "I know their ways well, and I will use my knowledge against them."

Joseph glanced over at Touching Sky. She had a worried look on her face. When she stood up and walked toward her wigwam, Joseph got up to follow.

She turned to face him. "I am worried about what the Paxton gang will do to our cousins in Philadelphia," she said. "Two of them have joined the Moravian Christians there. If the governor cannot protect the Conestoga in Lancaster, how can he keep the Delaware safe in Philadelphia?"

Silver Sage joined them. "There are more of Penn's followers in Philadelphia," she said. "They will keep our cousins safe from the Paxton boys."

Joseph turned to Silver Sage with the question that niggled in his mind. "Will many from our village follow Tom Lions to attack the settlements at Lancaster?"

Silver Sage shrugged. "Ordinarily, the men in our village would not follow Tom into battle," she said. "But after what they heard today, they might. I hope not."

Touching Sky looked at her with surprise. "Why not?"

"George Girty and James Sherrick are outlaws with bounties on their heads," Silver Sage said. "They are stirring up our people to more violence. The white man will take it as cause to push us even further off our land."

"Not all whites hate our people," Joseph said. "I heard James say that the Mennonites tried to protect the Conestoga."

Silver Sage nodded. "I give thanks to the Great Spirit for the people of peace who have inherited the spirit of Grandfather Penn. May their tribe bring peace to our troubled land."

Joseph sighed. There would be no peace as long as Tom Lions and the men from Paxton had their way. If only there were more people of peace like *Dat* and the Amish, who would never take up a weapon to kill others—whatever their race.

Later that night around the campfire, Joseph sat down next to James Sherrick. After a few moments, James turned to him and said, "You appear to be a fellow white man. Where are you from?"

"I was born in the Northkill in Berks County."

"I know where that is. The Amish live there among other German people. Tom Lions told me he helped take several captives from there."

Joseph's throat tightened. "Yes, Tom was in the raiding party that attacked my family." He looked down into the fire.

"I was born into a Mennonite family in Lancaster," James said. "I left there because I couldn't stand their strict way of living."

Joseph was startled. He was silent for a moment. "So will you join Tom Lions's raiding party?"

James stared into the fire. "I wouldn't kill the Mennonites, since they tried to save the Conestoga. Two of them warned the authorities about the Paxton Boys threat, and one of them provided a hiding place for the Indians for a time. Another gave his land as a burial ground for those who were murdered. But I'd kill almost any Scotchman or British soldier. Ever since Pontiac took up arms, they've tried to exterminate our Indian people by every means possible. They even spread smallpox among us."

"How could they do that?" Joseph wondered aloud.

"Haven't you heard? They sent blankets from the smallpox hospital at Fort Pitt out to the Indians."

Joseph felt his world turn upside down. *Blankets? But surely . . . oh no . . .*

"Do you mean someone could get the spotting disease by using a blanket from the fort?" he asked.

James nodded. "Of course. Smallpox is so contagious you must never let an Indian touch a blanket used by someone with smallpox. White people might get away with it, but Indians will most likely get the spotting disease."

Joseph's stomach churned. He got to his feet, then ran to the edge of the woods. *Oh no! Oh no!* Then he threw up.

I carried the blanket from Fort Pitt. I killed them both. I killed Nunschetto and Runs Free. I brought the smallpox to the village.

Joseph started to get up, but his legs buckled. He bent over at the waist, his hands on his knees. *No one must ever know.*

-28-

November 1764

I fear that something bad is going to happen to Swift Foot," Touching Sky said to Silver Sage as they stood just outside the wigwam, watching a light snow fall on the village. "Last night I dreamed that a great eagle swooped down from the sky and carried him away toward the rising sun."

"Let's hope that the dream means something else," Silver Sage said.

"I would rather die than lose my son." Touching Sky's voice was devoid of all emotion. She had lost too much.

"In the last several moons, I have often seen him with Summer Rain," Silver Sage said, turning to go back into the wigwam. "Perhaps she will sweep him away from you."

"That would not be a cause for mourning," Touching Sky said, pulling her blanket more closely around her and following Silver Sage through the door. "Although I would rather he marry a woman who was born a Delaware." She squatted to stir the fire back into life.

The fire was blazing when Joseph burst through the door. "The scouts say Colonel Bouquet is heading this way with a large army," he said. "He could be here in several days. This is the same warrior who defeated our people at Bushy Run."

Touching Sky looked at Joseph in alarm. "Custaloga said the governor is paying for Indian scalps. Some white people are killing Indians just to collect the money."

Silver Sage looked sober. "That's what I thought would happen. Too many men like Tom Lions, raiding the settlements. The time will come when it has to stop."

Joseph nodded agreement. "Things will come to a head soon. Custaloga set out to meet the other chiefs today."

Touching Sky sighed. It had barely been a year since the spotting fever had swept through; now an even greater threat loomed on the horizon. Nothing could be worse than the white man's army marching into the village. *I must talk to Custaloga as soon as he gets back.*

Custaloga returned a few days later. The moment Touching Sky saw his solemn face, she knew he carried bad news. Rather than going directly to the lodge, he stepped inside her wigwam. Joseph had gone hunting but Silver Sage was nearby.

"We have concluded a grand council with the one they call Colonel Bouquet," he said. "Turtle Heart, Guyasuta, King Beaver of the Turkey Clan, and other chiefs from among our brothers were there."

Touching Sky's heart sank. "Tell me the bad news," she said. "I want to know everything."

"The colonel spoke with fierce anger," Custaloga said. "He told us that he had brought with him the relatives of the people we had killed or taken as captives. He told us they were impatient to take revenge for the bloody murders of their friends, and that only with the greatest difficulty could he protect us against their just resentment."

"Was Swift Foot's father there?"

Custaloga shrugged. "I don't know. The army surrounded us on every side as we spoke. The colonel said it was completely in his power to destroy us. As chiefs, we knew this to be true, so we offered terms of peace."

"I hope you didn't give up our captives!" Touching Sky's eyes blazed.

"The colonel charged us with the worst cruelties that the human heart can imagine. He said he would tear down our villages if we did not return all of our captives and make peace according to his terms."

"Tell me. Did you agree to release Swift Foot to them?" Touching Sky could barely speak.

Custaloga's voice dropped. "It breaks my heart to see Swift Foot go, but we have no way to stop this great warrior. If his scouts come to our town and see that we have retained any captives, they will treat us badly."

"Let me speak with the colonel. I will tell him that my life depends on Swift Foot, and that he does not want to return to his former home."

Custaloga shook his head, deep lines on his forehead. "We told him that we no longer have captives. All of the white people among us wish to stay. He refuses to listen."

Touching Sky grasped at straws. "Then I will move away from this village and take Swift Foot with me. We will be out of the white man's reach."

"Where would you go? The colonel has taken hostages from among our people, as well as the Shawnee and Seneca. He already has two of our Delaware captains in custody; he will not return them until our deputies have made a treaty with Sir William Johnson. When we agreed to bring all the white captives to Fort Pitt in the next half moon, he extended his hand to us for the first time. This gave us great joy, knowing that our village will be saved."

"And my beloved Swift Foot will be lost. First it was my husband, then my son and daughter. I shall soon be all alone." Touching Sky's voice broke.

Custaloga put his hand on her shoulder. "I'm sorry," he said. "If I could have found any other way to save our village, I would have done it."

Silver Sage slipped her arm around Touching Sky's waist.

"How will I ever tell him? How will I let him go?" Touching Sky stood stiff, as if carved from a block of wood. Custaloga squeezed her arm and then slipped out through the doorway.

Silver Sage said nothing, just listened. The two stood in silence for a long time.

Finally, Touching Sky spoke again. "If Swift Foot has to leave, I'm going to walk back to the Northkill with him. I will not give him up to the colonel."

"My dear niece," Silver Sage said, her gentle voice softer than usual, "why should you take your life into your own hands? Remember that the scalp bounty is for women as well as men."

Touching Sky shook her head. "Then I'll ask Tamaqua to go along." She tried to focus her mind, numb with grief, on practical matters. "I have some dried corn and he can hunt game on the way. I'll speak to him now."

Silver Sage tried to comfort her. "You don't have to do everything right away."

But Touching Sky knew she had to let Joseph know right away. *He will wonder why I am grieving again, and worry.* She spoke with determination, "We'll leave in half a moon." With that, she walked out the door and strode toward Tamaqua's hut.

If we must do this thing, we will do it quickly. But how will I tell Swift Foot?

The next morning, as Joseph was getting ready to leave the hut with his bow and arrows, Touching Sky cleared her throat.

Joseph glanced at her with worry in his eyes. He had known something was wrong—something she was keeping from him. *Last night she seemed so sad. What now?*

"I know you have heard that Custaloga has been negotiating with the British army," she said.

"Yes, I hear they are threatening to destroy our village. I hope they don't find out that we have one of their horses," Joseph said.

Touching Sky nodded and cleared her throat again. "Custaloga says that the British will burn down our village if we—" Her voice broke.

Joseph stood next to her, waiting with bated breath. On the one hand, he wanted Touching Sky to hurry up and speak. On the other, he didn't want to hear what she had to say. *It has to be bad news. More bad news.*

Touching Sky started again. "They will burn down our village if—if we don't return all of our white captives." Her eyes were wet with unshed tears.

Joseph tried to take in her words. "Mother! Even the ones like me who have been adopted?"

"Yes!" Touching Sky threw her arms around him and the tears finally spilled out. She wept on his shoulder. "Oh my son, my son. I don't know what I will do without you."

Joseph was numb. "When must I go?"

"Within a half-moon. I will go with you. So will Tamaqua. We will not let you go alone."

Joseph held Touching Sky in his arms. She seemed thin and vulnerable. *How can I leave her?* They stood this way for a few moments, and then she pulled away.

"I have something for you," Touching Sky said. She reached for a basket hanging from the ceiling and pulled out a soft bundle.

"I hadn't planned to give this to you so soon," she said, unrolling the bundle to reveal the shirt Joseph's sister had made him. "Your father sent this shirt by the hand of Walks Proud two summers ago when he returned from the treaty conference in Lancaster. Your sister made it for you."

Joseph's breath caught as he stroked the new shirt with his hand and held it against his chest. *Barbara made this?* He traced the fine stitching at the seams with his finger. "Shall I—?"

"Yes, you can put it on now."

Joseph stripped off the worn shirt he was wearing and pulled on the new one. *So* Dat *is alive after all. I wonder if Christian is going home too?*

"Tamaqua and I want to meet your family," Touching Sky said. "He said it will be safest to go by the way of Fort Augusta."

Joseph searched for words. He had long since given up hope of returning to the Northkill, but he felt a faint flicker of longing that he hadn't felt in a long time. "This is my home now," he mumbled, but his stomach churned with feelings that spoke of a more complex story.

"We'll leave in a few days, after I sew some warm clothing. Silver Sage will help me."

Joseph nodded wordlessly. *This is moving too fast. I must talk to Summer Rain. Must she leave too?*

"I'm going to check our traps," he said, desperate to be alone.

Touching Sky struggled to keep her composure. "I hope you get a fox pelt."

Joseph walked into the cool air and headed for the woods. Hunting would clear his mind. He inhaled the smell of fallen leaves. He had come to love the forest more than he could have imagined. Hunting and fishing brought life to his soul. It wearied him to think of working on the farm again.

And—who would want to marry an Amish girl? They were beautiful, but in an unadorned way. *They don't wear feathers in their hair and jewelry like Nunschetto did. They don't have her cute nose and her wonderful smile.* His heart ached. Would he ever be able to forget her?

On the way back from the woods that afternoon, with a fox pelt in hand, Joseph stopped by to see Summer Rain. Her father met him at the door. "I'm sorry, but she just went to stay in the hut out back."

Joseph's shoulders sagged as he turned to leave. *I guess I won't get to see her for several days. I wonder what she'd say if I called for her?* He thought better of it and turned toward home.

When he got to the wigwam, Custaloga was talking to Touching Sky. She motioned for him to join their conversation. "I have told Swift Foot the sad news," she told Custaloga. "We must say goodbye in a few days."

"We shall miss you, my beloved nephew," Custaloga said, reaching out his hand to touch Joseph's arm. "You have been a loyal and faithful member of our tribe. I wish so much that you could stay."

"You have always treated me well," Joseph said. "I shall always love and respect the Delaware people for what you have done for me."

Custaloga pulled Joseph into an embrace. "Be assured that we will never make war against you or your house."

Joseph tried to swallow the lump in his throat. "And I shall never speak against your people or take up arms against you." It felt a bit strange to speak that way. It seemed like something that *Dat* might say.

On the day they were planning to leave the village, Joseph suggested that Touching Sky ride Star on the journey. "It's a long way to walk," he said.

"You're thinking like a white man," she said. "It would take a lot of corn to feed that horse! And what if we need to take a canoe part of the way? We should leave him behind." She wrung her hands. "And besides, he reminds me of Runs Free."

Joseph had suspected it. Ever since Runs Free's death, Touching Sky had not wanted anything to do with the horse. "What shall we do with him?" he asked.

"You decide. I have other things to worry about."

Silver Sage, who had overheard the conversation, stepped up to Joseph. "You might give your horse to Tom Lions."

Joseph studied her face. Was she serious? "Why should I give my horse to Tom rather than Miquon or some other friend?"

"Tom helped our family when he rescued Runs Free from the fire," Silver Sage said. "And he's had his eye on that horse ever since you got it."

She is *serious.* "I'll decide tomorrow," Joseph said, and headed out the door.

He walked over to stroke Star, who was nibbling at the heavy grass that bowed under the weight of the last snow. "You poor thing," Joseph said. "You need corn to eat in this cold weather, and we don't have much to spare."

He pondered Silver Sage's words. He wasn't surprised that she'd suggested he give the horse to Tom Lions. Ever since he'd read the Lord's Prayer in Touching Sky's purse and told them about *Dat*'s nonresistance, she'd pressed him to treat Tom with more respect. *What am I to do?*

He remembered the time he'd helped Tom build the sweat lodge and seen the tears in his eyes. Had he not shared that moment with Tom, he wouldn't even consider Silver Sage's suggestion. But now . . . What would *Dat* do?

It was a long time since he'd asked himself that question. But now that he was returning to the Northkill, and now that he knew *Dat* was alive, he pondered it. What would he tell his family about Tom Lions and the way that he'd treated him?

"What do you think, Star?" he asked the horse as he stroked his curved neck. "Do you want to go to Tom Lions?"

A crow cawed overhead.

Star lifted his head and looked up.

"Is that crow trying to tell us what to do?" Joseph asked. He laughed and looked at the crow, who stared back. Star nickered.

"Okay then, I'll give you to Tom Lions," Joseph said to Star. "Let's go."

Joseph took a rope from his bag, tied it to Star's halter, and headed for Tom's home. Tom saw him coming and stepped into the frigid air to greet him. "Hello."

"Hello," Joseph said. "Maybe you heard that I'm being forced to go back home."

"Yes."

"Would you like to take care of Star? Touching Sky doesn't want him. He belongs here, in the village."

Tom looked stunned by the offer. "Well, maybe. I mean, yes. Sure."

Joseph gave Star a pat on the rump and handed the rope to Tom. "He's yours. Be sure to take good care of him, for Nunschetto's sake."

"Thank you."

Joseph felt Tom's eyes searching him as he turned to walk back to his wigwam.

"Wait," Tom said. "I have something for you." Joseph turned to watch Tom walk into the wigwam where Nunschetto had died.

Tom returned a few moments later with a new pair of moccasins in his hand. "Nunschetto made these for her father— Walks Proud—after he left for battle. He never came back. Just before she died, she said she wanted you to have them."

Joseph's heart beat faster as he took the moccasins in his hand. "Thank you."

He studied the fringe of white beads that rimmed a finely woven pattern of red, green, and white on the front and sides of the new footwear. *I've never seen such intricate work. How she loved her father. And she gave them to me.*

Tom stood looking, with no hint of his thoughts.

Joseph stuffed the moccasins into his bag and turned to go. He didn't look back.

As he walked home, he decided to try to see Summer Rain one more time. He detoured to the little hut that lay behind her home. "Ho, ho," he said, hoping that Summer Rain was there and would recognize his voice.

After a few moments, Summer Rain stepped out of the hut with a blanket wrapped around her shoulders.

Joseph took a deep breath. "Have you heard?" he asked. "All of the white captives must return home. I'm going to leave the village today." His mind flashed back to their first meeting on a cold day seven winters back, when she'd dampened his hope of an escape.

She nodded. "I've been told I'll be taken to Fort Pitt. I'll miss it here but I look forward to seeing my relatives again."

"I'm going to miss you more than anyone else in the village," Joseph said, surprised at his boldness. He took a step closer to her as he spoke. "I have something for you." He reached into his bag and pulled out a wooden carving he'd intended for Nunschetto.

"Thank you." She turned it in her hand, feeling each curve and ridge. "I promise I'll keep it, and not pass it on the way we've been taught here," she said with a smile.

Joseph reached out to take her hands in his, not caring that Touching Sky had told him never to touch a woman who was staying in the hut. "We've been through a lot together."

Her eyes were bright as she stood with her hands in his in the morning sun. "I'll miss you too. You've been like a brother to me."

Joseph leaned forward so that their lips almost touched. "When you go back to Fort Harris you won't live too far from my home. Maybe I can come to see you."

She gazed into his eyes. "Yes, I would like that. I would like that very much. And I'd like my family to meet you."

Joseph's heart quickened. *Maybe . . .*

"Summer Rain!" someone called from the wigwam behind them.

"I've got to go," she said, turning toward her wigwam. Joseph let go of her hands reluctantly.

"I will never forget you," Joseph said. Now it made sense to him that she'd turned down a chance to be married, with the hope that the British would free her someday. He stood silently for a few moments as she headed toward the wigwam.

He paused for a moment and then headed to the place where Runs Free was buried. He stood next to the small mound and pulled the purple wampum bead out of his pocket. He stood there for a long time, remembering how Runs Free had helped him learn the Delaware language, ridden on his shoulders, and played hoops with him. "I'm so sorry you got hurt when you hiked with Miquon and me," he said, his voice husky with emotion. "I hope you're in a better place now, where you can run free again." The ground swam in his eyes as he knelt down and kissed the mound where he thought her head would lie.

He stumbled over to the place where he'd been told Nunschetto was buried. He hadn't been able to bring himself to go there before. He stood beside the grave and pulled the new moccasins out of his bag. "Thank you for the moccasins you gave me," he said, running his hand across the perfectly aligned rows of quills. He sat down and took off his old moccasins and put on the new ones. "I'll always think of you when I wear them. Touching Sky will be really pleased too."

He knelt there for a time in silence, and then he reached into his bag and pulled out a pair of earrings he'd hoped to give Nunschetto as a gift. "I have something for you." He took his tomahawk and scratched a hole in the mound, dropped the earrings into it, and closed it back up again. "I only wish I would have given these to you when you were alive. But you shall always live in my mind."

With that, he took a deep breath, and turned to walk to Miquon's home for yet another painful farewell.

Nearly a moon passed from the time Joseph left the village with Tamaqua and Touching Sky until they arrived at the forks of the Susquehanna.

"This must be Fort Augusta," Tamaqua said. "It's the place where Custaloga told us to turn Swift Foot over to the British."

"Let's sleep here tonight," Touching Sky said. "We can go to the fort in the morning."

Tamaqua shook his head. "It would be dangerous to sleep this close to the fort. There'll be scouts about who'll shoot without asking questions. Remember, they have a scalp bounty here."

Touching Sky's face darkened. "No, I'm afraid of how they will treat Swift Foot. Maybe we should go back."

Joseph glanced at the garrison. The British flag flapped in the breeze. *What will they do to me?*

"We could probably keep Swift Foot for a few more moons before the colonel's army would find us," Tamaqua said. "Swift Foot will have to decide."

Joseph squeezed his medicine bundle. If only his spirit helper could show them what to do.

"I'm afraid the soldiers won't let us come with you," Touching Sky said, worry creasing her brow. "Let's go back a little way and think about it."

A crow lighted on a branch nearby and cawed. Joseph looked up. It flew to a tree a little closer to the river and cawed again, as though beckoning.

Joseph glanced at Touching Sky, whose eyes were fixed on the crow. Did she recognize his spirit helper? The crow cawed loudly and then flew across to the island.

"Let's follow the crow," Joseph said.

Touching Sky nodded at Tamaqua, who picked up his bags and headed for the water. After the three of them had crossed, Joseph waved a white cloth and walked toward the fort.

A soldier with his long hair pulled back in a band spied them and strode up with his rifle at the ready. "Who are you?" he asked.

"I am Joseph Hochstetler," he said in broken German. To say the name felt awkward—like it belonged to someone else. "I was taken by Indians from the Northkill and have lived in Custaloga's Town for several winters. Now I am returning by orders from Colonel Bouquet."

The soldier's mouth dropped. "I heard about your family," he said in German. "I was assigned to Fort Northkill when the Indians attacked your farm and killed one of our soldiers. Many of your people moved away after that."

Joseph felt uneasy. What might this man do to Tamaqua and Touching Sky? Would he take vengeance on them for the attack on their farm and for killing the provincial soldier?

The soldier motioned for Joseph and his companions to follow him into the fort. "Please don't harm these people with me," Joseph said. "They are my adopted family and wish to meet my family in the Northkill." He hoped the soldier could understand his uncertain German, rusty from lack of use.

The soldier nodded.

Joseph hoped against hope that Tamaqua and Touching Sky would be allowed to accompany him to the farm. He had already harmed the people he loved by bringing smallpox to their village. Had he now drawn Tamaqua and Touching Sky into danger too?

-29-

Touching Sky's face reflected the glow of embers from the fire. She lay down for the night just outside the fort. Although the commander of the fort had invited her and Tamaqua to sleep inside with Joseph, she had refused. She needed some distance from the man who now had Joseph in his custody. He said they'd be leaving for the Northkill the next morning.

She begged for sleep to take away the pain of her grief. *I've been through this too many times.* She mourned her husband, her son, her daughter—all ripped from her grasp. Swift Foot would soon be taken as well.

She fell into a restless sleep, full of dreams. She was on the top of a grassy mound. Glancing about, she breathed deeply of the evening air, thick with the fragrance of flowers. She looked around, trying to figure out where she was. Nothing looked familiar.

Then she heard the faint sound of laughter. She followed a path that led past a small lake. Two deer, ignoring her, drank from the water's edge. Swallows darted around her as she entered a wood in the fading sunlight. The laughter of young children grew louder as she passed through the copse of trees and stepped into a small clearing.

She held her breath at what she saw—Runs Free was dancing as she'd done as a child. Her daughter threw back her head as she twirled, her laughter accenting the tinkling of the bells on her ankles. She tossed her head from side to side, swinging her looped earrings and showing off the red scarf that tied back her long black hair.

But Runs Free wasn't alone. A dozen boys and girls speaking different languages ran and played alongside three fawns that gamboled in the grass and a young wolf that cavorted with a bear cub. Touching Sky stood transfixed as her daughter took another girl's hand. They twirled each other in a broad circle, laughing and dancing like lifelong friends, casting shadows larger than life in the evening sun.

Touching Sky stepped forward to get a closer look at the barefooted white stranger in the long plain dress who danced with her daughter. The young girl's face glowed in the evening sun. She wore no earrings or bells. Two long braids of brown hair swung to her waist as she danced.

Touching Sky watched her daughter run freely. There was no sign of an injured foot, no pocks on her lovely skin. *This is life as it is meant to be*, she marveled.

The two girls paused, breathless, and walked hand in hand to a fruit tree in the middle of the clearing. Runs Free reached among the leaves and pulled off a piece of golden fruit tinged with red. She handed it to her friend. They both took a bite of it and giggled with delight.

Touching Sky's mouth watered as she watched. Was it an apple? A peach? Or something she'd never seen before?

I must speak to my daughter. Touching Sky took a step toward Runs Free but was stopped by an invisible wall that stood between them. She tried to speak, and then shout, but no sound came.

She started to wave, to get her daughter's attention, but she could not raise her arm. The two girls looked in her direction, but paid no heed. She clawed at the invisible barrier that separated her from her daughter.

Her breath came fast as she was roused from her sleep.

She pulled the blanket tighter around her in the chill of the night air. What had she just seen? Was Runs Free in the happy hunting ground of which the prophet had spoken?

She lay warmed by the blanket that staved off the chill, but she was comforted even more by the vision of a daughter released from the cruelties that had plagued her life. *I must tell my dream to Swift Foot.* With that thought, she fell into a restful sleep.

The next morning Touching Sky told Joseph what she had seen during the night. "Runs Free was so happy," she said. "She was among so many friends—children and animals alike."

Joseph listened intently. Touching Sky described the little girl who had danced and eaten fruit with Runs Free.

"It must have been Franey," he said, his voice deep with emotion.

"Who?"

"My little sister, whose name was Veronica. We always called her Franey. She was Runs Free's age when . . ." He paused and swallowed. "When I first came to Custaloga's Town."

"Oh." Touching Sky dropped her gaze when she saw tears form in Joseph's eyes. Perhaps he missed Franey like she missed Runs Free.

Touching Sky stirred up the fire as though to prepare a meal, but her mind was preoccupied with other thoughts. Who would be there to greet Joseph when they arrived at the Northkill besides the father he spoke of as *Dat*? What kind of welcome would she and Tamaqua receive?

On the third day after they left Fort Augusta, the soldier with the long hair led Joseph and his companions off the North Tulpehocken Trail toward the gap in the Blue Mountains, which he now knew as the *keekachtanemin.* The soldier pointed south. "We'll follow this trail to the Northkill," he said. "We should be there by evening."

Joseph's mind stirred with questions as they walked along. Had his father remarried? If so, who would his stepmother be? Someone he knew?

He glanced over at Touching Sky's face. What was she thinking? What would *Dat* say about Touching Sky? Would he invite her and Tamaqua to stay with them for a few days before they returned?

The questions came faster. Was this the same path his captors had traveled when he was first taken captive? Nothing
looked familiar except for the gap in the steep ridge that lay
not far ahead. Did *Dat* live in the same place? Had he rebuilt
the house and barn that they had left smoldering behind them
some seven summers ago? Would *Dat* expect him to work on
the farm as he had before? Much of what he had done in the
fields and garden as a child seemed like women's work now.

The foursome made their way through the gap and down
a rutted road, and Joseph now had a faint sense of familiarity.
The plowed fields lay fallow, but he could see short stalks of
corn poking their heads out of the furrows. It seemed like a
strange way to plant corn.

The sun was dropping when they approached the Northkill
Creek. Joseph's heart pounded in his chest. This was the place
where the Indian war party had forced him to leave his home
on that fateful morning seven winters earlier.

The painful memories he'd repressed for years came racing
back. He recalled the first time Tom Lions had jabbed a rifle in
his ribs, forcing him to march away from the only home he'd
ever known. He smelled the odor of the burning flesh of the
animals still trapped inside the barn, and heard the scream of
their panicked horse, Blitz, briefly trapped in the corral.

Joseph slowed his steps, dreading the first sight of the home
farm. It had been so long since he'd last been there. Would he
even recognize it? Would his family recognize him and accept his Indian ways? Would he find an Amish woman who
could cook as well as Touching Sky? Would he be allowed to
wear his beloved medicine bundle along with his breechcloth,
or would he have to wear Amish breeches and heavy-soled
shoes? Could he keep wearing his cherished earrings?

Joseph's stomach churned. To rejoin his white family might
be even harder than he had first imagined. He dreaded raising crops like *Dat*; he'd rather hunt and fish like the Indians.
Perhaps if it didn't work out to stay on the farm, he could
return to the Indian village after Colonel Bouquet's army

returned home. After all, he was of age now and *Dat* would not force him to stay against his will, at least if he didn't join the Amish church.

He wondered if Christian had been forced to return home. *He might be there now. Maybe if things don't work out, the two of us can go back to the Indians together.*

Joseph stopped and bent over, pretending to take a pebble out of his moccasin.

The soldier paused as Joseph shook his moccasin and put it back on.

Joseph slowly straightened up. *I can't go on. But what can I do? The soldier won't be satisfied until we get to* Dat's *doorstep.* His eyes met Touching Sky's. They were full of pain. She raised her eyebrows, inquiring. How could he explain his feelings to her? He felt as if he was being torn in two.

Joseph glanced at the soldier, who frowned and waved him forward. Joseph took a deep breath and followed, with Touching Sky and Tamaqua close beside. They reached the Northkill Creek—the creek where he had spent so many days swimming and fishing. The soldier bent over and drank deeply, then splashed a handful of the cold water onto his face. Joseph knelt down and sipped slowly from cupped hands, as did Tamaqua.

Touching Sky seemed impervious to thirst. She stood gazing at the trees that stood nearby. "Swift Foot," she said, "this is the place where I played as a child while my father was hunting. I remember that tree." She pointed toward a sycamore with an odd-shaped burl on the side of the trunk, just above a large cavity at the base. "I used to hide in it—it's hollow inside."

Joseph's mouth dropped. To think that Touching Sky had played here as a child! That she had loved this very spot of land as he and his family had . . . he could hardly take it in. That tree had been his sister Franey's favorite hiding place. He remembered the time when he'd huddled inside the hollow with her in the midst of a cloudburst, watching the rain fall. It was the place to which she'd vainly tried to flee on the day the Indians attacked.

His mind went to a long-forgotten phrase from the Psalms, words that his father had often read aloud during family prayers: "*Du bist mein Schirm; du wirst mich vor Angst be-hüten* (Thou art my hiding place; thou shalt preserve me from trouble)." There was more to the verse but it was all he could remember. That's what he needed now. Shelter. A secure hiding place.

A prayer rose to his lips from deep inside, words he had learned as a child. He mouthed them softly: "*Unser Vater in Himmel* (Oh, dear father in heaven) . . . !" As he repeated the words, he felt a knot loosening inside. He breathed a deep sigh of relief.

"Is this your home?" the soldier asked, pointing toward the barn built on a slope just ahead.

Joseph paused. The last glimpse of his home had been the timbers falling, and the remains smoldering to ashes. The pair of chestnut trees that framed the path to the barn looked familiar; they cast their leafy arms over the split-rail fence just as they had when he left so long ago.

The house looked quite new. Perhaps *Dat* had rebuilt it along with the barn? Off to the right was a springhouse that looked just like the one where he'd often gotten a drink. And yes, yonder on the side of a gentle rise beyond the house was the bake oven where he'd often stood with his mouth watering, waiting for *Mam* to pull out the hot loaves.

Joseph nodded. "*Jah,*" he said, surprised at the sudden huskiness in his voice. "*Jah*, this is the place."

"Well then, let's go." The soldier motioned them to follow.

Joseph nodded and forced himself to come after. He reached out with a trembling hand to grasp Touching Sky's arm as they stepped onto the cobbled path that led to the two-story wooden house. And then, as the setting sun shone red in the glass windows, a glimmer of hope stirred.

Could he—like the Joseph of Scripture whose story he had told to his Indian family, raised in the land of Egypt for God's purpose—be reunited with his family without leaving the way of life he had come to love? Could he bridge the divide between two sides—red and white—who clamored for his soul? Could he be loyal to two different families—two ways of life? With Touching Sky at his side, Joseph raised his hand to knock on the door of the house.

He prayed it could be so.

Acknowledgments

This book is the culmination of much research and many invigorating conversations with people who accompanied me on the writing journey. A number of individuals deserve my sincere, written acknowledgment.

Thank you to Beth Hostetler Mark, a librarian at Messiah College, who gathered archival sources relating to the Jacob Hochstetler family in the context of the French and Indian War. I often drew on her extensive bibliographic knowledge and sleuthing instincts when searching for historical sources.

Thank you to Becky Gochnauer, director of the 1719 Hans Herr House & Museum and the Lancaster Longhouse, who helped me make vital connections with the Native American community. I admire the work her organization has done to construct and interpret an authentic replica of a Native American longhouse. Even more, I admire the conciliatory spirit in which Becky and her team interpret the history of the Mennonites in the colonial context, including the colonists' role in the displacement of Native Americans in Pennsylvania.

Thank you to linguist James Rementer, director of the Lenape Language Project, the driving force behind the online Lenape Talking Dictionary. He responded promptly to my email queries about Delaware idioms and cultural practices.

Thank you to Cindy Crosby, who served as a coach and fiction editor from the conception of the plot to the submission of the manuscript. Thank you to Herald Press editors Amy Gingerich and Valerie Weaver-Zercher, who guided my work toward publication. The marketing staff at Herald Press, particularly Ben Penner and Jerilyn Schrock, also deserve my gratitude for their belief in and enthusiastic promotion of this book.

Thank you to readers James D. Hershberger, Beth Hostetler Mark, Becky Gochnauer, Rusty Sherrick, and Ruth Py, who offered feedback to an early draft. Rusty and Ruth are descendants of the Lenape-Delaware who serve as reenactors and interpreters of Lenape history and culture. Together with Becky, they served as my advisory group on matters related to the Native American tradition. I dedicated the book to them in appreciation for their commitment and expertise.

Thank you to Elizabeth Soto Albrecht, moderator of Mennonite Church USA, who supported me in this significant diversion from my daily work. Together we hope that the book will promote the vision we share as members of our denomination: "God calls us to be followers of Jesus Christ and, by the power of the Holy Spirit, to grow as communities of grace, joy, and peace, so that God's healing and hope flow through us to the world."

Thank you to Shirley Showalter and Gloria Diener, who meet regularly with me as a writers group. They offered creative suggestions or helpful critiques on scenes scattered throughout this book. Their encouragement helps me to keep writing even when I'd rather do something else.

Thank you to my wife, Bonita, for her loving forbearance throughout my journey of researching and writing this book. She listened with grace to my preoccupied musings about this project through its various stages. Increasingly, I approach writing as a medium of word painting, complementing the visual mixed media that grow out of Bonita's creative imagination.

Above all, I give thanks to God, the Great Creator, whose redemption through Jesus Christ makes possible a peace that transforms human relationships, even between disparate peoples. *Soli Deo Gloria*.

The Author

Ervin R. Stutzman was born into an Amish home in Kalona, Iowa, and spent most of his childhood in Hutchinson, Kansas. He serves as executive director for Mennonite Church USA and holds master's degrees from the University of Cincinnati and Eastern Mennonite Seminary, and received his PhD from Temple University.

Stutzman is the author of *Jacob's Choice*, book 1 of the Return to Northkill series; *Tobias of the Amish*, a story of his father's life and community; *Emma: A Widow Among the Amish*, the story of his mother; and several other books and articles.

Ervin is married to Bonita Haldeman of Manheim, Pennsylvania. They live in Harrisonburg, Virginia, where they are members of the Park View Mennonite Church. Ervin and Bonita have three adult children and four grandchildren.

Read all the books in the Return to Northkill series by Ervin R. Stutzman

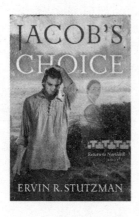

JACOB'S CHOICE
Return to Northkill, BOOK 1

PB. 9780836196818. $14.99 USD
HC. 9781513801681. $28.99 USD

Jacob Hochstetler is a peace-loving Amish settler beside the Northkill Creek in Pennsylvania when warriors, goaded by the hostilities of the French and Indian War, attack his family. Taken captive, Jacob finds his beliefs about love and nonresistance severely tested. After enduring a hard winter as a prisoner, Jacob makes a harrowing escape. Based on actual events, *Jacob's Choice* tells the story of one man's pursuit of restoration that leads to a complicated romance, an unrelenting search for his sons, and an astounding act of reconciliation.

Expanded Edition
HC. 9780836198751. $29.99 USD

The expanded edition of *Jacob's Choice* includes the novel itself along with maps, photographs, family tree charts, and other historical documents to help readers enter the story and era of the Hochstetler family.